Snowed In

BOOKS BY CATHERINE WALSH

One Night Only
The Rebound
Holiday Romance
The Matchmaker

CATHERINE WALSH

Snowed In

bookouture

Published by Bookouture in 2023

An imprint of Storyfire Ltd.
Carmelite House
50 Victoria Embankment
London EC4Y 0DZ

www.bookouture.com

ISBN: 978-1-83790-666-6
eBook ISBN: 978-1-83790-665-9

This one's for Lucy

CONTENT NOTE

This book features references to a controlling relationship. If this is potentially sensitive to you, please read with care.

PROLOGUE

MEGAN

I wish I wasn't wearing heels.

I wish I wasn't wearing a wedding dress either, but I really wish I wasn't wearing heels. It's very difficult to run in heels. It's also very difficult to run when your fancy new bridal bra is digging into your skin, and your scalp is being pulled by a hundred million hairpins.

I wish I hadn't decided on an updo.

I wish a lot of things right now.

Mostly I wish that Aunt Susan would get off the freaking phone.

I peek around the corner, watching her pace along the hotel hallway. She's wearing a bright pink dress and an elaborate white hat and, for some reason, has made it her mission to hold her very important conversation right in front of the elevators.

Why is she even here? Shouldn't she be at the church? I should be at the church, so she should definitely be at the church, but no. She's here. Talking loudly down the phone and blocking my escape route.

Escape route. Jesus. Try to be more dramatic, Megan. I dare you.

Aunt Susan laughs, turning my way, and I rest back against the wall, hiding from view. Maybe she's a sign. A bright pink sign telling me that this is a stupid decision and I should just return to my room and wait for the photographer. We spent a fortune on the photographer. We spent a fortune on the whole day but especially on the photographer.

Not as much as we spent on the food, though.

At least the food can still be eaten, right? It would be a waste otherwise. And we paid for it weeks ago.

I should have left a note on the mirror.

Sorry about ruining the day, but please enjoy the crab cakes!

Just thinking about it has me glancing back to the room, but then Aunt Susan laughs again, and it's so loud and sudden it's like a glass of cold water to the face. No. I'm not going back. I'm not going back because I have to go.

I have to go. I have to go. I have to *go*.

I straighten from the wall, imagining myself full of resolve and determination and not coffee and nausea as I leave the elevators behind and take off for the employee stairwell I passed earlier.

I swear I didn't know what I was going to do when I woke up this morning. I'm not this person. This rash, last-minute person. I'm usually pretty calm, pretty practical, but I just *can't*. I can't marry Isaac. And surely, it's better to come to this decision now than in six months. Better now than a lifetime of knowing I made the wrong choice.

It was Uncle Ted who made up my mind. Uncle Ted, who, an hour ago, came into the room with the rest of my family and handed me an unsealed envelope. The same kind of envelope he gave me at my communion, my confirmation, and every birthday and Christmas since I was a kid. One that contains a card in his neat, flowing script, accompanied by several crisp bills to *keep me going*.

As soon as he gave it to me, I made my decision. Maybe I was even waiting for it. Because I knew if I went too soon, if I broke this whole thing off with time to spare, everyone would just talk me back into it.

I have only my backpack with me, a ratty old school bag that horrified Mam, but I insisted on bringing for sentimental reasons. It holds nothing more than my phone, my purse, and the clothes I traveled to the hotel in, but there's no time to change. No time for anything other than to just leave.

Easier said than done.

Turns out, when you're a bride on your wedding day, you can't even go to the bathroom without three people helping you, and it took a lot of needling and *I just want to take a moment*s to get everyone to leave me alone. I probably only have five minutes tops before someone comes to find me, and I am in a big white dress. I'm pretty findable right now.

I thud awkwardly down the stairs, clinging to the handrail for support, and after what feels like an hour, but is probably only a minute, I emerge into a near-identical hallway and follow the neon green exit sign pointing to the back of the building.

There's no one else around.

I was banking on this. All the guests are at the church next door, and most of the hotel staff are in the lobby to cheer me out as I leave. There are pictures of them doing it on the website. One of their wedding package perks. I thought it looked nice when I saw the images, but now the idea makes me pick up my pace, bundling my skirts into my fist when they catch on my shoes.

I should have planned this better. I should have brought sneakers. I should have told someone.

I should have thought about whether or not this exit was alarmed.

The thought hits me as soon as I burst through the double doors, and I wince as I wait for a siren to blare or lights to flash. But nothing happens. They fall shut behind me with a shuddering clang, and that's it.

I'm out.

I catch my breath, waiting for the doubt to creep in, but there's nothing. Just my gut telling me to get the hell out of dodge, and beyond a few issues with dairy, it's never let me down before. I just need to find a taxi. I need to find a taxi, and then I can—

"You lost?"

I jump. I think I even let out a little squeak, and whirl around at the question to see a man standing right next to me.

Christian.

I pause before him, startled into stillness, and the first thing that pops into my mind, the very first thing my panicked, addled brain latches onto, is what the hell is Christian Fitzpatrick doing at my wedding? I didn't invite him. I've barely spoken more than two words to him despite sharing a classroom for our entire childhood, and since then, I've only ever had a brief glimpse of the man when he comes back to the village for a visit.

But I have my answer before I've even finished the question. Why wouldn't he be invited? My mother invited everyone. Third cousins twice removed, friends of friends of friends. It's that kind of wedding. She probably tracked down half the kids I went to summer camp with when I was twelve. Maybe even all of them. Of course, everyone I went to school with would be invited.

Including Christian Fitzpatrick.

He stands in the shade just to the left of the doors, his phone in one hand and a lit cigarette in the other. His dark hair is slicked back, and I can't help but notice he's wearing a tie. It's weird. I mean, I know it's my wedding, but not once, not *ever* during a single school day did he show up wearing the required tie, and now here he is, with a silky teal one knotted neatly at the base of his throat.

I'm bizarrely touched by the sight of it. Like he made an effort just for me. But then his eyes drop down my dress before taking in the bag, and I'm back on edge, my skin prickling under his gaze. Christian's not a snitch, but he was also the kid who thrived on chaos, and I can see him raising the alarm just to be entertained.

He finishes his perusal, meeting my eyes with an unreadable expression as he brings the cigarette to his lips and takes a slow drag.

Oh no. "Christian—"

"Megan." He says my name like a taunt, like we're back in the playground, but there's no bite to it. If anything, he sounds amused. "Need some help?"

I shake my head, and he takes another drag. Neither of us moves.

"Well," he says finally. "I won't tell if you don't."

He gestures with the cigarette when I just stare at him and blows a short stream of smoke from the side of his mouth.

"Go on then." His attention turns to his phone, and he starts to scroll, acting like I'm not even there. Like I didn't just...

Oh.

I wait another breath to see if he's playing with me before I take a hesitant step forward and then another and another until I hurry past him, my pulse pounding once more.

"Freedom's the other way," he calls, and I spin around, darting past again with a mumbled thank you. I'm never going to live this down. But that's the least of my worries right now.

This time, I feel his eyes on me as I race around the side of the building, but I ignore him as I round the corner and find myself in the hotel parking lot. It's jammed with cars but empty of people, deserted but for a couple of taxi drivers standing around as they save their spots.

I get into the first one I see, startling the poor man in the front seat, who had his head in a newspaper.

"What the—" His eyes widen in the rearview as I shut the door, and he twists around to take me in. "Are you the bride?"

"No." I shove my skirts out of the way and zip open the bag. Technically, it's not a lie. Not anymore. "Are you free? I have cash. Lots of cash. Literal envelopes of cash."

His expression softens at my increasingly hysterical tone, and he reaches out to pat my arm.

"Don't worry about that, love. I believe you."

"I know how this looks, but I—"

"I've been doing this for forty years. You think you're the first runaway bride I've had?" He turns back to the front, all business. "Just tell me where you're going, and I'll get you there."

I could almost cry at his kindness. "Dublin," I say. "Please." I booked a random hotel room under a fake name, and it's where I plan on staying until I figure everything out. I don't know anyone in the city, which means no one will think to look for me there.

But my driver is hesitating. "Ah," he says lightly. "I thought you were thinking of the train station. That's a bit of a drive if I could just see some proof of—"

I fling the envelope into the front passenger seat, and he immediately changes track.

"Right-o! Any radio preference?"

I shake my head, glancing out the back window as he puts the car in gear. I don't know what I expect to find. Isaac chasing after me? My grandmother weeping? All I see are cars and the other drivers casting curious looks my way. And though I still feel guilty about the party and the lying and the rather abrupt exit from what was supposed to be the rest of my life, I don't regret it. Turns out the right decision just happened to be the most dramatic one, and as my getaway driver pulls out of the parking lot, I feel nothing but relief as we leave the hotel, the church, and my future behind.

ONE

CHRISTIAN

Five Years Later

This pub smells like a gym. Specifically, it smells like the changing room of a gym. It smells like the changing room of a gym the first day back after Christmas, full of sweaty bodies and damp towels and too many people in my space. Because there are too many people in my space. Too many loud, shuffling people, including the woman behind me, who's trying to squeeze past my chair but is seemingly unable to do so without jabbing an elbow into my back.

I hunch forward, reaching for my drink as an excuse to get away from her, only to scowl as the group next to us bursts into noisy laughter. Tourists, by the look of them. Six fresh-faced people in expensive rain gear and practical walking shoes. German?

"Christian."

Or maybe Dutch.

"*Christian.*"

"What?" I drag my gaze away from them to find Zoe watching me from across our tiny table.

"Do you think I should get a fringe?"

"A what?" Another person squeezes past, another elbow in the back.

"A fringe," Zoe continues.

"Yeah," I say, distracted. "Sure."

"Not too long." She makes a chopping motion against her forehead, her expression deadly serious. "Like, to here."

"Sounds great."

"But will it look great?"

"How should I know if— *Watch it*," I snap as some guy in a cheap suit almost spills a glass of wine over my head.

Zoe frowns. "I feel like you're not having a nice evening despite my incredible conversation skills."

"I'm having a great evening," I mutter. "And I'm sure I'd love your incredible conversation skills if I could hear them, but I can't. You're bad at picking places."

Her mouth drops open. "This is my favorite pub."

"It's packed."

"It's a lot of people's favorite pub. And it's not usually this busy," she adds. "It's just raining."

It is raining. I can see the sharp, violent burst of a shower against the stained-glass window above her head. It certainly explains the damp smell everywhere. And the sudden throng of office workers all looking a little stale after a day at their desks.

"What about side bangs?" Zoe asks.

"What are you even—"

"For my *fringe*." She sounds exasperated now. As if I'm the problem and not our surroundings. "Be more helpful. I thought you'd be good at this."

"Why would you think that?"

"Because your hair is fantastic!" she exclaims. "Look at it! It's so thick and soft." It's now the tourists' turn to look at me as she practically shouts the words for the whole pub to hear.

"Zoe."

"Good hair is wasted on men," she continues, oblivious. "Like eyelashes. Why do you all have such long eyelashes? I pay fifty euro for my lash lift; meanwhile, you're just walking around like some Victorian doll."

I choke on my beer, setting the glass down before I can spill it.

"It's a compliment," she insists.

I'm sure. "If you're that worried about a haircut, just make Molly get it first. Then you can see if it looks good or not."

She starts to scoff before her eyes go wide, and she takes out her phone, presumably to text Molly, her identical twin. Said identical twin is dating my nonidentical brother, Andrew, and last December, our families decided to spend Christmas together in Chicago, where they live. As the designated sarcastic siblings, we ended up spending a lot of time together. There was nothing romantic about it, but Zoe is blunt in a way I enjoy and lives her life exactly how she wants to, so we get along more than I do with most. She was one of the first people I reached out to when I moved to Dublin a few months ago, and I was secretly relieved with how easily she accepted me into her life here.

Even if it is hard to keep up with her train of thought sometimes.

"Have *you* ever thought about a fringe?" she asks now, peering hard at my head, but before I can respond, a woman in a low-cut top and exceptionally tight jeans appears beside us, planting her hands on an empty stool.

"Excuse me?" she asks, already halfway to taking it. "Are you using— Is that a toddler?"

Zoe and I both turn to her almost two-year-old son, Tiernan, who sits next to her as he enjoys his daily allotted screen time via a tablet.

"I think so," Zoe says slowly. "He was here when we arrived."

"She's kidding," I say when the woman stares at her.

"I am," Zoe says. "Sorry. I'm just nervous. It's his first time meeting his dad." She turns back to me, suddenly emotional. "I'm glad you came."

And here we go. "He's not mine."

"I just need the chair," the woman says hastily.

"He's not mine," I repeat, as Zoe sniffs.

"If you could give us some privacy," she continues, and the stranger scurries away with the stool to a group of women who, after a few whispers, all swing in our direction.

I force down a sigh. "Are you ever going to get tired of doing that?"

"It's literally the reason I bring him."

"And did you have to bring Tiernan?"

"You love Tiernan," she admonishes, pretending to cover his ears.

"I do love Tiernan. But everyone assumes I'm his dad."

"So?"

"So," I say, as she kisses him on the head. "Kind of makes it hard to meet someone."

"You want to meet someone in the pub? What are you, old?"

"I'm—"

"You can't pick up women in pubs. We don't want that. If an unknown man so much as looked at me tonight, I would glare at him so hard he'd need a root canal."

"That's not a saying."

"I never implied it was." She sits back. "You are so grumpy tonight."

I am. I know I am. And it's not her, and it's not her child, and it's not this pub even though, yes, the pub is a big part of it. It's me. I've been in a mood for months now, and I don't know why I thought moving back to Ireland might be the solution, but if anything, it's made it worse.

"I'm just tired," I say.

"Uh-huh." She clearly doesn't believe me but drops it as my phone buzzes on the table. "If that's work, I'm confiscating it."

It's not work. It's an email from my older brother, Liam, with the usual list of what his kids want from Santa. I suppose you've got to respect the forward planning. December 1 and he's straight in there. But he knows I take the role of favorite uncle seriously, so I send him a quick thank you before checking to see if anything needs to be ordered now.

"Mam invited you over for Christmas?" I ask, as I look up some overpriced, elaborate dollhouse.

"She did," Zoe says. "But I'll probably stay in Dublin."

I glance over in surprise. Zoe's a mother, but she's also the only other single person connected to our immediate families, having chosen to pursue IVF so she could have Tiernan, and I was looking forward to some backup at the dinner table. In fact, I'd been counting on it.

"I thought that was the plan, though."

"That was the suggestion," she corrects. "But your mother has enough to worry about without a bunch more mouths to feed. Think we're going to go to my folks. Order Chinese food."

"But Molly's coming," I push. "You don't want to spend Christmas with her?"

Zoe shrugs. "She's going to come up for New Year's. Same vibe. Different night."

"It's nowhere near the same vibe."

"Maybe not for the Fitzpatrick family. What's the big deal? Worried things will be incredibly dull without me?"

"I always worry about that," I say, straight-faced. "But you should come down. Even just for the day. You can save me from all the couples who—"

"Ah."

I break off, not liking the knowing look on her face. "What?"

"That's what this is about," she says. "Another lonely boy having another lonely Christmas."

"I'm not—"

"You are so lonely. You are textbook lonely. Why else are you hanging out with a single mother and her two-year-old in a pub you hate on a Friday night?"

"Apparently, for a therapy session," I say, but she ignores me.

"You're a grown man. You don't have to go home for Christmas if you don't want to."

"Of course, I want to." The words are instant. Automatic. Zoe sees right through them.

"What happened to that girl you were seeing?" she asks. "Naoise. She seemed nice."

"She dumped me for a rugby player. And she wasn't nice. I'm also pretty sure she was stealing from me."

"And that brunette with the killer arm muscles?"

"Focusing on her career."

"What did she—"

"Influencer."

Zoe presses her lips together. "Maybe you should try dating a librarian. Or a Taurus."

"Maybe I should just accept bachelor life."

"But you're a lonely boy."

"I'm not a—" I break off when she smiles. "You're single," I point out. "And you're not lonely."

"I never said it was about being single. You can be with someone and be lonely. And you can be alone and not feel lonely at all. It took me ten years of dating and thinking something was wrong with me before I realized I was happier by myself. And now look at me. I'm so well-adjusted it's unfair on everyone else."

"Well, maybe that's me," I say. "Maybe I'm better single."

"Aw. Buddy." Zoe pouts. "No. You definitely need a girl-friend. Other half, two-become-one, that kind of thing."

"But you don't."

"No."

"Never? Never ever?"

"Nah." She shrugs. "I'd be open to it if it happened, but I'm good. Plus, I don't want to tie myself down too much."

"You literally have a child."

"I have a *what?*"

"Okay." I finish the last of my pint and stand as Zoe turns to Tiernan with a shocked expression. "That's officially old now."

"It's a classic," she says, wiping some chocolate spread from his chin. "Classics don't get old."

I beg to disagree. "Do you want another Diet Coke?"

"If you're buying."

"I bought the last round."

"And you're a true gentleman," she says sweetly.

"Tiernan?" I bend to meet his eye. We got along great when he was a baby, but now that he's developing into an actual human, he alternates between thinking I'm the best person ever and completely ignoring me. Tonight, it's the latter. "Are you thirsty? You want juice?"

"Juice?" Zoe repeats, and he manages a distracted nod before focusing back on the screen. "He'll have a whiskey sour," she says to me.

"On it."

I turn, only to dodge a waitress who flashes me a smile as she balances a tower of empty glasses in her hands. She looks back with obvious interest, and I pause, considering, but Zoe's pointed throat-clear ruins that little plan.

Fine.

Gearing myself up for the inevitable wait, I leave the safety of our table and join the masses at the bar. You'd swear it's the only open pub in Dublin given how busy it is, a consequence of being at the epicenter of tourist hotspots and office blocks. The smell of gym only gets worse as I approach, but it's not lost on me that I'm like those people stuck in traffic complaining about other cars, so I try to ignore it, and squash in behind a woman shouting her order over the chaos.

She looks as bedraggled as everyone else, with her brown hair settling into almost-dry waves along her shoulders while her blouse is soaked through, revealing the outline of a bra strap. I look away, but that only brings my attention to the man next to me, who's huffing and glaring every five seconds as if that will make the overworked staff move faster.

The whole thing is giving me a headache, and not for the first time do I question the life choices that brought me here.

I thought I'd be working in some skyscraper right now. In some glass-walled office with a glorious view and my future secured ahead of me. And I was there. For a while at least. And in that office, I watched the sun rise and I watched the sun set, and I sat in my ergonomic chair and I worked. I worked and I worked and I worked because that was what I was supposed to do. Because that was supposed to be the solution to everything.

I was, to everyone's surprise, the smart one in the family. I didn't want to be. I didn't try to be. I just was. School was easy. College was easy. I aced my tests, charmed my way through interviews, got a scholarship to business school, and off I went.

It didn't change anything.

I mean, on the outside, sure. I got the grades and the graduate programs, and the jobs. I made friends with people who went skiing and dated women with names like Venetia who always seemed to have a lot of money despite working at tiny publishing houses that only put out experimental poetry twice a year. I wore nice things and ate nice things and bought nice things. I invested my bonuses and donated to charity, and did everything a social climber was supposed to do, and still, I felt restless. Incomplete.

Everyone else seemed to know their place in the world but me. Like they'd all been let in on some big secret. And no matter how many things I did right, everything always felt wrong.

Zoe wanted to be a mother, so she became a mother. My siblings have their partners. My colleagues have their careers, and I have an empty apartment, a job I lose interest in by the day, and friends and girlfriends that come and go with such little impact on my life that I'm beginning to think something's wrong with me.

No matter how pretty my eyelashes are.

My phone vibrates again, but I ignore it as a group of office workers enters the pub, adding to the small throng around the bar. As they do, I finally make eye contact with the bartender, who hands a receipt to the woman in front of me.

Two things happen at once.

Someone in the group pushes me forward, trying to see what's on tap at the same time the woman picks up her glass and starts to turn, her eyes on her feet, watching her steps.

For a second, I feel a warm body pressed against mine and then a whiff of flowers from the stranger's hair. She clearly isn't expecting anyone to be right behind her and gasps as soon as she realizes there is, the sharp inhale ending in a curse as she's jostled into my chest, tipping the glass she's holding, and the 175 milliliters of red wine within it, straight down my shirt.

TWO

MEGAN

I am not having a good day.

I would actually go so far as to say that I'm having a bad day.

And that's fine. They happen.

It's just that today was supposed to be a *great* day. I was supposed to have my powerlifting class this morning, and I love my powerlifting class. And then it was our receptionist's birthday, which meant cake in the office. After work, I was going to go with Lauren from sales to give blood because Lauren from sales hates needles and needs constant support throughout. Then as a reward for the whole saving-someone's-life thing, I was going to go home, put on a facemask, and watch the cinematic masterpiece that is 1999's *The Mummy* before going to sleep at ten p.m.

A great day.

But instead of any of that, my class was canceled, so no endorphin rush, my meeting overran, so no cake, and then David, the guy I've been half-heartedly messaging, was like, *don't forget our date tonight!* And I was like, *sure won't!* Except I absolutely did forget our date tonight because I only agreed to it when I was feeling unloved and hormonal in that week-before-your-period way. So instead of giving blood with Lauren and feeling great about myself, I gave blood with Lauren while anxiously doing my makeup and then left before my allotted "stay here in case you faint" time because I was running late and then it *rained,* and then I arrived at this shitty pub, and David's all *I got caught up at work,* and now I've just spilled a glass of house red all over some guy's shirt.

"I'm so sorry," I say, watching the stain spread rapidly down his front. "I'll pay for dry-cleaning. If you give me your number, I'll—"

"Megan?"

My head snaps up, which is a mistake as the sudden movement makes little spots appear at the corners of my eyes, but through the sudden rush to my brain, I manage to focus on the man in front of me. The frustratingly familiar man, who looks like—

"Christian?"

It *is* Christian. Christian Fitzpatrick. Here. In Dublin. Which is odd because the last time I saw him was...

He starts to sway in front of me, which is weird until the whole world starts swaying, which is even weirder until I realize they're not moving at all. I am.

"Whoa." He grabs my upper arm, warm fingers wrapping around my bicep as he holds me steady. "You okay?"

"Yeah, I'm..." Nope. No, I'm not. "My knees feel funny."

"You take something?"

"Uh, I got the bus here..." I trail off as his grip tightens, tugging me out of the chaos. The small crowd parts as if pushed, all eyeing me curiously as I'm brought over to a row of tables next to the bar.

"She needs to sit down," he says to the nearest man, who just frowns at us.

"But I—"

"Move," Christian says, sounding *very* annoyed, and I smile a weak apology as the guy scrambles away. "Sit," he says to me, and that sounds like a great idea, so I do, feeling like I'm going to puke.

Actually, I'm definitely going to puke, and Christian must see it on my face because he doesn't even give me a warning as he plants a hand on my head and pushes it between my knees.

"Deep breaths," he orders, and I squeeze my eyes shut, waiting for my body to calm down.

"She okay?" another man asks.

"She's fine."

"Too much to drink?"

"No," he says tersely, and that's the end of that conversation.

Was he always so abrupt? I don't remember him being like that.

"Megan?"

Not that I knew him at all.

"You here with anyone?" he asks. "A friend?"

"I'm supposed to be on a date."

"Do you want me to get them?"

"I think he's a no-show. It's a first date." I sit up slowly, pleased when the world doesn't immediately tilt. "Sorry. I just gave blood."

Christian looks incredulous. "You gave blood before a first date?"

"I was fine until I wasn't." I try another breath, and the world remains as it is. "He bailed on me." God, I am so done with this day. "Sorry about your shirt."

"It'll wash. But you should—"

"You tried to flirt, didn't you?" A new voice interrupts as a pretty blonde woman appears beside him, carrying a toddler on her hip. "You tried to pick up someone in a pub, and now look. You've got wine on your shirt."

"I'm aware," Christian says, as she turns her curious gaze to me.

"Are you alright?"

"I'm fine," I say. "Just nauseous."

"He has that effect on people."

"This is Megan," Christian explains flatly. "I know her from home."

"Oh. Cool." The woman smiles at me. "Are you a librarian?"

"Okay, thanks, Zoe," Christian interrupts before I can respond. "You're going?"

"Yeah, he's getting cranky. I'll see you next week? Say bye to Uncle Christian," she adds, passing the kid over to him for a kiss before turning back to me. "You sure you're alright?" she asks kindly.

"I just need to sit for a while."

"I'll stay with her," Christian adds, handing the little boy back.

"If you're sure." The woman gives me another sympathetic smile, and then she's gone, slipping through the crowd with a final goodbye.

"Friend of the family," Christian explains, and I nod, which only sends my head spinning again.

"You don't have to stay," I tell him. "Honestly. I'll be fine."

"You don't look fine."

"That's just my general vibe."

"Uh-huh." We begin a short staring contest that he wins. "On a scale of one to ten, how much do you still feel like throwing up?"

"...seven? I'm grand," I add quickly. "Honestly. I'll just go hang out in the bathroom and— Or okay, you can come too."

I don't protest as he takes me by the elbow, helping me stand. Mostly because I do actually need the help, and I'm feeling too shitty to be embarrassed about it. Embarrassment is future Megan's problem. Now Megan just wants her bed.

Christian leads me over to the unisex bathrooms at the back of the pub, which are... not great. But they're empty, and there's a small basket of free tampons next to the sink, so, you know, bonus points. Or at least I think so. They don't seem to impress Christian, who's looking around the room like he's getting a disease just by standing in it.

"I'll get you some water," he says, and lets me go.

"You really don't—"

Yeah, he's gone.

Christian Fitzpatrick. Huh.

I don't move as the door swings shut, testing my stomach to make sure everything stays in place. When it does, I check my messages to see David's still left me on read.

Maybe he died.

Or got *arrested*. Or— Yeah, he bailed. Well, screw him if he thinks I'm going to hang around and wait for him.

This has been a shitty day, and I would like a nice end to it.

Which means pizza, facemask, and movies.

I swipe David's profile away and text my roommate instead. Maybe Frankie can tear herself away from the lab for one evening and keep me company.

I almost fainted in the pub.

She messages back immediately.

Attention seeker.

I'm serious, I send, and start to type out an explanation when she calls me.

"The fact that you answered me right away makes me think you're not working as hard as you should be," I tell her.

"I'm not working at all," she says bluntly. "I'm with Claudio."

"What? Why?"

"For an orgasm, Megan. Why else?" Frankie's a good room-mate. But a bad dater. Or maybe just a serial one. She flits from one guy to the next like she's trying them on for size, and in the two years I've been living with her, I've never seen her be with someone for more than a few weeks. She says she's not going to settle for anything other than her soulmate. But I just think she's picky.

"I thought you said he blinked weird," I say, organizing the tampons into little rows.

"He did. But it's grown on me. Did you know he plays the horn in an orchestra?"

"No."

"Well, he does. Do you know what that means?"

"No, and if this is connected to your future orgasm, I don't think I want to."

"What happened?" she asks, and I sigh, feeling sorry for myself.

"Nothing. I'm just dumb. I gave blood after work, and then I was rushing and got all light-headed."

"You said you fainted."

"*Almost* fainted," I correct. "Big difference."

"Small difference," she argues. "Do you want me to come home?"

"No. I thought you were studying. Orgasms are much more —" I lock eyes with Christian as he enters the room, and his brows shoot up.

"Much more important," I finish, accepting the glass of water from him with as much dignity as I can muster.

"You're important," Frankie says firmly. "I can orgasm at home."

"I know you can. I hear you all the time."

"So, I'll—"

"Frankie, I'm serious. I'm going to grab a taxi and watch TV. I was just trying to give you an excuse to take a night off."

"But—"

"Enjoy yourself," I say, glancing at Christian, who's studiously examining a poster for next week's karaoke night. "But thank you for offering to give up sex for me. I know it's been a while."

"I'm not even mad about the jibe because it's true. Text me when you're back."

"I will."

"Don't faint again."

"I won't," I promise, and Christian turns back as we hang up. "My grandmother."

"It's good to keep in touch," he says, without missing a beat. He peers at me, but his concerned expression clears slightly at whatever he sees. "You look better already."

"I do?" I feel better. I only realize it then and take a few sips of the water to make sure.

"Got you these as well," he says, brandishing a small packet of peanuts. "I wasn't sure what was best."

"Iron," I say. I watched two *what to do after giving blood* videos before I went into the clinic and then proceeded to follow none of the advice. "But I'm going to guess they're all out of spinach."

"It is a Friday, Megan."

I smile, taking the snack as my eyes drift down to the stain now covering half his shirt.

"If you offer to pay for my dry-cleaning again—"

"I wasn't going to," I say, even though I definitely was. "I think I'm going to go home."

"Are you sure?"

"Definitely."

As if on cue, the bathroom door swings open, nearly hitting

Christian in the butt as a group of women stumbles inside. They take one look at him and start giggling, all of them delightfully tipsy, but he doesn't seem to notice, holding the door open as he focuses on me. Our gazes meet like this is something we do every night, and then he tilts his head.

"I'll walk you out," he says, and he does just that, shepherding me through his new fan club and back into the din.

"Do you usually come here?" he asks, as I shrug on my coat.

"God no," I say before catching myself. Crap. This could be his local. "It's nice and all, but I usually... Uh..."

"Megan?"

I don't answer, distracted as I catch sight of two people making out in one of the nooks nearby. One a complete stranger and the other... well. You have to laugh, or else you'd cry, right?

Just kidding, I'm definitely going to cry later.

Christian follows my gaze, confused.

"Who's that?" he asks, and I don't bother lying as David pulls back, intending to catch the attention of a waitress and seeing me instead.

An officially bad day.

"My date."

THREE

CHRISTIAN

I barely get a glimpse of the guy before Megan plasters herself to my side, sliding her hand around my back as she all but clings to me.

"What are you—"

"Smile."

"What?"

"Smile!" She orders and waggles her fingers at the man. "Dickhead," she adds through clenched teeth. "I should have known by his profile. *Not looking for someone who takes themselves too seriously.* What does that even—"

She inhales sharply as I throw an arm around her shoulder, squeezing her to me. I don't so much smile as I do smirk at the idiot who obviously messed her around, the same one who now has the gall to look mad about it. But the last thing I want to do is get into a sloppy fistfight in the middle of this shitty pub, and so as soon as he stands, I turn us both and tow her away.

"Wait," she protests, trying to look back. "I want to—"

"Take the high road," I tell her, as he calls after her. "Let him flail."

"Or I could make a scene," she says hopefully, and I almost

laugh as I push our way outside. The rain has stopped, but it's left a minefield of puddles in its wake, pointedly highlighting every pothole and blocked drain along the street. A few brave souls risk the threat of another downpour as they huddle under an awning, including a group of men in the smoking area to the left of us, clutching their pints as they talk.

"Thanks for looking after me," Megan says, once we stop. "And for helping me save face."

"I'm sorry about your date."

"I'm not," she mutters, rubbing her hands together. She looks cold.

"You should eat something," I say, trying to think of a restaurant nearby, but she's already walking to the side of the road, looking expectantly at the line of cars waiting at the lights up ahead.

"I will at home."

I frown. "*How* are you getting home?"

"Taxi."

"In Dublin?"

"A fool's errand, I know." As if to punctuate her words, the line of cars moves forward, all of them ignoring her outstretched arm. She doesn't seem fussed though, just takes out her phone, and opens a rideshare app. It doesn't make me feel any better.

"You want me to walk you out a bit? You're not going to have any luck around here. Not at this time of night."

"I'm not that far," she says. "I'll give it five more minutes, and then I'll walk."

Alone?

Unease slithers through me, making me want to fidget. Well, actually, it makes me want to smoke, but I fidget instead, turning my lighter over and over in my pocket. The night has barely begun, but it's winter, and it's dark, and the thought of her going home by herself just doesn't sit right. "I'd prefer if I went with you."

She looks surprised. "You want to walk me home?"

"If that's alright with you."

"Hey." One of the men calls out to us, stepping away from his group. "You okay?" he asks Megan in a *is this guy bothering you?* voice.

I bristle, but Megan just nods. "He's a friend. Thanks, though."

"You sure?"

"Positive," she says with a smile. "Have a good night."

The stranger raises a hand in acknowledgment and leaves us be. I turn to Megan with an expectant expression.

"Friend, huh?"

"Best friend," she says. "It's a real honor, so you're welcome."

"You realize that means you're going to have to let me walk you now. As your friend."

"Best friend."

"Best friend," I echo, but still she hesitates.

"You don't need to."

"But I'd like to."

She glances back at the traffic, clearly torn, and I think that's it, and we'll say our goodbyes, when she looks down at her app and sees the ride she just requested is canceled.

"That's one good thing about bad days," I say, as her face falls. "They always end."

She slips her phone back into her pocket, pursing her lips. "I'm really not that far."

"Then it won't take that long. Please," I add. "My mother would disown me if I didn't."

"How is Colleen?" she asks, and I try not to show how surprised I am that she remembers my mother's name.

"She's good. Happy in the knowledge that she raised her children right."

Megan snorts, her face scrunching with indecision before smoothing out. "Okay. Thank you."

And just like that, I'm walking her home.

I'm embarrassed about my persistence as soon as we hit the main road. It's late, but it's not that late. Instead, it's that odd time of night when the after-work mob is leaving, but it's too early for the nightlife crowd, and the streets are a mix of office clothes and minidresses.

We dodge a group of tech bros with their branded backpacks and lanyards still swinging around their necks and almost walk into a group of women spilling out of another pub, lighting cigarettes with French-tipped nails.

I hold my breath until they're well behind us, keeping my gaze ahead.

It's been three months since I've gone cold turkey.

And it's *shit*.

It's my fourth go at it, but it's the longest I've ever gone, and I'm determined that this time will be the last time. That I'll quit them for good even though some days the cravings are so bad I feel like my throat is closing up, and some nights I can't sleep more than a few snatched hours, and I get so frustrated I can—

"So," I say, plastering a smile on my face. "What have you been up to since you... you know."

"Left my fiancé at the altar and skipped town?"

"Yeah. That."

"Well, I moved here, and now I work in marketing," she says, and I nod because what else are you supposed to do when someone says they work in marketing?

"Do you like it?" I ask politely.

"I do." And she sounds so earnest, so damn cheerful about it, that I check to see if she's joking.

She's not.

"I work for this company that does eco mold remover," she continues. "We've got a few products on the market now, but it's still pretty small. My boss started the business in her kitchen a few years ago, and now they're talking about expanding into Europe. The money isn't amazing, but I like working there." She pauses. "I think I love it, actually."

"You sound surprised."

"Everyone always thought I'd be a teacher."

"My parents thought I'd end up in jail, so you're doing better than me."

"There's still time," she says pleasantly and pulls the zip of her jacket up. "What about you? Have you been in Dublin this whole time?" She sounds skeptical, which I understand. Dublin's a capital city, but a small one, and it isn't unusual to regularly bump into people you know.

"I just moved here," I explain. "From London. My company started up an Irish branch and put me in charge."

"The fools."

"Tell me about it."

"How's it going?"

I shrug. "Fine, I think. No one's fired me yet."

"Do you like it?"

"I like the money."

"Ah. Work to live, is it?"

"That's it."

"So, what do you do to live?" Her voice is probing, unabashedly curious, and I get an honest-to-God flashback. Not a sense of déjà vu. Not a vague, *I've been here before*. But a crystal-clear memory of seven-year-old Megan sitting in class with her hand in the air and her forehead creased in a constant frown as she pesters our teacher over and over and over again. *Why?*

It used to annoy the hell out of me.

But now I just feel a vague sort of affection for the woman beside me. It's kind of comforting how so many years can pass, and yet a part of her is still exactly the same.

"I'm still figuring that part out," I say truthfully, and she seems to accept this as we cross a junction and enter into that middle space between city and suburbia. It's not exactly the nicest part of town. I can't tell if things are downtrodden in a hipster way or a real way, but Megan seems to know where she's going.

"What about everyone else?" she asks. "Liam?"

"Married," I say, thinking of my eldest brother. "Two kids. Weirdly normal and well-adjusted, so they take after their mother's side. Andrew's in Chicago and has got himself a girl-friend. And then Hannah's in college studying fashion."

"College?" Megan makes a face. "I feel old."

"What about you guys?" I know it's just her mam and her brother, but for the life of me, I can't remember his name. "How's..."

"Aidan," she supplies. "He's in Melbourne. Don't ask me what he's doing, but it's something with software for some other software, and it's one of those cult companies that he spent six months interviewing for, and now they keep him trapped in the office. Like every time he tries to leave, they add an arcade game or something. He's like a magpie."

"Is he coming back for Christmas?"

"Yep," she says, popping the p. "Big reunion time."

I glance over at the uncomfortable edge to her tone. "You guys get along?"

"Oh, no, it's not that," she says quickly. "He's great. Annoying but great. I want to see him. I'm just nervous about going home. It's been a while."

"How long's a while?"

"Since forever," she says, and it takes me a second to under-stand her words.

"You're joking? Since the wedding?"

"Didn't exactly leave on the best of terms with everyone."

"But that was years ago."

"I remember," she says testily, and I fall quiet as I try to recall what happened after she left. Not much if I'm honest. I was hungover enough on the day as it was, and I just remember a lot of people standing around whispering. Beyond my enjoyment of something happening to liven things up a bit, I never gave it much thought except for...

Well.

My eyes drift back to Megan as she jabs the button to cross the road, the image of her in that wedding dress suddenly as clear in my mind as if it had happened yesterday. I swear even now I can still feel the heat from that afternoon, the rigidness of my suit. I'd slipped away from the church to get a few minutes to myself and that's all I thought I wanted until she came bursting through those doors like an unstoppable storm.

A storm in stilettoes, but a storm nonetheless.

It was the moment she went from being someone I barely thought about to one of the most interesting people in my life. And then she disappeared.

"I promised Mam I'd go back this year," she says, dragging me back to the present. "But between the possibility of bumping into Isaac and seeing everyone else, I keep thinking of excuses not to."

Isaac. The ex. Another kid at the front of the class. This one not as cute, though.

"He still hanging around?"

"As far as I know," she says. "Our parents are still friends."

"Can't you stealth it or something? Sneak in in the dead of night and out again."

"Maybe. And yeah, if Aidan wasn't coming back. But he is, and Mam wants to make a big thing of it and..." She sighs. "You're right. I'm sure it will be fine. It's been years, but I'm just worried that I'll go back, and it will seem like five minutes. And my therapist would *not* be happy if I regressed. He said I made great progress, and it's incredibly important to me that I'm his favorite patient."

"A normal thing," I agree. "Well, hey. I'm not one to talk. I'm thinking about not going home either."

"For Christmas? How come?"

"Just…" I try to think of an explanation that doesn't head into pity party territory. "Family."

She waits for me to continue, only to nod sagely when I don't. "Family can be hard."

"Yeah."

A beat of silence. "Not as hard as my thing, though."

"No." I fight back a smile. "Runaway bride definitely wins."

"We should have Christmas together. Be each other's excuse."

"Excuse?"

"Yeah. 'My friend wants me to stay in Dublin' and so on and so forth. We could have takeout. Watch some movies. Get wine-drunk." She sounds wistful. "No showboating. No fake smiles."

"No questions about life choices—"

"Or life partners," she adds. "Just all the good stuff and none of the bad stuff. A black sheep Christmas."

"Is that what we are?"

"I'll buy us an ice-cream cake," is all she says, and leads me across the road.

She tells me more about her work as we go, and it's only another few minutes before she slows to a stop in front of a small, three-story building.

A low, buzzing noise emanates from the streetlamp over-head, the same one that casts an eerie orange glow over our little patch of pavement, but the rest of the road is dark. I peer down it, but Megan seems comfortable as she produces a fluffy pink keyring from her purse and gestures at the door.

"This is me," she says.

"It was nice bumping into you."

"Yeah."

"Say hi to the family?"

"Sure. And same."

It's a clear end to the conversation, but she doesn't move. Just continues to fiddle with her keys as she looks at me with a small line between her brows. And I'm about to say goodnight, already mentally mapping my route home, when she opens her mouth and erases every other thought in my head.

"You want to come up?"

I freeze, and I swear to God, even Megan looks startled by her offer, but she doesn't take it back. She doesn't blush or backtrack. She just waits, still spinning those keys, still staring up at me, and for the first time tonight, I take a proper look at her.

It's not the first time I registered that Megan O'Sullivan is kind of hot. Kind of beautiful, even. She always was. Gray-blue eyes, delicate features. Her brown hair falls to her shoulders in the same cut I remember from when we were young, but in the haze of the streetlamp, I spy strands of red scattered throughout, glinting in the artificial light.

She's done this before. That much I can guess by the confident way she holds herself as she waits for my answer. And it's that knowledge that helps me make up my mind. That, plus the little tug inside that made me walk her home in the first place, the pulling curiosity that doesn't want to say goodbye just yet.

The one that says screw it.

"I'd love to."

FOUR

MEGAN

Oh no.

Oh. No.

Maybe they took more blood from me than I thought.

That can be the only explanation for what just happened.

Do you want to come up? Do you want to come up and have sex with me, Christian Fitzpatrick? Then *step this way. Come right in.* Be my *freaking* guest.

That's thinking with the vagina and not the head. Except for my eyes. Because the eyes see what the eyes see, and I see... him.

Every one of my friends was in love with him growing up. Or at least love as in the preteen, "he has messy hair and sits at the back of the classroom" way. He doesn't have messy hair now. He has very tidy hair. Very dark, thick, tidy hair and nice clothes and a nice coat and an expensive watch on his wrist. It's why I invited him up. Because he's gorgeous. There's no depth to my intentions here. Nothing other than I haven't had sex in a few weeks, and I am a shallow lady with shallow needs. Needs that, let's be honest, that man looks like he would have no problem fulfilling. But ideally, he would also be a stranger while doing so. Someone who doesn't know about my past and who doesn't care about my future. Who's only thinking of tonight.

But then again, there's no rule saying I have to see the guy again.

And it's not like he said no. Not like he's... Oh my God, I'm considering it.

I drum my fingers against the sink as I stare at my reflection. Five years. It's been five years since I last saw him, and who's to say it won't be five before I see him again? Or ten? Twenty? Ever? I could drop dead tomorrow and—

Leave the bathroom, Megan.

Be a normal person and leave the bathroom.

I give myself a spritz of the communal perfume before (bravely) opening the door, half-hoping he's snuck out so my decision's made for me.

He has not snuck out. He's made himself at home exactly as I told him to before I mumbled something about needing to pee. His coat is folded neatly over the back of a chair, his phone is on the table, and the man himself is busy looking at a Polaroid of Frankie and me taped to the mirror.

He straightens when I emerge, turning around with a smile on his face. One that fades as soon as he sees the strained one on mine.

"Want something to drink?" I ask brightly. "I've got beer."

"Beer's good," he says, his hands slipping into his pockets as I make my way to the small galley kitchen. "Nice place."

"It's not, but thank you for lying."

"That your roommate in the photo?"

"Frankie. She's doing a PhD in microbiology."

"Impressive."

"It's mainly her snacking and crying, but I think it's all part of the process." I open the fridge, staring at it blindly as I babble.

"I'm lucky with her. In a place this small, we should be at each other's throats, but we get along okay. She's pretty easygoing." I grab two bottles from the shelf and turn around to find him examining one of the many baskets of wool dotted around the apartment.

I watch as he plucks a purple ball from the top, turning it over in his hands like he's almost certain what it is but wants to make sure.

"You paint?" he asks after a long second.

"I..." Huh? "No, I— Shut up," I say, and he smiles.

He full-on *smiles*.

It's a charming, eye-crinkle smile that thrusts me out of my childhood memories and into my teenage ones. A flash of the Christian I once knew, flirting with half the class.

"What?" he asks when I just stare at him.

"Nothing." But then: "Everyone had a crush on you in school, you know."

He props a shoulder against the wall, his smile turning to a grin. "I know."

Of course he does.

"Not you, though," he adds. "You didn't even know I existed."

"*Me?*" I pry the caps off the bottles, aghast at this complete rewrite of our history. "Other way around, Casanova."

"I knew you existed. It was hard not to. Always sitting at the front of the class, answering every question. I had to lean around your raised hand just to see the board."

"As if you ever looked at the board," I scoff, and he laughs. It's a nice laugh. Deep and husky and... I clutch the bottles, mulling over his words. He's not wrong. I knew he existed too. But it was in a vague way. A peripheral way.

I didn't have a crush on Christian because I had a crush on Isaac. I only ever had eyes for Isaac. To the point where it never occurred to me to so much as look at anyone else.

"I knit," I explain, gesturing to the wool. "I have a shop online."

"Oh yeah?" He looks mildly impressed. "You make much from it?"

"About minus twenty quid a month."

He laughs again, throwing the ball in the air before placing it back in the basket. "When did that start? The knitting."

"I can't remember." It's like asking when I learned to talk. For as far back as my thoughts allow, I always had needles in my hands.

"All your hats," he says suddenly, and I cringe as his eyes widen. I insisted on wearing every one of my creations as a child, whether or not they suited me. My mother probably thought she was doing the right thing by encouraging my interests, but looking back, maybe she could have hidden *one* of the uglier pieces and told me it shrunk in the wash.

"I'm better at it now," I say, but Christian's not listening to me, too busy reminiscing.

"And those cardigans you used to wear. With the holes."

"Some of those were intentional."

"And the socks. With the—"

"Pom-poms." I sigh, passing him one of the bottles. "Yeah."

"How did we not bully the hell out of you?"

"Because knitting needles can stab," I mutter.

"Do you make sweaters? Christmas ones, that kind of thing?"

"I mean, I can," I say, and he nods as if storing that piece of information away for the future.

There's a moment of silence, one broken only by the wail of a siren in the distance, and then he clinks his bottle against mine. "Cheers."

I murmur it back, taking a sip at the same time he does and all the while pretending that I'm not studying the strong column of his throat, the full curve of his lips. With the long nose and hint of cheekbones, he looks the same as he did back in school. Just older now. Better. The unruly hair has been tamed and styled, the boyish face grown into something sharper and stronger, traits that usually aren't my type, but tonight, definitely are.

He's studying me too, though he's being much more obvious about it, his dark eyes wholly on me until it becomes a bit of a game. Neither of us looks away. Neither of us blinks. When he takes another sip, I do too, and when he starts to smile, my mind starts to race, focusing in on those long fingers wrapped around the bottle, and imagining all the other places they could go. Imagining—

"You're buzzing."

"What?" Oh.

I wriggle out my phone from my back pocket, flustered. My mother is calling me.

"Let me just— Hello? Mam?" I point at the thing as though explaining to him what a phone call is. "You okay?"

"I'm fine!" She chirps down the line. "Can you talk?"

"I— Yes?" Christian's already moving away, taking another swig of beer as he takes a seat at the table. "One second," I say to my mother before going into my bedroom and closing the door behind me. One look at the place makes me extremely glad I did, and I put her on speaker as I move clothes from the floor to the laundry basket. "What's up?"

"I got an email from Aidan just now. He's back on the fifteenth."

"That's early."

"Said he's going to make a month of it. He can work from home, apparently. You know how it is these days."

"I do," I say, making the bed.

Aidan didn't come back for Christmas last year because of a deadline, and the year before that, Mam and I flew out to

Melbourne to be with him for the novelty of it. And at the time, it was a novelty. He was only supposed to be gone for a few months, but every time the topic of returning home came up, he'd make some excuse, or he'd get a promotion or a new girl-friend, and he'd push it back. No one expects him to return permanently. No one that is, except my mother, who still talks about the whole thing like he's gone backpacking for the summer, and not, you know, emigrated ten thousand miles away.

"So, what day can we expect you?" she asks now. "I think it would be nice if you were here when he was."

"Uh..." I re-tuck my fitted sheet, checking for errant socks as I go. "I guess I haven't really thought that far ahead."

My mother makes a disapproving noise, letting me know that that was the wrong answer. "You said that last month."

"And I'm saying it this month. Christmas is weeks away."

"You're still coming home, aren't you?"

"Of course, I am," I say, feeling a twinge of guilt at the suspicion in her voice.

It's not like I don't understand it. I was telling the truth to Christian earlier. I haven't stepped one foot in the village since I ran out on my wedding. Of course, she doesn't believe me. *I* wouldn't believe me.

But while Aidan may be covering the physical miles, I'd be covering the mental ones, ones I'd happily cross a few oceans to avoid. I didn't think about the repercussions at the time, but it wasn't just my fiancé I left behind at the altar. It was everything.

I was fifteen years old when Isaac first asked me out. He was the first boy I ever dated. The first boy I ever kissed, and we became the kind of couple where you didn't hear one name without the other. Where you didn't exist apart.

And when I left him, I was no longer Megan from down the road. I was the girl who broke his heart. Unfriended, unliked, and unsupported. The level of animosity wasn't something I was used to. So I stayed away. For everyone's sakes. And now I was coming back. Single and broke and... no, that's it, actually. That's me.

"I'm not asking you to make an announcement in the village square," Mam continues as though reading my mind. "But I'd like you to be at the fundraiser."

Her Christmas fundraiser, she means. The one she hosts every year. A snazzy, decadent affair where we dress up, drink up, and raise a lot of money for the local hospice. She's thrown one every year since I was a kid, and it's a big deal to her. She works hard on it, she looks forward to it, and she's never once pushed me to go since the wedding. Not until now.

"I'll be there," I promise. "I'm looking forward to it."

"Good."

I can tell she doesn't believe me.

"I bumped into Sophie O'Meara yesterday," she adds, and I still.

"What?"

"She wanted to know how Aidan was getting on."

But not me. Not her actual friend. Or her ex-friend.

"She's a teacher now," Mam continues in a "just like you were going to be" tone. "Moved into that old cottage by the church."

Fantastic.

"Mam, please don't speak to Sophie."

"Why not?"

Because she doesn't speak to me. The words are on the tip of my tongue. But I don't say them. Because if I did, I'd sound like I was twelve.

"Megan—"

"You're right," I say. "Never mind. That's great news about Aidan. I'll let you know the timings, but I've got to go, okay?"

"If you're just hanging up to—"

"I'm not. I've got someone over." And knowing it's the only thing that will get her off my back, "A date."

She instantly changes tune. "A date?"

"Uh-huh."

"Well, why didn't you say anything?" she asks, sounding half-annoyed and half-delighted. "Is he—"

"I'll talk to my boss on Monday," I interrupt. "And book some time off. Alright? Love you! Bye!"

I hang up, dropping my head back as I allow myself one moment of stressing about everything before letting it all out. There'll be plenty of time to worry later, but right now, I deserve to relax.

And luckily for me, I know just how to do it.

Or at least who to do it with.

I do another quick check of the room, making sure it's presentable before slipping back out to find Christian sitting on the couch, his beer abandoned with mine on the table. He looks up when I appear, and I linger a little obviously in the doorway, but when he just sits there, I decide to join him.

"Sorry about that," I say. "Parents."

"You're grand," he says, as I adjust the cushions. "You weren't kidding about your mam, were you?"

I'm confused for a moment before I realize he must have heard every word.

"Sorry," he says, seeing the look on my face. "The walls are..."

Paper thin. Crap. "I guess I shouldn't complain," I say. "*Oh, no. Help. My mother loves me.* But it's like..."

"I know."

"It sounds silly, but I just—"

"Megan," he interrupts gently. "I get it. Don't worry."

I hesitate, but he seems to mean it. And I believe him. I don't know why. It's not like anyone else ever tried to understand. Usually, they were too busy trying to convince me otherwise. But Christian's looking at me like he knows exactly what I'm going through. And more than that, like it's okay that I am.

But even with that, even after the terrible day I've had, I'm still surprised to hear myself blurt, "Do you want to get a coffee sometime?"

His brows pinch together, and I hurry on.

"Not now," I say. "That would be ridiculous for our sleep cycle. But at home. At Christmas."

"Christmas?"

"Yeah. Since we'll both be back and miserable, we could be miserable together." I pause. "Okay, that doesn't sound very fun."

"No," he agrees, but there's an odd tone to the word, one that matches the odd look on his face.

"I guess I'm just asking if you want to have a buddy system. I know you'll be busy, but if you ever need a break from your family, I'll be around, so we could grab coffee or..." I trail off, as he just stares at me like he's figuring out some intricate puzzle. Or like he took something and is trying very hard to behave normally. "Or not," I finish.

"Like backup," he says, and I perk up, relieved.

"Exactly."

He nods, his eyes searching my face. For what, I don't know, but he must find it because his confused expression changes, turning almost pensive. "When are you going home?"

I blow out a breath, thinking back to what my mother said. "Fifteenth? Sixteenth? Whatever that Saturday is, I guess. If they'll give me the time off," I add, even though they will. The office basically shuts down for Christmas, anyway.

"I was planning a few days later, but I could do that."

"Do what?" I ask, only to straighten when he shifts closer to me. So close our knees touch. Or almost touch. If he'd shuffle over an *inch* more, we'd—

"I'm just thinking out loud here," he says. "But I want to ru₁ something by you."

"Okay." The word comes out a little breathy, and I cringe, but Christian doesn't seem to notice.

"Why don't we go back together?"

"For Christmas?"

"Yeah."

"Like carpool?"

"Like a couple."

Like a... "A couple of what?"

His lips twitch. "The way I see it is neither of us is looking forward to spending Christmas single, but neither of us really has a choice if we don't want to let our families down. So why don't we do it together?"

I'm beyond confused. "As a couple?"

"Not a real one."

"Oh, okay, that's super clear." I go to push myself off the couch, thinking he's making fun of me, but stop when his hand lands on mine, his palm warm and dry and—

"Megan?"

"Yeah? What?" I clear my throat as he looks at me with this open, earnest expression that makes my heart flutter a teeny tiny bit.

"Will you be my fake girlfriend for Christmas?"

I wait for the punchline. I wait for anything, but he just looks at me, and I just... "No?"

"Think about it," he continues, but I'm barely listening, too distracted by the feel of his hand still atop of mine. "Having someone by our sides would make things a lot easier, wouldn't it? You wouldn't be so worried about bumping into Isaac. I wouldn't be the only single member of my family for another year. We'd each have a partner in crime. Backup."

"That's not what I meant."

"I know," he says. "But it's what I think we should do."

s more complicated than it is," he says, growing

h word. "All we need to do is go back together.

we tell everyone that we met in Dublin, which we did. We just embellish a few things. We say we hit it off. That we started seeing each other."

"No one's going to believe that."

"Why not?"

I stare at him. "Because it's *dumb*?"

"I admit we don't have that much time to prepare—"

"You think?" I tug my hand free of him, needing a clear head.

"We'll only have to do it for a week," he says. "Two at the most. I'll be your date for the fundraiser. I'll back you up if you see Isaac. I'll do everything an actual boyfriend would, but it will just be..."

"Fake," I say flatly, and he hesitates.

"Let's say pretend."

"You're serious about this."

"It makes sense."

"Not really," I say, even if everything he just described feels like it was plucked directly from my own private fanfiction. "Because yes, I admit I can see in some strange alternate universe what I get out of this plan. But it's not like your ex-fiancé is running around the place reminding everyone that they hate you."

"No," he admits. "But I do have a family who are so coupled up it's starting to feel personal, and if I have to spend one more Christmas with them sending me pitying looks down the dinner table, I don't think I'll manage another. I'm tired of them asking the same questions in the hope of a different answer. Just one year, I'd like them to be off my back and enjoy myself."

"There are other ways to do that."

"Such as?"

"My one!" I exclaim. "We stay here and get drunk." I slump back against the cushions, suddenly suspicious. "How many people have you asked to do this with you?"

"Today or...?" He smiles when I scowl. "Just you, Megan." And something about the way he says my name melts my aversion just a bit, but before I can respond, my phone chimes with a text. It's Frankie.

Turns out Claudio's promise of a private horn performance wasn't a euphemism.

"My roommate's coming home," I say reluctantly, but Christian just nods.

"I guess that's my cue." But he doesn't move. He doesn't move, and I don't want him to move and I—

"I was going to take this to the bedroom," I say, and his brow lifts in amusement.

"I'd hoped you would."

"I just want you to know what you're missing. I would have let you stay until morning and everything."

"A real hostess," he says, but he turns serious as he gets that confident look again. "This way is better."

Is it, though?

"Cleaner," he continues, as he swipes the phone from my hands and starts to type. "No messy feelings."

"Yeah, feelings are gross."

He hands the phone back, ignoring my sarcasm. "I texted myself. You have my number."

"Great." My enthusiasm is half-hearted at best, but my hopeful fling turned new fake boyfriend doesn't seem to notice as he stands and grabs his coat.

"Let's get a drink next week. It will give you some time to consider."

"You're really committed to this bit."

"Not a bit. How about Monday?"

"I—" I break off with a laugh. A perfectly reasonable reaction, all things considered. "Fine."

"Promise me you'll think about it."

"Sure," I say, but I'm lying.

I will not think about it.

I will not think about it at all.

Because it is the dumbest idea in the history of the world.

FIVE

CHRISTIAN

"You're a genius."

"I know." I fit the plastic lid over my steaming cup of coffee, warming my hands with the cup as I turn to Zoe.

"It's just a faultless plan," she continues beside me. "It makes sense. It's well thought-out. It's in collaboration with someone you know well and trust. Truly, I'm amazed people don't do this all the time."

I pause, letting a group of people squeeze past me as she waits by the door. "You're being sarcastic, aren't you?"

She puts a hand to her chest. "Me?"

"It's a good idea."

"No," she says. "It's not. I can't believe you even got her to agree to it in the first place. I mean what did you—oh my God, you didn't, did you?" She gapes at me. "She thinks it's as stupid as I do."

"She'll come around."

"I thought you were supposed to be the smart one," she says, following me out of the café and into the sharp bite of a Monday morning. It's not even eight a.m. yet, and the sky is still dark, but the city is bustling with bundled up workers heading to the office, all of them looking less than pleased to be doing so.

"You didn't hear her talk about going home," I explain, as we join them. Wind rips through the street, sending Zoe's scarf flying, and she grabs it with a scowl. "She sounded miserable."

"And pretending to date you will help with that? You, who's never held onto a girlfriend for more than a few months?"

"We're talking about a week, Zoe. Two at the most. We'll hold hands, help each other out, and go our separate ways. It's simple."

She goes quiet, grimacing at nothing as we cross the street. "You know I was just teasing in the pub, right? I don't actually think you're lonely. I just—"

"I know," I interrupt. "But for the first time in years, I'm not dreading going home for Christmas. I'm honestly annoyed that I didn't think of this before."

"If you were that serious about it, you could have just asked me," she says, dodging around a slow walker. "We could have— What?" she adds at my look. "I think we'd have a blistering chemistry if we put our minds to it."

"And when I break up with you and your toddler a month later, I'm sure they'll forgive me."

"Alright, good point."

"Just don't tell Molly about it, okay? The only reason I told you is because you're not going to be there."

Zoe makes a face. "I tell Molly everything."

"No, you don't."

"I don't," she admits. "But she thinks I do."

"Just promise me you won't say a word."

We stop outside her building, and she takes a sip from her coffee, her expression pensive. "I promise," she says eventually. "But this is assuming Megan will even say yes."

"She will."

"Your confidence is scary."

"I'm going to woo her."

She pulls out her lanyard with a snort. "Good luck with that. But do you know what might be better than introducing a fake girlfriend you barely know to your family during one of the most stressful times of the year?"

"What?"

"Adopting a kitten."

I raise my coffee in goodbye. "Have a good day at work."

"Feel like you'd make a great cat guy," she calls, as I leave her on the steps. It starts to drizzle as soon as I do, but it's only another ten minutes to my own office, and I barely notice the rain as I cross the River Liffey, watching the sun finally start to rise.

I know my plan is a little out there. But all the best ideas are.

We get along. We know each other's histories, each other's families, and if anything, she's got even more hang-ups than I do. Hang-ups that I can easily solve for her if she does the same for me.

We don't even have to spend that much time together if that's what she's worried about. A lunch here, a walk there. Christmas dinner will be tricky because Christmas dinners are always tricky, but we'll be ready for that when the time comes. Some rehearsed lines about how well I'm doing. An inside joke or two. We could start practicing right now if she'd just answer my text.

I messaged her Saturday morning, and she still hasn't replied, and fine, I can take a hint, but like calls to like, and I think she needs this just as much as I do.

She just needs to see that I'm serious about it.

I reach my office in plenty of time and swipe my way through the turnstiles as I head to the elevator.

I got my job at Away Homes two years ago, trading luxury real estate for luxury vacation homes because once you're in the property game, it's kind of hard to get out of it. I only went into the business because a friend at college convinced me the bonuses would be worth it. And they were. The hours were long, and the competition could be fierce, but selling ugly penthouses to rich people was mostly easy when clients have more money than sense, and I saved up enough that when the chance to head up the Dublin office came about, I was able to set myself up here pretty comfortably.

Now I spend my time managing a growing team that provides premium accommodation and short-term stays for digital nomads. Namely, social media influencers looking for content and wealthy software engineers who want seaside cottage inspiration for their podcasts on *logging off*.

I don't mind the job. Some days I even like it. But I never let myself get too comfortable in any workplace. Not when it's just a step on the ladder. A ladder to what, I'm not sure, but I was taught to climb it, and so climb I do.

I say hello to the few people here before me and aim for my desk at the back of the room. I've just hung up my coat when my phone vibrates.

And just like that, I'm instantly alert.

Megan.

Thanks for seeing me home the other night. I know we were supposed to meet this week and talk about that thing, but something's come up. Chat soon!

I read it twice, knowing she's been thinking about this for a while. She sent the text at five past eight on a workday because she knew I'd be going to the office. She probably hoped I'd be going straight into a meeting. Which means that the last thing she wants is for me to text back straight away.

So that's exactly what I do.

You're not even going to give me a chance to persuade you?

I'm sorry. I wish you luck with your search, but there is nothing you can say that is going to make me agree to this.

I go to type before pausing, watching the status update under her name flash from *online* to *last seen* to *online* again. Like she can't stop herself from checking.

Like I've got her attention.

I delete the message and put the phone down. Let her simmer.

Let me think.

I don't need to for long. It takes less than five minutes for me to solve the problem. An internet search for mold remover, a couple of clicks, my credit card, and that's that.

I push Megan O'Sullivan to the back of my mind and start my day. I go into my meeting. An hour later, I come out of my meeting. I answer some emails and listen politely when Sinead, three desks down, complains about her kid. I get a salad in the deli across the street for lunch and get some actual work done. And at twenty minutes past three in the afternoon, my phone lights up with a call.

Megan.

I stare at the screen, letting her wait.

Five... four... three... two...

"Hello?"

"What the hell!"

I'm full-on grinning now. "Sorry, who's this?"

"Christian—"

"You don't like roses?"

"Not five bouquets of them," she snaps. "Everyone thinks I've got a boyfriend."

"Oh no," I say cheerfully. "Sounds awful."

"They're asking me questions, and I don't have answers."

"You do have an answer. The answer is yes."

"I—"

"That's just a hint of what I have up my sleeve. Imagine that but ten times bigger when Isaac walks through the door."

"Going to make me the most popular girl in school?"

Heavy sarcasm. But I'm sincere. "If that's what you want."

She goes quiet on the other end of the line. But quiet is better than a refusal. I've got her considering it.

"Look, I get where you're coming from," she says finally. "I do. But I'm not looking for a relationship right now."

"Neither am I." At least not a real one. I don't think I could handle something serious for a while. It's been nothing but one breakup after another these last few years, and I'll admit it, I'm tired. But something like this? With a controlled outcome and clear communication? It's all of the benefits and none of the pain. "I'm not trying to trick you," I tell her. "I'm asking for your help to make the next few weeks a little more bearable for me, and I hope a little more bearable for you. I'm completely serious."

"I think that's what I find most confusing. What are we going to do? Show up and hold hands? No one's going to believe that."

"Why not?"

"Because we barely know each other?"

"People meet people all the time," I remind her. "They *get* to know each other."

I hear her sigh, but she doesn't hang up. Doesn't sound so mad anymore either.

"Just give me a shot," I say. "For old time's sake."

"*Old* time's sake?"

"Yeah. Where's your village loyalty?"

"In the village graveyard," she mutters, but she hesitates. "I guess it would be nice to have a date for my mother's party," she adds reluctantly.

"I can be much more than that," I promise her. "You still free tonight?"

"Maybe."

"Can I come over? Talk this through some more?"

"I haven't agreed to it yet."

"I know. Can I come? Around seven?"

"Fine. But no more flowers."

"No more flowers," I promise. "I'll see you then. Wear something nice."

"What? Why?"

The suspicion in her voice makes me smile. "Because I'm taking you out on a date."

SIX

MEGAN

Wear something nice. What does that even *mean?*

"Frankie!" I throw another five dresses on my bed, hoping one of them will magically catch my eye. Because it should. Because I am a clothes person. I love clothes. I love outfits and pieces and fashion and trends, and I like buying them, and I like making them, so you'd think finding something for a simple date night shouldn't be a problem. You'd think that. But you would be wrong. *"Frankie!"*

"I'm right here," she says, sauntering in. "You don't have to yell." My roommate is a tall, pink-haired bombshell with the most perfectly toned arms you've ever seen. As well as being quietly incredibly intelligent, she's also a high jumper, a cook, and a part-time DJ. I told her exactly what happened with Christian the other night because I tell her everything, but she wasn't helpful, seeming to view the whole thing as an experiment and not telling me what I resolutely should or should not do, which is what I actually wanted.

"He told me to wear something nice," I say, as she eyes the mess that is my room. "I don't have anything nice."

"Yes, you do."

"No, I *don't*," I moan, throwing another dress on the bed. "Help me."

"I'm going to need more information," she says. "Nice because you're meeting his grandmother, or nice because he's going to sex you up?"

"He's not going to sex me up." At least I don't think he is. "Surely there is a nice in-the-middle of those two options?"

"There is, but they're not fun." She sighs, leaving me for approximately five seconds before returning with a modest green dress in her hands. "Here," she says. "Ankle boots. Your black coat. It's a classic."

"You're sure?" I ask, even though I'm already pulling the thing on.

"Very sure. Maybe heels?"

"I don't know how much walking we're going to be—" I break off as the buzzer goes. "That must be him."

"You think?"

"Who else would it be?"

"But he's early," Frankie says, as the buzzer goes again. "He's also impatient," she adds, following me into the kitchen. I press the button to let him in and pull the heels on, unusually nervous.

"I'm not ready yet."

"So make him wait."

"That's rude."

"That's power. But you're ready. Just put your hair down. Maybe muss it up a little," she adds, doing just that until I bat her hands away.

"I thought you were going to the library."

"I am," she says. "I just want to see—"

A knock on the door.

"—what all the fuss is about."

"There's no fuss."

"But there's fluster," she says, perching on a stool. "You're flustered."

I give her a look, silently telling her to behave and undo the lock.

I spent all weekend pretending I wasn't thinking about Friday night. All weekend thinking about what he said. And thinking led to imagining which led to full-on fantasizing about all the things he'd proposed. About arriving home with someone like him on my arm. About not feeling alone during the loneliest time of the year.

I'd meant what I said on the phone. I'm not looking for a relationship. Not a serious one, anyway. But even still when I open the door, caution tinging my every move, I can't deny my reaction to the man. The way my mood lifts at the mere sight of him.

Christian just smiles like this is something we've done a hundred times before, and okay, as pretend boyfriends go, I could do a lot worse.

He's wearing that nice coat again and smells incredible, his cologne earthy and spicy and expensive, and I kind of just stand there sniffing it for a second before I realize what I'm doing.

"You're early," I say, and he raises a brow.

"I said seven. It's seven."

"That's early."

"It's literally not."

"No one comes when they say they're—"

"Let the man inside, Megan," Frankie calls, and I step back, letting him past.

"This is my roommate, Frankie. Frankie, this is Christian."

Christian nods a hello while Frankie just stares, unabashedly taking him in from the top of his head to the tips of his toes before turning to me.

"I'd fake date him."

Oh my God. "You said you were—"

"I'm going," she says, as Christian grins at her. "I'm gone. You two kids have fun."

"It was nice meeting you," Christian says. She waits for him to turn back to me before motioning something *very* lewd and then disappears through the door, slamming it shut behind her.

"That's Frankie," I say lamely.

"She seems fun."

"She is."

"You told her about my plan?"

"I figured it was okay since she wasn't from home."

"And because you're considering it."

"Where are we going, anyway?" I ask, choosing not to answer.

Christian examines one of the many handfuls of roses I'd filled the apartment with. I ran out of vases, so these ones are in an empty wine bottle. "It's a surprise," is all he says.

"I don't like surprises."

"It's a nice surprise."

"Well, am I dressed appropriately for the nice surprise? Do I look *nice*?"

"You look great," he says like I'm his sister, which just isn't going to cut it. Not if he wants me to go along with this.

"Okay. No." I drop my purse on the counter and take a step back.

Christian looks confused. "What did I say?"

"It's not what you said. It's how you said it." I cross my arms under my chest, pushing the girls up slightly. "You're trying to convince me to be your fake girlfriend? That you're madly in love with me? Then right now? In this dress? With these shoes? I do not look *great*. Try again."

He doesn't do anything for the longest moment, and I'm surprised how disappointed I feel. For all his talk, I thought he might—

I stiffen as he steps toward me, the movement slow and

purposeful. All of a sudden, it's difficult to meet his eyes, and I feel my face heating with every pulse of blood as his own gaze gentles into something approaching reverence.

"You're right," he says, and my eyes widen as he tucks a strand of hair behind my ear. "I'm sorry. You look incredible, Megan. You look..." His fingers skim over my cheek, sending a tingle down my spine, and I can't breathe. My stomach is doing somersaults, and my mouth is drying up, and I—

Oh my God.

"Get the hell away from me," I snap, and he laughs, the spell instantly broken.

"Good, huh?"

That's one word for it. "How do you do that?" I press a hand to my heart, pretending to exaggerate my reaction even though the thing is going a mile a minute.

"It's a skill," Christian says, opening the door. "And there's plenty more where that came from."

———

I trail behind him as we wander into town, our pace slow because of my shoes. But Christian doesn't seem in a hurry, content to stroll when I say no to a taxi. I'm glad he is. I always think you can see so much more of a city walking through it. And I love Dublin at this time of year. There's an extra buzz in the run-up to Christmas, one that brings everyone out despite the cold. That means roaring fires in pubs and busking choirs and just a little extra *something* that makes you smile that bit brighter. A sense of anticipation that's even nicer than the day itself.

The streets are busy, and I grow more and more curious as we pass restaurants and bars, trying to guess where he's taking me. But Christian just keeps moving.

"Are you going to tell me where we're going?"

"Impatient, are we?"

"Thirsty," I correct. "A drink wouldn't go amiss."

"We'll get there," he says. "This is a multistep date."

"What's the first step?"

"I thought you'd never ask." He gestures to a building across the road, swiveling to face me as he slows his steps. At first, I think he's joking.

"The Dead Zoo?"

"It's open late tonight. They've got a special exhibition."

"Of dead animals?"

"Of history," he corrects. "Which also includes animals."

The affectionately named Dead Zoo, otherwise more professionally known as the natural history part of the National Museum of Ireland, is an old Victorian building just off Merrion Square, housing an admittedly impressive collection of taxidermied animals, flora, fauna, and all manner of things. I'm pretty sure the last time I visited it, I was eight, and so I still think Christian's kidding right up until he walks us through the doors and wanders off to pick up a leaflet.

Guess not.

Feeling overdressed, I pull my coat tighter around me and gaze up at the skeleton of what the little plaque tells me is a 10,000-year-old elk and then glance around the room. It's pretty, I'll give him that, with brass fittings and glass cases and dark polished wood floors that creak under my every step. What's most surprising is that it looks like we're not the only ones here on a date. Couples roam around the large ground floor, speaking to each other in hushed voices as they peer at the exhibitions, and I'm more than a little confused.

Whatever happened to dinner and a movie?

Christian comes up beside me, clutching a pamphlet behind his back, and I point to a particularly bloated-looking fox in a case next to us.

"That's you."

He doesn't look impressed. "Let's go find some sexier animals."

"Like what?"

"Tigers," he says like it's obvious, and we head farther inside, passing bears and badgers and otters and gulls.

I try not to look too much at them, suddenly squeamish, but the extinct ones I can handle, and I pause beside a couple more skeletons of ancient Irish deer that look like they could eat me in one bite.

"You know," Christian says conversationally. "One of those guys has an antler span of 3.5 meters."

"Sounds like he's overcompensating," I quip, as I head down an aisle with a much prettier display of shells. "I haven't been here since I was a kid," I add, peering into one.

"I come here all the time," Christian says. "Or at least since I got back."

"Really?"

"Yeah. Mam and Dad used to bring us whenever we came up to Dublin. I think it's my favorite place in the city."

Any snappy retort I was about to make quickly dies. "It is?"

"It's peaceful, isn't it?" He scratches the back of his neck, looking utterly sincere. "I guess I wanted to take you somewhere that meant something to me."

Oh God. "Well, now I feel bad for my jokes."

"You should."

I sidle closer to him as another couple drifts past. "Sorry," I mutter. "I didn't know you were giving me insight into your soul."

"We've got a lot of catching up to do. We haven't even started on my favorite foods yet."

"The true way to any man's heart."

He closes another inch between us, and I have to crane my neck to meet his eye.

"You're thinking about it," he states, looking more curious than he does smug. Like he's trying to figure me out.

"A little," I confess, not wanting to lie to him. "I wouldn't be here if I wasn't."

"And do you maybe want to put me out of my misery and tell me which way those thoughts are going?"

"And ruin the suspense?" I tsk and move past, glancing up at the biggest shark I've ever seen hanging from the ceiling.

How many skeletons does this place *have*?

"Kind of cool, huh?" Christian says, joining me.

"Kind of morbid."

"Oh, come on." I can hear the smile in his voice, and I know he thinks I'm just teasing him. "You don't like creepy taxidermy?"

"Not really," I say, as he takes out his phone for a picture of the thing. "I'm a vegetarian."

———

"You didn't know," I tell him for the hundredth time as we head up the stairs of a nearby cocktail place. He's so horrified that I'm starting to feel bad that I told him. He's also so horrified that it's a little funny.

"You try and think outside the box," he says. "You try and be cute with your dead zoos, and then your date turns out to be a vegetarian."

"I liked the shells," I assure him. "And the architecture."

We're shown to a small table at the side of the room, and Christian lets me order a boujee red wine for both of us, probably still feeling guilty.

"I'll bring you somewhere better next time," he promises when the waiter goes.

"Next time?"

His eyes narrow in the dim light. It's the only warning I get before he leans in. He leans in so much that I move back, watching as he crosses his arms on the table and tilts his head, studying me.

"It's bad manners to put your elbows on the table," I tell him.

"Says who?"

"... the French?"

"You're killing me here, Megan. I've laid out my cards. I've been up front. I'm about to pay for the third most expensive wine on the list—"

"It's actually the second."

"And you still haven't given me a yes or no," he finishes. "So please. Tell me what you're thinking."

"So you don't have to pay for the wine?"

"So I'm not wasting your time. Or mine."

I make a show of looking around the room, stalling. "I think," I begin slowly. "That it isn't the most ridiculous idea in the world."

"I guess that's a start," he says when I don't continue.

"I just want to make sure you know what you're getting into. I said before I didn't leave on the best terms with everyone, and I meant it." I pause. "But there are some things you could help with."

"Your mother's fundraiser."

"It would be nice not to go alone," I admit. "Very nice. Extremely nice. But it's not just a few drinks and a photo opp. It involves dressing up. It involves standing by my side all night when I have to talk to her friends. It involves looking at me like I'm the most beautiful, captivating person in the room, *and* being my excuse whenever I need to escape."

"I can do that."

"But it's not just the party," I insist. "Isaac will be home. I know he will. And while I don't intend to walk around, trying to bump into him, if I do, then we have to be united."

"Done."

"And if I'm not there, but you bump into him—"

"Megan," he interrupts. "I promise that if we do this, whenever Isaac Quinn is so much as in the same room as us, I will look at you, touch you, treat you like you are the most important person in the world to me. I promise that if I meet him, I will be thinking of you and only you, and I will make sure he knows that. I'll make sure everyone does. Does that sound okay?"

That sounds freaking amazing. But I just nod.

"Is that all?" he asks.

"That seems like a lot to me," I mutter, crossing my legs. "Why? What's your game?"

"No game," he reminds me. "And exactly what I said before. Backup. I want to bring home someone that my family will actually like. Someone who will make my mam stop questioning me about my life, my siblings stop looking at me with pity, and my dad stop sighing in disappointment whenever he thinks I'm not paying attention."

"So you want someone boring?"

"There's nothing wrong with boring. And beyond a few family gatherings, I promise I won't ask for much."

"And then what?" I ask. "What happens a month later when we fake break up and everything's back to normal?"

"Would you believe me if I said I'm not thinking that far ahead?"

"No."

"Well, I'm not," he says. "And if we want, we can keep things going for a little while longer. It's not like they'll be here to check up on us. This is a short-term solution for a short-term problem. Unless you guys also go all out for Easter."

"Don't you dare make fun of the Easter egg hunt." I tap the edge of the table with my fingers, trying to think of more potential problems and not finding any. "Okay. Fine. Family dinners.

Sit and smile. I can do that. But you're forgetting one very important thing."

"What's that?"

"That in order to make this believable, we'll have to pretend to be in love."

"That's the general idea."

"But that means..." I gesture between us, and he goes deadly serious.

"It doesn't mean anything. We don't have to do anything you're uncomfortable with."

"But we'll have to do *some* things," I say. "It's not going to work otherwise. We just have to be clear about what those things are."

"Agreed," he says, and I force back my awkwardness.

This is definitely the weirdest conversation I've had. But Christian seems set on this, and I can't help but think of my roommate before Frankie. A pretty, petite girl named Lisa, who was into the kinkier side of relationships. She once showed me a checklist she kept for when she met with potential partners. I found it so clinical it was funny, but she explained that it made her feel safe and that it kept everything clear between them. And that's what we need here. Rules. Rules and rules and rules.

"No kissing."

He doesn't even blink. "We'll have to kiss a little bit."

He's right. "No tongue," I amend. "And we keep it to the face area." I pause. "Except for my hand. If you want to do a cute bit and kiss my hand, you can do that. And my shoulder."

"Why would I kiss your—"

"It's romantic."

He nods solemnly, but I can't seem to shut up now.

"Nothing in the—" I motion to my chest. "Area. We can hug, but—"

"Hands where you can see them," he finishes. "Anything else?"

"Yes." I clear my throat. "I don't want you to be with anyone else."

Christian looks taken aback. "I'd assume that's a given," he says, but I'm not convinced.

"Is it?"

"What do you think I'm doing at Christmas? Throwing myself at women before heading home for some turkey?"

I doubt Christian Fitzpatrick has ever had to throw himself at anyone in his entire life, but point taken.

"Just promise me you won't."

"I promise," he says. "But only if the same goes for you. No holiday hookups. No crushes on childhood friends or handsome strangers visiting for the weekend."

"What if he's *really* handsome?"

"We can revisit the terms if the circumstances are exceptional," he says, not taking his eyes off me as the server sets down our drinks. "This is going to be good, Megan."

"Says Mr. Confident." I take a large gulp of my wine and set the glass down on a napkin, only to immediately take another mouthful. "I'm getting drunk now," I tell him.

"I can see that."

Another healthy sip. "Whose house are we going to eat Christmas dinner in?"

"Mine, obviously."

"Why, *obviously*?"

"You've got your mother's fundraiser; I've got Christmas dinner at my house."

"We still have Christmas," I protest. "We watch movies."

"So do we."

"But ours is a *thing*. We put a projector in the living room. We have mulled wine. Mam falls asleep twenty minutes in." My heart gives a painful thud just thinking about it. That's what I've missed the most. "It's my favorite tradition."

"So we'll eat separately."

I make a face, and he sighs. "So we'll do two."

"Two Christmas dinners?"

"Couples do it all the time."

"Just remind me not to fill up on bread," I mutter. "Fine. Two." I sit back as someone starts to play piano across the room. "Should we be keeping a note of this?"

"That's not a bad idea," he says, and I watch as he reaches into his pocket for a...

"You carry a pen?"

He seems surprised by my surprise. "I'm a grown man. Of course, I carry a pen."

"Not a grown man in nineteen sixty-two, though."

"What happens if I need to write something down?"

"You use your phone."

"Like an animal?" He clicks it once, pulling the now-stained napkin toward him when I pick up my glass again.

"So you carry a pen, but not anything to write on *with* the pen."

"Terms and Conditions," Christian says, ignoring me. He writes the words as he speaks, underlining them with a flourish.

"We already went over them."

"And now we'll have them in writing. Makes it official. Number one," he continues. "No tongue."

Christ. "A little louder, please. I don't think the people in the back heard you."

"Number two—"

"Let's just say nothing the other person is uncomfortable with," I say, and he writes it down. "No putting one family above the other. No made-up stories beyond what we've agreed to. It will be way too much to keep track of." I take a moment, thinking. "No telling anybody. No cheating. And no... no backing out."

Christian notes every word and signs his name at the bottom. "No backing out," he echoes and hands me the pen. I sign a quick scrawl, and then he folds up the napkin and tucks it into his pocket.

I stare at it for precisely ten seconds before sighing. "Is this going to be the stupidest thing either of us has ever done?"

Christian just picks up his wine, his gaze holding mine as the corner of his mouth curves. "I guess we'll find out."

"Reassuring."

"Always. Merry Christmas, Megan."

"Merry Christmas," I say, and clink my glass with his before downing it in one.

SEVEN

CHRISTIAN

There might be a pounding in my head the next day, but there's also a spring in my step that I can't seem to shake. I'm almost whistling when I enter the office a little after lunch, having taken the morning to work from home/nurse a hangover.

I dump my bag at my desk and head straight to the individual breakout rooms that make up the wall opposite. They're meant for private phone conversations and are supposed to be completely soundproof. That theory was disproved two months ago when Pilar from HR broke up with her boyfriend. You could hear them screaming at each other from five desks away.

Now I lock myself in the nearest one and dial my mother on the speaker phone while I open my laptop to order more things to annoy Megan with.

It takes her three rings to pick up.

"To what do I owe *this* pleasure?" she asks crisply. "Or are you calling to tell me you died?"

"Not yet. And I don't think it will be me who does that."

"I haven't heard from you in weeks."

"I'm sorry. I've been busy."

"Yes, I'm sure. Very busy. You know you missed your Aunt Alma's birthday."

"She's not my aunt."

"She might as well be."

"And yet, she's not. Listen, I wanted to—"

"I know she's not the easiest woman to get along with," Mam continues. "But you should have been there."

"It was a Tuesday afternoon," I remind her. "I was working."

"You could have taken some time off."

"For tea with my non-aunt Alma, who was probably a bitch the whole time?"

"*Christian.*"

"I'm just reading between the lines here."

"It's not like I was over the moon to be spending an afternoon with her myself. I know her knee has been troubling her, but I think the woman needs someone to have a strong word with—"

"I'm bringing someone home for Christmas."

Silence. Surprised, hopeful silence. "What's that?" she asks.

"My new girlfriend," I say, bookmarking a few bakeries near Megan's house. "I'd like to bring her over for Christmas if that's okay with you."

"Of course it is," Mam says, and though she tries her best to sound nonchalant, I can hear the delight in her voice. The kind of delight that is so rarely directed at me. "Must be serious."

"Her name's Megan."

"Megan!" You'd swear she'd never heard a more beautiful name in her life. "And she's from Dublin?"

"Actually, she's not." I switch tabs, zooming in on some cupcakes. "She's from home. It's Megan O'Sullivan. From school."

This time her pause is more strained. "Emily's daughter?"

"That's the one."

"I thought she moved to Canada."

"She didn't. She's here."

"You're *dating* Megan O'Sullivan?"

We're saying her name so much it's starting to lose all meaning.

"Is that okay?"

"Yes, it's just..." She hesitates. "Well, you know how it is. Small towns. People talk."

I frown at that. Megan said she didn't leave on the best terms with everyone, but still.

"That was years ago, Mam."

"No, I know," she says hurriedly. "I just—"

"You'll like her."

"Of *course* I will if she's caught your eye." She's on the back foot now, but I'm not convinced.

"Would you let Dad and the others know? I want to make this as easy as possible for her. She hasn't been home in a while."

"Not since the wedding," Mam says, her voice dropping to a whisper.

She might as well have said *the murder*. "Mam." I sigh, my good mood deflating. "I like her."

"Then I'm sure I will too," she says, which is probably the best that I'm going to get out of her.

"I'll call more often," I promise. "I love you."

"I love you too. Text your Aunt Alma."

We share our goodbyes before hanging up, and I feel oddly disappointed by the conversation. Then again, I don't know what I expected. More fawning, maybe? Some more excitement? Maybe I should bite the bullet and ask Megan exactly what went down after the wedding, just so I know what I'm working with.

Or if I need to find someone else.

My gut immediately rejects the thought, but before I can

get too worried, my screen lights up with another call, and I'm puzzled to see Andrew's name flash. It's early morning in Chicago, which means he would have just woken up.

"Brother."

"Christian. Mam said you're bringing a girl home."

Oh, for the love of— "I literally just told her. How does she move that fast?"

"What can I say? The woman's starved of gossip."

"Has she told everyone?"

"Well, I'm her favorite, so she probably told me first," he muses. "Who's the lucky lady?"

I tilt my head back, staring up at the ceiling.

I had fully planned to tell him myself. But our mother's reaction has thrown me off slightly. Not to mention that I'm a little jealous of my brother. I've always thought of him as a bit of an idiot, but I love him. And while he may be an idiot, some- how, in the last few years, he's done a lot better than me in every way possible.

A bunch of badly paid freelance gigs turned into a full-time career as a photographer.

Couch surfing in Chicago turned into a two-bedroom apartment.

And a string of random girlfriends led to him falling in love with his best friend, his soulmate in every sense of the word.

I know he worked hard. I know it didn't all fall into place, but damn, if he didn't make it look easy sometimes.

"Christian," he presses now. "What's her name, where does she live, and what do her parents do for a living? Or I'm calling Mam back to ask."

I bite the bullet. "Megan O'Sullivan."

There's a short pause on the other end of the line. And then: "Why does that name sound familiar?"

"Because she went to school with me and left Isaac Quinn at the altar."

Andrew lets out a low whistle. In the background, I hear a dog barking and Molly shouting for it to stop. It does not.

"The runaway bride, huh?"

"She's not a runaway bride."

"She literally is, but I mean no offense." He sounds thoughtful. "I thought she moved to France."

"She didn't. She's in Dublin."

"Well, obviously. What's she up to now?"

"Marketing. And she knits," I add. "She has a store online."

"Okay." He sounds amused. "You seem a little defensive."

"I'm not."

"I'm sure she's great."

"She is." I do sound defensive. And I don't know why. "I bumped into her at the pub."

"Old school. Nice." He sounds genuinely excited for me. It's why I almost feel guilty about lying to him. My brother is a happy person. Always has been and probably always will be. Maybe I should have told him first.

"She's nervous about coming back," I admit. "She hasn't been home since the wedding. I think she's lost touch with everyone."

He makes a sympathetic noise. "That's got to be hard. I remember hearing about it. Think Mam spent an hour on the phone telling me all the details."

Great. "Can you ask Molly to... I don't know, be her friend or something?" The thought comes out of left field. I don't know if Megan would even want one or need one, but I like the thought of her having someone not from the village on her side. Especially if everyone else is going to react the way Mam did.

But Andrew sounds doubtful. "I don't know," he says slowly. "Molly's kind of a bitch."

"I can *hear* you!" Molly calls, and Andrew laughs.

"I'm sure she'll be happy to," he says. "I will also not be an asshole."

"I appreciate that." I might be overpreparing a bit, but I don't care. I know Megan agreed to this, but it's still my idea. The last thing I want to do is make it any harder for her.

"Anyway, this is brilliant news," Andrew continues. "Bet Mam's delighted."

"She sounded weird when I told her."

"She just worries about you. It'll go great. Besides, I, uh, might have something to help take the heat off you this year."

"Meaning?"

"Meaning..." There's a soft click as he closes the door on his end. "I need your help with something. And you can't tell anyone."

"Pass."

"You don't get to pass."

"Just did. Ask Hannah."

"Hannah, who's never kept a secret in her life?"

"Andrew, I'm busy. I don't have time for whatever—"

"I'm going to propose at Christmas."

Surprise shoots through me, making me momentarily speechless. "To Molly?"

"No, to my barista. Yes, to Molly."

"That's..." Wow. "Huge. Congratulations."

"Yeah." He clears his throat. "Thanks."

"And there I was, thinking you guys were going to wait another ten years."

"Very funny. Can't wait to hear that joke a hundred more times." His voice muffles until it's a whisper.

"Are you lurking behind a curtain or something?"

"I'm hiding in the closet. Literally. Not metaphorically. Molly has freakishly good hearing."

"But terrible taste in men, so it all balances out."

"You said your new company does romantic getaways?"

"We might."

"And is there a family discount on said getaways or—"

"A few weeks out from Santa time? You're paying full rates, big brother." I pull up our website, filtering through availability.

"I swear this isn't that last minute," he says, as I type. "I thought about doing it at the airport, but figure she'll kill me if it's in public. So, I thought I'd do it when we got back home. That way, she doesn't hate me, but it's still a surprise, and we can celebrate with everyone."

"That's assuming she'll say yes."

"Again, a hilarious joke."

"There's not a lot of options," I say, looking through the places we still have left. It's slim pickings, but we usually set a few to the side and hike up the prices for any last-minute bookers. Season of giving and all that. But there's got to be some perks to being the boss. "I've got a penthouse in Dublin and a cottage and a cabin in Cork. Take your pick."

"What would you choose?"

"The cabin is isolated, with minor horror movie vibes, but it's the biggest and comes with a hot tub. The cottage is closest and small, but it looks the best and has a heated pool."

"The cottage has a *pool*?"

"Welcome to modern Ireland."

"Alright. Then I'll take the cottage with the pool."

"The cabin is also five hundred quid cheaper."

"Then I'll take the horror movie cabin with the hot tub," he says just as cheerfully. "What could go wrong? Don't answer that."

"It's nice," I assure him. "About two hours out from the house. I can throw in food and champagne as a welcome gift."

"Well, Molly's particular about food," he muses. "And I'm sober. So again, I don't see what could go wrong."

"I'll add it as a freebie. Just bring the stuff home. Rose petals?"

"Too much."

Disagree, but I keep my mouth shut and add them in,

anyway. The way I see it, if you're going to propose to the love of your life, you might as well go all out.

"You're going to need to pay in full," I tell him. "Nonrefundable. It's too short notice for just a deposit."

"That's fine. I'm ready. Got the ring and everything."

"Got or picked out?"

"Got," he says, sounding confused. "You've got to get the ring to propose."

"No, you get a dummy ring," I say. "Then you let *them* pick out the real one."

Andrew makes a dismissive noise. "I know what she likes."

"How? How do you know what she likes? She doesn't even wear rings."

"How do you know she doesn't—"

"Because I'm observant."

"Well, stop observing my future wife," he says before he pauses. "Oh, that sounds good. *Wife*."

"Let's get through the proposal first."

"Stay away from my wife," he continues in a mockingly deep voice, and I double the order for the petals.

"I'm booking you in. You'll get an email in a few minutes."

"Thank you," he says, and there's some rustling where I picture him moving through clothes. "I'd better go. I'm going to be late for work, but I wanted to tick one thing off." He pauses, sounding nervous. "It feels more real now that I've told someone."

"You'll be fine. And you don't have to do anything big. Molly doesn't care about that stuff."

"No, I know, I just... I want it to be special. She deserves it."

"She does," I say. "She's great, Andrew."

"She is, isn't she?"

I smile at how happy he sounds. The same way he always sounds when he talks about her.

"Any excuse for a party, right?" he adds.

"We'll make it a good one," I promise. "And I won't say a word."

We hang up as I stare at the main picture of the cabin, a staged photo of a beaming couple drinking champagne in the hot tub, and take out my phone, pulling up my photo album. I must have taken dozens of Megan on our date, but I choose one from the end of the night. One which she's barely even in. Just the left side of her. With her brown hair swept over her shoulder, a peek at the gentle slope of her nose, and the hint of a smile as she starts to look back at me.

I send it to her, seeking permission, and five minutes later, her answer comes through.

Okay. And then: *You can tag me.* And then: *Do it before I change my mind.*

I take her at her word, uploading the photo, and announcing our relationship to every social media account I have. It takes only a few seconds for the first few likes to start coming through. Only a few seconds to make it official.

And that's it.

We're coming home for Christmas.

EIGHT

MEGAN

Just over a week. That's all the time we have before we go home. All the time we have to rehearse, to learn, to get as comfortable as we can around each other. If this were a movie, we'd be meeting every day, we'd be going for walks in frost-covered parks, our heads bent in deep discussion. We'd be sitting in coffee shops, pouring over weirdly intricate family trees. We'd be in the best montage ever and yeah, okay, *maybe* I thought that was what was going to happen. Maybe I was even looking forward to it. But of course, it didn't.

Number one we both had full-time jobs (and in Christian's case he made it sound like full-time plus overtime) and number two... it was Christmas. Or the run up to Christmas. The run up to Christmas when we'd both be taking two weeks off. We were busy. I had the office party, two different friend group parties, plus the most important party, the Frankie and Megan party, where we eat as much pizza as we can and watch a BBC period drama of our choice.

I devoted one evening on top of that to shopping for presents and two to getting Christmas-ready. That meant hair, nails, wax. Buff, polish, shine.

It was chaotic. It was fun. And it left very little room for anything else.

We didn't have time to meet in person. But that was okay. Because what we did have was emails. Emails and texts and voice notes, back and forth, over and over.

Instead of laying out our life stories to each other, Christian decided it would be better if we shared the smaller parts of ourselves. To drip-feed information so it was less rote memorization and more get an idea of each other's habits. Our likes and dislikes and whatever else springs to mind.

Unfortunately for Christian, I took this to mean I can tell him whatever I want, whenever I want, and again, on a week with no less than three Christmas parties, I told him a lot.

I don't think we should explore the ocean.

Do you mean as a couple or...

I think we should just leave it alone. We don't need to go down there. Ever. We should just stay where we are. No more exploring.

What about space?

Oh, I don't think about space. None of my business.

Noted.

Will you knit a Christmas sweater for Andrew?

Is this a joke or not a joke?

Not a joke. I want to give him one as a present. How much do you charge?

??? Don't be dumb. I'll do it for free if you're serious.

I'm serious and I'm paying you. How much?

It's grand!! Just buy me a coffee.

This is why you're making minus twenty quid a month.

It's a hobby.

It's a skill.

Buy me two coffees then.

Should we have pet names for each other?

No.

guess what I'm a little grank.
Drank
drink

Drunk?

Yes!! ☺ ☺ ☺

Where are you?

*In a taxi. His name is Hank.
The driver not the car.*

**I figured. Please tell me when you're
home.**

☺ ☺ ☺
Hank said the car does not have a name. ☹

I don't get soup.

Is this you telling me you're home?

I can eat it. I just don't get it.

**Please send me a picture of your apartment
if you're home.**

...

Thank you.

It's just liquid food.

Goodnight, Megan.

I told my mother. Think she bought the whole "just bumped into each other" thing.

Is that why she followed me on Instagram ten minutes ago?

SHE DID WHAT???

I'll pick you up at 1 p.m. tomorrow.

For what?

Funny.

Are you up?

I'm at the gym. Are you okay?

I'm fine.

Actually I lied! I'm not. I'm backing out.

You can't back out. You signed a contract.

I signed a cocktail napkin.

You just have last-minute nerves. This is going to be good, Megan.

Or it could be bad.

It won't be.

How do you know?

I know.
I'll see you at 1. Okay?
Megan?

Okay.

"This is so weird." Frankie stares at me from where she sits cross-legged on my bed. She's wearing a pair of fuzzy socks that I made for her, and her hair is currently halfway through dying what looks like some sort of vivid purple. "Like, I can't believe you're doing this; that's how weird this is."

"If it helps, I can't believe I'm doing this either." I stuff another handful of underwear into my bag and check the time: 12.56 p.m.

"You're going to have to kiss him."

"Not all the time."

"New couples do. In-love couples do. And if you want to be convincing, you have to act like you're in love. You do realize this?"

"We're just helping each other out. It's not like we're getting married or anything. As long as we stick to the rules, no one's getting hurt. I'll be fine."

"And if you're not, you can just come home." She sounds like she's saying it more to herself than to me, but it still makes me pause. Home. Meaning these four walls and Frankie's cooking and the shower you can only use for exactly three minutes before it starts deciding its own temperature. "Promise me you'll give me a call if you need me to— Okay. Love you too, Megs."

I hug her so hard she falls back on the bed, and there we stay until my phone buzzes with a text from Christian, telling me he's outside.

"Make good choices," Frankie says in her *don't be an idiot* voice, and then I'm off, dragging my biggest suitcase down the stairs where Christian waits just by the door, a Santa hat on his head.

"Seriously?" I ask.

"I got one for you too," he says, tugging it on over my hair. "Although, on second thought, that might be too much red."

He steps back, gazing at my coat, and just for a second, I feel a hint of an old self-consciousness I'd fought so hard to forget. I get it. It's a big coat. A very big, very red coat that I found in a charity shop when I was nineteen and fell completely in love with it. It falls mid-thigh and has white wooden buttons and a hood that does *not* fall back at the first hint of a breeze and is perfect even though, yes, I am aware it makes me look a tiny bit ridiculous.

"Did you make that too?" Christian asks.

"No."

"So you... exchanged money for it."

"Do you not like my coat, Christian Fitzpatrick?"

"I love your coat," he says seriously. "It's very important to me that I'll be able to see you in a blizzard."

"You can make fun all you want, but I will be warm and cozy all winter."

"On our trip to the Arctic?"

I hand him my suitcase. "I have three more bags."

"You— What?"

I don't answer, running up the stairs where Frankie hands me the rest of my stuff.

"How much are you bringing?" Christian asks when I come

back down. He doesn't sound annoyed, just starts a game of Tetris with all the luggage in the car.

"A lot," I say. "I don't have any clothes at home." I keep my knitting bag on me, as well as my purse, but by the time I shove my coat into the back and slide into the passenger seat, we've used up nearly all the space. And that's saying something because there is a lot of it.

I run my hand over the beige leather seats, marveling at the feel of them as he gets behind the wheel. "I think I'm attracted to your car."

"Well, so am I, so that's just another thing we have in common. Here." He holds out his hand, offering me a pink paper-wrapped box. "Happy Christmas, Megan."

"It's mid-December."

"Take the damn present."

I do, peeking inside to see a swirl of vanilla frosting. "You got me a cupcake?"

"I did." He clicks his seatbelt in while I stick a finger in the buttered sugar. "This is going to be good, okay?" And he sounds so confident, and he looks so confident, that all of my earlier worries vanish from my mind.

"Okay," I say, as he pulls out onto the street. I tuck the cupcake carefully back into its box, not wanting to get crumbs everywhere. It's one thing I'm beginning to suspect about Christian. The man is tidy.

"Pick your poison," he says, gesturing to the dashboard where a screen shows a range of music apps.

"I get to choose?"

"You are the passenger princess, which means you can do whatever you like."

This is true, so I do, putting on a generic playlist called Classic Christmas Hits before taking out my knitting.

"That for Andrew?" Christian asks, eyeing the wool with interest.

"It is." I unfurl the patch of blue I'm working on, smoothing it out on my knee.

"You can knit in the car?"

"I can knit anywhere."

Christian watches me with a thoughtful expression as the stream of traffic crosses in front of us. "Will you have time to do one more?"

"You want to give him two sweaters?"

"A matching one for his girlfriend. Or fiancée, I guess."

"I can try," I say, even though I know I'll definitely be able to. But, you know. Love to be humble. "Wait. Fiancée? Andrew's engaged?"

"He's going to propose over Christmas."

"That's brilliant!" I exclaim, and he glances over at my enthusiasm.

"I'll send him your regards."

"No, I mean— Yes, do, but that's great news. It means all the attention will be taken off us."

He looks a little grumpy at that. "I wouldn't mind if *some* of the attention was on us."

"A new relationship is not going to compete with an engagement."

"So, you're saying we should also get fake engaged to keep up appearances."

"Cute," I say, as the light goes green. But I feel a lot better now. An engagement. We can definitely fade into the background with that. "I'm warning you now, though. A potential wedding will cause some side-eyes."

"What do you mean?"

"Runaway bride, remember? I've got baggage."

"You've also got me," he dismisses. "I'll deal with any side-eyes."

"Oh yeah? What are you going to do?"

"Punch 'em," he says, and I laugh as I check my bag for

more wool. I'll have to stop in town on the way and pick up some more if he wants another sweater. "What does she like?" I ask. "Andrew's girlfriend?"

"Something colorful," he says casually. "And very Christmassy. With pom-poms."

"I don't have any— Wait." I totally do. "No, we're good."

He glances over again as I cast on a fresh set of stitches. "I feel like you're going to poke your eye out."

"Well, drive carefully, and I won't. But thank you for your concern."

He doesn't look convinced, and I swear he even slows down a smidgen, but he doesn't make me put them away, and I'm soon lost in the familiar click of the needles, my hands moving like they've got a mind of their own.

"Do you think I should make something for your parents too?" I ask.

"Nah."

"What about your sister?"

"You can't buy my family's love with sweaters," he says, seeing straight through me.

"What about scarves?"

He just smiles. "You're nervous."

"Uh. Yeah." Duh. "Of course, I'm nervous. You're not nervous?"

"I have faith in you."

"I have faith in me too, but I'm still nervous. I want them to like me. And we can learn as much about each other as we want, but we've still got to improvise." All it takes is one slipup for someone to get suspicious, and if anyone finds out I pretended to be in a relationship to save face, then I definitely, *definitely* can never step foot in my village again. "We should always hold hands," I say. "All the time. Whenever anyone else is with us, we are holding hands."

"Very normal behavior," he agrees.

"You can also touch my hair. Add that to the list."

"Okay, but you're not going near mine."

"Maybe we should have a diagram," I add absently. "Or go over the appropriate touching areas so we can— What are you *doing*?" I jolt as his hand lands on my thigh. Not my knee. My *thigh*. His big broad palm heavy and warm, his fingers wrapped around my leg.

"I'm touching you appropriately."

"*In*appropriately." I fight the urge to clench my legs together, knowing if I did, it would just trap him there.

"Appropriately for a girlfriend I'm madly in love with," he says. "You're right; we can't discuss PDA in contract terms every time I want to hold your hand."

"Again, this is *not* holding my hand."

"So tell me to stop. We'll practice now." He drags his hand ever so slightly higher, moving closer to the danger zone. Even so, I bite my lip and say nothing, staying perfectly still until he hesitates, his eyes darting to mine.

"I didn't say stop," I say, and his gaze narrows as I start to smile.

"Okay, see that?" he asks. "That laughing? That is not an appropriate reaction to my seduction. You should be incredibly turned on right now."

"Well, move those fingers more, and I might be able to make it more believable."

He gives me a look, bringing his hand back to the gear stick as he returns his attention to the road. But I'm having too much fun now.

"What's your favorite move in the bedroom?"

"Megan."

"I'm serious. What if someone asks me? What if we're having girl talk, and they ask me how good you are at sex?"

"I would hope you'd be charitable."

"Come on."

"I don't have one."

"Everyone has one. Tell me yours, and I'll tell you mine."

"Show me yours, and I might consider it."

"That's definitely not in the contract."

He shakes his head but relents when it's clear I'm just going to keep pestering him. "It depends on the girl," he begins. "On what she likes to— What?" he asks, breaking off when I groan.

"On what *she* likes? Seriously? You're such a liar."

"Oh, well, apologies if you've only been with selfish lovers, Megan. I can't help that I'm generous in the bedroom."

"No one is generous in the bedroom. Or you think you are, but all you do is get her off, and then you're like, *cool, my turn.*"

He's laughing now. "I have *never* said—"

"It's what you're all thinking."

"What's your move then?" he asks, glancing at me when I don't respond. "Come on."

"I just did it," I say, doing it again. "I do lots of pelvic floor exercises."

He's confused for an instant before recognition dawns on his face. "That's cheating."

"I've had no complaints."

"How did we go from knitting to this?"

"It's the quiet ones you have to watch out for," I say, and watch him smile as he makes a turn and drives us out of the city.

———

We make great progress until we hit the motorway, when we slow to a near halt, with everyone else trying to get home for Christmas. When my stomach starts to rumble after forty minutes of crawling along, Christian mutters something under his breath and turns off at the next exit, pulling into a roadside pub.

Despite all the traffic on the road, the place is nearly empty, and we're waved over to a small booth where we get tap water and plastic-covered menus, to which a bubbly waitress informs us they only have half of. I order a club sandwich. Christian gets the roast of the day.

It's a nice place. The lounge is worn, but they've made an effort with the decorations, with plastic garlands hanging from the bar and a small tree in the corner with fake presents underneath. A family nearby has a baby who won't stop staring at me, and despite making several *hilarious* faces for her, doesn't seem impressed, so I turn my attention to Christian who barely gave his order before he started checking his phone.

"Work?" I ask.

"Yeah. I'll probably have to do some while we're back. Nothing too much, but I'm technically on call."

"Whatever you need to do," I shrug. "We don't need to be tied at the hip, do we?"

"Not unless that's something you're into," he winks. I throw a napkin at him. "No, I don't think so. Though, if you like, we can disappear for an afternoon or two. Give ourselves a break from pretending."

"Can we go to a cinema?" I ask, and he smiles. "What? Not romantic enough for you?"

"The cinema's very romantic," he says. "But projectors at Christmas. Movies on our day off..."

"I'm a film girl," I explain. "But the *Jurassic Park* kind. Not your kind."

"What's my kind?"

"Probably ones without dinosaurs," I say, and a waitress arrives with our drinks.

We spend the next hour chatting about a million different things while we eat. Our jobs, our colleagues, the last television show we watched, the pub we both like that's closing down. I get apple pie for dessert while he has a coffee, and when we're done, we stay right where we are, talking easily until we're politely asked to free up the table. Aka, to leave.

"Regretting that pie yet?" he asks, as we navigate our way back to the car.

"No." Yes.

"Told you not to get it."

"If you offer to pay for dessert, a girl is going to order dessert. This is on you." We stop at the car, and I shuffle my feet, grateful as always for my big warm coat, as Christian checks one pocket and then another. "You lose your keys?"

"No."

"You lost your keys."

"It's a new jacket," he says, patting down his pockets. "I don't know where the— Found them."

He takes them out with a smug smile, and I mock clap as I glance around. The parking lot is busier now as dinnertime approaches, and there's a traffic jam by the entrance. I watch, distracted, as a man in an SUV tries in vain to squeeze through the crush, and catch sight of two people a few rows down from us.

It's the woman I notice first. A tall brunette in a thick black sweater. She's on the phone, gesturing as she talks, and she waggles her fingers at the man next to her, who dutifully hands over a water bottle. He has his back to me, but something about the way he moves holds my attention, and an instant before he turns, I realize why.

Isaac.

My breath mists in front of me as I exhale, watching with a kind of eerie serenity as he grabs a jacket from the back seat and pulls it on.

He's cut his hair short.

He wore his hair long when we were in our early twenties and always threatened to shave it. He hated any kind of upkeep. Any kind of style.

I begged him not to do it. I loved running my hands through the strands. Loved it even if he didn't.

He said he kept it to make me happy.

Said that was all he wanted to do.

And now he's shaved it all off.

"What's wrong?" Christian asks, noticing my hesitation.

Nothing. Everything.

"I..."

And Christian follows my gaze just as my ex-boyfriend, ex-*fiancé*, glances in our direction.

Our eyes meet, and panic surges through me, taking over all reasonable thought.

Oh my God. Oh my *God*. "What do I do?"

"What we agreed," Christian says, his voice low and soothing as they start walking our way. "Just remember, we met in Dublin. We hit it off, and we fell in love."

"Right. Okay." Met in Dublin. Fell in love. Met in Dublin. Fell in love. I repeat the words over and over in my mind as nerves jostle my stomach. They're close now. Only a few cars down.

"Or we could just leave," I say quickly. "Pretend we didn't see him."

"You're literally staring at each other." He steps closer to me, his hand finding mine. "You've got this."

Do I, though? *Do I?*

It sounded like a movie when Christian talked about it before, but this is real life, this is now, this is the man I left at the altar staring at me like he's seen a ghost.

Met in Dublin. Fell in love.

Met in Dublin. Fell in love.

Three cars away. The knot in my stomach moves to my throat.

"Megan?"

I drag my eyes to Christian, and I swear it's like my brain

shuts off. It's the only explanation I have for losing all rational thought. All I can think about is *ex-boyfriend* and *fake boyfriend* and *kiss here, not there,* and before I'm even aware of it, I'm fisting the front of his jacket, rising up on my toes, and pressing my lips to his.

NINE

CHRISTIAN

This is not how I envisioned this going.

Megan freezes as soon as she touches me, her every muscle tensing until she's as stiff as a board. I can practically hear the alarm bells ringing in her mind, the *now what*s coursing through her. It would be funny if I didn't know why she did it in the first place.

Three seconds pass before she tries to retreat, and when she does, I follow, cupping her cold cheeks and slanting my mouth over hers until there can be no mistaking what's happening here.

Her lips are soft if unsure, hesitant against mine until she grows bolder, following my lead as I try and forget the world around me and make this believable. It's not exactly hard. She tastes like sugar and apples, her breath sweet as it skates across my skin, and just for a moment, I feel her relax into me, the tension in her jaw easing, the grip on my jacket loosening.

I break away only when Isaac clears his throat behind us and I catch a brief glimpse of Megan's dazed expression before I snake a hand around her back, drawing her into me as close as her coat will allow. She stumbles into my side, breathing heavily, and we turn as one to face him.

I would say he's just like I remember, but to be honest, until Megan and I started hanging out, I didn't think about the guy at all. Never got my membership to his fan club. Not like everyone else in the village, who treated him like he could do no wrong. Maybe it was because he was so polite. Always *please* this and *thank you* that. Used to irritate the hell out of me.

He looks older than the smooth-faced profile photo he has online, and he's recently had his hair cut somewhere between a buzz and a trim, like he couldn't decide what he wanted. It doesn't suit him, making his broad face even broader and his big forehead even bigger.

His eyes are on Megan, but they go to me when I turn, shock making him slack-jawed.

"Christian?"

"Hi, Isaac," I answer, enjoying this more than I should. "You're looking well."

He nods, his gaze flickering between us before he finally seems to remember the woman at his side.

"This is Natalie," he introduces, and she lifts a hand in greeting.

Megan flinches, and at first, I think she's sizing her up, but then I realize what she's looking at. The small but unmistakable diamond on her left hand.

"You're engaged?" Megan blurts out.

Both Isaac and Natalie look surprised, looking down at Natalie's finger as though they'd forgotten all about it.

"Uh, yeah," Isaac says, scratching his jaw. "Sorry, it's kind of new."

"I keep forgetting it's there," Natalie murmurs, tucking her hand into her pocket. She looks embarrassed, and silence falls over our small group, the tension stretching and stretching until Megan offers a smile.

"Congratulations," she says, and I squeeze her hip in support, only for Isaac to zero in on the movement, staring at my hand like he didn't know I had one.

"I didn't know you guys were together," he says after a beat. The words are careful, but there's no mistaking the accusing tone beneath them.

"Also new," I say. "We thought Christmas would be a good time to make it official to everyone back home."

Isaac's brows rise at that. "You're staying for Christmas?" he asks Megan.

"Aidan's coming home, so..."

"Right. Yeah, my dad told me that." There's a pause as Natalie edges away, but Isaac doesn't budge. Nor does he stop staring at Megan, something that's starting to piss me off. "We were just going to go get some food if you guys want to—"

"Already ate," I interrupt. "Going to try and get back before it's too late."

"Traffic's terrible," Natalie agrees, latching onto neutral territory. "We should let you guys go. I'm hungry," she adds to Isaac, who gives her a distracted glance.

"Right. Yeah."

"Happy Christmas," I tell him, and it takes another nudge from his fiancée to finally get him to move.

"Bye," Megan chirps beside me. His smile comes a beat too late, and then he's gone, walking with Natalie toward the pub.

Megan doesn't move, gawking after him like she's trying to commit the back of the guy's head to memory.

"You okay?" I ask when they disappear inside.

"Yeah."

"It's okay if you're not," I continue, especially considering this is exactly what she was worried about.

"I'm fine. I just..." She shakes her head. "He hated this coat."

"What?"

"He said it made me look like a child." A line appears on her forehead, but before I can say anything else, she gets into the car and pulls the door firmly closed.

As soon as we're back on the road, I realize how much I'd gotten used to talkative Megan. Snapback, quippy, teasing Megan. This Megan, the one currently sitting next to me, is quiet. Withdrawn. And it's kind of freaking me out.

She's silent the whole way back to the village. And I mean silent. Not a word. Not a peep. She just turns her head to the side and stares out the window, lost in thought.

And I hate it.

I hate it even more that I don't know her well enough yet to drag her out of it. So I sit there in silence too, growing progressively angrier every time I think about Isaac freaking Quinn.

She was glowing on the way up here. I thought I'd have to spend the ride convincing her not to call the whole thing off. Hence the cupcake. But instead, her good mood was so bright it was infectious. She was excited. And now it's like it's all been sucked out of her. Leaving her lifeless. And it's all because of him.

Which is going to be a big problem if it happens again.

No one's going to believe we're madly in love if she freaks out every time her ex walks into the room. And chances are she'll be bumping into him. It's a small village, and we'll be here for two weeks. It's going to happen again.

And if other people see her react like that...

I gaze out at the dark road as I consider it. Did she still have feelings for him? Was that why? Maybe not so much seeing him as seeing his new fiancée? I hadn't considered it before, but I guess it's a possibility. I never felt it was my place to ask why she ran out on the guy, but I assume she just realized what a complete waste of space he was and left while she had the time. But maybe that wasn't the case. Maybe something else happened and she still loves him.

Maybe that's why she never came back.

The thought stays with me, sitting uncomfortably in my stomach as I drive through the village and out the other side to where her family is. The only thing that distracts me is when I make the turn for her house and remember one very important thing.

Megan is rich.

Or at least her mother is. I know her dad left the picture when she was pretty young, but her mother is some property tycoon heiress alongside her own job and did just fine. More than fine. They lived about a mile from the village in a house that was big, even by countryside standards. I'd grown used to living in cities. Box rooms and tiny apartments. Any place with more than a handful of rooms might as well be a mansion to me. But Megan's actually *was* a mansion. And a big one at that.

"I forgot you were loaded," I say, as I slow the car. There are no streetlamps out here, and I have only the headlights to show me where I'm going.

Megan frowns, but it's the first bit of life I've seen from her in ages, so I'll take it. "I'm not loaded."

"Your family is."

"I guess."

"I'm not judging," I add. She sounds uncomfortable, which wasn't my intention, but I don't know what else to say when I pull up to the large gates that mark the entry to her property.

"You can just leave me here," she mutters, but I ignore that.

"You might get lost in the five miles it takes to get up your drive," I tease, but she doesn't answer; just takes out her phone and calls a number to open the gate.

The driveway is graveled, and even in the dead of winter, the plants on either side of the doorway look fresh and manicured. Not like Mam's enthusiastic but forgetful garden phases, where flowers seem to bloom and die within the week.

The house itself is a big, three-story block painted light yellow with white shutters on the windows. Thick stone pillars bracket the front door, and the steps leading up to it are decorated for Christmas with garlands of ivy and carefully strewn fairy lights. The lights in the house are on, but no one comes out to meet us, and as soon as I stop the car, Megan is all business, grabbing things like her phone and her knitting and the two lip balms, one water bottle, and the bag of homemade trail mix she'd left in the side pocket.

I leave her to it while I get her bags out, lining them up by the door as she gets out.

"I'll pick you up tomorrow?" I ask, and she nods, her attention on anything but me, and the curdle in my stomach sours even further.

"Is this it?"

"What?" She's distracted, double-checking she's got everything.

"Are you backing out?" I ask. "Is that what's happening here?"

That stops her in her tracks. Her gaze swings my way, and the surprise there makes me feel better. But I still have to know.

"Do you want to stop this?" I ask. "Because if you do, you need to tell me right now."

"No," she says quickly. "I'm not backing out. I swear, I'm just..." She sighs. "Isaac threw me. That's all. But I wouldn't do that to you, I promise. And I'm sorry," she adds. "I shouldn't have kissed you like that."

"Kiss me like that anytime you need to," I say. "It's what we agreed. Maybe a little more enthusiasm next time, but—" I break off as she pretends to kick me, and I'm relieved to see she doesn't look as miserable as she did. "Alright then. We're doing this."

"We are."

"I'll pick you up around eleven."

"You'll— What? Why?"

"Lunch with my family," I remind her. We agreed to a rough schedule a few days ago. "You sure you don't want to get this over with now?" I add, gesturing to the front door. I thought I might introduce myself to her mother, but she just shakes her head.

"I'm tired. I'll be better tomorrow. I promise."

"You're perfect now," I assure her. "Don't stress about this."

She nods, definitely still stressing, so I do the only other thing I can think of right now and don't give her a chance to respond as I wrap my arms around her, pulling her into me.

"What are you doing?" she mumbles into my shoulder.

"Hugging you. This is a supportive hug. Plus, I think your mother is watching us from the window."

I smile to myself as she stiffens and pull back to press a kiss to her cheek. Megan's eyes widen in surprise. Behind her, the curtains twitch.

"I'll see you tomorrow."

"Okay."

"And Megan?"

She waits, her hands clenched into fists at her side.

"It's a great coat."

And finally, she smiles.

TEN

MEGAN

I wait until Christian leaves before I ring the doorbell, cursing myself all the while for being the dumbest person alive.

I can't believe I kissed him.

I mean, I *can*. It was an instinctual reaction, but all that tells me is that my instincts are dumb. And yes, I know we both agreed to it, and I know it was going to happen at some point, but A: I didn't think I'd be the one to initiate it, and B: I didn't expect for it to be in a pub parking lot in front of my ex-fiancé. I wasn't prepared. I wasn't prepared at all.

Not to see Isaac. Not to meet Natalie.

Not to kiss Christian.

Christian and his hands on my cheeks. Christian and his cheerful hello as he tucked me into his side. Christian and this bizarre idea.

He's holding up his end of the deal. I wouldn't have blamed him if he freaked. I didn't exactly give him any warning. But he went with it exactly like he promised he would. He stood beside me, and he didn't let me down. Which means I can't let him down. Which means we're doing this. We're actually doing this. And it all suddenly seems so real.

I roll back my shoulders as I wait on the porch, surprised Mam didn't come out to meet us. But as soon as the bell goes, the door flies open, revealing the woman herself standing in the hallway.

"Were you lurking?" I ask, as her eyes flick behind me.

"No."

Yes. "Mam. You could have come out."

"I wasn't lurking," she protests. "I was waiting for you in the living room."

Lurking. But I let it slide as she steps forward to embrace me, the jasmine scent of her perfume tickling my nose. It's the same one she's worn all my life, and just like that, I could be seven years old again, breathing her in.

I was obsessed with my mother when I was a child. To mini-Megan, she was this magical, movie star–esque figure who was always the best-dressed person in the room. Even when it was just the three of us at home for the night, she'd be made up to perfection, like she was ready for visitors at a moment's notice. And we had lots of visitors. We had friends and family and colleagues and acquaintances, a revolving door of people who would come for an afternoon, a night, a summer.

Emily O'Sullivan is a social creature, someone who would throw a party every night if she could. But she's also a good parent. My abiding memories of her are of someone who was patient and kind and never raised her voice until my brother and I turned into moody teenagers. She wanted us to find happiness, no matter what that looked like, and even though I know she doesn't always understand the decisions I make, she tries to, which is all that I can ask for.

"Welcome home," she says, pulling back to look at me. Her once-brown hair is now a soft shade of gray, and she's cut it since the last time I saw her, so it curls around her ears. She looks older, but carefully so, with Botox and makeup and something a little more surgical that she'll probably tell me about after two glasses of wine. "How was the drive?"

"We hit some traffic, but it was okay."

"That's good," she says, examining me as though searching for any changes. "I made up your bed," she adds, taking my biggest suitcase as I toe off my sneakers. "And left you out some towels. Are you hungry?"

"We ate on the way."

The place is spotless, as always. She'd probably collapse if she saw the state Frankie and I keep the apartment in. I was never very good at tidying up beyond the basics, preferring a spring clean on Sunday morning with *Mamma Mia!* on the television.

Here, the only bit of clutter I can see is through the doors to the living room, where her laptop lies open on the desk, surrounded by folders. She ran her own interior design business for thirty years, and though she's technically retired, she still does a lot of freelance work around the country. Says she'd get restless otherwise. Do something stupid like sell her belongings and live in the woods. I presumed it was an exaggeration, but sometimes with my mother, I can never truly tell.

"Is that a new chair?" I ask, eyeing the latest velvet piece in the corner.

"It is," she says proudly. "Aidan didn't notice."

"Where is brother dearest?" I ask, stretching out my back. I feel stiff from sitting in the car for so long.

"Catching up with some friends," she says. "He said not to wait up."

Of course he did.

"Sit in it," she says, ushering me over to the chair. I acquiesce because she takes these things seriously.

"Very comfortable," I proclaim, and she beams at me.

"A girl in Kildare makes them. I wasn't sure at first, but it's different, isn't it?"

"Nice different," I assure her, and she nods, even as a hint of worry enters her expression.

"What?"

"Should I have invited him in?"

"Who? Oh, Christian?"

"I didn't mean to lurk," she says. "I just didn't want to crowd you. It's the first time you've wanted to introduce me to one of your boyfriends since—"

"It's not an introduction," I interrupt, uncomfortable. "You've met him a bunch of times."

"Yes, but it's different now," she insists. "You were just children, and now you're..." She frowns. "I saw his mother in town the other day. She didn't say anything."

I fight the urge to roll my eyes. "Did you say anything to her?"

"Well, no, but—"

"Mam."

"You're right, you're right." She makes a weird shrugging movement and wanders toward the kitchen. "I'll write her a note. Maybe they could all come to the fundraiser," she adds. "Or I could throw a dinner! Do you think they'll like that?"

"Maybe," I say, following her. "But we're trying not to make too big a deal of it." Or at least I'm not. "Okay?"

"Yes, yes, that's fine. New love and all that."

"Not love," I say firmly. "Just dating."

"Sure," she says brightly, and I swear to God I can see wedding bells in her head. "Now. What would you like to drink?"

———

The rest of the evening is actually pretty nice. I take a quick shower and change into my pajamas, deciding to leave the unpacking until tomorrow. Mam's waiting for me with a glass of celebratory prosecco when I come downstairs, and she puts a comedy panel show on the television and tells me about the latest renovation she's considering for the main bathroom and how she's finally going to tackle the garden and the way her book club has gone downhill ever since someone named Sorcha joined and keeps expecting them to have actually read the books.

She asks about my job and Frankie and whether I used that Pilates voucher she got me and tells me my skin is looking much clearer than it did. She seems giddy to have me home. Giddy enough that I get excited too. And all worries about Christian and Isaac get pushed from my mind as I let my mother fuss over me. It's been a long time since anyone has.

It's a nice night. The nicest I've had in a while, and by the time she finally lets me go to bed, I'm so exhausted by the day that I figure I'll probably sleep until tomorrow afternoon. As it is, I barely get a few hours in before I'm woken abruptly by a heavy weight collapsing on top of me. My brother is back from the pub.

"What the... Aidan!"

A grunt comes from somewhere above my head.

"Move," I hiss, catching a whiff of beer as I try to push him off.

"Merry Christmas."

Ugh. I shove him again until he rolls partially over and hits the wall. "Go to bed."

"I am in bed."

"Your own bed."

"Your mattress is better."

I tug my pillow away from him, squinting in the darkness. He's left the door open, and from the soft light left on in the landing, I can just make out his face, flushed from the cold or, more likely, the alcohol. He's grown in the few years he's been away. Gone is the chubby-cheeked brat who used to terrorize me, and instead is a young man who seems to have inherited all of Mam's best features. The straight brows, the square jaw, the brown eyes so much warmer than my own dull gray ones. He's probably got a tan and everything, though I can't tell in the dark.

I haven't seen my brother in person in nearly two years, but right now, I couldn't care less.

"Get out," I tell him when he doesn't move.

"I saw a massive spider in here the other day."

"Shut up. No, you didn't." I twist his wrist toward me, ignoring his noise of protest as I check his watch. Three a.m. "Did you just get home?"

"Maybe."

"Who were you with?"

"Friends." He makes a show of pushing himself off the bed. Not all the way, though. No. He just sits on the side of it, peering down at me with those slightly dazed, *I'm still buzzed* eyes, and I have to admit, I'm jealous at how easily my brother has just slotted back into his life here. He probably had a million invitations when he told people he was coming home. Just another reminder of how firmly I'd shut the door on this place.

And then he flicks my nose, and I'm back to being annoyed again. "Stop."

"Where is he?"

"Who?"

"Your boyfriend," he says. "Is he in the guest room? I don't want any funny business if I'm across the hall."

"He's not here."

Aidan looks confused. "Mam said you were bringing someone home for Christmas."

"He's staying with his family," I mutter, rearranging the blankets around me.

"In Dublin?"

My eyes snap to his, only to see he's being serious. She didn't tell him it's Christian.

"No," I say. "He's from here." I don't know why I'm so wary. But I thought Mam might have spread the news around and save me from conversations such as this one.

"What?" Aidan asks. "Who?"

"Christian. Christian Fitzpatrick."

My brother goes quiet, and I can tell he doesn't believe me. At least not at first, but when I don't say anything more, he seems to sober up real quick. "Christian *Fitzpatrick*?"

"Yeah," I say, defensive now.

He gazes at me as though he's struggling to process this little nugget of information. "Isn't he in jail?" he asks eventually.

"*No.*"

"But he was in jail."

"He was never in jail," I say firmly. "He was brought home by the guards *one* time because he skipped school, and his parents freaked." I only remember it because it was all anyone could talk about in class for a month. "And he's not fifteen anymore," I remind him. "He's different."

Aidan still looks unhappy. "How did you even meet?"

"In Dublin. He works there now."

"And you just... caught up like old friends."

I plant a hand into the mattress, pushing myself into a sitting position. I am done with this conversation. "You want to know if we had sex?" I ask. "You want to know if your sister made *love*? If she—" I bat his arm away as he tries to cover my mouth. "What are you doing?" I ask, as he takes out his phone. The screen is cracked because, of course, it is. Some things never change. "Aidan. What are you—"

"Googling him."

"Why?"

"Because I want to. Hey." He holds his arm out, so I can't reach his phone. "No touching."

"Stop looking."

"No."

He gives me another push, infuriatingly stronger than me, and my anxiety notches up several levels as Aidan goes quiet, scrolling through the phone. The websites for Christian's job come up first, and then his social media. Aidan pauses on the most recent pictures, focusing on one in particular.

It's the picture of Christian and me at the cocktail bar the night we agreed to do this. We were at least a bottle in at that stage, as evidenced by the wide smiles on both our faces.

Another flick of Aidan's thumb and there I am again, leaning against a brick wall outside. A string of fairy lights above casts me in a white glow, and I make a mental note to grab that one off him because I look pretty hot, not gonna lie.

Aidan keeps scrolling, moving past Christian's Dublin era and back further to London.

Suddenly my fake boyfriend is standing next to big glass buildings and posing with friends in sun-scorched parks and slick bars. Random family members pop up now and then, but it's mainly women I see. All of them beautiful, all of them as well-groomed as he is, with perfect hair and low-key clothing. He stands with his arm around one as they pose on a balcony, in a suit with another at someone's wedding, then next to a blonde in a beige trench coat, drinking white wine on a Soho street.

Jealousy stabs at me, along with a wriggling hurt that's just ridiculous, and I try and lift my legs to dislodge my brother.

"Aidan," I warn.

"I'm just looking."

"No, you're not." I shove him hard enough that he falls off the bed, and he lands with a thump on the floor, his phone forgotten.

"You're so mean to me," he grumbles, getting back up. "I had a long flight."

"Yeah, you smell like you did. And you— Get *out*." I whisper-shriek the last word, clutching my blanket as he tries to yank it off me.

He gives it another tug, but it seems to be his final act of being irritating as he straightens with an aggressive boy yawn. "Watch out for that spider."

"There's not a—"

I break off as he leans down, patting me on the head like a child. "Glad you came home," he says, and while the action might be sarcastic, the words are anything but. They're unusually sincere, especially for him, but before I can respond, he slips out, closing the door gently behind him.

ELEVEN

CHRISTIAN

The next morning, I wake to cold air and a stiff neck, which tells me two things.

One is that I should have brought my expensive pillow from home, and two, the radiator is on the fritz. Everything in this house is always on the fritz. The place is old and drafty, and when I was growing up, if something couldn't be fixed, it didn't always mean it would be replaced. It's not that we were destitute or anything. We had everything we needed, but four kids on a small farmer's salary did not a trip to Disney World make.

Nor, apparently, a working heating system.

I lie on my old bed in my old room, gazing up at my old ceiling. I slept badly, tossing and turning and thinking of everything and nothing. My apartment building back in Dublin has a twenty-four-hour gym, and usually, when insomnia hits, I exhaust myself there until my body has no choice but to recoup its energy. I'll have to make do with a simple run here, but I didn't have time to unpack my stuff yesterday; too busy being fussed over by my mother. It was only her here to greet me. Hannah was out with friends, and Andrew and Molly hadn't landed yet. My dad was already asleep, but I'd have to see him this morning, something I wasn't exactly looking forward to, and even knowing I have Megan by my side now, my chest still tightens with that familiar sense of dread.

It doesn't help that I also badly, desperately want a cigarette.

I used to have one every morning, and waking up is always a trigger. I quickly go through my routine to distract myself, reaching for my glass of water first and then the book on my nightstand, only this time as I do, I'm reminded of how Megan reaches for her knitting, her fingers always moving like she can't keep still.

The thought of her stays with me, and I'm barely a few pages in when I abandon the paperback, impatient to get a start on our plan. With a brief scroll through my phone, I slip out of bed and head to the bathroom, putting a sock on the door to keep other members of my family from barging in.

The room smells like strawberries, which is my first indication that this won't be the best shower of my life. If Hannah washed her hair, it means there's going to be no hot water left, and sure enough it takes a good minute for the trickle to warm up to something just short of icy. But I'm not bothered to wait for the boiler to restart, and so choose violence and brace myself under the freezing stream for as long as I can bear.

Afterward, I get to work unpacking, hanging up my clothes, and hiding the various presents for everyone under the bed.

Including the one I got for Megan. It's a simple silver chain that cost me an arm and a leg. Jewelry is always a risky gift, but I noticed she wears a few staple pieces and thought it was safest to get something she could simply add to her collection and, in a few years, forget it was even from me.

I place it carefully next to the new phone I got Hannah and, feeling more myself now that everything's where it should be, I finally seek out my family.

Hannah's door is open, but my sister is nowhere to be seen.

Liam's old room, the now guest room, is where Andrew and Molly are supposed to be sleeping, and the closed door means they probably still are.

I find Mam in the dining room, sorting through her Christmas card list. In two weeks, the place will be spotless for dinner, but now it's like Santa's workshop, with the table littered with boxes and envelopes and recycled wrapping paper from last year, neatly folded and ready to be used again.

"Did you sleep okay?" she asks when I appear.

"No. My room's freezing."

"Don't exaggerate."

"Fine. My room is very, very cold. I'm going to call someone to take a look at the heating. And this time, if they say to replace the boiler, you're replacing the boiler." I'll pay for it myself if I have to. My parents don't like when I send money home, but I figure they won't be able to protest if I just do it without them knowing. "Where are the emigrants?"

"Asleep," she warns. "And they're going to stay like that for another two hours at least. Don't go waking them just because you're bored."

"I'll try to control myself," I promise, leaving her for the kitchen. I pop a slice of bread in the toaster and put water in the kettle for some tea, my movements so instinctual it's like I never left.

"I'll have a cappuccino," a familiar voice calls from the adjoining room, and I head through the archway to finally find Hannah.

My baby sister sits cross-legged on the floor in front of the television, surrounded by textbooks and legal pads filled with her impatient scribble. She's still in her pajamas, and her long dark hair is pulled back into a thick plait, kept off her face with a dozen butterfly clips.

"With oat milk," she adds, not looking up from her work.

"Dad lets you have oat milk in the house?"

"I told him it's good for my brain and that I need it for my exams."

"What exams?" I joke. "You're studying fashion." I toe one of her books out of the way, tilting my head to read the title. "Or is it history now?"

"Both. I've decided I want to work in the film industry."

"Sounds like a stable career choice."

"Can we go to the lake later?" she asks, ignoring me. "I want to show Daniela, and the weather's supposed to be nice this afternoon."

Daniela is Hannah's latest girlfriend. One of many I've been introduced to over the years. Turns out my sister is a bit of a player. This one appears to be sticking around, however.

"You're still with Daniela?"

"*Yes*. She's coming over for lunch, and I want to show her the lake."

"We can do that." I pick up another book. "We can show Megan too."

"Who?"

"Funny." But when I glance up from the title, it's to see genuine confusion on her face. "Megan," I repeat. "My girlfriend."

Her mouth drops open. "Your *what?*" she asks, just as our mother hurries into the room.

"I knew there was something I forgot to do."

She can't be serious. "I told you to tell everyone," I say.

"I thought Andrew would."

"Andrew knows?" Hannah asks, obviously hurt. "Andrew knows, but not me?"

"Plus, I didn't want to go spreading it around," Mam adds.

"She's not a *disease*," I say.

"Hello?" Hannah gets to her feet with a pout as Mam starts tidying up the room, flustered. "I want to hear about the girlfriend."

"Did you tell Dad at least?" I ask, ignoring her.

"Of course I did."

"So everyone knows except me," Hannah says.

Mam pauses. "I don't think I told Liam."

Jesus Christ. "Mam was meant to tell you," I say to Hannah. "Stop with the wounded-puppy eyes. I posted about her."

"Oh, *sorry* if I didn't pay attention to a picture of you and some random woman. What a rare occurrence in your life."

"It's Emily O'Sullivan's daughter," Mam interjects, as we glare at each other.

"And I'm bringing her around later, so if everyone could be semi-normal, that would be just great." I take out my phone to text my eldest brother but stop at Hannah's sudden wariness. "What?"

"Megan O'Sullivan?" she asks. "Didn't she dump her fiancé at the altar?"

"She didn't dump him. She left him." The dumping came after.

"But she still ran from her own wedding."

I pause at the tone of her voice, surprised by the hint of disdain I hear there. "Yeah," I say. "She did. But that was a long time ago. You weren't even there. You were like two at the time."

"I was fourteen."

"Same thing. You have no idea what went on."

"I know it was rude," she says. "I know Isaac was heartbroken."

"How the hell do you know that?"

"Because I've known him since I was seven," she says hotly. "He used to coach camogie."

He did. I'd forgotten all about that. Every Saturday morning, he spent several hours of his free time teaching a bunch of kids how to hit a ball. Mam once said he had the patience of a saint. And the way Hannah's looking at me now makes me think he's more than wormed his way into her good books.

"He took a whole season off after she left," she continues. "Mr. Heaney had to take over. And Mr. Heaney was shite."

"Hannah," Mam cautions.

"He was! We lost every match."

"I don't care, just keep your voice down. Your brother is sleeping."

"She basically destroyed him," Hannah says. "No one likes her."

"I like her," I say firmly. "And you can be team Isaac all you like in private, but she's coming over later, and you're going to be nice."

"Of course, she's going to be nice," Mam says, even though the stubborn look on Hannah's face tells me otherwise. "And Megan's more than welcome here. I used to go to her mother's parties every year. They're a very nice family."

"They are," I say, staring at Hannah. "Thanks, Mam."

My mother retreats to the kitchen, muttering something about extra plates, while Hannah drops back down to her study nest.

"She sent her engagement ring back in the post," she says, her eyes on her notes. "She didn't even send him a text."

"How do you know that?"

"People talk."

"People gossip, you mean." But I cross my arms, feeling like I'm the one on the back foot. "I think you'll like her if you give her a chance," I say finally.

"I'm sure I will," Hannah mutters.

It doesn't make me feel any better.

———

It's only an hour later when I've helped Mam with the dishes and signed my name to what feels like five hundred Christmas cards, that I finally hear my dad out front.

My relationship with my father growing up was complicated at the best of times, and as the years went by, they didn't get any simpler. He's a quiet man. A pretty calm one too. Patient and hardworking. He encouraged all of us to pursue our own lives, but he always thought I'd take over the farm.

He never said it to me, but I know he did. Liam was the obvious choice, but his wife Mairead's family left her land, so it made sense that he helped her in looking after that. He grew interested in the business side of things anyway and was more at home balancing the books than mucking out the stalls. Andrew came next, but he never had the heart for it. Or the head. Photography was his thing, and now he's staying in Chicago; there's no hope of it. Hannah's a straight-up no. She'd rather lose herself in her drawings, and me...

As a kid, I loved helping him out. As a teenager, I couldn't think of anything worse. I probably broke his heart, as all shitty kids do, but I know he always thought I'd get back to it. Honestly, so did I. I just assumed it's where I'd end up, and that was maybe why I rebelled so much back then. It was only when Andrew left for the States that I realized it was even possible to *leave*. That you don't have to stay in the same place you grew up. Once I figured that out, I never looked back.

And I don't think he ever forgave me.

"Need some help?" I call, as he strides across the yard. He's dressed for the cold in a heavy-duty coat and hat and looks the exact same as the image I have of him in my head: a tall, burly man with weathered, reddened skin from working outside. Bushy brows, dark eyes, and an unruffled aura around him, like as long as he gets up every day and does his tasks, the world will keep on spinning.

I give him a hug, the smell of earth and animals filling my nostrils before I step back.

"You're alright," he says easily. "I hear you've got yourself a girlfriend."

"Megan. She's—"

"The knitting girl."

I pause in surprise. "Yeah," I say. "How did you know that?"

"The O'Sullivan daughter? She used to knit hats for the lambs when she was a child. Her mother would drop them over, bring her sometimes."

"I don't remember that."

"She was only a young thing," he says, and I smile. The knitting girl. She'll like that.

"Most people think of her as the runaway bride," I tell him, and he grunts.

"People like to talk," he says before he pauses. "Be nice to her, yeah?"

"How do you mean?"

"Ah, you know."

I tense. "I don't," I say, already knowing where this is going.

"Just don't play around with her," he says, sounding exasperated, and I feel the tightness building in the back of my shoulders even as I keep my voice calm.

"I don't play around."

"I don't mean anything by it," Dad says placidly. "I just don't think I've ever heard you mention the same girl twice. And that's fine when I don't know her, but you're not the one who'll have to see her mother every other week in town."

"That's what you think I'm doing?"

"I don't know what you—"

"No," I say. "You don't."

Dad falls silent, his expression shuttering, and I remind myself that this, this right here, is why Megan and I came to our agreement in the first place. So he'd stop thinking of me like I'm...

"I'm not playing around with her," I say, calmer than before. "I didn't play around with anyone else either, but that doesn't seem to matter."

"Christian—"

I'm already heading toward the car. "The heating still isn't working, by the way. I told Mam, but I'm going to call someone to come take a look at it. You guys can't keep relying on hot water bottles."

"Where are you going?" Dad calls after me, and I can hear the frustration in his voice.

"To pick up my girlfriend," I say shortly and slide inside, slamming the door shut.

TWELVE

MEGAN

Christian arrives an hour earlier than I expect him to, and I'm still drooling into my pillow when my mother calls my name.

I've never gotten up so fast in my life, not even taking time to see how I look before I'm out the door and rushing down the stairs so fast it's a miracle I don't fall over them.

I needn't have worried, though. I skid to a halt to find them in the kitchen, sitting at the island with cups of tea. Both happy as clams.

"Good morning," Christian says, smiling as though the very sight of me has made his day. I blink at him, lost, until he surreptitiously indicates the chair beside him. Right. Act in love.

"Christian brought cookies," Mam says like he just bestowed a mountain of gold upon her.

"My mother made them," he explains.

"Great! Yum." *Yum?* Ugh. I sit down, meeting his eye. "You're early," I whisper.

"I couldn't wait to see you," he says in a normal voice as Mam roots through the cabinets. As soon as she turns, Christian grabs the bottom of my seat and drags me closer. The chair makes an ungodly screech against the tiles, but when Mam glances back we just smile at her.

"Quit it," I mutter.

"Are you always so grumpy when you wake up?"

"Yes."

His lips twitch before his eyes drop to my mouth, lingering in a way that puts me even more on edge.

Is he going to kiss me good morning? Do I want him to kiss me good morning?

Our gazes catch.

"Nice retainer," he murmurs.

Oh my *God*.

I tug the thing out and shove it into the pocket of my bath robe as Mam turns back around.

"Megan tells me you were in London," she says, pushing the plate of cookies toward us.

"For a few years," he says, while I grab one, nibbling on the edge. "Nice to be back, though."

"And what is it you do? Megan mentioned real estate."

I seem to have mentioned a lot of things in the one five-minute conversation we had about him.

"It's luxury holiday homes at the moment," Christian says. "A branch of the company I was working for in London opened up a Dublin office, so I put my hand up to help get things running here. I figure I'll spend a few more months with them and then see what my options are."

"And what is it you do there?" Mam continues. "Sales?"

"Seriously?" I ask.

"What?"

"It's too early for an interrogation."

"It's not an interrogation," she says, defensive. "I'm asking him questions."

"I'm more in the management side of things," Christian says as if we're not about to start snapping at each other.

"He's in charge of the whole office," I say because he's being needlessly modest. "He's the boss."

"It's a small team," he clarifies. "But they're..." he trails off as Aidan appears in the doorway, one hand freezing mid-scratch against his stomach when he sees us.

"Well, look who's alive," Mam says pointedly, but Aidan doesn't seem to hear her, all his attention focused on Christian.

Christian who acts like they're best friends. "Aidan," he says cheerfully. "Welcome home. How's Australia?"

"Warm," he grunts, shooting me a look before heading over to the fridge.

"You remember Christian?" Mam asks. "He went to school with—"

"Yep," he says, not looking at any of us.

Oh boy. I glare at my brother as he pours a glass of orange juice, but Christian doesn't so much as bat an eyelid.

Mam also seems to sense her son's tone and shifts on her stool, drawing our attention back to her. "You never told me how you two met."

"She poured a glass of wine over me," Christian says and looks at me with such convincing affection that I almost blush. Then he ruins it. "While on a date with another man."

"I wasn't on a date," I protest. "I was supposed to be on one, but he... never showed," I finish, not exactly wanting to tell her that I saw him making out with someone else.

"Megan," Mam says, disapproving. "You shouldn't speak to men who treat women like that."

"Everyone treats everyone like that," I mutter.

"It all worked out," Christian says easily. "For me, anyway."

Aidan's expression sours further, and he doesn't look at us as he grabs his cereal bowl and vanishes back up the stairs like he's twelve.

Mam pretends she doesn't notice. "So, what's the plan for today?"

"I was hoping to bring Megan around for lunch," Christian says. "Introduce her to the family."

You'd swear my mother had never heard better news in her life, and I feel a little guilty at how happy she looks. "We should have your parents around too," she says. "Do you think they'll have time before Christmas?"

"I'm sure we'll make time," Christian says, as my stomach keeps twisting.

"I'll go get dressed," I mutter, and I rush out of the room. I don't feel too bad about leaving him alone with Mam with the way they're getting on, but I don't love it either, so I throw on a pair of dark jeans and my favorite sweater before slapping on some foundation. Mascara, earrings, and a classic messy bun help complete the look of Christian's-nice-new-totally-normal-girlfriend, and I tug on my boots as I leave my room.

Aidan's door remains firmly shut the entire time, and I'm definitely going to give him a piece of my mind later, but Christian doesn't seem too fussed, waiting for me at the bottom of the stairs, my red coat in his hands.

"Your Mam's phone rang twice before she felt she had to pick it up," he explains, when I look around for her. "I think it's the caterers."

"She likes you."

"Of course, she does," he says. "I'm extremely likable."

"Humble too," I say, as I follow him out. It's a sunny day, but early enough that there's still some frost on the hills.

"Your brother, on the other hand," Christian continues.

"He's just hungover."

"I thought he was going to threaten me to a duel."

"Please," I grumble. "Your family's going to be a million times worse."

"How do you figure that?"

"Because there's more of them?" I say, kicking at the gravel as he leads me to the car.

"This is the hardest part," he promises. "Once we get through this, we can get through anything."

He's clearly never been to my mother's parties.

It's only twenty minutes to his house, and as we drive through the village, I see a few new additions to the otherwise usual handful of homes, offices, and shops. The old phone box on the main street is apparently now a Wi-Fi hub. The gardens in front of the school now given over to rewilding. There's a new café where the old shoe shop used to be, and the corner store has been taken over by a chain, the peeling signs replaced by digital displays urging me to play the lotto and buy three boxes of chocolate for the price of two.

Eventually, Christian pulls up to a sprawling white farm-house that looks annoyingly familiar, even though I'm sure I haven't been here before. If you'd told me to draw a picture of Christian's house, I wouldn't even know where to begin, but now that I'm here...

I get out, looking at Christian over the roof of the car. "I think I used to knit hats for your sheep," I say, and he grins.

"Apparently. In this family, you're known as the knitting girl."

"I am?" I ask, unable to hide my delight.

"According to my dad at least."

"He remembers?"

"He does." Christian shepherds me toward the house, and I feel lighter as I try to picture his father, but all I can remember is the sensation of rough hands lifting me over a fence, of someone helping me pet the small animals on the other side.

"Ready?" Christian asks.

"If I say no, can we leave?"

He laughs and pushes open the front door to reveal a long, narrow hallway with a staircase right in front of us.

I don't know why I expected the Fitzpatricks to be lining up like the von Trapp family or something, but I feel better when we're met with nothing but silence. Silence and... mess.

We barely take a step inside before we're met with our first obstacle, two suitcases taking up most of the hallway. Shoes and coats are strewn everywhere, but thankfully Christian doesn't just throw his over the banister like the others, instead hanging it carefully up before doing the same with mine. Shopping bags stuffed with presents sit by the door, probably waiting to be brought somewhere, and everywhere I look screams Christmas. The miniature manger on the hall table, the green and gold tinsel adorning the stairs. The house even smells like the holiday, with the scent of sugar and cinnamon wafting from the kitchen. After the serenity of my home, it feels like pure chaos.

I kind of love it.

"Please tell me you made that," I say, pointing to a faded child's drawing of several stick figures trapped in a glitter snowstorm.

"That looks like Hannah's creation. I was more of a numbers kid. Though there's definitely a stocking I made somewhere. Sewed it myself and everything."

"You sewed?" I ask, and he points at my face.

"That?" he says. "That impressed look? Look at me like that all the time, and we'll be fine."

"I want to see the stocking."

"It's probably by the—"

"Christian."

We turn our attention upward as someone appears at the top of the stairs.

She's vaguely familiar, and I realize with a start that she looks just like Christian's friend from the pub, which means this must be Molly, Andrew's girlfriend. She's pretty, with long blonde hair and a blinding white smile. She's also tiny, barely coming up to my shoulders as she hurries down.

Christian grins at her as she does, and I stand there awkwardly as she throws herself into his arms.

Okay, maybe that's a bit of an exaggeration.

She pauses on the bottom step, rising up on her toes to kiss him on the cheek. "Hey, stranger."

"Hey, yourself," Christian says. "Molly, meet Megan. Megan, Molly."

We smile at each other, and I try not to do the jealous-girl thing because you're not supposed to do the jealous-girl thing, and I definitely shouldn't do the jealous-girl thing because, hello, fake relationship, but I can't help but notice how very put together she is even though she's obviously jetlagged. Her makeup is light, her hair curled, and she isn't wearing a spot of color on her, which has me second-guessing the bright red and green I picked out for her sweater.

"When did you get in?" Christian asks.

"A few hours ago." She rolls her eyes. "Some of us are taking it better than others."

"My ears are burning." Another voice calls from above, and a second later, Andrew appears. Unlike Molly, who's fully dressed, he's still in flannel pajama bottoms paired with a thick navy fleece, his hair sticking out in all directions, much like my own brother's. He was a few years older than me, so I don't have as many memories of him as I do of Christian, but he smiles warmly as he comes down.

"Megan O'Sullivan," he declares, coming to a stop beside Molly. His hand slides around her waist, squeezing her hip, but his eyes are on me. "You free for a swim later?"

"A swim?" Christian asks before I can answer. "Hannah said she just wanted to show Daniela the lake."

"Yeah, and one thing led to another, and now we've challenged each other to a race."

"I tried to stop it," Molly tells us.

"We were thinking about bringing lunch with us. Go for a walk. Freeze to death. You know. Christmas things."

Christian doesn't look happy. "I don't—"

"That sounds great," I say before he can make an excuse. The whole point of this is that we spend time as a couple with his family. If this is what they do, then this is what we do. "Some fresh air would be nice."

"See," Andrew says, turning to Molly. "People like activities."

"I like activities," she says. "I just don't like *your* activities. You want some coffee?" she asks me. "I'm the only one who really drinks it, so I bring my own."

"Coffee sounds good," I say, and she smiles, heading to the kitchen. Andrew flashes me a grin and follows as if being in a different room to her is incomprehensible.

"So they're like *in love* in love," I whisper to Christian when they're gone.

"Sickening, isn't it?"

"Do we have to be in love in love?"

"Not unless you want to change the touching rules."

"I mean, a shoulder massage wouldn't be frowned upon," I say, and his hand lands on my back in more of a thump than a caress as he steers me toward the kitchen. I can hear Molly and Andrew inside, along with another voice, older and softer, which I guess is his mother. My nerves, which had been churning quietly away, kick up a notch, and I ground my heels in, forcing him to stop.

"I have to nervous pee," I say truthfully, and his mouth contorts like he's trying not to smile.

"Down the hall on your left," he says, pointing up the stairs. "Wash your hands," he adds loudly, and my glare is met with a smile.

I'm glad one of us is enjoying ourselves.

I find the bathroom easily enough but linger when I'm done,

double-checking my makeup and smoothing down stray hairs. I'm just delaying the inevitable, but I want to make a good impression on his family. Between Isaac and Mam, I feel like he's been doing all the work.

When I'm finally happy, I head back toward the stairs, glancing through the open doors as I pass, only to pause when I spy a familiar suitcase.

This one must be Christian's room. There are two beds inside, one of which has been stripped bare while the other is carefully made, and curiosity pulls me further in before I can keep moving. His clothes hang neatly in the closet, a mixture of casualwear and the subtle, expensive pieces I've come to associate him with. At the sight of them, I realize how I've never seen where he lives in Dublin, even though he's been to my place a few times now. The image in my head is of something very orderly and stern. Dark colors and sleek lines. More or less the exact opposite of the house I'm in now.

I definitely don't picture any books there. But they're everywhere in here. Stacked on the bedside table, packed tight along the windowsill. An old case shoved against the wall is crammed with them, and I run a finger over the top shelf, hoping for some random insight into the man.

I thought they might be very serious history tomes, and there are some there. But also, an assortment of crime and old copies of *Goosebumps* with battered spines and yellowed pages. I assume they're all from his childhood, but the top one on his bedside table looks newer, with a torn sheet of paper slid halfway through it, acting as a bookmark.

Starting with You, the title reads, and then, in smaller print below that, *Rebuild Your Life Step by Step.*

"Can I help you?"

My heart leaps into my throat as I spin around to find a young woman standing in the doorway. She's nearly as tall as Christian, with a slender figure and wide-set green eyes that are now narrowed in suspicion. She looks like she's in her late teens. Which means...

"You must be Hannah," I say. "I'm Megan."

Her expression doesn't change. "Are you snooping?"

"I— No," I say because what else can you say? We both know I was snooping. I was obviously snooping. But the way she says it makes it sound like I was stealing her mother's jewelry. "I was just—"

"Hannah!" Andrew yells before I can think of an excuse. "Someone's here claiming to be your girlfriend? She's way out of your league, though, so I'm not sure if I believe her."

Hannah's gaze flicks around the room before landing back on me, and then she turns without another word and disappears.

Well. That's not good.

I scurry after her and find my way to the kitchen, a large, charmingly hectic room that is clearly the heart of the house. Every inch of space along the countertops is filled with food and utensils, and the sugary smell I caught earlier is revealed to be another tray of cookies cooling by the sink. Hannah's gone straight to the table where she's laying out bread for sandwiches while Molly and Andrew stand by the kettle, counting out mugs. They both look up when I come in, but my attention is on Christian, who's chatting with who must be Hannah's girl-friend, a young woman in a neon green puffer jacket with box braids down to her waist. At any other time, I'd try to get to know a fellow lover of bright colors, but I only smile apologeti-cally at her as I steal Christian away.

"What's wrong?" he asks when I pull him into the corner.

"Your sister doesn't like me."

His smile comes a beat too late.

"Oh my God."

"Well, your brother doesn't like me, so I think we're even."

"She caught me in your room."

"Why were you in my—"

"I was snooping! Girlfriends are allowed to snoop. She looked at me like I was catfishing you."

"Isaac used to teach her camogie," he admits, and I almost groan.

"She hates me."

"She doesn't know you. It will be fine."

"But—"

"And this must be Megan!"

I shut up as Christian's mother, Colleen, enters the kitchen, wiping her hands on a dishcloth. She's about my height, with graying hair and laugh lines around her eyes.

"I've heard so much about you," she continues.

"She hasn't," Christian says. "She's just being polite."

"Well, at least one of us is," she says, eyeing me. "Has no one offered the girl a drink?"

"I'm making coffee," Molly pipes up.

"And what about food? Are you hungry?"

"We're making lunch to go," Andrew says, as Hannah starts cutting thick slices of cheddar. "I've challenged your only daughter to a race to the death."

"I'll get your father to update the will," she mutters. "Just get back before the weather turns. It's supposed to get icy later."

"Apparently, it's going to snow this year," Hannah says, as Molly holds up a carton of milk, shaking it at me.

"Just a splash," I say, lingering awkwardly by Christian as she makes me a coffee, and I'm just thinking that there's nothing worse than being the new girlfriend next to the almost-part-of-the-family girlfriend when I make the mistake of catching Hannah's eye across the kitchen.

Nope. Sibling hate is much worse.

"I'd love some snow," Molly says wistfully. "It's so pretty when it falls here."

"Not always," Hannah says. "Do you remember the big storm a few years ago? We almost ran out of bread."

"We didn't run out of bread," Colleen huffs, clearing space along the countertop.

"I know we didn't; that's why I said almost. Dad's car got stuck, remember that?"

"*Yes*, Hannah," Colleen says. "We remember. It won't be like that."

"I'm just saying we're going to need to be more prepared."

"Then maybe you should stop making two sandwiches for every person here."

"But we're racing," she protests, as Molly hands me a mug. "We need fuel."

"You *need* to go easy on that butter, or you're going down to the shops to get me more. Now is everyone okay with ham and cheese, or does anyone want chicken? Because if not, it's going in the freezer. We need to clear space in the fridge."

"We need a just cheese one," Christian says.

"We've got plenty of the ham," Colleen says, uncovering a tinfoil-wrapped leg of it. "I roasted it last night. From the new butcher in town," she adds to Molly, who nods.

"Megan can't eat ham," Christian continues before I can stop him.

"Well, the chicken's a little dry, but—"

"She's a vegetarian."

I swear you'd hear a pin drop. Everyone's attention goes to me, except for Colleen, whose eyes drop to the ham like she doesn't know whether she should fling it out the window or not.

"Vegetarian," Christian repeats when no one says anything. "Not a serial killer."

"What would you eat at Christmas then, Megan?" Colleen asks, her voice too bright to be normal.

"Oh, she can still eat turkey," Andrew says. Molly whacks his arm.

"You don't need to go to any trouble for me," I say. "Honestly, I'll be fine."

"You have to eat at Christmas," she says like the alternative is unthinkable.

I smile cheerfully. "I will. We're going to go to mine afterward."

"Afterward?"

"We're doing two Christmases," Christian says, which doesn't seem to help.

"I see," Colleen murmurs, still looking troubled, and there's an awkward beat where no one seems to know what to say before Daniela grabs a bowl from the table.

"We've got tomatoes?"

"Perfect!" I say quickly. "Cheese and tomato would be brilliant, thank you. I can make them my—"

"Hannah's making them," Christian says, and Hannah presses her lips together as she slaps a slice of bread down onto the counter.

I take a sip of coffee, just so I have something to do, and Christian's arm slides around my back.

"You're doing great," he whispers, and that's when I come to understand that my new fake boyfriend is a big old liar.

THIRTEEN
CHRISTIAN

"They love walking," Molly mutters to Megan when we leave the house thirty minutes later. "And being outside."

"Christian warned me," Megan says, as I take her hand. Her eyes drop down to it, but she doesn't pull away.

Hannah, Andrew, and Daniela all power ahead, laden down with bags of towels and food, while the three of us slow-pokes take up the rear.

"It will be nice not to be completely outnumbered by the Fitzpatricks this Christmas," Molly continues. "There's only so many in-jokes a girl can take."

I nearly point out that she'll be a Fitzpatrick soon enough, but I manage to keep my mouth shut.

"Your scarf is beautiful, by the way," Molly adds. "Where did you get it? I'd love a big one like that."

"Oh, I made it."

"You did?" Her eyes brighten. "Jesus. I'm surrounded by artists. Hannah!"

I tense as Hannah glances over her shoulder, still marching ahead.

"Megan makes clothes too!" Molly calls, but she just nods

before turning back to the front. Megan practically wilts beside me, and I feel a rare surge of anger toward my sister, but Molly at least doesn't seem to realize anything's wrong.

"So, how did you guys meet?" she asks. "Andrew said you went to school together?"

I launch into the same spiel I told Megan's mother that morning, and then Molly tells Megan her own little love story, and just like that, the two of them are doing that instant best friend thing girls seem to do. They keep it up the whole way until we round the bend, and the smile drops from Molly's face.

"What's that?" she asks, confused.

"It's the lake," Andrew says, jogging back to us.

"*That*'s the lake? I thought it was going to be a pond or something."

"Then it would be a pond," Andrew points out. "And not a lake."

And it is most definitely a lake. A sparkling blue circle of one, nestled in the middle of the sloping hills. It's where we spent most of our summers when we were kids and might as well have been a massive waterpark to us with the way we carried on. But I have no desire to dip so much as a toe into it today.

"Let's go get a good seat," I say to Megan. There's a grassy bit near us that looks like it's been in the sunlight long enough that it will be dry, but Megan doesn't budge.

"We're not going to race?" she asks.

"*We're* not, no."

"Christian doesn't do anything unless his personal trainer tells him to," Andrew tells her.

I give him a look. "Christian likes not contracting the flu before Christmas."

"The flu's a virus," Hannah pipes up. "You can't get it just from being cold."

"But you can get a cold from being cold," I say. "That's why they call it a cold. Let's go."

I tug on Megan's hand again, but she just gazes at the lake, an odd expression on her face. "I can race," she says, and I frown, dropping my voice so only she can hear me.

"You don't have to."

"I know, but…" Her eyes latch on to Hannah. "I don't mind. I want to."

"Megan—"

"I'll race," she says loudly, breaking away from me.

"You don't even have a swimsuit," I protest.

"She can have mine," Molly volunteers. "There's no way I'm getting in that. I like all my fingers and toes attached to my body, thank you very much."

"But—"

But nothing, it turns out. The girls all head to the small public bathroom by the side of the lake while Andrew undresses there and then, stripping down to his trunks, even though it's so cold I can see my breath.

"I told her we were just having lunch," I say, exasperated, and he laughs.

"Ruining a romantic plan, am I? She doesn't have to get in."

"She wants to impress you."

"Well, consider me impressed," Andrew says lightly. "Relax. She's doing great."

I grunt. "Hannah's being a brat."

"She's just stressed about her exams."

"No, she's just being a brat."

"Well, I'm staying out of it. And her and Molly seem fine." His gaze drifts over my shoulder, and I turn to see the two of them standing by a bench, Megan with her back to Molly as the other girl adjusts the straps of her swimsuit. The swimsuit that is at least half a size too small, the bright blue polyester leaving nothing to the imagination.

"Honestly, she's brilliant," Andrew says, clapping me on the shoulders. "I love her already."

"Do you mind?" I ask when he keeps looking their way. "She's getting changed."

"She's already changed."

"It doesn't mean you need to gawk at her," I say, but he just smiles. "What?"

"Nothing," he says, smiling harder.

"Andrew—"

"I didn't say anything." He holds his hands up as Hannah and Daniela emerge from the bathrooms, Hannah clad in her own swimsuit while Daniela remains in more practical clothes.

They go to the water while Megan darts to my side, her nose already turning pink from the cold.

"To the island and back again?" Andrew asks, pointing to the tiny bit of landing in the center. "It's not that far. A minute tops?"

"Sure," Megan says, and he and Molly go over to tell the plan to Hannah.

"You don't have to do this," I say again when they're gone.

"I know," she says. "But I want to race. It's fun."

"What if you get cold?"

What if she gets *cold*?

"Let's go, losers," Andrew calls before I can sound like any more of an idiot. Daniela gives Hannah a good luck kiss before racing over to us, and I turn to Megan, intending to do the same, but she's already joining my siblings, bouncing up and down as she tries to keep warm.

"She's not some secret Olympic swimmer, is she?" Molly asks, as she joins my side.

I don't answer because I don't know, and I can only stand there and watch as Daniela starts the timer on her phone and yells for the race to begin.

The three of them go screaming into the water, Andrew's

quickly dissolving into curses as they start to swim, and I take an involuntary step forward when Megan briefly disappears under before splashing back again.

"Holy shit," Molly laughs as she overtakes him. "She's fast."

She is.

Megan doesn't so much as glide along the water as she does power through it, a lot stronger than she looks. So strong she even catches up with Hannah, who's been taking lessons since she was five.

She doesn't slow down either. Daniela and Molly shriek encouragement at their respective partners as they reach the island, but it's Megan who ekes out in front as they head back. Barely a minute has passed, and I step closer to the shore, not taking my eyes off her as they head into their final few strokes.

I've never been competitive, never needed to be, but an unfamiliar sense of pride fills me as I watch her, the urge to shout like the other two growing stronger as I get caught up in the moment.

Andrew falls back and it's just Hannah and Megan now, side by side, as they kick their way back to us, and I swear my heart thrums with each splash, willing her on.

"She's amazing!" Molly yells, shaking my arm in her excitement, and I can only nod because, yes, she is.

Hannah eventually beats her to the post, much to Daniela's delight, but Megan doesn't seem to mind. She's smiling when she hauls herself out of the lake, even as her body shudders, and I stride over with the towel, only to falter when she stands, jogging the final few steps to me. The straps of her swimsuit fall as she does, revealing the curve of her breasts before she pulls them back up, and my eyes stray for a full second before another shiver runs through her, this one almost violent in its intensity, and all other thoughts are wiped from my brain.

"You're freezing," I scold, as she wraps the towel around her. "Where's your coat?"

"I left it in the— it's going to get wet," she protests, as I shrug off my own and put it around her shoulders.

"It will dry," I say, tugging it closed. Not like her hair, which is plastered to her head. That's still wet. Not just wet. Soaking. And she doesn't have another towel for it. Isn't that a thing? Wet hair in the cold? She needs another towel. She needs—

"Andrew," I bark, and Megan looks up at me in surprise. "Megan needs another towel."

"Don't yell," she whispers.

"I didn't."

"You did."

I shrug, watching my equally cold brother jog over to the bags for another towel.

"Are you annoyed that I didn't win?" Megan asks.

"What?"

"Are you pissed at me because I didn't win the race?"

I drag my attention back to her, beyond confused. "Of course not."

"Then why are you mad?"

"I'm not."

"Then why are you scowling like that?" She's smiling as she says it, even as she continues to shiver, which only baffles me more because I'm not scowling; she's just cold, and—

I fall still as she reaches up, pressing a finger to the spot between my brows. "Right there," she says, poking me lightly, and it's at that moment Andrew chooses to appear, a towel in his hand.

"You're on my team next time," he says. "You swim?"

"A bit," she says, only to grin when he laughs. For some reason, the sight of it only makes my mood worse.

"Thanks," I say, a little pointedly to Andrew as I take the towel from him. He just lopes back over to Molly as I shake it out.

"I thought you wanted *me* to have the towel," she says, still sounding giddy. Maybe that's a symptom of hypothermia.

"I can do it," I mutter, opening it up before glancing at her hair and realizing, no, I can't.

She snorts at my obvious confusion and grabs it back from me, flipping her head forward to do some complicated twist that makes it stay in place.

"Witchcraft," she says when she straightens, and she starts tucking in the stray hairs around her face. "You're staring."

"Sorry."

"Am I bright red?"

I shake my head, even though she is. But that's not what caught my attention.

Megan O'Sullivan has freckles.

Dozens of them. Maybe hundreds. I've never seen them before because I've never seen her without makeup, but whatever she was wearing washed off in the lake, and now she's here with her face tinged pink and dotted all over and her gray eyes so bright you'd swear they were lit from within.

Something squeezes in my chest, and it becomes hard not to stare at her. Hard not to feel like a piece of shit either.

This is the best mood I've seen her in since we got back here.

And I'm ruining it.

"You didn't tell me you swam," I say eventually.

"Well, we've gotta keep some mystery to the relationship," she jokes. "I got into sea swimming when I moved to Dublin," she adds. "I'm used to the cold."

"You were brilliant."

"Thanks." She turns shy and wriggles away from me. It's only then I realize I'm rubbing her arms up and down.

"Are you still cold?"

"I'm warming up," she says, and I cast an eye over her without trying to be too obvious about it. Her legs are covered in goosebumps, and I'm relieved when she lets me lead her back to the others, where they've gathered to unwrap the food.

Megan pulls her shoes on and exchanges my coat for her red one while I grab a ham and cheese sandwich from the box and root around for another.

"Where's the tomato one?" I ask, as Hannah digs into hers.

"Tomato?"

"For Megan."

Hannah doesn't look at me, purposefully evasive, as she takes another bite. "I just made ham and cheese."

I stiffen at the fake innocence in her expression. "I told you she's a vegetarian."

"Sorry," she says, not sounding sorry at all. "I forgot."

"I can just pick the ham off," Megan murmurs beside me, but that's not the point, and she knows it.

"Alright," I say, dumping my sandwich back in the box. "That's enough."

"Christian—" Megan tugs at my sleeve, but I easily break away. "Honestly, it's fine."

"It's not. Hannah," I say, loud enough to draw everyone's attention. "Can I have a word?"

She frowns around a mouthful of bread. "I'm eating."

"I don't care."

"But I'm— Hey!" She garbles a protest as I grab her hand, tugging her away from the others.

Megan looks like she's about to come after us, but Molly, my official hero of the day, quickly distracts her with a flask of hot chocolate as I drag my little sister around the bend to a small picnic bench we passed earlier.

"What is your problem?" I snap.

"Says the grown man throwing a hissy fit." She yanks her arm away and tries to head back, only to glare when I step in front of her.

"You know the first thing Megan said to me when she met

you?" I ask. "She said that you didn't like her. And it made me feel like utter shit because it's scary enough meeting your partner's family for the first time without them being dicks about it. I asked Andrew if Molly would make an effort with her, but I didn't think I'd need to ask you. I thought you just would."

"I don't not like her. I don't know her."

"Didn't stop you from fawning over Molly when Andrew brought her home."

"I didn't *fawn*," she says, the tips of her ears turning pink. "That was completely different."

"How?"

"Because she's... Oh, come on! It's obvious."

"Is this about Isaac?"

"No!"

"Because it's a little creepy that you're so obsessed with your ex-camogie coach."

"It's about you, you idiot! She's using you." Her mouth slams shut as soon as she says the words, instantly embarrassed.

"She's what?"

"She's using you," she says, softer now like she's trying not to hurt my feelings. "I'm sorry, Christian, but it's as clear as day to everyone but you."

To everyone? I shove away that little nugget to worry about later. "Why would she be using me?"

"Oh, I don't know, because you grew up? Because you dress in nice clothes and have a good job? Her whole family is loaded. She wouldn't have looked at you twice before you got all successful."

"Successful, huh?"

"Christian, I'm serious! I have a sixth sense about these things, and I'm never wrong."

"Oh, well *then*."

"You don't think it's a little odd?" she continues. "You don't think it's even a *little* suspicious that her ex-fiancé gets engaged, and after years of being away, she coincidentally returns to the village with you on her arm? She's using you to make her look good."

"She's here because it's Christmas," I say. "And her brother's come all the way from Australia. She's here because it's her home, and she can come back whenever she likes. And if she wants to use someone, I'm sure she can find someone a lot better than me."

Hannah scoffs like that's ridiculous, but whether that's due to her opinion of Megan's options or my standing in her eyes, I'm not entirely sure.

"She doesn't love you," she says bluntly. "I know when people are in love with each other. And I know when they like each other. I'm a romantic."

"You're annoying is what you are."

"Mam and Dad. Andrew and Molly. Me and Daniela. We all—"

"Hang on," I interrupt. "You're in *love* with Daniela?"

"We told each other three months ago," she says defensively, and I blink, trying to merge the nineteen-year-old in front of me with the ten-year-old in my head.

"That's great. What did you guys—"

"You're not distracting me," she says, eyes narrowed. "Something's up with that girl. I know it."

"And what if there is?" I ask, starting to feel tired. "What if I don't care? I'm not in love with her either, Hannah. We're just taking things as they come. But I like spending time with her, and she likes spending time with me, and I would really, *really* appreciate it if you stopped making her feel like shite every time you look at her."

Hannah's hands go to her hips, her glower turning more into a pout. "I just don't want to see you get hurt."

"Well, I don't want to see her get hurt," I say. "So, I'm asking you to give her a chance. You don't think she's nervous enough as it is coming home for the first time after everything that happened? She's trying. And that's the least you can do too."

"But—"

"Hannah. If you don't trust her, then trust me. Drop it, okay?"

She slumps before me, the stubborn hold of her shoulders easing as she sees how serious I am. "Okay," she says. "I'm sorry."

"It's not me who needs to hear that."

The scowl comes back. "I'm not going to apologize to her," she says. "Because that will be awkward, but I'll... I don't know. I'll make it up to her." Her gaze hardens. "But if she does anything to you, I swear to God, I'll—"

"Again, you're an idiot," I interrupt, looping an arm around her shoulders. "But thank you for protecting my honor."

"Someone has to," she grumbles but leans into my side as I lead her back to the others.

FOURTEEN

MEGAN

I'm still shivering by the time Christian drops me back at my house. The water was the kind of cold that creeps into your bones and takes hold no matter how many blankets you have, and I know it will be a few hours before I feel normal again. It was worth it, though. Years of early morning dips in the freezing Irish Sea hardened me to the initial shock of the lake, and even if I lost, I like to think I proved myself a bit. Christian definitely looked at me like I did.

He fussed over me afterward and wanted me to take a shower back at his, but I figured there would be a long enough line for their bathroom, so I insisted he take me home instead. That was the reason I said out loud, anyway. The other was Hannah, who still definitely doesn't like me even though Christian said he took care of it. But not even she can ruin my good mood as I let myself into my blissfully warm house.

I need a bath, but I didn't have a sandwich like the others, and all that exercise has left me starving, so my mind is fully on toasted bread and melted cheese when I come to a halt in the kitchen doorway and find my mother sitting with someone at the island.

Isaac's dad.

Padraig Quinn is a big, quiet man, who I'd once heard someone refer to as a gentle giant. He's polite and soft-spoken and was always kind to me growing up. His hair is whiter than I remember, his skin more lined. But his eyes are the same, and he still wears the same blue shirt and brown corduroy pants ensemble that I used to see him in every day.

It's something people rarely talk about when they discuss breakups, especially with long-term relationships. You lose a partner, you might lose their friends, but you also lose their family. And Isaac and I had known each for so long that his parents were like mine. I used to get on well with Padraig, but now we stare at each other like strangers. Which I guess, in a way, we are.

"Megan," he says like I haven't been gone for five years. "You look like you've been in the wars."

"We went swimming."

"Swimming?" Mam's nose wrinkles. "Where?"

"The lake," I say, tugging at my coat. "I didn't see your car," I tell Padraig. The words are apologetic like I'm telling him if I had, I would have run five miles in the other direction.

"I walked over," he says, stretching out his leg. "Bunged my knee up a few months ago. Trying to get into the habit of stretching it out."

"I'm sorry to hear that," I murmur, and he nods, glancing between Mam and me before clearing his throat.

"Well, I should probably head," he says gruffly, getting to his feet.

"You're very good to stop by," Mam says.

"Not at all." He turns to me with a hopeful look. "You should drop by the house sometime. I'm sure Alice would love to see you."

"I will," I say, even though I absolutely will not. His parents still don't know what went down between Isaac and me. But

I've always wondered if they've had their suspicions. The way Padraig's looking at me now, with a hint of embarrassment, only makes them grow stronger.

Mam sees him to the door, and I start pulling together my sandwich, trying not to listen to their murmured conversation. She returns a minute later, but says nothing, watching me go through the motions.

"He stops by every now and then," she says when I finish. "Both him and Alice. And he sends his apologies. He dropped over some Christmas presents but didn't know you were back. Otherwise, he would have included you." She hesitates. "He also said that Isaac's—"

"Engaged," I say. "I know."

"You do?" She's too surprised to hide it.

"Christian and I met him on the way down."

"Oh. Okay then." She straightens a place setting on the island, lining the corners up just so.

My smile is grim. "Thought I was going to freak out?"

"I never know what you're going to do," she says, not meeting my eye. "Not anymore." And with that, she leaves.

———

Later that evening, after a very long, very hot shower, a detailed skin-care routine, and a frozen pizza that I only partially burned, I sit on my bed with a show on my laptop, determined to get a good chunk of Andrew's sweater finished. It's the only plan I have for the rest of the night, and I'm just about to start a snowflake pattern along the front when my door swings open, and Aidan strolls inside.

"Watcha doing?" he asks, flicking the end of a scarf hanging nearby.

"Knitting."

"It's a Saturday night."

"I'm aware," I say, trying to concentrate. It's kind of hard with him in my room. Especially when he settles back against the dresser, staring at me.

"Where's your boyfriend?"

"Hiding under the bed." My laptop buffers, and I huff, pausing it so it doesn't skip ahead. "You can leave now," I say when he doesn't move.

"Let's go out."

"No."

"Come on." He jerks his head toward the door. "We'll go to the pub."

"Aidan, I'm tired. I was socializing all afternoon trying to make a good impression on Christian's family, and I don't have the energy to smile for a bunch of your friends."

"My friends aren't there. Or they might be, I don't know."

"Then why do you want to—"

"I thought we could catch up," he says, and I frown. He sounds sincere, and he looks sincere, but Aidan and I were never the kind of siblings who hung out when we were kids, and we literally live on separate continents as adults, so...

"We can watch a movie?" I suggest.

"There's no point in you making a big thing about coming back for Christmas if you're just going to hide in your room the whole time."

"I'm not hiding! I'm knitting." I gesture at the laptop in front of me. "And I'm nearly finished with season three."

"Of a show that finished fifteen years ago." He's scowling at me now. "I'm not going to ditch you if that's what you're worried about."

I pretend to count my stitches, embarrassed that he can see right through me. That's exactly what I'm worried about. The last thing I want to do is put myself in a situation where I'll bump into people I don't want to bump into, but I also haven't seen my only brother in a year, and yeah, I wouldn't mind spending some time with him.

"Saturday night," he reminds me. "You can be an introvert on a Sunday, Meg, but this is getting sad even for you. It's Christmas."

"It's not Christmas, it's mid-December."

"Come to the pub for a drink," he says slowly. "Stop hiding in your bedroom."

I stare at him for a moment before my eyes drift back to the laptop, to the beautiful doctor and her ruggedly handsome patient with the incredibly rare, incurable disease. The one I know that in about nineteen minutes, he'll die from because I have seen this episode twice already.

"I'm not going to leave until you say yes," he continues. "I'm just going to stand here and look at you."

"Feels like a waste of your time."

"And a ruin of yours. I hear O'Donoghue's has a pool table now."

I smooth out the sweater, knowing my decision even though I pretend to mull it over. "Fine. *One* drink," I add at his triumphant look. "I'm tired."

"Sure," he says, all smiles now that he's gotten his way. "Also, I had a beer with dinner, so you're going to need to drive, and if you could stick to the nonalcoholic— Okay, see you downstairs!" He calls and ducks out of my room just before I throw a pillow at him.

———

Twenty minutes later, with the addition of some makeup and clothing that does not simply consist of a wearable blanket, I drive us to O'Donoghue's, a large pub a few minutes outside of the village. Aidan spends the entire journey telling me about some big project he's working on that I can barely understand, but I do my best to keep up since he's clearly excited about it. Excited enough that I start to get pumped too, until we arrive at the pub, where I take one look at the parking lot and balk.

It's busy. Busier than I thought it would be. I can't even find space in the lot itself and have to park off the road like I see a few others doing.

As soon as we get out, Aidan swings an arm around my shoulders, the move feeling less like a show of brotherly affection and more like he's trapping me to his side so I don't run away. Probably because I do want to run away. Or drive away at least. But he gives a subtle flex when I try to shove him off, his arm like an iron band around me.

"What are you, like a gym bro now?"

"Work pays for it," he says easily.

"Oh, does it? Pays for all your meals too, right?"

"You sound jealous, Meg."

"Of working twenty-hour days? You know they give you all those perks because they never want you to leave the office, right?"

"We're also getting beanbags next month," he says, and I roll my eyes as we enter the pub. As soon as we do, I'm hit by the familiar smell of leather stools and spilled beer. It's comforting. Like everyone else in the village, Isaac and I spent a lot of time here, and Mam, Aidan, and I used to come for lunch every Sunday.

The bar takes up the middle of the room, a long oval that splits the lounge in half. On one side, booths and tables occupy the space, while the other is cleared for the promised pool tables. The large television screen that usually shows sports now has *Die Hard* on mute, the automated subtitles showing up a few seconds after the actors speak.

"You hungry?" Aidan asks, as we linger just inside the door.

"I guess," I say, glancing around. "If they have anything sweet left, I wouldn't say no to..." I trail off, tensing as I catch the eye of a tall, curvy redhead standing by the pool table. She's staring right at me, cue stick in one hand, a soda in the other, and a look of complete shock on her face.

Sophie O'Meara. We were close once. Very close. And out of all our friends, she was the one who took my supposed betrayal of Isaac the hardest. She sent me a long text message the week after it happened. One that I deleted without reading because I took one look at the first line, *breaking his heart... how could you*, and felt like I was going to be sick. By the time I was strong enough to contact her a few weeks later, it was to find she'd blocked me on everything.

I still think about her sometimes. I still miss her. But if I thought remaining at the heart of our community meant she'd be privy to any and all gossip, I'd be wrong. It doesn't look like news of Christian and I has spread as much as he'd hoped. In fact, judging by how she's looking at me like I've just stepped through a magic portal, it doesn't look like it's spread at all.

"I thought you said no one was going to be here," I say, as the two people she's with, her brother Cormac, and Jason, another friend, all look our way. One by one, their smiles drop.

"I didn't say that," Aidan says. "I said I didn't know if they were going to be here or not."

"We should go."

"What?" He sounds incredulous. "They're your friends."

"No, they're not."

But he ignores me, raising a hand in acknowledgment and doing that *hey* chin lift that boys do. No one does it back. No one waves. No one calls over, and after a second, Sophie leans over and whispers something urgent to the others, and my face heats so hard I'm surprised the sprinklers don't go off.

"I told you," I whisper, because now my brother, my cool, easygoing, *just relax!* brother is stiff as a board, and I know he's surprised by their reaction.

I can't help but feel a little justified.

Everyone always thinks I'm exaggerating. Sometimes I think I'm exaggerating. But then things like this happen, and I want nothing more than to be back in my childhood bedroom with my twenty-year-old television shows and my knitting.

"See?" I say dully. "Can we go? We can come back tomorrow and— *Aidan*." Shit. I follow him as he heads to the opposite side of the pub, ignoring my obvious unhappiness as he dumps his coat in one of the booths and gestures pointedly inside.

"We're staying," he says, and he's got that stubborn look on his face I remember so well.

"You're making it a thing."

"I'm not," he says. "What do you want to drink?"

"Can't we just—"

"This is your home too," he interrupts. "Sit down, Meg."

I do. Shuffling along the seat until I'm squeezed in by the wall, as far away from the others as I can be. The table hasn't been cleared yet, so Aidan grabs the remaining glasses, all business. "You want a Coke?"

"We're just staying for one," I remind him.

"We'll see," he says calmly and strides off to the bar. As he does, I catch the eye of Jason across the room. Jason, who quickly looks away.

Great.

Just great.

FIFTEEN
CHRISTIAN

My first proper evening at home is a long one. I'd forgotten how busy the house gets when we're all back, especially when Liam brings the kids over. Mam makes chicken with rice, and everyone squeezes around the table as best they can. It's the first time in months we've all been together, and it's a noisy, messy affair, but I wouldn't have it any other way. Liam leaves soon after dinner with his two exhausted children, while Andrew disappears with Molly, and my parents settle down in front of the television. This leaves me with Hannah. Hannah, who's been acting extra clingy since our conversation by the lake. So much so that I'm not surprised when she finds me a little after nine, slinking into the back room where I'm trying to read. It barely takes two minutes of sighing and wheedling before I agree to take her to the pub.

It's not exactly a unique idea in the village. The place is so busy I have to park on the side of the road, and I'm tired just thinking about all the people inside, but Hannah's practically skipping as she walks alongside me, delighting in being out after hours of studying. "My hand is cramping," she says. "I have essay cramp."

"That's not a thing."

"You know what will solve it?" she continues sweetly. "A vodka lime. Bought by you."

"I drove. Why do I have to buy?"

"Because I'm a poor student," she says with a *duh* voice and pushes open the swinging door with her shoulder. She stops immediately with a dramatic gasp, and I almost walk straight into her. "Sophie's here," she says, grabbing my arm. "I'm trying to get her to be my model for our summer showcase, but she keeps saying no."

"I can't imagine why," I say, shaking her off me. I look around for somewhere to sit, already tired. "Alright. How about you grab some stools and I'll—"

"Are you *serious*?" she interrupts, and I swear I'm just about to turn around and head home when I follow her gaze across the room to where Megan sits stiff-shouldered in a booth, talking to a man in a knitted beanie. Her red coat is cushioned between her body and the wall, and there's a novelty snowflake clip in her hair that she somehow makes look elegant. "You planned this," Hannah continues.

"No, I didn't," I say. "If I had, I would have made you stay home. And this was your idea in the first place."

She makes a dismissive noise. "Who's that? Her other boyfriend?"

"Funny." But I feel oddly nervous until the man finally heads to the bar, and I get a view of his face. "It's her brother."

"He says, relieved. I'm going to play pool."

"No, you're not." I grab her wrist before she can run off, sensing an opportunity. "You're going to say hi first."

"But—"

"And you're going to give her a chance," I finish, glancing back to see Megan's spotted us. She holds up an awkward hand when our eyes meet, and I smile in response, even as Hannah tugs on my hold.

"This was supposed to be a sibling night out."

"Don't even try it. You were just about to desert me for Sophie. Now be nice, or I'll drop an ice cube down your sweater."

I don't dare release her as I cross the room, not stopping until we're right by Megan's table. We stare at each other for a beat, and I almost expect a repeat of the awkwardness in her mother's kitchen when she straightens with a cheerful look.

"Hi!"

I try not to smile at her fake enthusiasm. "Hey. Didn't know you were out tonight."

"Neither did I. Aidan dragged me." Her eyes flick to Hannah. "Hello."

"Hiya," she chirps, perfectly polite. And not even a second later: "I'm going to go play some pool."

"Cool," Megan says before I can respond, and Hannah doesn't hesitate in scampering over to the other side of the room.

"I was hoping you guys could talk," I grumble, sitting opposite her.

She shrugs. "I'm too tired to play nice. I promise I won't make you speak to Aidan."

"I can speak to Aidan."

"Well, he doesn't want to speak to you," she says with a hint of amusement. "I don't think he likes you."

"What?" I look over to where he's waiting at the bar, oblivious to my presence. "What did I do?"

"Date his sister?"

"He should be happy about that. I'm considered a real catch around here."

"Who considers that?"

"My mother," I say, and she rolls her eyes, flipping a coaster over and over again.

"It's okay that I'm here, right?" she asks, suddenly sounding a little wary.

"Why wouldn't it be?"

"Because I didn't tell you I was coming?"

I give her a strange look. "I'm not a stalker, Megan. You do you."

"I just feel like I've ambushed your night. You came here to spend time with Hannah."

"I didn't come here to spend time with Hannah. Hannah dragged me here because Daniela's visiting family tonight and if she stays in the house, Mam will give her chores. And then she'll give me chores."

She smiles, but she's not really listening, her attention flicking back and forth between me and where Hannah went.

"You were brilliant today," I say, and she brightens slightly.

"Yeah?"

"Yeah. Mam thinks you're great, and Andrew won't stop talking about your swimming."

"So I passed?"

"Flying colors."

She looks so relieved that I'm mad at myself for not telling her earlier, but then her attention darts away once more, and the coaster flips again.

"Ignore Hannah," I say, and she's confused for an instant before she realizes what I mean.

"Oh, no, it's not her. It's nothing. Sorry. I'm distracted."

As if she can't help herself, she glances over again, and I follow her gaze to the bar, where her brother still waits to order. He hasn't noticed I'm here. Instead, his eyes are on the pool tables, where Hannah now stands with a small group of people who look like they're several beers in. I recognize them immediately, even though I'd never have considered them friends back in school. But in a small place like this, you know people even if you don't *know* them, and as if on cue, one of them looks in our direction before quickly turning away again.

"Aren't they your friends?"

Megan stiffens, confirming my suspicion. "Not really."

The little liar.

"They used to be," she concedes when I just wait. The coaster keeps flipping, and I realize what's different about her tonight. What's bothering me. It's that for the first time since I met her, she looks self-conscious. She didn't look like that when we met Isaac. She didn't even look like that when she almost threw up in the pub, and the sight of it grates on me, igniting a protectiveness I didn't expect.

"Were you going to call me?" I ask, suddenly very glad Hannah insisted we go out.

"What?"

"If I didn't arrive tonight, would you have called me? Asked me to come?"

She looks baffled. "Why would I do that?"

"Because it's part of the agreement?" I remind her. "If someone makes you feel like shit, you're supposed to tell me."

"They're not doing anything."

"Yes, they are. They know it, and you know it, and if someone says something and I'm not there, you call me. If someone side-eyes you, you call me. You call me, and no matter where you are or what time it is, I'll pick up and I'll come running. That's the whole point of this."

The vulnerability in her expression is almost painful to see, but she nods, her hands finally stilling.

"Maybe you could act like I just said something really funny?" she suggests hopefully.

But I just frown. "You?"

"Christian—"

"I'm the funny one in this relationship."

"But you're so good at pretending."

"No one's that good," I say, and she starts to smile just as the group across the room breaks into laughter, then she's back to looking like she wants a sinkhole to swallow her up.

And just like that, I know what I need to do. Even if she's going to hate me for doing it.

"Okay. You'll thank me later," I say, grabbing our stuff.

"What are you— *Christian.*"

She tries to pull back when I take her hand, just like I thought she would. But I also know she doesn't want to create a scene, so beyond making a strangled noise of threat, she lets me drag her across the room, straight into the viper's nest.

We're nearly at the bar by the time anyone notices our approach. Aidan does first, his eyes widening when we go past, but we're at the pool tables before the others finally see us, all turning our way with expressions of minor alarm as I break the rules of... well, whatever this is.

"Hey," I say, as I bring us to a stop. "Happy Christmas."

They echo it back automatically, and Megan offers a weak smile as I try to get my mind around the group dynamics. Cormac's the ringleader of the lot, that much, I can guess. He was best friends with Isaac, and I presume not much has changed because nothing ever changes around here. My sister is currently standing beside *his* sister, Sophie, who I remember as a skinny, timid thing. I'd barely recognize her now if Hannah hadn't pointed her out. Jason seems the friendliest, even if he's not exactly welcoming us with open arms, so it's him I decide to start with right before we're interrupted.

"So what have you been—"

"Happy Christmas." Aidan appears at Megan's side with a beer and a Coke and a wide smile on his face. "Mind if we join for the next round?"

He hands Megan the soda before anyone can say no, and perches on a stool next to Hannah.

"Aidan," he says, holding out his hand. "Megan's brother. You're Hannah, right?"

"Right." She shakes it with a smile. "I'm glad you're here.

Maybe *you* can help me since these guys won't. I'm trying to get Sophie to be my model. She keeps saying no."

"She just wants you to flatter her more," he says, barely glancing at the other girl.

Sophie says nothing, suddenly very interested in her phone.

"You still in Berlin?" he asks Jason, and he stares at the guy, a clear challenge in his gaze. The silence stretches out a beat too long before it breaks.

"Two years now," Jason says. Megan lets out a small breath beside me. "How's Australia?"

And just like that, everyone cautiously moves on. Aidan launches into what sounds like a rehearsed speech about life Down Under, and the attention slowly fades from us as it turns back to the pool table.

Megan pulls at my hand, obviously wanting to go, but that would just make the whole thing even more awkward, so I grab the only chair free and sit myself down before gesturing to her.

She gives me a confused look until I pat my knee.

Then she glares. *No.*

I smile back. *Yes.*

"I'll stand," she mutters, shifting on her feet. Or at least she does for approximately two seconds before I tug her down onto my lap. She lands awkwardly, and I fight back a wince as she lands onto what can only be described as a sensitive area.

"Relax." I say the word so quietly that only she can hear it, and to my relief, she does. It's not easy for her. I can feel how twitchy she is, but after a few seconds, her shoulders lower, and her back eases against my chest until she's resting against me. And while it's still not the most natural of poses, she no longer looks like she's sitting on burning coals.

I drape a loose arm around her waist, keeping her steady while I place my other hand on her thigh, feigning interest in the game. I hadn't thought much further than this. Nothing more than getting her over here, reintegrating her with her friends. I believed Megan when she said that people treated her differently after she left Isaac, but the fact that she never came back also never gave anyone a chance to get over it. I just need to get them talking.

"I know what you're doing."

I tense as she leans into me a little more. She does? "You do?"

"Your hand?" she murmurs, and it takes me a moment to realize she's referring to the one on her leg. As if someone flipped a switch, I'm suddenly extremely aware of the heat of her body beneath the denim, and I shift under her, feigning casualness.

"This hand?" I ask, dragging it higher. "The one you're making no move to stop?"

"I'm not going to stop you because you're not going to do anything."

"That a dare?"

"That's a fact."

"Sounds like a dare."

"Christian—"

"Megan." I inch higher, curving down her inner thigh just like I did in the car, but I barely brush the seam of her jeans before she grabs my fingers in a death grip. I go lax, accepting her limit, but she doesn't move me away. And the pink splotches on her neck go a whole shade deeper.

"So, how long has this been going on?" Cormac asks, and I bring my attention back to the others to see Sophie eyeing us with barely concealed distaste.

"A couple of months," I say, waiting for Megan to chime in. I pinch her leg when she doesn't, but she just pinches me back.

Try, I want to tell her, willing her on. And after a beat, she does.

"How's your mother doing?" she asks Jason, who immediately perks up. "I heard she went back to college."

"She did," he says. "She's studying art history. Costing a small fortune, but she's happy."

"You know that's your inheritance," Cormac jokes, and the tension eases further as he takes another shot.

"What about your mam?" Jason asks. "She making you do her fundraiser again?"

"I don't mind them," Megan says. "Not like there's much else to do around here."

"You should come with us to the city next week," Jason says, earning himself a sharp glance from Sophie. "We're going ice-skating."

"Oh. Uh..." Megan looks at me, and I shrug. I can skate. "I suppose we could—"

"I think it's all booked out," Sophie says quickly, and Jason falls quiet.

Hannah looks between them confused. "But you just invited me to—"

"That was the last spot."

My sister's smile falters. Mine disappears altogether. Jesus Christ, how old is this woman? Nine?

Cormac seems to think so too. "Soph..."

She just takes a sip of her soda, not meeting anyone's eye.

"Maybe the lake will freeze over," Hannah suggests when no one continues. "We could skate there too."

"It's supposed to get that cold?" Jason asks.

"Apparently."

"Hannah's the resident weather girl this year," I explain.

"At least one of us will be prepared."

"Hey." Jason turns to Megan with a sudden grin. "Do you remember the year the river flooded? We had to stay at your house Christmas Eve because our entire ground floor was ruined."

Megan smiles. "How could I forget? You wouldn't stop

crying because you thought Santa wouldn't know where you were."

"And you were convinced that all we needed to do was head back to mine at midnight."

"It made sense!"

Jason laughs. "My dad was *furious*. We got caught immediately," he explains to the rest of us. "Picture two seven-year-olds in nothing but their pajamas trying to climb over the fence. We didn't even make it past the—"

A furious clatter interrupts him as Sophie dumps her cue back on the rack.

"No," she says, and pins her gaze on Megan. "No, I'm sorry. I don't care that it's been a while. I don't care that it's Christmas, and I don't care that you're dating the guy who used to pull everyone's hair in the playground. You can't just show up here like nothing happened and expect us to pretend we haven't seen you in five years."

"I never pulled anyone's hair," I say, insulted.

"Don't you have a car to steal?" Sophie says, and I scoff as Hannah frowns at her.

"That was one time, and I literally drove it halfway down the road before they caught me. It was funny."

"It kind of was," Jason mutters, and Sophie glares at him. "He was going at ten miles an hour!"

"Plus, I'm pretty sure this isn't your pub," I remind her. "We can show up where we like."

"You can," she agrees. "But don't expect me to like it. Not after ruining Isaac's life."

The group goes deathly silent, and okay, maybe bringing Megan over here was one of my rare yet giant miscalculations. But before I can do anything about it, she speaks up.

"Isaac's got himself a brand-new fiancée," Megan says, and there's an edge of resentment in her voice that I haven't heard before. "Doesn't look like his life is ruined to me."

"You didn't see how he was after you left."

"Sophie—" Cormac begins.

"No," she says to him. "He's your best friend. You saw him. She didn't. She didn't see how destroyed he was. It wasn't some comedy where the bride skips out, and everyone claps. I've never seen him so upset. It was selfish." She turns back to Megan. "*You* were selfish."

"Hey," Aidan says sharply, and Hannah's gaze bounces between the two of them as if suddenly aware she's bang smack in the middle of everything.

"I never said I wasn't," Megan says, but Sophie doesn't seem to hear her.

"And now you waltz back home like nothing ever happened. Like you didn't disappear without a word."

"I tried to get in touch with you."

"Yeah, months later," she mutters, crossing her arms.

Jason clears his throat. "Okay," he says mildly. "Why don't we take a breather? We've all been drinking and—"

"I haven't," Megan and Sophie say at the same time.

"Well, I have, and I need some fresh air," he says.

"Or maybe we can just finish the game," Cormac says tiredly, picking up Sophie's cue stick. "Soph, come on. It's your turn."

"You could have told me what was wrong," Sophie says, ignoring him, but Megan shakes her head, standing from my lap.

"You would have talked me back into it."

"Into marrying the love of your *life*?"

"He wasn't the—"

"And you don't know what I would have done," she continues. "Not that that matters anymore."

"Guys—" Cormac tries again at the same time Jason looks over at us.

"Maybe you two should go."

I don't like that. Neither, as it turns out, does Aidan.

"They don't have to go anywhere," he says, as I stand by Megan's side. "And can you stop ganging up on my sister?" he asks Sophie, who falters under his stern gaze.

Now it's Cormac's turn to look mad. "Don't speak to her like that."

"Don't treat Megan like she killed the guy."

"We're not."

"You are," Aidan snaps back. "Maybe she was right to leave him, Soph, ever think of that? Maybe she didn't marry him because he's a boring, self-righteous dickhead, who wouldn't know a joke if it laughed in his face." He takes a pointed swig of his beer as Sophie turns the full force of her glare on him, a glare he only smirks at.

"You don't even know him," she says.

"He was at my house every day for ten years. I think I did."

"He's a good guy."

"What an incredible endorsement. Write it on my tombstone."

The two of them stare at each other, something flashing in Aidan's eyes before Sophie turns back around, looking like she's about to lose it.

"Okay. Look." Cormac steps in front of us as if to physically block his sister's view of Megan, but that just riles everyone up further. And I'm wondering just how much yelling will be allowed before we're all kicked out when three things happen at once.

Across the table, Jason, bored of waiting for the game to resume, fumbles his shot and knocks over an errant beer bottle balanced on the ledge of the table. The resulting smash is enough to draw everyone's attention, and Cormac whips around to see the commotion, bringing the two sticks he's holding with him. One narrowly avoids Megan's forehead as I tug her back, and I'm so focused on her that I don't see the other one until it's too late.

She gasps as the heavy wood connects with my face, and for a split second, I hover in that gray area between impact and pain.

And then, just for a moment, everything goes black.

SIXTEEN

MEGAN

Christian grunts as the stick smashes into his nose, his hands flying to his face, and I swear a collective wince goes around our small group.

"Okay," he says after a beat. "Ow."

"Shit." Cormac puts the cue down, panicked. "Are you okay? I didn't mean to—"

"I'm fine," he says thickly, tilting his head back.

"Don't do that," I say, trying to see if it's bleeding. "Is it broken?"

"I don't know."

"What does it feel like?"

"Like *pain*?"

"Can you get a first aid kit?" I ask Hannah, who's watching her brother with a real *yikes* look. "Maybe an ice pack too?" She nods and scrambles over to the bar. Everyone else has gone quiet, tempers dying as quickly as they flared.

"I swear it was an accident," Cormac continues.

"I know," Christian assures him as I peel back his fingers. "I'm grand."

He is not grand. He just got hit in the face with a big wooden stick and is now bleeding from his nose.

"Come on," I urge, ignoring the others as I bring him to the bathrooms. "I need to look at that."

"If I start crying, just remember that's manly now," Christian says, following me blindly. "Toxic masculinity is dead."

"Yes, it is." I pull him down the hallway and into an empty cubicle, where I sit him on the toilet lid. "Now let me see."

He drops his hand, breathing through his mouth as I inspect the damage. Bleeding, but not too bad.

"I don't think it's broken," I say, pulling some toilet paper free of the container. "You probably just burst a blood thingy."

"Is that a scientific term or...?"

"I watched a video on it once." I press the tissue to his nose at the bit of blood I see there. "Lean forward."

"Not back?"

"Not unless you want to vomit," I say, crouching before him, and he does as he's told as we wait for it to pass.

I am instantly more comfortable now that it's just us again. Compared to the tense atmosphere outside, the moment is nearly peaceful despite the fact my fake boyfriend almost broke his nose, and we're huddled in a pub toilet. Could be worse, I suppose. They're cleaner than most I've seen, and a pleasant lavender scent wafts from the automatic dispenser over our heads.

"I'm sorry," Christian murmurs after a few seconds. "I don't think I made it any better with your friends."

"They're not my friends."

"They used to be."

"You sound like Aidan," I say dryly. "And they weren't really my friends back then either."

"What do you mean?"

I shrug, checking his nose before pressing the tissue to it

again. "They were Isaac's," I explain. "They always were. He was the popular one. I was just the girlfriend."

His brow furrows. "I don't know if you're being humble," he says. "Or just looking for compliments, but if it's the latter, you just have to ask, Megan. No need to put yourself down."

"I'm just realistic." But even as I say the words, I know they're not wholly true. There was a time when I was friends with the people on the other side of the door. But that just makes me want to deny it all the more.

"I think the bleeding's stopped," I say, changing the subject.

"Oh yeah?" He takes the tissue away, showing me his bloody, messy face. "How do I look?"

"Terrible."

He chokes out a laugh. Or he does for precisely half a second before his face contorts with pain. "Don't make jokes."

He leans his head down again, and I run my hands through his hair, an apologetic, instinctive act of comfort that I do over and over again until I realize I am.

"That feels nice," he murmurs when I stop, and when I don't continue, he lifts his head, his gaze catching on mine.

He has the tiniest white scar near his hairline.

I've never noticed it before. Because I've never really looked at him before. But now I am, and now I see. The scar right there and the random freckle near his temple, and the faint line across the middle of his forehead, one that I'm itching to smooth out.

"I think this is going really, really well," he deadpans, and my laugh comes out like a snort. "You don't think it's going well?"

"I think you got hit in the face with a pool stick," I tell him. "I think everyone is suspicious as hell, and I think we still have to get through Christmas."

"We can do it."

"I told you this was a dumb idea."

"You still said yes," he murmurs, and how does he look so sure of himself, so damn charming, when he's got drying blood all around his nose?

"Yeah," I say, letting myself comb his hair one final time. "I did."

His eyes flutter closed, the line on his forehead disappearing. "You did good back there. Standing up for yourself like that. Sophie was way out of line."

"She wasn't really." Now I'm no longer being stared at, I'm feeling a lot more charitable toward her. "I understand it. Leaving like I did."

"You had your reasons," he says. "Though I guess I never asked you what those reasons were." His eyes open, and I find myself unable to look away.

"Did he cheat?" he asks.

"No."

"Did you?"

I shake my head. *Just tell him*, a little voice says. *It doesn't matter anymore*. But it does. And my mouth runs dry as nerves curdle, an echo of an old embarrassment I thought I'd dealt with. It must be clear on my face because Christian's gaze gentles until he's the one comforting me.

"I still think about it sometimes, you know."

"About what?"

"You. The hotel." His mouth curves and I realize I'm holding my breath. "When you—"

But whatever he's going to say is lost as the door opens with a bang behind us, and I spring back so fast my ass hits the floor in a way I know is going to bruise.

"Shit!" A voice exclaims behind me. "Are you okay?"

"Hannah, what the hell?" Christian reaches for me, but that just makes the bleeding start again, which makes me start to get up, which makes our heads bump together, making this the most ridiculous moment of my life.

"Sorry," Hannah squeaks, and I twist to see her standing in the doorway. "Are you guys alright?"

"No," Christian snaps at the same time I say, "I'm fine."

"Sorry," she says again. "I have the pack."

She holds it out to me as if I'm in charge, which I guess I kind of am with all my unverified internet knowledge.

"Knock before you enter," Christian says, sounding like the grumpiest person alive. He swaps out the tissue as I pass the ice to him, wincing when the cold hits his face.

"Your brother's waiting for you," Hannah says to me. "I think he wants to go."

"How are you guys getting home?" I ask Christian. "You can't drive like this."

"We'll just—"

"I called Dad," Hannah says, and Christian stiffens beside me.

Hannah notices it too. "What?"

"You called *Dad*?"

"Yeah," she says, confused. "He always drives me home from the pub."

"Perfect," Christian bites out, and Hannah scowls at him. A scowl that vanishes as soon as she turns to me.

"I'll go get your stuff," she says and slips out of the room as quickly as she came.

"You're only telling me now that you've got Daddy issues?" I ask, and he sighs.

"Some other time. But while we're on the subject, you couldn't knit me some more of those lamb scarves, could you?"

"It was hats. But anything for my boyfriend."

"Throw in some adorable boots to be sure."

I can't help but smile. "Do you seriously think your dad's going to be mad at you for this? You're not a kid anymore."

"He won't be mad," Christian says, standing carefully. "Just disappointed."

"Ah. *Those* kind of Daddy issues."

The bleeding's stopped now, and when he cleans up his face in the sink, he almost looks normal, if not for the still watery eyes.

We head back into the lounge, where everyone is still hanging around, waiting for us. To my surprise, Hannah stands with my coat, and she lurches forward with it as soon as she sees me.

"This is really pretty," she says, and I pause, not entirely sure if she's making fun of me or not.

"Thanks."

"Where's my coat?" Christian asks.

Hannah blinks. "Did you bring one?"

"*Yes.*"

It's Cormac who has it, and he approaches with a string of further apologies as Aidan glues himself to my side like it wasn't his plan to come here in the first place.

"You ready to go?"

"You're not having fun?" I joke, but he doesn't smile.

"No," he says, and that's that.

"It's fine, Cormac," Christian says behind me. He tries to wave his accidental assailant off, his attention on me, but I just mouth a goodbye as we head to the door.

Jason offers a limp wave, and from the corner of my eye, I see Sophie step toward us, but whatever she wants to say, Aidan doesn't let me hear it, guiding me through the pub and out of sight.

———

The next morning, I sit at the kitchen island with my brother, who's being *extra* nice to me. Despite the other night being an unmitigated catastrophe, it also kind of wasn't. Hannah didn't seem to think I was the worst person in the world anymore, and Aidan finally opened his eyes to the fact that not everyone was pleased to have me home. Which is probably why he walked into the kitchen twenty minutes ago, insisting he make me breakfast.

It's not going well.

"You put the egg in the bagel," he says. "You bake the bagel. And then you have an egg bagel. It's not hard, Meg."

"Those eggs are too big."

"They're not."

"They are," I say, as he takes them out of the carton. "They're going to spill over the side."

"I made the hole bigger."

"It's going to spill."

"It's not going to—"

"It's a *disaster*," Mam shrieks, and Aidan drops the two eggs he's holding. They fall to the tiles with a cartoonish splat, and I raise my coffee mug in a mock toast.

"Good job," I say, as he scowls. "You alright, Mam?"

"No, I'm not alright," she says, striding into the room as Aidan grabs a dishtowel. "Fionnula canceled on me."

I try to remember if Fionnula is the girl who does her hair or the one that—

"At the hotel," she continues. "There's a burst pipe in the kitchens. They won't be back up and running for another week."

"So you can't have the fundraiser?"

"Not at Cliffside, anyway," she says before she notices the state of her kitchen. "Aidan, what are you doing? That's the good dishcloth."

"Why do we have a good—"

Mam plucks it from his hands and hands him a roll of paper towel. "It's fine," she says, more to herself than to me. "I mean, it's not because I'll have to update all our invitations and the suppliers and the girl doing the decorations, but I've already rung around, and we've confirmed space at—" She cuts off abruptly, her eyes widening in alarm.

"What?" I ask when she just stares at me.

Aidan straightens, dumping the eggy paper towel in the bin. Whatever's wrong, he figures it out before I do, and I know he does because he starts to laugh.

"Mam?" I ask.

"They have space at the Regency," she says reluctantly, and my stomach doesn't so much drop as it does plummet straight to the floor.

The Regency Hotel. Where I was supposed to get married. *That's* where she's throwing it?

"*Mam*," I protest, and she waves a hand, ruffled.

"I forgot you were coming."

"You asked me to!"

"I know, I know," she says. "But I wasn't thinking, and we held it there a few years ago, and it was lovely, and they have the space, and they know me, so they didn't overcharge, and there we have it." She taps a finger against the counter, biting her bottom lip. "You don't have to go," she adds reluctantly.

"Of course, I'm going. I came back just to go." But I know she's two seconds away from canceling the booking just for me, which would be so dumb, and I just—

"It's fine," I lie. "Seriously. It's a building."

"That you escaped from," Aidan mutters, and I am *this* close to throwing a bagel at his head.

"I can find somewhere new if you want me to," Mam says.

"Of course, she wants you to," Aidan calls, leaving the room. I sit there silently, neither confirming nor denying.

"Whatever you want to do, I'll do it," she says gently, and I know she means it. I know in a heartbeat that if I told her I wasn't fine, she wouldn't go through with it. She wouldn't go through with any of it.

But this fundraiser isn't about me.

This Christmas isn't about me.

It's about her and us and our family, and I swore to myself that this year I wasn't going to ruin it.

"It's fine," I say. "Mam, honestly. It's just a hotel. You're not going to be able to find anywhere else."

"If you're sure," she says, relenting a little when I just stare back at her. "Alright. Thank you for understanding."

"You're welcome."

"And I suppose now is a good a time as any to tell you I collected your dress from the dry cleaner's yesterday."

"My dress?"

"You don't have to wear it. It's one of your old ones, but I thought you might like some options on top of whatever you brought back for yourself. It's hanging up in my room. Shoes, I can't help you with. Not with my clown feet."

"You don't have clown feet," I say, getting up.

"Tell your brother to come down and finish whatever he's doing with this mess," she calls after me, and I give her a thumbs-up as I jog up the stairs, only to find Aidan already waiting for me.

"I was promised egg bagels?"

"Well, you shouldn't have been so dismissive of them," he says, as I go past. "You need to stand up for yourself."

"Excuse me?"

"With Mam. I know you don't want to go back there."

I pause in the doorway of her room. "It would just upset her."

"She'll be more upset if you're unhappy," he points out. "But you need to actually tell her. She doesn't know what to do with you half the time. Let alone how to talk to you."

"That's such an exaggeration."

"Is it? You make all these choices that she would never make, and she tries to understand you, but she doesn't. And I know this because I'm the one who has to act as the go-between the two of you." He pulls back his shoulders as he adopts an eerily perfect imitation of her. *"Ask your sister ABC. Do you think she'd like XYZ? You need to tell her the truth more, or she's never going to know how you really feel."*

I say nothing to that, conflicted, but Aidan's already moving on to the next thing.

"You're bringing Christian to the fundraiser?"

"Is that a problem?"

He shrugs. "Might be for him."

"It's a party. He'll be fine. It's a few drinks and finger food."

"It's ballroom dancing and a bunch of bored rich people. You might want to warn him if you're putting him on the spot. There's going to be a lot of assholes there."

"Thanks for the concern," I call, as he disappears into his bedroom, and I glare at his door since I can no longer glare at him.

In Mam's room, I find the dress in her closet as promised. It's a simple dark blue cocktail one that I remember from a few years ago, and that was actually one of my favorites. The sight of it just makes me even more confused about Aidan's words. My mother might not know how my brain works, but she knows what clothes I like. She knows me. And I don't want to lie to her. I just don't want to worry her.

I hold the dress up to the mirror, flattening it against my body, as I picture the shoes I brought with me.

Warn Christian. I don't need to warn him. Warn him about what?

Everything, I guess.

I just subconsciously assumed that he'd be okay. That he'd fit in. And I'm sure he met all sorts of fancy people in London, but there's a difference between city rich and country rich. A difference when everyone's known you since you were a child. When they know everything.

What kind of fake girlfriend would I be if I just threw him into the deep end like that? Not a good one.

A pretty bad one, actually.

Shit.

SEVENTEEN

CHRISTIAN

"You'll need a new one."

I look up from my emails to find the boiler repair guy standing in the doorway of my room, radiating judgment.

"Should have replaced it years ago," he continues, and I force a smile.

"I'm aware. How much?"

"I'd say around four grand."

"Four *grand*?"

He shrugs as if to say, *Tell me about it*. "If you want to make an appointment for January, I can—"

"How much to get it in by Christmas?"

"Christmas?" He hesitates, looking like I just asked him to build a rocket ship. "That's just over a week away."

"I know."

"Christian?"

Shit. I check the time as Dad calls up the stairs, feeling like I've been caught stealing from the liquor cabinet again. He's usually out of the house until lunch.

"Just a second," I yell down as I shut my laptop. "Can you do it this week?" I ask the repairman.

He spends a moment huffing and puffing. "I can," he says eventually, his expression grave. "But it will cost you an extra—"

"That's fine," I interrupt. "As quickly as you can. You've got my details?"

We finish up, and he agrees to go out the same way he came in, quietly and without drawing attention to himself. If anyone asks who he is, he's to tell them he's here to fix my work phone.

My parents won't accept any money from me. I know they won't. Which means it's best to just do it myself and let them be mad at me afterward. At least they won't be living in a cold house for the rest of the winter.

When I'm sure that Mam's still out shopping, I leave him to it and head down the stairs, annoyed at the hint of nerves I feel.

Besides the nosebleed and a headache this morning, nothing was broken, bruised, or sprained, but still, Dad took one look at me when he picked us up last night, and you'd swear I was sixteen years old in his eyes, getting into fights in the schoolyard.

He isn't in the hall, but the front door is open, so I head outside, squinting in the winter sunshine as I spy him next to his Jeep. I'm halfway across the yard before I realize he's not alone.

Megan rounds the tractor, dressed like she's about to head into a snowstorm in her coat, scarf, and hat. She looks so at odds with my father, who's in his dark, roughened work jacket he's worn every day for the last twenty years, but that's not what's so strange about the scene.

It's that a moment before, they were both laughing.

My father is not a man who laughs regularly. A smile is as about as good as we get, so to hear the deep timbre of it, to see him in a rare moment of ease, is enough to stop me in my tracks. Only as soon as I do, they look my way.

"Look who I found," he says, his voice as warm as I've ever known it.

"Your dad was just reminding me about the time I *apparently* tried to take a lamb home," Megan says.

"You stole it right from under me," he tells her. "You tried to convince your mother that I'd given it to you as a gift."

"I have no memory of this," Megan sniffs, but she looks toward the fields with undisguised interest. "Do you have lambs now?"

"We won't have any until February. You'll have to come back and see them then."

I take a hasty step forward as her smile slips, and hold out my hand. "I'm sure the cows would love some earmuffs, though. You want some tea?"

"That would be great."

She fits her gloved hand into mine and turns back to my father. "Thanks for the mini tour. I'll see you at Christmas?"

"I suspect so," he says. "I hope you have your party piece ready."

Alarm flashes across her face, but Dad's mouth doesn't so much as twitch as he climbs into the car.

"There's no party piece," I tell her, as we head back to the house. "Except for Riverdance."

"I can't tell if you're joking or not."

"Do you know any Yeats off by heart?"

"How's your nose?" she asks, peering up at me.

"Smells a bit funny, but..." I side-eye her when she doesn't respond. "Really? Nothing?"

"Do you own a tuxedo?"

I blink at the change in conversation. "Of course."

"Really?"

"No. No one owns a tuxedo," I add over her groan. "You rent one."

"Then can you rent one?"

"For your mother's party? Yes. I've already reserved it."

"And shoes," she adds worriedly. "Do you have shoes?"

"Oh, you didn't tell me this was going to be a shoe kind of a thing."

"Christian—"

"Calm down," I say, amused. "You're making me anxious just looking at you." I lead her into the living room, where she plops onto the couch and starts to unwind her very long, very green scarf.

"It's a big night," she says. "It's the most important night of the year for Mam. She spends a lot of time on it, and she raises a lot of money and all her friends are there, and I've known them all my life, and a lot of them are lovely, but a lot..."

"Aren't," I finish, and she sighs.

"The politicians are fine. The businessmen are fine. It's everyone else who's the problem. The people who just want to get their pictures taken and stock up on a year's worth of gossip. They're retired, rich, and bored, and they want some entertainment."

"And you think I won't be able to handle it."

"I just want you to be prepared. I want you to know what you're getting into, and I should have told you more about it before you agreed to it." She takes a breath, looking like she's steeling herself for something horrible. "If you don't want to go, we can make an excuse and—"

"I'm going," I cut her off. "I once dated a girl whose dad owned half the antique stores in London. I can schmooze."

"But—"

"Megan. Look at me. I'm not backing out. I'm not doing that to you."

Her eyes flit across my face, looking for any sign that I'm lying. "Okay," she says, relaxing. "Thank you." She pats my knee before folding the scarf on her lap. "And you're okay with the singing thing, right? It will only be one song, I swear."

I pause at that, an automatic yes on the tip of my tongue when her words suddenly register. "I..."

"Gotcha," she whispers, and Mam chooses at that moment to make her entrance, appearing with a tray of assorted mugs.

"I saw you outside," she says, sounding delighted. "Thought you might want tea. Is this your mother's fundraiser you're talking about?"

Megan just nods. "Are you going, Mrs. Fitzpatrick?"

"Me? No. Too close to Christmas this year, I'm afraid. Liam's eldest has a starring role in the school play the same night, and I'll be the worst grandmother in the world if I miss it. But his father and I used to love them. Milk or sugar?"

"Just milk," Megan says, as she hands her the cup, and I wait for Mam to leave. She doesn't, of course. Too busy reminiscing.

"I can't remember the last time I danced to a live band," she says. "I used to love dancing. Proper dancing now, not whatever grinding you two do."

"That's us," I say. "Noted grinders."

"Your father and I used to dance all the time," she continues, ignoring me. "It's not that hard once you find your feet. I think he still has his old suit lying around," she adds, glancing about the room as if it will suddenly appear, and I'm about to ask her to go find it so we can have some privacy when a thought occurs.

"Can you teach me?"

Megan glances at me in surprise as a delighted look crosses Mam's face.

"I suppose I could," she says, sounding a little girlish.

"We don't have to dance," Megan tells me. "Not if you don't want to."

"Who said I don't want to?"

"No one but..."

No one ever wants to. Meaning Isaac didn't want to. Meaning, now I have to.

I get to my feet. "Let's do it then."

"Now?"

"Good a time as ever!" I say the words so cheerfully that both women look baffled, but I ignore them as I start pushing the furniture back so we have space. Mam doesn't take much more convincing, and deftly connects her phone to our cheap speaker system, crooning out some old big-band music as for the next twenty minutes, she leads me around the room. It's hard to do with all the wrapping paper and decorations scattered about, but we pretend they're other couples and keep going as she corrects my posture and steps and more or less everything I'm doing because, apparently, it's all wrong before finally the timer for something in the kitchen goes, and she leaves me to collapse on the couch next to Megan.

"You're getting there," she says. "I have to check the nut roast."

I make a face. "When have we ever had a nut roast?"

"It's a practice one for—" She breaks off abruptly, glancing at Megan, who looks predictably embarrassed.

"You don't have to go to any trouble for me."

"It's no trouble at all," she says. "What are you going to do? Eat a plate of parsnips all night?"

I scoff. "We have a million side dishes she can—"

"And now she'll have a main too," Mam says firmly. "We can all have some," she adds though we both know it will be a cold day in hell if Dad ever eats a bit of a nut roast for his Christmas dinner.

"Sorry," I murmur when she leaves the room. "I know it's the most clichéd vegetarian dish in existence."

"It's kind of her," Megan says.

"I told you she liked you. Almost as much as my dad, by the looks of things." I meant it as a compliment, but her smile dims.

"What?"

"I just didn't think they'd be so nice."

"Did I make them sound that terrifying?"

"No. but... Doesn't it make you feel bad about what we're doing?" she asks. "Lying to them about us?"

"The whole point of this is that they like you."

"I know, I know, I just... What's it going to be like for them when we break up?"

I pause at that. "Breaking up is weeks away."

"Yeah, like one," she jokes, and my mood dips. Can't we just focus on the now?

"Let me worry about my parents. But if you want me to be less charming to your mother, I'm going to need one to two business days. I can't just turn it off that easily." The words are teasing, but my skin feels tight, and I pull her to her feet, restless. "How's your spine?"

"What do you— Christian!" My name is said on a laugh as I dip her to the floor. "All about that back bend," I say, bringing her back up. She blows her hair out of her eyes with an exaggerated puff, but she's smiling.

I start to move us to the music, bringing her closer as I count the steps.

"Sorry about freaking out," she says.

"Don't be sorry. This is a big deal to you."

"Honestly, I'd barely thought about it until Mam brought it up this morning. I think she's extra nervous with me and Aidan at home this year. She's going all out. Even though Aidan hates it," she adds dryly. "He always did. Can't stand the suit-and-tie affair. Can't stand her friends. Can't stand any of it. At least he's old enough now to pretend for her sake."

"Are they that bad?"

"No, they're fun. They are!" she adds when I give her a look. "I used to really like them. I mean, sure, when I was a child, it was boring, but when I got older, it was like I could play dress-up for an evening. And then, with Isaac there, it was... Well, he was good at talking to people. He didn't like the dancing part, though," she admits.

Called it.

"We'll dance," I say decidedly, and she shrugs a reply even though she looks pleased. Or at least she does for a second before something else starts worrying her.

"It's at the Regency this year," she says. "It's the hotel we stayed at for the wedding."

"I remember. And I'm going to guess you haven't been back there either."

"My general approach to that part of my life has just been a real head-in-the-sand vibe. If I'm not there, it doesn't exist. And if it doesn't exist, it didn't happen. It makes perfect sense in my mind."

"Please tell me this isn't something you learned in therapy."

"Oh, no that's all me. Much easier than whatever he told me to do."

I fight back a smile as one song bleeds into the next. At some point, we'd stopped dancing and started swaying, gentle, tiny movements that I only grow aware of when her hand on my shoulder inches down, curving around my bicep.

She doesn't seem to realize how close we are, her gaze distant as her thumb sweeps over my arm.

"Mam thought I'd been kidnapped," she says absently, and it takes me a second to follow her train of thought.

"When you ran?"

"Aidan had to talk her down from calling the police. In case you wonder where my dramatic side came from."

"Was she furious with you?"

"Eh." She tilts her head left and right as though weighing up her answer. "I don't know. I don't think so. Once she knew I wasn't, you know, *dead*, I think she thought it was cold feet. Everyone did. That once I calmed down, I'd come back. But when she realized I wasn't going to change my mind, she did everything she could to help me. She contacted an old friend of hers whose daughter had a spare room in Dublin, and a day later, she came up with a bunch of stuff from home."

"She sounds like a good mother."

"She was. She is. We're just very different people. And back then, I was... I mean, you have to understand, I'd been with Isaac since I was fifteen. Do you know how much you have ahead of you at fifteen?"

"A lot?"

"A lot," she confirms. "And it was all intertwined with him. I went to the same college as him so we could be together. I applied for jobs to be close to him. And then, all of a sudden, I was by myself. Just like that. Twenty-five years old, and I might as well have been a kid with how much I knew about being alone. I was terrified."

"That sounds brave to me."

"Being brave would have been stopping it months before it happened," she says with that little frown. "There was nothing brave about letting it go on as long as it did. Spending the money, getting everyone's hopes up."

"A runaway bride is a lot cheaper than a divorce. And a lot more fun."

"Stop trying to make me feel better."

"Never."

Her smile grows sad, lost in thought, and I have the strongest urge to comfort her, to wrap my arms tight around her and hold her close. But even though that's well within our rules, and even though we did a lot more at O'Donoghue's the other night, it somehow feels like a lot more intimate than what we've agreed to, so I stay where I am, my hand on her arm until someone clears their throat nearby.

My sister.

"Hi." Hannah slinks into the room, her attention on Megan in a way that tells me she's been eavesdropping for a while. "You guys training for your mam's party?"

"I wouldn't call it training," Megan says, her voice a lot lighter than it was before. "But Christian's showing off if that's what you mean."

"Sounds like him." She takes another step, unusually hesitant. "I was wondering," she begins, her eyes flicking to me. "If... well, I thought I could make you a dress."

I think my surprise is matched only by Megan's, who looks at Hannah like she's never seen her before.

"A dress?"

"Yeah. To say sorry for how I acted. I thought... I don't know what I thought. But I know I don't think it anymore, and I..." She blows out an annoyed breath, looking to me. "I'm not good at this," she says like that's my fault. I just shrug. After how she behaved, she's on her own until she makes up for it.

"I've been working on a gown for my final project," she continues. "Nineteen-forties movie star shit, and I'd like you to wear it. It's green," she adds. "You'd look great in green. And it's beautiful. It'll probably get full marks."

And there's the girl I know. "Hannah—"

"I think it would really suit you," she says, ignoring me as she focuses on Megan. "I'll have to make a few alterations, but no one else will be wearing anything like it. Really, you'd be stupid not to—"

"Hannah," I interrupt.

"Right. Sorry. What I'm saying is, I'd love to dress you. If you like it, of course. And if you don't already have something in mind." Her face falls. "Do you?"

"No!" Megan says the word so quickly that I know it's a lie. "I was going to go shopping tomorrow, so you'll be saving me a whole morning of trouble. That would be incredible, Hannah. Thank you."

"Really?"

"Yes. And apology accepted."

Hannah beams at her, and just like that, everything that's come before is instantly forgotten.

"You're going to look *amazing*," she says. "Honestly, I'm so good at this stuff. I know just the lipstick to wear with it as well. Do you like makeup?"

"I love makeup."

"And what cup size are you?"

Megan stiffens. "Uh—"

"Don't worry," she says. "I can let it out. Let's go."

"Go?"

"We can use my room for the fitting," she says, grabbing her hand. "I'll need to start on it now. Unless you guys still need to practice?"

She directs the last bit at me, and I shake my head, trying to hide my smile as Megan sends me a panicked look.

"She's all yours," I say and wave my goodbye as Hannah drags her out of the room.

EIGHTEEN

MEGAN

The next few days are taken up wholly by my mother's party. So much so that I barely get to see Christian because I'm so busy helping put the final bits and pieces together.

On the day itself, Aidan goes early to check on things after Mam had a dream where the food didn't arrive, while the two of us take our time getting ready. When I was younger, she used to hire a hair-and-makeup girl to come to the house, but the older I got, the more I liked doing it myself.

I've always liked dressing up. Clothes. Makeup. Hair. It was fun to me, and though the odd person in my life tried to make me feel vain or vapid because of it, they never succeeded. Show me someone who can draw their eyeliner as sharply as I can, and then we can talk. Tonight, I pin my hair back for an effortless look that takes a lot of work and go for a smoky eye. Red lipstick. Light jewelry. A slightly heavier foundation to see me through the next few hours.

And, of course, Hannah's dress. A strapless empire-line, emerald-green wonder whose full skirt falls to my ankles in a whoosh of satin that brushes pleasantly against my knees.

She'd meant every word of her apology, as awkward as it

had been, and treated me like we were best friends as she spent hours lowering the hemline and adjusting the waist. She chatted incessantly as she did and was incredibly easy to talk to despite her not-so-subtle prods for more information about her brother and me. It wasn't long before I felt guilty again that Christian and I were lying to her. But when I confided as much to him, he just brushed it off, so I tried to do the same.

I think he was just happy I was getting on with her. That I was getting on with everyone. That's all he's ever wanted. In fact, it's reached the point where I feel like he's gotten the raw end of the deal. Attending formal functions, getting pool sticks to the face. All I have to do is hang out with his family every now and then, and after the initial nervous introductions, it's become something I actually look forward to doing.

I'll make it up to him after tonight. I'll fawn over him on Christmas Day. I'll wash all the dishes after dinner and miraculously heal his relationship with his father. I'll be the best fake girlfriend ever.

"Well now! Don't you look lovely."

I dump my makeup bag onto the table as my mother appears in the doorway wearing her favorite purple gown.

"It's the dress."

"It's the girl," she says, and when I meet her gaze in the mirror, her lips twitch.

I raise a brow. "You're in a good mood."

"I've had half a bottle of champagne."

"*Mam.*"

"I'm kidding," she says, smiling fully now. "I'm just excited. I'm allowed to be excited, aren't I? It's the first time in years we'll all be there together."

"And ten quid says Aidan will still hide under the table."

"He's grown up a lot," she chides. "He'll suffer through one night for me. Just like you will."

"I'm not suffering anything."

"Still," she says, watching me sort through my lipsticks. "At least you'll have Christian there. It's good you two found each other." She shakes her head, looking wistful. "The way he looks at you..."

"Like he's madly in love," I joke, searching for the one I want.

"Like he sees you." And the sheer honesty in her voice makes me turn around.

"Isaac never saw you," she continues, a thoughtful expression on her face. "I get that now."

"Mam," I begin slowly, but she cuts me off with a wave of her hand.

"We've never really seen eye to eye, have we?" she asks, and I frown.

"I think we've done alright."

"I'm glad to hear that," she says, amused. "But having you back home these past few days has reminded me how proud I am of you. And I don't know if I ever told you that, but I am. What you've done, and the life you've made for yourself, I might not have always understood it, but I'm proud of you for doing it. For standing on your own two feet." She shrugs, blinking back the fresh glimmer in her eyes. "Makes me think I did something right raising you."

"You did," I say, bewildered by the whole conversation. "You were brilliant. You still are."

"I'm glad you're coming tonight," she adds. "I know it will be hard for you, but the support means a lot."

"I want to go. This is important to me too." I go to hug her, mindful of both our makeup. "It's going to be great," I say firmly, and she nods, letting her nerves show for the first time. "And we're going to squeeze every last cent out of them."

She smiles then, looking at me with such affection that I have to hug her again.

She leaves soon after when a taxi comes to collect her, and

I'm just putting the finishing touches to my brows when I hear Christian's car roll up. A second later, the doorbell goes.

"It's open," I call and grab my coat, a long navy one that I've only ever used for fundraisers and funerals.

"Megan?"

"One second!" Perfume. Double-check teeth for lipstick. Deep breath. Another deep breath. And off I go.

My heels clack rapidly against the wooden floorboards as I stride toward the stairs. Frankie always moans about how I can wear stilettos without falling flat on my face, refusing to believe it's just practice and gel pads, but despite what she calls my superhero calves, for one of the first times in my life, I falter as I turn the corner and look down.

Christian stands just inside the entranceway in a classic black tuxedo, single-breasted and utterly divine. The man inside it doesn't look too bad either. His hair is brushed back, his jaw freshly shaven, and while I miss the shadow he usually keeps, I decide that scrubbed-up Christian is just as nice. Just as handsome. Just as—

"What?" he asks, and I realize I'm staring.

"Nothing." I clear my throat. "Just didn't think I was getting picked up by James Bond tonight."

"It's got a pocket and everything," he says, gesturing grandly at his jacket. "You ready?"

"As much as I can be." I force a smile. "Let's go."

"Whoa." He takes a step to the left, blocking the door. "Nuh-uh. Big reveal first."

"What?"

"Show me the dress! Hannah's been keeping her door shut. I'm dying here."

Oh. Right. My palms grow clammy, unusual shyness overtaking me as I put my clutch on the hall table and slip the coat off my shoulders, smoothing the skirts in a nervous tic.

Christian's whole body goes still as he takes me in, his gaze dropping to my heels and back up again, lingering on the bodice. I hold my breath, anticipation thrumming through me as his face flickers with something unreadable, an emotion gone too quick for me to catch.

And then he smiles.

It's a... nice smile.

A normal smile.

A normal, friendly, pleasant smile, and one that I'm immediately disappointed by.

"You look stunning," he says, and while the words are right, I'm instantly transported back to my apartment, moments before our first "date." *You look great,* he'd said back then, in that same exact tone, and I just thought... I don't know what I thought.

"Thanks." I pull my coat back on, covering it up again. "You look nice too."

"Tied my own bow tie and everything," he says, holding out his arm, and I place my hand on the crook of his elbow and let him lead me out of the house and into his car.

"Nervous?" he asks, as he pulls onto the road. He doesn't wait for an answer, taking one look at my expression before smiling.

"Yes," we say in unison, and he laughs.

"Here." He fiddles with the radio, finding some festive music, and turns the volume up as he heads away from the village.

It weirdly helps, and I'm doing fine until we are near the hotel, when my stomach starts twisting with anxiety. It's not so bad that I ask him to turn around, but it's enough that I wish I had followed my mother's example and did a little pre-drinking to take the edge off.

Hey! I want to point out when he pulls into the parking lot. *This is where I fled in a taxi. And over there is where I thought you were going to rat me out. See that window up above? That's the one I spent thirty minutes at, wondering if I could Rapunzel my way down with a bedsheet.*

"You good?" Christian asks, and it's only then I realize we're parked.

"I'm something. You'll tell me if I get sweat patches?"

"I thought that was why I was here?"

I take more time than I need getting out, but Christian's patient with me. He doesn't say a word while I fuss over my dress, adjust my heels, check my hair. Just lets me stall for time, even though I'm buying mere seconds at most.

"We'll stay an hour," he says when we finally wind our way through the parked cars toward the entrance. "One hour, and then if you want to leave, we'll leave. We'll tell them I had some bad oysters, and that's that."

I nod jerkily, my gaze on the train of my dress. Hannah did a beautiful job with it, and it's a perfect fit, but I haven't worn anything like it in a while, and as we climb the steps, I'm extra careful that nothing catches on my heels.

"People will want to talk to me," I remind him as we reach the top.

"So we'll talk."

"And you need to act like we're—"

"Megan." His finger goes to my chin, and he tips my head up so our eyes meet. "Not alone, remember? I've got this. I've got you."

"Right. I know." I blow out a breath. "Thank you."

"Just remember," he continues as he leads me over to a server with a tray of champagne. "I'm really, really good at this."

"At what?"

"Pretending," he says, and he gives me a wink as we enter the ballroom.

Mam's really outdone herself this year. I know it wasn't her climbing the ladders to drape swathes of red velvet ribbons around the room or dust the glittering chandeliers that hang above us, but it's a lot of work organizing something on this scale, and she puts a lot of time into it. Several hundred people mill about the main ballroom, all dressed in their finest as photographers slink in and out, and the whole place feels alive with excitement. It will get messier later. It always does. But right now, a few days out from Christmas, everyone's on their best behavior. Not a drink spilled or a hair out of place.

I just wish I could enjoy it more.

"What's over there?" Christian asks, looking to the side of the room where small lines are forming.

"Bidding tables," I explain. "It's a silent auction for hotel stays, restaurants, that kind of thing. Besides one-off donations, it's the main source of money."

"This isn't the kind of event where they bid on me, is it?"

"You'd like that, wouldn't you?"

"I'm just saying if you want to make some real money, then—"

"Megan!"

Oh God. I stiffen as the first of what feels like will be *many* people makes their way toward me, practically shouting my name for the whole room to hear.

"Kathleen Finnegan," I murmur, as the tall, slender woman approaches. "Used to play tennis with my mother. Married to some pharmaceutical millionaire and has more money than sense."

"Nice or not nice?"

"Not nice," I say, smiling broadly as she gets within earshot. "Hi, Kathleen."

"You look beautiful, dear." She kisses the air beside my cheek as her eyes flick to Christian. "And who's this?"

"Her lucky date for the evening," Christian says, holding out his hand. "Christian Fitzpatrick."

"Annette's son?"

"No," he says and leaves it at that.

"Thank you so much for coming," I say, drawing her attention back to me. "Have you bid on anything yet?"

"Not yet," she says, her gaze still bouncing between the two of us. "I have to say I wasn't sure I'd make it, but when your mother told me you'd be joining us again, I had to see it with my own eyes."

"Well, here I am," I say with a rigid smile. "In the flesh."

"And looking so well," she says like I'd been infirm the last few years. "I don't think any of us expected to see you back here after what happened. And in this hotel!" She gestures around us. "It must be so *strange* for you to—"

"Is that a Constantin?" Christian interrupts, and the two of us stare at him before Kathleen's gaze drops to the watch on her wrist.

"Oh." She looks pleased. "It is."

"It's exquisite," he says. "Do you mind if I—"

"No, no, go ahead," she says, preening under his attention as she holds out her arm. "I'm surprised you know them. No one under the age of forty seems to wear watches anymore."

"I had a friend whose father collected them. I've always admired them. You have excellent taste."

I shoot him a look, convinced he's laying it on a bit thick, but Kathleen seems enthralled, and I stand there forgotten as the two of them chat about white versus rose gold and how no one appreciates true craftsmanship anymore.

When she finally goes, flattered enough to see her through the rest of the night, Christian just sips his champagne, looking about the room as if nothing happened.

"What?" he asks when I stare at him.

"You know what," I say, and he takes my arm again.

"You go swimming in ice-cold lakes, I break out my luxury jewelry knowledge. Fair's fair."

"Is this what you were doing in London all those years?"

"I also know a lot about polo," he says, and I laugh as he

leads me into the center of the room, where we're soon stopped by the next person. And the next, and the next, and the next.

Over and over, they approach with the same questions and the same comments, some a little more pointed than others. But I am my mother's daughter, and our chat earlier reminded me what I need to do. With each question, I get better at answering what I want to and brushing off what I don't. Christian charms them and then I swoop in, reminding them to bid, marveling at the auctions. Mam even joins us for the first little while but leaves us to it when she sees we're able to handle ourselves. And we are. More than able.

Christian plays the part perfectly.

He laughs and talks and listens to those I introduce him to. He smiles at them.

He smiles at me.

And I can forgive him for not falling to his knees at the sight of my dress with how well he pretends to be utterly and completely captivated by my mere presence. He doesn't stop touching me for the rest of the evening. His hand on my back, my arm, my elbow. Like he knows I need it. Because I do. The little ball of anxiety doesn't go away, but it eases bit by bit until I even start to enjoy myself, and when the band takes to the stage, and the dancing starts, he pulls me to the floor without hesitation.

We're still there thirty minutes later, taking only short breaks to catch our breath. Maybe he realizes we don't have to talk to anyone if we're moving. Maybe he just likes it. He certainly acts like he does, spinning me around like we're the only two people there. Like this night is just for us.

During a slower song, one of Mam's old golf friends strikes up a conversation beside us and as Christian chats easily about greens and irons and fairways, I use the opportunity to study him from the corner of my eye, admiring all the angles and edges to his face that would have been severe on anyone else, but on him seem to fit perfectly, softened by his intelligent eyes and quick smile.

He laughs at a joke, his crow's-feet creasing in a way that already feels familiar to me, and expertly moves us away, his hold on my body comfortable and sure, like we've done this a dozen times before.

And just for a moment, just for one fairy-tale second, I wish we had.

I wish this was real.

All of it.

As if feeling the weight of my attention, his gaze snaps back to me, and my heart skips a beat, launching into something new. Something sweet and delicate that I've never felt before.

The band keeps playing, but our steps slow as his grip on my hip tightens, and I wonder if he can feel my pulse racing beneath my skin.

"You okay?" he murmurs, dropping his voice so no one else can hear. I nod, and it must be convincing because something playful sparks in his eye. "You want to do our signature move?"

"What's our—" I break off in a gasp, delighted as he dips me until my hair nearly brushes the floor. My head spins as he pulls me back up, and... *iron tablets, Megan, take your iron tablets.*

"You dizzy?" he asks, as he twirls me around. And I am. I am, but I like it. I like it so much that I ask him to do it again, and he happily obliges.

"Okay, stop," I plead even as I laugh. "Stop, stop, stop." A bead of sweat trickles down the small of my back, and I know my face is flushed. "Air," I demand.

"You want some champagne?"

"Of course, I want champagne," I say, and with a swish of my dress, Christian brings me to a halt. He pauses there on the edge of the dancefloor, gazing down at me as he lets me catch my breath. I'm aware that we're being watched. The other couples look our way curiously, indulgently, and I couldn't care a bit. I'm smiling so wide, my cheeks hurt, but I can't seem to stop. And I don't want to. "You're a good dancer," I tell him, and though he starts to respond, no words come out.

He's staring at me now, but for once I don't mind being stared at.

The silence stretches, and Christian's brow furrows for an instant before he abruptly steps back, his hand dropping mine like it's on fire.

"Two minutes," he says, and he waits for me to nod before disappearing into the crowd. I feel oddly bereft once he's gone and linger awkwardly, before making the mistake of meeting someone's eye. Not wanting to rehash the same conversation for the hundredth time, I turn before they can approach, aiming for the patio doors on the other side of the room.

It's quieter out here. Colder too.

My skin prickles with goosebumps as soon as the fresh air hits me, the sweat cooling irritably on my skin. But it's refreshing, and I can already feel my head beginning to clear as I step farther onto the patio, looking out at the dark gardens of the hotel.

I wonder if I can tempt Christian into exploring them with me. There's a playground around here somewhere, and I freaking love a swing set. A bottle of champagne, talking the rest of the night away under the stars. Just the thought of it makes me smile. I'll need to get my coat, but—

"Megan?"

"That was quick!" I say, turning eagerly. But it's not Christian behind me.

It's Isaac.

He moves closer, stopping a short distance away as though he's not sure what's appropriate anymore. "Hey."

"Hi." I lick my dry lips, glancing over his shoulder for Christian but seeing only the backs of other guests instead. "I didn't think you were coming tonight."

"I wasn't going to. But Dad's knee was acting up and Mam didn't want to come alone, so I... This is his tuxedo, actually," he adds, looking down at the ill-fitting suit with a rueful smile. "I suppose better too big than too small. You, on the other hand..." He smiles at me. "You look beautiful, Megan."

"Hannah made it for me. Well, not for me. It's a school project, but she wanted me to wear it."

"Hannah?"

"Christian's sister."

His smile dims. "Right."

"It's good of you to come," I offer. "For your Mam. I know you used to hate these parties."

"Was I that obvious?"

No. Not to the others. He'd laugh and talk with the best of them, but as soon as we'd be alone, he'd start complaining, no matter how much I told him I was enjoying it.

"A little," I say, as a breeze wafts through the pillars. I shiver from the chill of it, and Isaac immediately shrugs off his jacket.

"Megan," he chastises, and before I can tell him not to, he holds it out to me. That's all. He doesn't put it around my shoulders like he might have done a few years ago. Just another reminder of the distance between us.

Still, I take it, slipping my arms through the sleeves. I regret it immediately, overcome with awkwardness.

This is weird. This is very, very weird.

"Cormac said he saw you at O'Donoghue's," he continues, and I tense.

"Is that not allowed?"

He frowns. "Of course, it is, I just—"

"Don't worry. I didn't stay long." I swallow, remembering the look on Sophie's face. "They hate me."

"They don't—"

"They do," I say, watching him carefully. "They think I ruined your life."

He gives me a look as if to say, *Didn't you?* But masks it instantly. "I never wanted them to think that," he says after a long second. "Besides, it's in the past, right?"

"Right," I say, but I'm not sure I believe him. "Is Natalie here?" I ask, changing the subject. It just makes him look even more uncomfortable.

"No. She's... she's not feeling too great. She sends her apologies."

"Oh. I'm sorry."

"Yeah."

"A cold or—"

"Something with her stomach, I think."

"Is she pregnant?" I hear myself say, and Isaac stares at me, taken aback. "Sorry. That was a terrible joke."

"No, I know," he says quickly. "She's not, though."

"Cool. I mean..." Christ. "So, when's the wedding?"

A strange, pinched expression crosses his face, and I feel a surge of frustration.

I'm trying to be nice here. I'm trying to be an adult. He's the one who came out to talk to me and I just—

"There's not going to be a wedding."

I pause, choking on the mini-rant I was about to unleash. "Excuse me?" I ask because, surely, I misunderstood. *Surely,* I misheard or—

"It's not happening," he continues. "The wedding. The relationship. Any of it. We broke it off six weeks ago."

"But you—"

"Her dad's sick," he explains, scratching the back of his neck. "Seriously sick. Nat asked if we could keep it up for his sake, just for the next few weeks, but we're not getting married. She's moved out and everything. She's staying with her sister." His hand falls to his side. "So that's it. No wedding."

No wedding. No... "You're pretending you're still in a relationship?"

"Pretty dumb, huh?"

The noise that comes out of me is borderline hysterical. "Does anyone else know?"

"Just her sister. I haven't even told my parents yet." He winces at the last bit, looking utterly woeful.

"I'm sorry," I say because I don't know what else I *can* say. Isaac just laughs, the sound bleak.

"Me too. Two failed engagements and I'm not even thirty." He shakes his head. "It's like a soap opera."

My sympathy dims at the bitterness in his words. He makes it sound like the universe is out to get him.

"You seem to be doing well, though," he adds, and I tell myself I'm imagining the accusing note in his words.

"I am."

"You and Christian."

"And other things," I tell him. Hobbies and holidays and friends and plans. A job. An apartment. A life. One without him. "I'm doing great," I say, and to that, he has no response.

I shrug his jacket from my arms, no longer cold. I'd panicked when I saw him in the parking lot. And I thought I would feel that way again. But right now, I feel nothing. After all the time we spent together, after the explosion that was our breaking apart, I look at this man, and at most, I get a vague sense of irritation that he's here, and I don't want him to be.

"I'd better go back in," I say. "Christian's probably wondering where I am."

Isaac looks annoyed. "He can wait a few more minutes. You owe me that at least."

"He's getting me a drink."

"But I— *wait.*" He grabs my hand as I move past, and I immediately tug it from his grasp, shocked. He doesn't reach for me again. If anything, he seems surprised by my reaction. Like I'm the one in the wrong.

"No," I say, my voice calm even if the rapid beating of my heart is not. "You don't get my time anymore."

"I only wanted to—"

"And I owe you nothing." I shove his jacket at him, furious I accepted it in the first place. "Goodnight." And before he can do anything else, I turn my back and hurry inside.

NINETEEN

CHRISTIAN

Charm a girl. Dance with a girl.

Leave a girl alone in the middle of a ballroom because you lose all ability to function.

I glower at the back of the man's head in front of me, trying to get a hold of myself. Two minutes has turned into five, the line at the open bar several people deep, and I'm impatient to get back to Megan, even if it means making an even bigger idiot of myself.

But that damn dress.

I don't think I've ever seen anyone more beautiful than her tonight. I don't know if it was the clothes or the hair of whatever shimmery makeup she's dusted along her chest that makes her body glimmer every time she catches the light, but every time I look at her, I have to keep reminding myself that this *isn't real*.

I could barely breathe when I saw her back at the house. Could barely think.

I still can't.

I look over my shoulder, trying to catch a glimpse of her through the crowd. It's the last thing she needs right now, for me to betray her trust in this. In us. Our rules were agreed. Signed.

Toasted to. And from the beginning, she made it clear that this was an important night. One I'm at risk of ruining because I can't keep my hands off her.

As if feeling the tension radiating from me, the man in front of me glances back and returns the polite smile I quickly adopt before turning back around.

I can't help but feel amused at it all. I mean, *this*? This is what she was worried about? A bunch of old snobs starved for gossip? She handled them like a pro. I could have spent all night watching her do it, but I guess then I would have missed having her all to myself. That was even better. The champagne, the dancing, the food.

Food. I should get her more food.

I glance around for a server, only to catch the eye of Megan's mother instead, standing near the band. She beams at me as soon as I see her, offering a wave as I smile back. I don't know what I expected from Emily, but she's been nothing but warm to me. And is scarily good at getting money from people. I may or may not have bid a chunk of my savings on a boat.

And for the first time, I feel that twinge of guilt Megan's always talking about. That her happiness for us will be short-lived, but before I can feel too bad about it, my phone vibrates in my pocket, and I sidestep out of the line to check it.

Andrew.

"I'm at Megan's fundraiser," I say when I answer the call. "So unless this is an emergency—"

"I feel like I should have a speech."

"What?"

"When I propose," Andrew says. "I should have a speech."

God help me. I tilt my head to the ceiling, watching the chandeliers glint. "You don't need a speech. You just ask her to marry you."

"But I should say something first."

"No, you just ask. Don't put more pressure on yourself."

"Right. You're right. Okay." A pause. "You know when I said I didn't want rose petals?"

"I ordered them, anyway."

I can practically feel his relief down the line. "You're the best brother ever. Do you know that? Way better than Liam."

"I'll be sure to tell him."

"You having a good time?"

"I was," I say pointedly, and he laughs.

"Message received. I'll tell Mam not to wait up." And with that, he hangs up the phone.

I'm never going to let him live this down once he's done. I've never seen him so nervous before. It's getting to the point where I feel like telling him to just pop the question. That Molly wouldn't care how he did it. That she'd probably be happiest with just the two of them. But he wants to make it special. And if that's what he wants, then I'm going to help him.

I finally reach the bar, where I order a glass of champagne for Megan, and cast about for a waiter to grab us some food. I've just pinpointed a man carrying a tray of pastries when someone clears their throat nearby.

Aidan stands behind me, clutching an empty pint glass. He's dressed in a similar tuxedo to mine, and while he looks the part, there's a stiffness in his body that no amount of tailoring can mask. He looks uncomfortable, like a kid at the grown-up table, and not for the first time do I wonder how he feels coming back here. Leaving his real life behind to play the younger-brother card. It can't be easy for him. But it's not easy for any of us, so I find my patience wearing thin when he keeps acting like I'm the bad guy here and not everyone who's treated his sister like shit.

Protective brother. I get it. I feel the same way toward Hannah. I feel the same way toward all my siblings. But it's not as fun being on the other end of it.

"Is this where you tell me to stay away from Megan?" I ask,

cutting straight to it.

"Feels dramatic."

"And yet here you stand."

"She can do better than you," he says flatly. "She deserves better too. She's had a rough time these last few years, and the last thing she needs is to get her heart broken again."

"Who says I'm going to break her heart?"

"The dozen different girlfriends featured on your social media? She's softer than she thinks she is." And something in his voice makes me bite back my retort. "She cares. She tries. And she's..." He looks at me then. Looks at me like he can see right through me. "You're the first boyfriend she's told us about since Isaac, you know that?"

I didn't.

"You're a smart guy; everyone remembers that. And you left here to make something of yourself, but you failed, and now you're back, and you've latched yourself onto her to hide it."

What's funny is that he's not even wrong. The only thing that hasn't occurred to him is that Megan's using me to hide too. But while I can't tell him that, I'm sure as hell not going to put up with him speaking to me like he has a right to her.

"Let's get one thing straight," I say. "I make your sister happy. And that's all I care about right now. So, I'm going to dance with her at her mother's fundraiser. I'm going to get her champagne, and I'm going to talk her up to everyone here, and I am going to do all the things you pretend you want nothing to do with. And you? You can just fly back to Australia for all I care. You don't get to come home and play the brother card just because it suits you. And what your sister does and who she does it with is none of your business." I clap him on the shoulder with more force than I should, and raise my voice. "Merry Christmas, Aidan. Have a good night."

And with that new spike of adrenaline humming through my veins, I go off to find Megan.

It doesn't take long. As soon as I turn back to the room, I spot her hurry through the patio doors on the other side. But any good mood I had at the sight of her drops as soon as I see the look on her face, tight-lipped and unhappy, and not how I left her.

I weave my way over, keeping my smile bright.

"What happened?" I ask as soon as I reach her side.

"Nothing," she lies. "But I think I'm done."

"Done?"

"Yeah," she says, not meeting my eye. "Social battery and all that. Can we go? I just need to say goodbye to my mam. She won't be mad."

I'm about to try and talk her out of it, confused as to where this sudden change came from before I remember this is what I promised her.

"No problem. Let's go find Emily."

She relaxes at my quick agreement and starts looking through the crowd, unaware of the figure who emerges from the same door she just came through.

Isaac steps back into the ballroom with a false smile on his face that does nothing to hide the angry line on his brow. His eyes go straight to Megan, and he takes a step toward her before he finally sees me. He stops instantly, and for a moment, the two of us just stare at each other before he turns swiftly in the other direction.

And I don't know what it is. Maybe the conversation with Aidan, maybe her obvious unhappiness at whatever happened in the few minutes we've been apart, but possessiveness surges through me, heavy and intense, and it's only the touch of Megan's hand on mine that stops me from going after him.

Not my girlfriend, I remind myself. Not my place. Not real.

But I wasn't lying to her before. As I follow her across the room to her mother, I realize I'm getting so good at pretending that I'm starting to fool myself.

TWENTY

MEGAN

Christian's acting weird.

He's been acting weird ever since I asked him if we could leave, ushering me through the required goodbyes before striding out to the car with his hand on my back the entire way. Maybe he thought I was about to freak out. And maybe I was. But I feel better now we're out of the lights and heat of the ballroom. Better in the darkness. Better just us.

I thought he'd drive me home or that we'd go to the pub to continue the evening. But we haven't gone anywhere. A minute ago, he closed his door, and for that minute, we've been sitting here. He hasn't even turned the engine on.

"Are we going to stay here all night?" I finally ask.

"No."

Okay. "What's happening right now?"

"Your brother had a word with me tonight."

I fight back a wince. "Was it to tell you how handsome you looked?"

"More along the lines of 'get your hands off her.'"

"Ah."

"Yeah."

I fidget in my seat, embarrassed, but also...

"You're happy about this?" Christian asks, catching my expression.

"I just..." I spread my hands out in a *what do you want from me* gesture. "He's my younger brother. It's cute. He thinks he's looking out for me."

"Which would be fine, except I'm not the one he needs to look out for." He sits back, one finger tapping against his knee as he gazes out the window and I realize what happened.

"You saw Isaac," I guess.

"I saw Isaac." And then: "I didn't know he was coming."

"Neither did I," I admit, and Christian grunts. The tapping stops, his hand just resting on his leg now, and I have a sudden flashback to the first time we were in this car together, and it was on mine. He'd been teasing then. I couldn't imagine him teasing now.

"I don't like you upset," he continues, and doesn't that just make my heart melt a little?

"I'm not."

"You were."

"And now I'm with you, so I'm not," I say, the truth tumbling out before I know what to do with it.

"You want to talk?"

"About?" I ask, and he gives me a look.

"Don't do that."

"Do what?"

"Lie to me," he says, and undoes his bow tie with a few swift tugs of his fingers. "You can't do that if this is going to work. You were fine when I left you and then you spend five minutes with the guy, and you suddenly can't wait to get out of the place. Why was he even there?"

"His parents are still friends with my mother. She must have invited them."

"Even though she knew you were coming."

"I didn't tell her not to. I'm okay with them."

"But not with him. So why the hell did he show up?"

I frown at his obvious frustration. "Do you think *I* invited him?"

"No, I just—" He knocks his head back against the seat, not finishing as he undoes the top button of his shirt. I allow myself to study the hint of skin on show there for precisely two seconds before forcing my eyes back up. "I don't get it," he says finally. "You and him. Any of it." His gaze lands on me, dark and steady and demanding my attention. "Why did you run?"

A lock of hair falls free from whatever gel he'd put in tonight, curling slightly around his ear. He brushes it back with an impatient gesture, but it just messes the rest of it up, his slick style vanishing in an instant.

"Christian..."

"Never mind." He sits up, suddenly all business. Like he's snapped back into a role. "It's nothing to do with me."

He reaches for the keys, only to still when I grab his hand. He immediately zeroes in on my fingers, not moving until I sit back.

"For a hundred million reasons," I say softly. "That's why I ran. But I guess the tipping point was when he sabotaged my career."

"What?"

"He pretended to be me and turned down a job I wanted. I found out the night before the wedding."

I'd made it through four rounds of interviews for a big internship in Dublin. Everyone was surprised I'd gotten that far, but none more than me. I'd never stood out to anyone before, but I'd clicked with the hiring panel and my would-be manager, and I wanted it badly. Badly enough that when the deadline to hear back came and went, I was still refreshing my emails the night before the big day, hoping there was just a delay. Isaac had supported me at first, though I realize now it was because he never expected me to actually get the job. When it became clear that I might, he changed his tune, and we fought about it daily. Still, I didn't suspect anything. It was only then, when I was scouring through my spam and trash folders, that I saw the deleted email. The stiff, formal note from someone claiming to be me removing myself from considera- tion. I knew instantly what had happened. I would have been stupid if I hadn't. He was the only other person with access to my email.

"I guess I technically hadn't gotten it yet," I clarify. "But I was confident. They'd told me it was just formalities from then on, and I was devastated when I didn't hear anything more. I thought I'd misread them completely, but it turns out, it wasn't just in my head. Isaac had contacted them days before pretending to be me and pulled me out of the running. That was my last straw. And that's why I ran."

I can see Christian's trying to hold back. Trying and failing. His hands are clenched so hard they have to hurt, and he still hasn't moved a muscle.

"Why would he do that?" he asks eventually, and he says it so calmly, so damn politely that I laugh.

"Sorry," I say when he stares at me. "I'm sorry. I just..." I shake my head, still smiling. But I know it's not a warm one. "Because he was a controlling dick," I say. "Because he had been for years. We did what *he* wanted to do. All the time. Always. School, college. What restaurants we went to. What we did on the weekends. He had our whole lives planned out. I was just along for the ride."

That was how he viewed it, anyway. Even on the rare times I argued back, he'd always win.

Sometimes he'd pretend to go along with me and then privately do what he wanted to, anyway. By the time I found out, it would always be too late.

"It was small things at first," I explain quietly. "We'd been together for so long I was used to them. I thought they were normal. But it got worse when we got older. When we started making decisions that would affect our future. That role was the first thing I ever wanted that was just for me, and he couldn't handle it. I tried to compromise. I suggested we move somewhere in between our jobs, but he refused. I said I'd commute, but he said it would tire me out too much. They offered a few days remote, but then he said it was just a trick and that they'd change their policies as soon as I signed the contract. It was the first and only time in our relationship that I stood up for what I wanted, and he acted like I was trying to break us apart. And maybe I was. Deep down, anyway. But the email sealed it for me. That's why I left him. I maybe could have chosen a better time, but I was running out of it by that stage."

"And you didn't think anyone would believe you. That's why you didn't tell anyone."

"You know how he is," I say, aware of how bitter I sound. "He's charming. He's handsome and polite and easygoing and everyone thought we were so in love. No way would they have believed me. At least not at first. They would have said it was nerves and talked me back into it. And I was easily talked into stuff back then."

"It doesn't explain why you haven't told anyone since."

"Because it's embarrassing?" I admit. "I know it's not supposed to be. I know I'm not supposed to blame myself or whatever, but I think about how much I used to let him get away with it and I just—"

"It's not your fault."

"I know. But knowing it doesn't magically get rid of every insecurity. And who's to say they'd even believe me now? You saw how Sophie reacted. Even Hannah had a grudge about it, and she didn't even know me. I don't need to reopen old wounds."

"But he's walking around like he's—" Christian cuts himself

off, his expression shuttering as he realizes something. "Is that why you didn't tell me? Because you didn't think I'd believe you?"

"No," I say quickly. "That's back to the embarrassment. I don't like who I was back then. I didn't want you to know me as her. I wanted you to think of me as I am now, and I... I wanted you to like me."

And there it is. In the simplest, rawest terms. I take a deep breath, but that's a mistake because my head fills with the woody, spicy smell of him, and I swear I can feel it, whatever the new thing is between us. Feel it like it's a tangible thing.

"I like you," he says, his voice rough. "I like you a lot."

"Oh thanks," I say, trying to make a joke of it and failing miserably.

But Christian isn't done. "I'm sorry you had to go through that."

"It's okay."

"It's not, Megan."

But it has to be. "It feels like a long time ago."

We're just staring at each other now, neither of us moving.

"I don't want to think about it anymore tonight," I tell him. "It was perfect otherwise. I don't want him to ruin it."

"You want to go home?"

"Not yet." I shift a little in the seat, turning my body toward him. Christian watches me do it silently, his eyes drifting over my dress.

"You want to go back inside?" he asks eventually.

"No."

"You want to—"

"I want to stay here," I interrupt. *With you.*

A muscle jumps in his jaw, but still, he doesn't move.

"How much champagne have you had?"

"Um." I swallow, trying to remember. "Two glasses. Maybe three?"

"Are you drunk?"

"No."

"Tipsy?"

"Not anymore." It's the truth. My head was light when we were dancing, but I'm pretty sure that was all the spinning. And the cold air blew any remaining fuzziness away. "I'm fine."

"You sure?"

I nod, and he smiles. The genuine, heart-skip one that I want all to myself.

God, I love it when he smiles. I love it when he—

The noise I make when his lips meet mine would embarrass me in any other circumstance with any other man, but with Christian, I quickly forget about it as we collide in a messy, slightly desperate way that sends a bolt of heat through me.

His fingers delve into my hair as he deepens the kiss, tugging gently as the pins come loose. I know they do because I can feel my hair start to fall from my careful updo, locks of it brushing against my shoulders, making me shiver.

This is new.

We haven't kissed without reason before, without an audience, but there's no one watching us now, no one to convince or deceive, just him and me and the sudden harshness of our breaths when we come up for air.

My hands go to his jacket, and he rolls his shoulders, helping me take it off, as he climbs over to my side of the car. I start on the buttons of his shirt, and my fingers trail down before Christian pins my wandering hands to the seat. I gasp loud enough that he pulls back to look at me.

"Are you okay?"

"Do that again."

"What?"

"New kink, new kink," I tell him urgently, and he catches on, tightening his grip as he leans in to suck a hickey to my neck.

All the blood rushes to that point, and I raise my hips instinctively, furious at the levels of clothing between us.

Why didn't we do this before?

A fling. That's what I want.

That's what I've wanted since the night I bumped into him.

Christian releases my neck to capture my mouth, wasting no time as his tongue moves against mine, hot and heavy and skilled enough to make my head spin.

"Let me go," I tell him, between licks and half bites, and when he does, I'm on him, nails sinking into his shoulder blades in a way that makes him shudder, as he finds the lever for the chair, and tilts us back a few inches.

I wriggle up as he moves fully over me, one hand fisting beside my head while the other tries to find an opening in my skirts. He doesn't succeed.

"I take it back," he says. "I don't like this dress."

"It's not the dress's fault," I protest, as his hand slides behind my neck. "It didn't know."

"Next time we—"

"Next time?" I tease, and he bites my bottom lip.

"You're mouthy when you're turned on. You know that?"

"This is where I make a joke about mouths," I say. "And how good I am at—" I smile into the kiss as he presses me into the seat. "Hold me down again," I order, and he does, gripping my wrists as our lower bodies press as close as we can to each other, straining against our formal wear. But it's not enough. It is extremely not enough.

"I need..."

"What?"

I don't know. Friction? Fingers?

When I don't respond, he goes back to kissing me, and his left hand leaves my wrists to slip behind my back and catch the zip. I curve my spine, arching into him as he pulls it, revealing my breasts. Or at least he would have if I didn't have a band wrapped around them.

"What's that?" he pants, glancing down.

"It's boob tape."

"What?"

"I can't wear a bra with this dress. It would ruin it."

"Megan."

"But the girls are a little heavy," I explain. "They need support."

He gives me an exasperated look. "How do you get it off?"

"Carefully," I admit, and his eyes close briefly before he drops his forehead to my chest, pressing a hot kiss to the top of my cleavage.

My hands go back to his hair, spearing through the strands as he palms my breasts, grazing my nipples through the tape as he tugs down the—

"Careful," I say, and he freezes. "With the dress," I clarify. "It's your sister's project."

"Please don't mention my sister right now."

"Please be careful with the dress," I counter, and he sighs, though it comes out as more of a pant the way his breathing is so heavy.

"We could take it o—"

"No," I say sternly, and the hopeful expression on his face drops so quickly I laugh. "We can still... you know," I smile, bringing his head down to mine. But whatever person the universe is rooting for, it is clearly *not* me tonight, as no sooner do our lips brush than a fist knocks sharply on the window, making me yelp.

Christian immediately covers my body with his, shielding me from whoever's outside.

"Get a room," someone yells as laughter sounds, and I quickly pull the fabric back up before stopping a murderous-looking Christian from opening the door.

"They're already going," I say, and he glances back at the smile in my voice.

"It's not funny."

"It's a little funny," I whisper, and he looks at me for a long moment before groaning.

"If you tell me this was a bad idea, I swear to—"

"It wasn't," I say. "I needed that." We both did if the frustration in his body is anything to go by. I sit up, and his eyes drop to my lips, but he quickly climbs over to his own seat, sitting back with a sharp exhale.

He looks like a mess. A delicious sexy mess. And I'm the cause of it. I'm almost flattered.

"I ruined your hair," I tell him as he rebuttons his shirt.

"I ruined yours."

I shrug, tucking it behind my ears. "Are we friends with benefits now?"

He tries and fails to hide his smile.

"What?" I demand.

"You say the weirdest things sometimes, you know that?"

"Is that a no?"

"I didn't say that. You want to be?"

"Could be complicated."

"Could be," he agrees. "We'd need to update our terms."

"I can't even remember our— No way." I gasp as he opens the dashboard compartment and takes out a familiar though now very crumpled cocktail napkin. "You do *not* still have it."

"Our extremely official contract?"

I pluck it from his hands, examining his neat handwriting.

"Number one," I read out. "No tongue."

"I don't remember that bit."

I hold out my palm. "Pen. I *know* you have one," I add when he just looks at me. He hands me one from his side pocket, and I smooth the napkin out, making a careful line through the words.

"*Some* tongue," I announce, adding in the correction.

"Much clearer."

"We'll figure it out." I put my seatbelt on as he pulls onto the road, reading through the rest of our terms. "We're pretty good at this."

"You think?"

"Yeah." The word is muffled by a yawn. "I think we should do it every year."

Christian goes quiet, his smile fading, and I rest my head back against the seat, letting my eyes drift shut in the darkness as he drives me home.

TWENTY-ONE

CHRISTIAN

I wake with a mini hangover the next morning, which, considering I didn't have a drop to drink, feels extremely unfair. It's much later than I'd usually get up as well, but I couldn't sleep when I got back, insomnia making me toss and turn until eventually I took out my laptop and got some work done. Now my phone tells me it's after ten, but you wouldn't know it by the light outside. Or rather, the lack of it. It's dark today, the sky an angry, ominous gray. The first thing I do is check my weather app, which tells me there's a thirty percent chance of light snow. The second thing I do is get a text from Megan.

> *My horrifically hungover mother requests your presence at lunch tomorrow. I believe a charcuterie board was mentioned.*

> **Hmm. Do friends with benefits do family lunches?**

> *They do if they want their brother's Christmas present. I'm almost finished.*

I sit up as she sends through a photo of a chunky navy sweater with snowflakes covering the front. It's perfect.

I added pom-poms to Molly's.

Even more perfect. It's become a bit of a running joke in our family how much Molly hates any kind of festive clothing. She always makes an effort when she's with us, like we'd care if she dressed up or not, but it's fun seeing how far we can take it.

I'll swing by later to collect.

And to see me.

And to see you.

And to bring me a little treat. For the sake of our ruse.

I grin, slumping back against the pillows as I type back. I have to admit I'm relieved. I thought for sure she'd wake up this morning regretting what happened last night, but if anything, she seems even more comfortable with what we have now than what we were before.

Friends with benefits.

It feels a little more than that. The softness of her skin is practically burned into my fingers. It was one of the hottest moments of my life, and we didn't even get that far.

We keep texting back and forth until she stops replying, and only then do I force myself up and out of bed.

I'm still tired as I make my way to the kitchen and find most of my family inside. Andrew's wearing an old Christmas sweater while Molly is dressed like a normal person. Hannah's texting on her phone, most likely with Daniela, judging by the smile on her face, and Mam stands over the stove, making eggs.

There's a chorus of hellos as soon as I enter, except from my mother, who takes one look at me and frowns.

"Are you coming down with something?"

"No?"

"You look like you're coming down with something."

"I'm not."

"Mam's right," Hannah says. "You look like shit."

"Well, you look like—"

"*Christian*," Mam warns, and I give up, taking a seat at the kitchen table.

Molly pushes a plate of toast toward me, and I shoot her a grateful look even as my stomach rebels at the thought.

Maybe I *am* coming down with something.

"I want you to invite Megan for dinner on Saturday," Mam says. "We're having the whole family around."

"You want the whole family around for dinner three days before Christmas?"

"She wants to practice vegan food," Andrew explains.

I sigh. "Mam, she's vegetarian, not vegan. Just don't slip a turkey leg into her potatoes, and she'll be fine."

"What about beef?" Andrew asks, as our mother flusters behind him. "Can she eat beef?"

"I'm not talking to you this morning."

"What about chicken?"

"Seriously, Mam," I say, ignoring him. "She wouldn't want you to go to too much effort. We're having lunch at hers on Saturday, anyway. She'll fill up there."

At this, Mam perks up. "You're having lunch with her family?"

"Well, with Emily," I say, highly doubtful that Aidan will show up.

Andrew lets out a low whistle. "Lunch with the mother. Things are getting serious."

Hannah finally puts her phone down, her expression intense. "Show me the pictures."

"Of what?"

"Of her *dress*."

"Her dress?" The main thing I remember about her dress was when I tugged down the bodice to suck on her—

"Preferably with her in it," Hannah says, tearing into a piece of toast as I take out my phone.

"I've only got a few," I say, showing her some pictures of Megan I took at the beginning of the night. "I'm sure she'll have more. I can ask her to—"

I'm cut off by Hannah's squeal as she grabs the phone from my hand. Molly immediately rushes to her side so they can look together.

"Oh wow," she says, squeezing Hannah's shoulder. "You did an amazing job."

"You have to let me make one for you now," she says, as Mam joins the little group. "I'm working on this satin pink slip that you'd look *perfect* in. Right, Andrew?"

"Right," he says, watching Molly with such an obvious puppy-dog expression that I have to kick him under the table.

They're supposed to go up to the cabin this afternoon, but whether he's popping the question today or tomorrow, I don't know.

"Have you told her yet?" I whisper, as the others continue to fawn over the dress.

"No," he says quietly. "She thinks we're just going out for a drive. I've got a bag packed for her in the car."

"Sneaky."

"I couldn't sleep. I kept dreaming I lost the ring."

"You'll be grand. She's going to say yes."

"I know. I just want it to be special."

I reach for the butter, trying not to smile too much. My big brother always was a big softie.

"The fundraiser went well then?" he asks.

"Yeah. Megan seemed happy."

"That's all that matters," Andrew says, as his eyes drift back to Molly.

"Alright," Mam says briskly. "Who's having eggs? Molly dear, thank you for that seasoning, but I've left it on the side just in case it's a bit too much for—"

She's interrupted as the doorbell rings, and Hannah stands so abruptly her chair almost topples over.

"Oh my goodness," she says loudly. "Who could that be?"

She doesn't wait for an answer as she runs from the room, leaving the rest of us to exchange blank glances.

"Do you think it's Santa?" Andrew asks Molly.

"Maybe. Or maybe it's— *Zoe*?"

As one, we turn to the figure in the doorway. It is Zoe. A very cold-looking Zoe wearing a hundred layers with a light dusting of snow on her head.

"What are you doing here?" Molly exclaims, as Hannah walks in behind her, carrying her bag with a smug look.

"Surprise!" she calls, as the two sisters hug.

"The traffic is awful," Zoe grumbles when they break apart. "An inch of snow and the country goes berserk."

"I think it's more than an inch, Zo," Molly says with a smile. "Where's Tiernan?"

"Oh, I got bored of him. I gave him to this nice lady at the bus stop." She takes off her coat, glancing around the room. "He's with Mam and Dad. Thought I'd come down and see you when they offered to babysit. Then I thought I'd make it a surprise. Hope that's okay, Mrs. Fitzpatrick," she adds to Mam, who looks like she just won the lottery. My mother loves nothing more than a full house.

"Are you staying the night? You can bunk with Christian."

"Oh, he'd love that," Zoe teases. "Unless he's too busy with the new girlfriend." Her eyes swing my way, full of trouble. "What was her name again? Mildred? Margaret?"

I smile in warning. "Megan."

"Megan!" She snaps her fingers. "That's the one. Your loving girlfriend, Megan. Is she here?"

"She'll be here for dinner on Saturday," Mam informs her. "You should join us."

"Unfortunately, I'm just around for the day," she says, finally leaving me be. "But I'll stay this evening if there's room?"

Mam nods, all business as she leaves for the dining room, probably to get out the good plates as opposed to the terrible bad plates her regular family uses.

"I was also hoping to take this one away for the next few hours," Zoe adds, turning to Molly, and Andrew, who had been smiling at the scene, immediately stops.

"I thought we could go shopping," she continues, as some twin communication happens between them.

"Yeah?" Molly asks.

"Yeah," Zoe says lightly, and they start grinning at each other, and now I'm very confused.

"Shopping?" Andrew asks.

Zoe nods. "Girls only."

"We actually have plans," Andrew says. Molly frowns at him.

"No, we don't. You said you just wanted to go for a drive."

"I know, but..." he trails off, and I can practically see the wheels turning in his head. "You also wanted to go."

"Can't we go tomorrow?"

"No."

"But—"

"We can't."

"Why not?"

"It's a surprise."

I kick him again, but this time he doesn't so much as flinch.

"What's a surprise?" Molly asks, as Zoe's attention flicks to me.

What? she mouths, but I just shake my head.

"Andrew—"

"I booked a cabin," he says before I can stop him. "One of Christian's ones. As a surprise. It's your Christmas present."

Silence in the kitchen.

Molly looks confused. "A cabin?" she asks. "Where?"

"In the woods."

"The *woods*?"

"Yeah?" He starts to sound nervous. "Why?"

Both sisters stare at him. And then Zoe tsks. Loudly.

"Woods freak me out," Molly tells him.

Andrew goes very still. "What?"

"They freak me out," she says. "You know that."

"No, I don't."

"Well, they do," she says, while Zoe nods.

"She saw a horror movie when she was a kid about this serial killer who lived in a forest?"

"Zoe—"

"He had this mask—"

"Okay," Molly says, holding her hands up. "I remember it, thank you."

Andrew doesn't respond, clearly panicking, while Hannah glances between us as though starting to realize she might have picked the wrong side in something.

"I think cabins are nice," she says pointedly, as loyal to the Fitzpatrick clan as ever. "You should do that instead."

The sisters share another look.

"Can we go tomorrow?" Molly asks Andrew again.

"Can't you?"

"No," Zoe says firmly. "I'm only here for the day." But she also looks worried. "I'm sorry, Andrew. I didn't mean to ruin your afternoon. I should have called ahead."

"You've got the place for two nights," I remind him before everyone can get miserable. "Make it a third and come back on Christmas Eve. There's no booking after you. Just go tomorrow."

He doesn't want to go tomorrow. Everyone knows he doesn't want to from the look on his face. But only I know it's because he's worried enough about something going wrong that this must be tipping him over the edge. But I also know he'd never deny Molly anything. And she hasn't seen her sister in months and clearly wants to spend the day with her. Basically, he doesn't have a choice.

"Sure," he says finally, forcing a smile on his face. "You're right. Of course, we can go tomorrow."

Molly comes over to kiss him, winding her arms around his neck. "Thank you for my present," she says. "It was very sweet of you."

"I know it was."

"I'll make it up to you," she says, her voice dropping to a low whisper. It's only because I'm sitting right beside them that I can even hear her. "I'll do that thing you like where I—"

"No," I say loudly as Hannah looks at them like it's the most romantic thing she's ever seen. "I'm eating."

"Go have fun," Andrew says. "But I get to ruin a day in Zoe's life of my choosing."

"Agreed," she says and turns back to her sister. "Just let me get dressed," she adds and grabs Zoe's hand to tug her up the stairs, leaving the three of us alone.

"What?" Hannah asks as soon as they're gone.

"Nothing," we both say. Because there's no way she can keep a secret.

"Something's going on," she insists, only to glare when we keep our mouths shut.

"I wish I had sisters," she grumbles and hurries after Molly and Zoe.

Andrew turns to me.

"So we're scrapping the cabin plan," he says, and I snort.

"Just ask her tomorrow."

"We're going to lose a whole night."

"From the sounds of it, she doesn't want to even be up there, anyway. How did you not know your girlfriend is afraid of the woods?"

"Because every day I learn something new about her, Christian. It's a blessing and a curse." His words are light, but he looks nervous as he runs a hand through his already messy hair. "I need you to go up there for me."

"Excuse me?"

"I ordered some special food that she likes on top of everything else. It's supposed to arrive this morning. It's just going to be sitting out there."

"It's a two-hour drive."

"What else are you doing?"

"What else are *you*?" I ask pointedly. "I'm spending the day with Megan."

"So, bring her too. Use the hot tub. I don't care. *Mi casa* is literally *su casa*."

"Andrew—"

"I've got to completely rethink everything I had planned and go to the bakery and tell them to delay the *Kvæfjordkake*."

"The what?"

"*Kvæfjordkake*," he repeats, completely serious. "It's Norwegian."

"*And*?"

"I don't know, Christian. It's a cake! It's her new favorite cake, and she found it last year, and she won't shut up about it, so I got the recipe online, and I brought it to the bakery, and they're making one for tomorrow at an extortionate price, but now I'll have to—"

"I get it."

"Please," he finishes. "I'll help you propose to Megan when it's your turn."

"If this is how you go about it, you're not helping me propose to anyone." But the more I think about it, the more I come around to the idea. A hot tub with Megan? A few hours, just the two of us? It's not the worst way to spend the day.

"Do you remember when Mam found your stash in the shed, and I convinced her it was Liam's?" Andrew continues.

"No, because you didn't convince her of anything. She didn't believe you."

"Yes, but I *tried*, and—"

"Okay," I interrupt. "I'll do it." And he looks so relieved that I pat him on the back. "It's going to be fine."

"I can't believe she's scared of the woods," he mutters, and rests his head against the table as I finish my breakfast.

I give Megan a call soon after, and though she's initially confused, she gets *very* excited about the mention of the hot tub and quickly agrees to the change of plans. We arrange to meet up later that morning, and I pack a change of clothes before heading down to the back room to work. It has the best Wi-Fi in the house and has become my unofficial office since Hannah's taken up the living room with her studying.

It's stuffy, though, or maybe it's just my head, and I crack open the window as I sit down, the chill keeping me alert as I check in with work. It's the longest I haven't been in the office since I started, and while I'm usually not bad at separating work from home life, it's a busy season, and there are only two junior people doing holiday cover.

It's not that I don't trust them, but I do feel responsible for them and sure enough, no sooner do I send a message telling them I'm around for the next while do I start getting forwarded some *didn't want to bother you but* emails that make the time fly by. It's another two hours before I get on top of things, and I'm wrapping up to go get Megan when heavy boots stomp down the hall.

"Working away, are you?"

My dad stops in the doorway, shaking off his coat.

"Still snowing?"

"It's light," he says. "But wanted to get the cows sorted just in case."

"Need some help?"

"It's all done," he says to my relief. He glances at my laptop, his expression unreadable. "Thought you were on your holidays."

"I'm just checking in."

"They're not working you too hard, are they?"

"Well, I'm the boss, so... no. I like my job," I add.

"There's a first."

Deep breaths, Christian. Deep, calming breaths.

"It's freezing in here," Dad adds, and I log off as he comes over to shut the window. He pauses halfway across the room, though, his eyes shooting to me suspiciously.

I tense, knowing instantly where his mind went. "I'm not smoking. I haven't had a cigarette in months."

"You shouldn't have started in the first place."

Jesus. I snap my laptop shut.

He doesn't like that either. "Where are you going?"

"To get Megan."

"You don't need to go just because I'm—"

"I'm not," I interrupt. "I'm not doing anything because of you. I told her I'd meet her in a few minutes, so that's what I'm going to do." And then, stupidly: "Wouldn't want to mess her around."

The words are a mutter, but he catches them anyway, his face falling as I stand and start gathering my things.

"Christian—"

"I'm going to be late."

"Now, hold on a second," he says, his face going pink as he rubs at his forehead.

"I don't have time for a talk."

"I'm not giving you a talk, but I think it would help if you stopped taking everything I say the wrong way."

"Well, maybe you could start by not assuming the worst of me every time I do anything."

"I don't assume the—"

"No?" My voice rises before I can stop it. "Sure feels like you do."

He doesn't deny it this time. "I'm just trying to understand you."

"What's there to understand? I've done every single thing I've been expected to do in my life, and you still think I'm a disappointment."

"I don't think you're a disappointment, I think you're unhappy."

"Unhappy?" No. "I'm not unhappy. Why would I be unhappy? I've got a promising career, a great apartment, a girlfriend who—" I cut myself off, swallowing the lie.

Dad's brow furrows at my silence, but I don't let him get a word in. "Who's going to be waiting in the snow if I don't get going," I finish. "I'm going to be late."

"Christian—"

"I've got to pick her up and help Andrew, and I've got six million emails to respond to, and my head is..." Pounding. It's pounding now. I'll have to stop off at the chemist in the village. I stuff my laptop into my bag, swinging it over my shoulder. "Your heating's fixed, by the way. Thought I'd forgo the gift voucher and get you a new boiler for Christmas. And I still maybe need to learn a lot of things, but at least I ask for help when I need it. I'll see you tonight."

"*Christian,*" he calls in his dad voice, but I ignore him, my chest tight as I head out of the house and away from him.

TWENTY-TWO

MEGAN

It's shaping up to be one of those Very Good days.

I mean, as if I would ever say no to a hot tub. *Yes, Christian, I will help you collect some food in exchange for spending a few hours in a luxury cabin I'd never be able to afford otherwise. I will make that sacrifice for* you. You're welcome.

That is to be my afternoon, and this morning I woke up to snow. Proper snow. Not crappy melty snow. No. This was a big white fairy-tale blanket of it. That coated the entire garden and came down for a good hour in thick white smudges that blotted out the entire sky. The news reports said it might stick around for Christmas Day and everything, which made me giddy and Mam worried, so I wasn't surprised when she asked Aidan and me to pick up a final few pieces in the shop before "people started losing the run of themselves."

I didn't mind, just packed a change of clothes and texted Christian to meet me in the village when he was ready. I want to take some pictures in the cabin, so I take my time getting ready, taking care with my hair and makeup until Aidan has to come and physically yank me from my room because he "doesn't have all day" even though he literally does.

He's in a bad mood. That much is obvious. I didn't hear him come home last night, and he slept in as usual, so the version of my brother who insists on driving is a grumpy silent one. One who doesn't like me attempting to make conversation or singing along, which is too bad for him because I love Christmas songs, which means I am singing along a *lot*.

"What's got you in such a good mood?" he finally asks halfway through "Wonderful Christmastime."

"What's got you in a bad one?"

"I'm not."

"You are."

He doesn't respond, his eyes darting to my knitting, where I sew on the final adjustments. I may have gone overboard with Molly's sweater, but I'm hoping that's the vibe Christian meant. "Who's that for?" Aidan asks.

"You," I lie, and he huffs. "You don't like it?"

"It's a bit much."

"It's for Andrew's girlfriend. Christian wanted it festive."

"Well, whatever he wants," Aidan mutters, and I almost laugh.

"Why are you trying to pick a fight with me?"

"I'm not."

"You *are*." I actually do laugh now, which seems to just make him madder. "Has this got anything to do with last night? Christian said you had *words* with him."

Aidan scowls. "He's such a snitch."

"I thought it was cute." He bats my hand away when I try to pinch his cheek. "My overprotective little brother. Every sister should have one."

"I will throw you out of this car," he grumbles.

"But then who will protect me? Who will— *Ow*." I glare at him as he flicks my arm, and rub it before it can bruise. "You don't have to worry about him, you know," I say more seriously. "We're just having fun."

Aidan doesn't respond. He doesn't respond for so long I don't think he's going to, and I'm scrolling through the playlist for another song when he finally opens his mouth.

"I guess he's not the worst."

"No?" I ask lightly, and he shrugs.

"He gets you."

I watch him for a few seconds, waiting for him to expand, but instead he changes tack entirely.

"I'm not doing this just because I'm home, you know."

"Doing what?"

He gestures vaguely with one hand. "This. You. I think about you guys all the time. Just because I'm away doesn't mean I don't."

"I know that," I say, bewildered. There's a stark look on his face I've never seen before, one I don't think he's even aware of because, otherwise, he'd never let me see it. "You know not to take Mam too seriously, right? When she asks about you moving home? She knows how hard you're working over there. We all do. It's a great opportunity."

"I know," he says, but he doesn't sound convinced. He doesn't act it either, just stares straight ahead like he's never been down this road before.

"But we'd be happy if you did," I say carefully. "Come home."

"And do what?"

"Whatever you want," I shrug. "There are jobs here. Maybe not with the same perks, but you'd get something good. Or you could work remotely. No one would think you'd—"

"Given up?"

I ignore that. "I'm just saying the option's there."

"It's a good job," is all he says. The words are automatic, and I force down a sigh. It's what people used to say to me about Isaac. *A good guy, Megan. He's a good guy.*

"So long as you're happy," I say. "But for the record, I wouldn't mind if you came back."

"Oh yeah?" he asks, and his lips curl in the first glimmer of a smile I've seen on him all day.

"I think I look better when you're here. Comparison-wise."

"Puts things in perspective, huh?"

"I'm just saying, you can't be the golden son if you're... oh, we should help." I sit up as I spy two figures hunched over the back of a stalled car up ahead. "*Aidan*," I warn when he doesn't slow down.

"I don't want to be stuck for thirty minutes in the cold."

"But it's alright if they are?"

"They're fine," he dismisses, as we pass them. "They've probably had a million people stop already."

"Then we'll be on our merry way when they tell us that," I say sharply, and he gives me a withering look but eventually slows and starts to reverse down the road.

Only when he pulls to a stop a few steps away, do I see whose car it is.

I spot Sophie first. It's hard not to with the shock of red hair under her hat. She gets out when we stop while one of the figures at the back straightens with a wave.

Cormac. Great.

"I'll stay here," I mumble, and Aidan sighs but thankfully doesn't push it.

"Two minutes," he says. And then, to the others, "Need a hand?"

A blast of cool air hits me as he gets out of the car before the outside world muffles as the door slams shut again. I turn off the music, feeling awkward as I watch them talk. Sophie glances over more than once but doesn't make any move to approach, and I don't want her to. I should have listened, and we should have kept going. I can already feel my spirits start to fall the longer I sit here, my good mood deflating like an old balloon.

And then it gets worse.

Isaac.

I freeze, watching him in the rearview as he dusts his hands free of snow and heads toward the others. He stills when he sees Aidan and then immediately looks to the car, meeting my gaze.

I fight the urge to duck down like a child, watching instead as he exchanges some terse words with my brother...

Before making his way toward me.

I groan softly, wishing I hadn't played the good Samaritan card because this should *not* be my reward, but I get out, meeting him with a polite smile.

He looks hungover.

The skin around his nose is an irritated red like he keeps rubbing it, and there are dark circles under his eyes. Maybe he didn't go to sleep last night.

Aidan doesn't move from where he stands with Cormac and Sophie, but nor does he take his eyes off me. It's only when I give him a nod that he leaves me be and, while he doesn't look happy about it, goes to help Cormac give the car another push.

Isaac watches them only briefly before focusing on me. "Can we walk for a bit?" He points to a small gap in the wall, one that leads to one of the many walking paths that dot the countryside around here. "Just for a second."

I don't want to.

I really don't want to.

But the others are doing their best to give us some privacy... and Isaac's already walking off, not waiting for my answer.

And just like I always used to do, I follow.

The ill feeling gets worse with every step, and the tips of my toes quickly get wet in the snow, but we don't go far, just a minute down the path toward the old castle ruins. It's usually a popular place for walkers, though today it's empty with the weather, leaving us alone.

"I'm sorry about last night," he says when we reach the

stone walls. "You were right to be, but I didn't mean to make you upset."

"That's okay."

"Aidan said you guys needed to get going, but I was actually going to swing by your house later, so this saves us both some time." He smiles at me, a polite, patient smile. "I wanted to make sure we were on the same page. About Natalie."

"What do you mean?"

"Just that..." His tone grows rueful. "Look, I'd had a few drinks. I was feeling particularly sorry for myself. I wanted to tell someone. Anyone."

"I get it," I say awkwardly. "Don't worry about it."

"Her dad's sick."

"Yeah, you said."

"Right. I just wanted to remind you in case..." He pauses like he's choosing his words *very* carefully. "In case you were thinking of sharing it with others."

And I realize at once what this is. "You think I'd tell them about you and Natalie breaking up?"

"I know you don't think much of me. But just know it would probably hurt her more than it would hurt me."

"I would never," I say, shocked he'd even think that. "Hang on, you think I want to *hurt* you?"

"Oh, come on, Megan. Is that not why you came back?"

My eyes go so wide they start to hurt. "I came back because Mam asked me to. I came back because my brother flew halfway across the world. I came back to spend Christmas with my family. Not to see you. I was doing everything I could to *avoid* just that."

"I didn't—"

"Not everything I do is about you!"

"*Alright*," he says. "Jesus. Lower your voice." His eyes skip back up the path, but there's no sign of anyone else. "I'm sorry," he says. "But can you blame me for being suspicious after what you put me through?"

And there it is. I stare at him as the real Isaac starts to peek through. The one I knew. The one I...

"What I put you through?" My voice sounds separate from my body, like I'm listening to someone else speak.

"Running from our wedding?" he reminds me, a hint of sarcasm peeking through. "Embarrassing me in front of our family and friends? You didn't even leave me a note."

"I didn't need to leave a note. You know why I left."

"Because you wanted to make a point."

"Because I couldn't stand you." And the quiet venom in the words is enough to freeze him to the spot. "Because I didn't love you. Because you're a manipulative asshole, and if I'd stayed, I would have been miserable."

He just looks confused now. "What are you talking about?"

"You took away my dream job," I say, and surprise flickers across his face. Surprise that makes me *furious*. "Did you think I wouldn't find out? You emailed them *as me* pulling me out of consideration, and you didn't think I'd notice? You really thought you'd just get away with it?"

His expression smooths into a blank kind of calm that I remember all too well. *Don't be silly, Megan. Don't be ridiculous.*

Calm down, Megan.

Calm down.

"I told you I was going to—"

"*No*," I say, my voice like a whip cracking through the air. "Don't you dare try and change what happened. Not now. Don't you *dare*."

"We'd discussed it," he says, his voice low and earnest. "We decided to—"

"*We* didn't do anything. You discussed it. You decided. I said I wanted to give it a go."

"You would have had to move to Dublin."

"I wanted to move! I wanted to try it! You were the one who didn't want to go. You wouldn't even consider it. I would have been three hours up the road, but you acted like I was moving to Siberia. Like I was leaving you."

"You had a job here."

"That I didn't give a shit about! And you knew that. You knew I was unhappy, but you didn't care. Because I always had to be the one to follow you."

"That's not true."

"Yes, it is. *Your* college, *your* apartment, *your* job. I had to mold my entire life around yours, and I couldn't go to the pub with my friends without running it by you first. I couldn't turn my phone off during a movie because I had to be in constant contact with you, and God forbid I didn't answer your text in five minutes, or you'd call me. I couldn't even wear this coat because you didn't like it and I love this coat. I *love* it." I jab my chest so hard it hurts, but I ignore the pain. I ignore everything but the man in front of me and the gall he has to still look me in the eye.

"I didn't know any better because that was all I knew," I say. "Because you told me you loved me, and I believed you. So did everyone else. You put on this face for your family and your friends, but you're not like that at all, are you? You're controlling, and needy, and you *lie,* and you never listened to me. You never even knew me, and I—"

My mouth slams shut as his attention darts over my shoulder and stays there. As if someone flicked a switch, his face goes so white you'd swear he was going to faint.

Already guessing what I'm going to find, I whirl around to see the other three standing a bit up the path, staring right at us.

But it's not them I focus on. That would be Christian, who looms behind them, a tight expression on his face.

Shit.

Shit.

There's a rushing in my ears, like a river in the distance, and even Isaac seems at a loss for words, his mouth opening and closing like a gaping fish.

Oddly, it's Cormac who speaks first. Cormac who's looking at his friend like he's never seen him before. "What the hell is she talking about?" he demands.

"She's not... she's..." Isaac's gaze bounces between the four of them like he doesn't know who to focus on or what to do. "Nothing," he says, a defensive note entering his tone. "She's just being dramatic."

A humorless laugh bursts out of me before I can stop it.

I just can't.

I can't deal with this. I can't deal with any of it.

Sophie straightens as I approach, a pained look on her face, but I brush by her, my heart beating so hard I feel like I'm going to throw up.

"I want to go," I say to Christian, who just looks at me. "*Now*," I plead, and march past him with a glance back at Aidan. Aidan, who's not looking at me, who's staring at Isaac with an expression I've never seen on him before. One that puts my "overprotective brother" comment into pale comparison.

My chest tightens at the sight, and I hurry back to the road and grab my bag from the back seat of Mam's car. Cormac's car is free from the snow and Christian's is parked a little way up. He must have stopped to help just like we did.

I make a beeline right for it, only vaguely aware of him following me.

"Megan," he calls, but I ignore him, waiting by the passenger door until he presses a button to unlock it. As soon as he does, I scramble inside.

"Please just drive," I say when he joins me a moment later. "Please don't say anything and just drive."

"Are you seriously running away from this?"

"I'm *trying* to," I say pointedly.

"You need to go back there and tell them everything that—"

"No."

"Why not?"

"Because I don't want to!" I exclaim, and put my seatbelt on. Because I'm angry and embarrassed and the one thing about coming home I didn't want to happen just did. "I was fine," I continue, the words as frantic as my feelings. It's like a dam burst and everything's spilling out. "I was perfectly happy before this. Before coming back here and before—"

You.

I bite my tongue before I can say the word, but from the look on his face, he knows exactly what it was.

"I was doing *fine*," I say, and my voice breaks on the last word. "Can we just go?"

"I think you need to—"

"I don't care. I don't care what you think. We're not really together, remember? So you don't get to advise. You don't get to do anything."

I clutch my bag to my lap, staring straight ahead, and ignoring the weight of his gaze on me. We stay like that for a full five seconds before he shuts the door, and a moment later, the car reverberates to life around me. His movements are choppy and frustrated, and I probably went too far, but I don't care. My emotions are swinging so wildly right now I'm not even attempting to understand them.

"I'll drop you home," Christian says, and my head whips toward him.

"You said I could come to the cabin."

"That was before—"

"Before nothing."

"You can't just keep ignoring what happened between you two," he tries again. "What he did."

Watch me.

"Can we please just go to the cabin?" I ask, my voice significantly calmer than before. He doesn't move for a long moment, and I think he's going to stay or argue with me some more or both. But he doesn't. He just takes a breath and puts the car in gear, his expression wiping clean as he drives us off into the snow.

TWENTY-THREE

CHRISTIAN

Megan simmers the entire drive up. I know she does because she doesn't talk to or even look at me other than to glare when I get annoyed at some idiot driver. She just sits there, angry-knitting. I don't know if angry-knitting is a thing, but I'm coining the phrase now because I've never seen her work those needles so fast. And I'm fine with it. Silence is good. Silence also lets me simmer. Also lets me stay mad. Or at least it does for the first thirty minutes, and then I'm just confused as to how she makes me so mad in the first place.

I've had fights with girlfriends before. Real girlfriends, anyway. Snapping ones, yelling ones, slamming bedroom door ones. You work stressful jobs in stressful cities, and you're bound to take it out on those closest to you. But it was always on their end. I never yelled. I never slammed. Never. It wasn't in my nature.

Or maybe I just didn't care enough.

But right now? I care. Maybe it's the headache or the run-in with my dad. Maybe it's the fact that something so simple as being in the same place as Megan usually cheers me up except for now.

But I guess I shouldn't be surprised. Ever since I bumped into her, she's had a habit of making me feel things I didn't normally. The only thing that irks me more is that I don't seem to have the same effect on her.

So we drive in silence. There's barely any traffic, and none at all when we start traveling up the mountains. The snow on the roads gets progressively worse as we do, the higher ground and fewer people making them more difficult to get through, but if this is as bad as it gets then we can manage. I'm only planning to stay a few minutes tops anyway. I think the best thing to do is to put the stuff away and get going, maybe find a pub some-where on the way back where we can have some privacy and hash this out between us, but that little plan goes flying out the window when we get stuck halfway up an incline, the car refusing to budge another inch.

I curse as the engine makes a noise I don't like, and Megan's fingers pause briefly before she continues knitting again. After a few seconds of trying and failing to restart it, I get out and round the hood to find the snow too deep to get any farther.

We're jammed in.

I straighten, glancing through the windshield, but Megan's so focused on her work that I have to knock on the passenger window before she realizes something's up.

"Car's stuck," I tell her when she rolls it down. "I'll be able to get us out for the way down, but we're going to have to walk the rest of the way."

"*Walk?*"

"It's just around the bend."

Still, she looks troubled. "I'm not in the right shoes."

"So wait here. I won't be long."

"But—"

"We don't have to stay, okay? I just need to put the food in the fridge."

"The world is a fridge," she mutters, and while I agree with her, I don't like the thought of it sitting out on the porch.

"I'll be ten minutes tops," I promise and take off up the slope, but I'm barely a few feet away before I hear a thump and a muffled curse. Turning, I find Megan sprawled face down in the snow, one of her shoes stuck in a lump of it.

"Don't say anything," she warns, pushing herself into a sitting position.

"You mean like how I told you to—"

"I know," she grumbles, as I help her to her feet. She tugs her boot free and shoves it back on. "But I need to use the bathroom," she says, dusting off her clothes. "So if we can just—Christian!"

She shrieks as I lean down, sweeping her into my arms.

"Put me down!"

"You're just going to slip again."

"I'm not arguing with you on that point, but you don't need to carry me."

"How else are you going to get up the hill?"

"With great caution," she says, glancing back at the car as I start walking. "Christian. I'm serious."

"So am I." And it's not that big of a walk or that steep of a hill. A minute of hiking and I spy the property between the thick trees, the triangular slope of the cabin's roof peeking out over the top.

Megan remains tense against my chest as I speed up, her hands in a rigid grip around my neck as if convinced I'm going to drop her.

"Where are we even... Oh my God."

And just like that, I'm so smug you'd swear I built the thing.

Megan peers up at the two-bedroom, eight-hundred-euro-a-night log cabin with her mouth agape. The pictures of it on our website feature it in the summer, with sunny blue skies and the firepit out front. But it looks just as nice in the snow too. Better even.

Maybe I should get Andrew to take some pictures when he's up here.

Megan clears her throat. "When you said *cabin*..."

"What part of luxury rentals do you not understand?" I ask, my mood lifting as I bring her up the driveway and to the front door. It's a huge wooden slab with floor-to-ceiling windows on either side, and in front of it lie several boxes of food and drinks. Most of it looks nonalcoholic, with Andrew being sober, but I spy a few bottles of wine meant for Molly.

"Just how much did he order?" Megan asks, as I set her to her feet.

"He likes to overprepare." And at least it's here. When I didn't see any tracks from the delivery guys, I assumed they got stuck in the snow the same as we did, but they must have come early enough this morning when it wasn't so bad.

I unlock the front door and let Megan inside before turning to inspect the packages. I've just heaved the first one up when she calls me tentatively inside.

"Um... Christian?"

"There should be a bathroom on the ground floor."

She doesn't respond, and I adjust the weight of a box simply labelled DESSERT (1 OF 3) as I follow her in. "Next to the kitchen," I say when I spy her in the foyer. "Could you help me check what needs to be put in the..."

She turns to face me, her eyes wide, but my attention is on the scene behind her, and the reason for her silence.

We're standing in what should be the showpiece of the entire property, a large, open-plan living room that takes up most of the entire ground floor. Low couches and armchairs all face the stone fireplace on the left-hand side and a small bar takes up the back wall, right next to the towering bookshelves.

It's supposed to radiate rustic elegance and cozy comfort.

And it would do if it weren't for the fact that it's been completely trashed.

"Did someone break in?" Megan asks in a hushed voice. I can see why that would be her first guess. Discarded food wrapping, dirty plates, and even a broken glass or two litter the space, along with a wine stain over half the rug.

I shake my head, lowering the box to the floor. "No, they... no." The door was locked, and the room is warm enough that I can guess no windows are broken. "It must have been the previous guests. They left yesterday."

"Do you not have a cleaning crew between visits?"

"We do," I say, confused. "Usually. I was working this morning. No one flagged any issues." But as soon as I say it, I realize what must have happened. Like a slow-motion movie playing in my head, I see myself booking Andrew's accommodation, bypassing our usual system to add in the perks. The usual system, which would have scheduled something in automatically. Which I didn't.

"Shit," I mutter, but Megan doesn't seem to hear me, wandering farther into the mess.

"Guests actually leave places like this?"

"You'd be surprised." Bitterness fills me as I look around. The more I do, the worse it seems, and I kick a McDonald's bag out of the way, wrinkling my nose at the smell. We get this a lot. People don't care about paying a deposit because they have the money to do it. All cash and no decency. But seeing it firsthand is something else.

"Can you get someone up?"

"In the next few hours, this close to Christmas?"

My head is really starting to pound now, the dull pain from this morning increasing tenfold, but I can't let Andrew bring Molly here with the place like this.

"Okay," I say, pinching the space between my brows as

though trying to force the pain away. "Okay, I just need to—What are you doing?"

Megan dumps her coat on the stairs and starts rolling up her sleeves. "What do you mean? We need to clean up."

"You don't have to help," I tell her. "I can—"

"Of course, I'll help," she says, sounding insulted. "I just need to pee first. Are there supplies here?"

Something warm flares in my chest until it becomes almost painful to look at her.

And that's it.

Her standing there in snow-soaked jeans pushing all her anger and hurt to the side to help me. Her with her hands on her hips and her smudged mascara from rubbing her eyes in the car.

Something changes in that moment, and all of a sudden I wish I'd never thought of this plan. I wish I could go back to her apartment that first night and sit on her couch and kiss her like she should always be kissed. Like how she should be right now. And there'd be no pretending about it.

"Christian," she says when I don't answer, and I clear my throat.

"Yeah. Should be. Not much, but—"

"We'll make do," she says, and takes one look around the room before disappearing down the hall. A second later, I hear a door snap shut.

I sigh and strip off my own coat, ignoring how my skin now aches with every brush of my clothes, and head back outside for the rest of the food.

————

It takes us three hours.

Three long hours.

Once I get past the initial shock, I realize the place isn't that bad. But we don't know our way around or where anything is, so it takes time to go through everything.

We tidy up all the trash first and then open the windows and doors despite the cold to try and air the cabin out. I clear the fireplace while Megan removes any cushions with stains on them. She catalogs each one without me even asking, taking pictures to aid in all my paperwork later. Upstairs is in better order. They must not have been doing much sleeping as one of the bedrooms is untouched, and the other just needs the bed to be stripped. Leftover toiletries are discarded, and we wipe the (thankfully) mostly clean bathrooms down before setting all the furniture back in place.

And all the while, my skin grows tighter, and my brain grows fuzzier, and despite the odd answer to a question or to tell her what to do, Megan doesn't say a word to me, lost in her own head.

But she does help. Diligently and without a word of complaint, she helps me put everything back in order, so that by the time darkness falls, it looks just like it should.

It's late by the time I put the final load of washed and dried towels into the cupboard upstairs, and when I head back down, it's to find Megan standing by the window in the front room, gazing out at the falling snow. She's put on one of her knitted sweaters, a giant dark green thing that dwarfs her, but that she must love judging by how worn it looks. She might as well be back in the ball gown for all I care. I could still look at her all night. And that's what I'm doing for a good minute before I realize I am, and I make a point of being extra loud as I come down the final few steps.

"It's really coming down out there," she says when I approach. "Probably too late to use the hot tub, huh?"

"You can try it, but if you blow away, I'm not running after you." I join her at the window, and she turns to face me. "I'm sorry," I say. "About earlier. You're right. I overstepped, and it wasn't my place."

"Christian..." She sighs, looking miserable. "You don't need to apologize. I was just upset. *I* should apologize for snapping at you."

"Yeah, you really hurt my feelings."

Her eyes shoot to mine, concerned for a second before she sees I'm joking. When she does, some of the tightness leaves her expression. Not much. But some. "You're trying to make me feel better again."

"I can't help it."

"It had nothing to do with you," she continues. "You know that, right? I'll be grand by tomorrow. I promise."

"You mean for dinner?" I shake my head. "I'm not worried about that."

"Well, don't worry about lunch. Mam's half in love with you after last night."

"I'm worried about *you*."

"You don't need to be," she says softly. "I'm not backing out."

"I don't mean the—" I break off, frustration building. "I don't give a shit about that anymore, okay?"

"But I agreed to—"

"I think what we agreed to pretty much went out the window after your mother's party," I say, and her cheeks go pink. "Don't tell me you're getting shy now."

"*No*," she says pointedly, even as her blush deepens. "But we should probably talk about that."

"We did."

"I mean *actually* talk about—" Her mouth slams shut as I step even closer, leaving only inches between us. "That's cheating."

"How is that cheating?"

"Because you smell nice."

"What?"

"You smell really nice all the time and— stop *laughing*." She groans as I ignore her, and this time, I wrap my arms around her. She goes willingly, resting her forehead against my chest. "It's been a bad day," she mutters.

"I know."

"A really, really bad day."

I tighten my hold, feeling her warmth through the thick wool of her sweater.

"But this is nice," she adds quietly, and I have to agree. I don't know how I never noticed it before. How she fits so perfectly against me. The top of her head reaching the bottom of my chin, her soft body sinking against mine.

I don't know how long we stand there like that, but I swear even the pain in my head eases. And I wonder how the hell am I going to explain what I'm feeling to her, when I don't even know it myself, when a shrill ringing sound cuts through the silence, making us both stiffen. Megan breaks away.

"That's your phone," she says when I don't move, and I fight back a sigh.

"Stay right there," I tell her, as I fish it out of my coat pocket. It's Zoe.

"You have bad timing," I say to her while holding Megan's gaze.

"Well, you have bad— *Molly*! Get back in the car."

I frown as a sharp wind blusters over the line, along with the faint sound of people yelling.

"Are you guys okay?"

"No. Well, yes but no. Extra no because Molly's made an arch enemy with the man behind us and she keeps—" A car horn blasts somewhere nearby, cutting off her words. Zoe curses sharply in my ear, and a second later, I hear a thump as she closes the car door.

"There," she says on an exhale. "Right. So. Super fun update: we're stuck."

"Stuck where?"

"On the road back from town with seemingly every car in Ireland. It's bumper to bumper. Can you tell your Mam we won't be at yours for dinner? And that we'll probably die out here?"

"Zoe!" I hear Molly hiss.

"Or that we'll be another few hours at least. Christmas traffic and snow. The perfect combination."

"That's shit," I say. "Are you guys alright?"

"We're fine, honestly. Just annoyed. Everyone okay there?"

"I wouldn't know," I tell her. "I'm not home either. Andrew sent me up with Megan to get things ready."

"You're at the cabin?" She sounds bewildered. "But what about the storm?"

"What storm?"

Megan yelps as the window beside us shakes, the glass shuddering violently as a flurry of wind and snow smashes against it.

That storm.

"Do *not* drive in this," Zoe continues. "It's chaos out here and it hasn't even got to us yet." There's a muffled conversation and then she comes back on. "Okay, new plan. You call your Mam, and Molly will call Andrew and then thoughts and prayers, I guess."

"*Zoe*," Molly snaps.

"Talk soon!"

I leave Zoe to deal with her sister while I rejoin Megan at the window.

"Holy crap," she whispers, as the wind continues to howl. "Is it supposed to be like that?"

"Maybe it's because we're so high up." I check my phone to confirm, seeing the weather alert pop up. "Or maybe not."

"How bad?"

Very. But I just shrug, playing it down at the worried furrow of her brow. "Enough that I don't think we're getting out of here tonight."

"I don't even want to try," Megan says, peering out at it. "Do you have signal?"

"For now."

Our eyes meet and I know we're both on the same page.

"Can we sleep here?" she asks. "Let everyone know?"

"It shouldn't be a problem," I say, thinking it through. "I'll see what time Andrew wants to come up, but we'll need to be gone by nine if we want to make lunch with your mother."

"That should be okay."

We both speak at once.

"The front bedroom should be big enough for both of—"

"I guess I'll just choose a room and—"

"Yeah, great," I say quickly, smiling too wide. "Pick away. Ladies' choice."

Megan frowns. "What were you going to—"

"Nothing. Same thing."

She hesitates but doesn't push me on it. "Okay," she says slowly. "I guess I'll see you tomorrow then?"

I nod, still smiling like an idiot and stay right where I am as she grabs her bag from the hall and disappears up the stairs.

Smooth.

TWENTY-FOUR

MEGAN

I'm ready at nine a.m. the following day. I'm ready before that, but I don't want to be too desperate, so I wait in my bedroom, and scroll through my phone before going down the stairs an acceptable ten minutes before I'm supposed to.

I'm weirdly nervous. I'm not saying I *expected* a knock on my bedroom door last night, but I wasn't not expecting it either. I might have fallen asleep waiting for it. I might have woken up twice thinking I'd heard it. But there was no knock. There was nothing. Because I am reading into things.

Christian's a protector. I get that. It's why he looked after me in the pub. It's why he walked me home. And yesterday when he saw me with Isaac, his brain went *damsel* and *distress,* and he did what he could to make me feel better. And that's it. Which means I have to stop second-guessing every look and get my head in the game.

We still have to get through Christmas. And now I'll have to deal with Sophie and Aidan on top of that. So as soon as Christian comes down those stairs, I'm going to be polite and friendly, and we're going to continue on like nothing's changed.

Except that nine a.m. comes and goes, and he doesn't appear.

I give him some leeway, even though he's Mr. On Time, but when five, then ten minutes pass, I grow restless. I text him at nine fifteen and get no answer. At nine twenty, I get annoyed.

"Christian?" I stand at the bottom of the staircase, staring up it as I call his name.

There's no answer.

Nothing but silence and the rustle of my coat as I shrug out of it, already sweating in the warm house.

I hang it on the banister and try again.

"Christian?"

Nothing.

Fine.

I march back up the stairs and down the short hallway to his room.

"Hello?" I knock and fall quiet, straining to hear any noise on the other side. "I'm coming in, so don't be naked."

The handle opens easily under my touch, and I poke my head in to see a small but nicely decorated room. I barely noticed it when I did my initial tour of the house, but this one is actually nicer than the bedroom I picked, with views over the tall trees in the back and big windows that lead onto a small balcony. There's an en-suite to my right and a large closet to my left and a king-sized bed pushed up against the wall.

Christian's lying in the middle of it with the covers pulled up to his chin. He doesn't stir when I step inside.

Is he asleep?

Drunk?

Dead?

I creep around the bed, eyeing him warily. The curtains are drawn back, meaning he either got up this morning or didn't pull them closed last night. His phone lies charging on the table beside him, and a change of clothes lie neatly folded next to his duffle bag like he started packing halfway through and gave up.

"Christian?" I move around to his side of the bed until I can see him properly and stop as soon as I do.

The man is asleep. He's actually asleep.

I click my tongue off the roof of my mouth, exasperated, and check the time again. We're definitely going to be late now.

"Get up," I say, grabbing his bag and shoving the rest of his clothes inside. "Christian."

There's a noise halfway between a grunt and a groan, but I take it as acknowledgment.

"I thought you said you were an early bird," I grumble but pause when he turns over onto his back, his eyes still closed. I can see his face better now, including the faint sheen of sweat covering his skin, like he's just gone for a run. He doesn't look like he's come back from a brisk five miles, though. He looks awful. He also doesn't make another sound, even though I'm making enough noise that he has to know I'm there.

I abandon the bag as I go back over to his side.

"Christian?" This time I say his name gently, and when he still doesn't answer, I drop to my knees beside him and give him a proper shake. He doesn't open his eyes, but his forehead twists into the most god-awful frown, which might be funny if I wasn't so worried.

"What the hell, Meg?" he grouses, and I blink at the familiar nickname. He must have heard Aidan use it.

"Are you okay?"

"I'm fine. I just have a headache."

Or a fever. I press my hand against his forehead to make sure, and he leans into it, the frown lines smoothing as he seeks my touch.

"Keep that there," he mumbles.

"You don't have a temperature." But he does look pale.

I sit back, ignoring his noise of protest when I stop touching him, and glance over my shoulder as the sun streams through the window.

"Go back to bed," he says. "It's early."

"It's not early. We were supposed to be on the road thirty minutes ago."

He doesn't answer, and I twist back to him, finally admitting what's staring me right in the face.

"You're sick."

He cracks open an eyelid, peering at me blearily. "I'm fine."

This time when I press a hand against his forehead, he turns away because, apparently, being told you're ill is the worst thing you can say to a man.

"I'm not sick," he says into his pillow. "It's just a headache."

"Or a migraine," I tell him. And a bad one at that. The man looks like he's at death's door, and disappointment crashes through me when I realize what that means.

"There's no way we'll be home for lunch."

"Don't be stupid," he grumbles. "You want to go home? I'll take you home."

"Christian—"

"I'm up. See?" He shifts in the bed, trying to get the covers off, and I quickly push him back down.

"You need to rest," I tell him. "You can't drive us back like this, and I can only drive automatic. We'll go back after lunch if you're feeling better, and if you're not, I'll get Andrew to come up and collect us."

"Just tell him to come get me now."

"So you can throw up a million times in the car back? How are you even going to get down the stairs?"

"I'll walk."

"Oh yeah? Lift your head for me."

"What?"

"Lift your head."

He glares up at me but otherwise doesn't move other than a weak twitch that was probably all the effort he could give.

Christ.

"You need water and rest," I say. "You're just going to be miserable if you have to travel right now. Believe me. Give it the morning."

"Megan—"

I put my hands on my hips, staring down at him until he sighs.

"Yeah, okay."

"I'm going to get you some painkillers and something to eat."

"I'm never eating anything ever again."

"You have to eat."

"I beg to disagree."

He turns his body away from me in a real *can't see you, can't see me* move, but I'm already leaving him, heading back down to the kitchen, where I throw some plain crackers onto a plate and grab a large mixing bowl and some kind of fruity sports drink. I add them all to a tray I find next to the sink and carry them back up along with a glass of water.

Christian hasn't moved an inch when I return, and he watches with groggy eyes as I set everything on the bedside table.

"What's the bowl for?" he asks.

"It's in case you throw up."

I might as well have told him he was going to die. "This isn't happening."

"You might not," I say. "Can you sit up?"

"Of course, I can sit up," he says hotly. But he doesn't. I bite back a smile.

"You're like a kitten," I tell him as I ease a pillow under his neck. "Like a little newborn kitten."

"Megan."

My name is a warning, but I'm having far too much fun with him like this. I wish he wasn't feeling like shit, but knowing how embarrassed he'll be when he gets better makes it very funny to me.

"You shouldn't even be in here," he says, as he pops the two pills into his mouth. "You'll get sick too."

"You can't catch a migraine, genius."

"I might have the flu," he points out. "If I have the flu, then you'll get the flu. That's how viruses work."

"Except I get my flu shot every year," I say sweetly. "And you don't have the flu because, believe me, you wouldn't be talking to me right now if you did. I know it sucks, but in all seriousness, you just need to rest and let me look after you."

"Don't look at me at all," he mutters. "If I look how I feel, I don't want you looking at me."

"I like looking at you," I say absently, and he goes very, very still. "I mean—"

I rear back as he sits up, his expression carefully blank.

"What are you doing?" I ask.

"I need a shower."

"You need to lie down."

"I feel like my skin is made of sweat and pain, and if I'm going to sleep away the whole morning like you want me to, then I'd like to do it feeling more like myself."

He sits at the edge of the mattress for a long second and then pushes himself up, swaying slightly. Besides a T-shirt, he's only in boxer shorts. Black, silky boxer shorts that my eyes are immediately drawn to as he staggers over to his bag and pulls out a sweater. When he heads to the bathroom next, I follow, concerned he might be weaker than he looks. But my caring nurse act must be edging into hovering because he makes it to the door in one piece before turning to face me.

"You want to help me in the shower or—"

"I'll tidy up out here," I blurt, and he smirks as he closes the door.

I wait until I hear the water turn on, and only when I'm sure he hasn't fallen over and *died* do I get to work opening the window for some fresh air and organizing the stuff I brought up earlier. As I do, my attention strays to the bed and before I know what I'm doing, I start stripping the covers off. Fresh sheets. Everyone loves fresh sheets.

I know from my rooting that there's spare linen in the cupboards, and by the time Christian comes out again, I'm wrestling with the corners.

"You don't need to do that," he says as soon as he sees me.

"It's fine."

He watches me finish with a slightly glazed look in his eye, which is how I *know* he's sick because a non-sick Christian would have made a joke and batted me away before doing the job perfectly, but instead, he just stands with his shoulders slumped like some kind of normal person.

When I'm done, he takes a few shuffling steps over and falls onto the mattress with a dull thud. "Smells like clean," he mutters.

"That's good." I give him a light shove to make him roll over and then drape the sheet over him. I've got more blankets by the side of the bed, but I don't know if he'd be too hot or too cold or if it's like in the movies where he says he's cold, but really, he's roasting and yeah... I would not make a good nurse.

"I'll leave you to get some rest," I tell him when his eyes close, but I've barely said the words when his hand shoots out, finding mine with unnerving accuracy where it rests on the mattress beside him.

"Or you can stay."

"You need to sleep."

"I'll sleep," he says, the words so muffled I can barely make them out. "I'm just saying you can stay. If you want to."

If I want to.

"Okay," I say, and his grip loosens enough to let me go. I tell myself it's fine. I'd just be coming in here to check on him every two minutes, anyway.

There's a large armchair in the corner of the room, and I drag it closer to the bed. I'll wait until he's asleep before I go and get my knitting, but for now, I just sit there, folding my legs under me as I watch his chest rise and fall.

It's only then I realize I forgot to close the blinds. The sunlight still streams through the windows, hitting him right in the face, and I stand, annoyed with myself but not sure if he wants them like that or not.

"Christian? Do you need me to..." I trail off, as a soft snore is my answer.

He's out like a light.

TWENTY-FIVE

CHRISTIAN

I wake to disorientation.

And a really dry mouth.

There's an ache in my neck from sleeping strangely and a stiffness in my limbs that makes it difficult to move, but I no longer feel like my head is being hit by a mallet, so I guess that's something.

I blink my eyes open, grateful, when I spy a glass of water on the bedside table. I'm even more grateful when I'm able to reach for it like a normal person. I sit up carefully, testing my body, and then drink the whole thing in three gulps, eyeing the dull daylight outside. The sight of it is a relief. I must not have slept that long if it's still bright. I must have just—

I freeze as the sheets shift around my legs, suddenly aware of another presence in the bed, and look down to see Megan curled into a ball beside me, a small patch of drool on her pillow.

Huh.

She's on top of the covers, in thick cotton leggings, and a navy T-shirt. She's also fast asleep and looks like she has been for a while.

I ease myself out of bed, draping the sheet over her legs before I reach for my phone. Two p.m. I must have slept through the whole morning, which means definitely no lunch with her mother. We probably won't even make it back for dinner with mine.

There are a few messages waiting for me, along with a dozen emails, but I decide to deal with them later as I head to the bathroom, glancing out the window to check the... avalanche?

I hesitate, staring out at the blanket of snow in case my eyes are playing tricks on me.

Okay, not an avalanche. But it's not just snow either. It's a lot of snow. A lot more snow than was there last night.

Not wanting to open the balcony door in case I wake Megan, I instead turn back to the room. My clothes have been packed haphazardly into my bag, but I don't even care about the creases as I throw on the first things I find and slip into the hallway.

My body is still a little slow, and there's a hollowness in my stomach that tells me I definitely missed breakfast. We could stop somewhere on the way back before dinner, but even as I'm planning out the rest of our day, I know deep down that none of it is going to matter. Not with what I feel I'm about to open the door to.

With grim resignation, I shove my feet into my boots, grab my coat, step outside, and immediately pause.

Yeah. We're not going anywhere.

At least not anytime soon.

It's not like the snow is above my head or anything, but it's heavy, and I'd definitely have to dig out the car.

I visited Andrew in Chicago last year and grumbled the entire time at how well-equipped the city was to handle its weather. We have nothing like that here. And even if they did get the roads cleared, they'd focus on the main ones first. Not up the mountains.

It's a shame because if I weren't so annoyed by it, I'd find it beautiful. It blankets the driveway in a thick white sheet, looking like something out of a children's book from long ago. Untouched by nothing except what looks like a fox's footprint circling the house.

Somewhere in the trees, a bird calls to another, and I take a deep breath, filling my lungs with the fresh air as I linger on the porch. You can't hear the traffic all the way up here. You can't hear anything.

I stand there until the cold gets too much, at which point I return inside, shrugging off my coat as I head back upstairs to wake Megan. As it is, I barely hit the landing before she bursts out of the bedroom, stumbling to a halt when she sees me.

"What are you doing?" she asks, her voice still raspy from sleep. "You shouldn't be up."

"I'm fine. I think I slept it off."

"Slept it off?"

"Yeah," I say, confused. She's acting like I was a step away from death and not just spending a few hours recovering from a headache. "Look, I don't think we're going to make it back in time for dinner."

She just stares at me. "Dinner?"

"With my family," I remind her. "We've already missed lunch. Did you call your Mam?"

"I... Yes, but—"

"I'm going to text Andrew. See if he still wants to come up here or wait until—"

"Christian." She rubs her face, looking confused. "It's Christmas Eve."

"What?"

She steps in front of me when I try and go past, blocking my path. "It's the twenty-fourth of December," she says, and I pause, taking her in properly for the first time. Taking in everything.

The snow outside. Megan in her pajamas. The way my body still feels like I ran a marathon.

"Of what year?"

"I'm being serious," she says, clearly in no mood for jokes. "You slept for a whole day!"

"I think I'd remember if it was that long."

"How could you? You were out of it. You'd wake up, take some painkillers, complain, and go back to sleep."

"For a whole day?"

"More or less," she says, rubbing one eye. It's only then I notice how frazzled she looks. Her hair is a mess, half falling out of her scrunchie, and there are deep pillow grooves on her cheek.

"You looked after me for a whole day?"

Her expression turns wary. "What was I supposed to do? You had a migraine, not the plague. And you're probably still recovering from it. Please get back into bed."

"I need a shower and shave," I say instead, feeling a pang of hunger for the first time. "And breakfast."

"You *need* to rest," she says. "At least for a few hours. I told your Mam we'd be back after lunch, and I still need to— What?" she asks, suddenly wary when she sees my expression.

"That's what I was coming up to tell you," I say. "I don't think we're going to get on the road today. Looks like it snowed pretty heavily last night. We're not getting that car free."

She huffs, not believing me, but when I just stand there, she whirls around, storming back into the bedroom, where she comes to an abrupt stop.

"Did you think I was lying?" I ask, as I follow her to the window.

"What the hell?"

"It was forecast."

"Not this much," she says, staring out at the snow. "What are we going to do?"

"Stay here." I shrug. "Even if we can dig out the car, the roads will be blocked. We're halfway up a mountain."

"That doesn't mean they can't clear the roads."

"No, but not this quickly. It will probably take them a few days."

"Days?"

I pause at the hint of panic in her tone. "We're fine here," I say slowly, but she doesn't seem to be listening, her eyes darting around the scene outside like she's looking for an escape.

"What if there's a power cut?"

"Why would there be—"

"Because of the snow," she snaps. She opens the sliding door, heedless of the cold, and steps out onto the balcony.

"If there's a power cut, we've got a working fireplace and a shed full of chopped wood," I remind her. "As well as enough food and drink to last us two weeks."

"But what if—"

"Here's what I think is happening," I interrupt, as her voice climbs higher. "And please tell me if I'm wrong. But I think you're freaking out about the storm, and understandably experiencing some form of claustrophobia, and now you're looking for the worst possible outcome wherever you can. Yes, we're stuck. But it will be a day or two at most. We have plenty of food and plenty to do. We'll be fine."

"But—"

"If you really want to go, we can go. It's not going to be easy to get out, and we'll need help, but we're not trapped here. We can leave whenever we want to, and it's not like no one knows where we are."

Her lips press together, but she looks mollified. "We can call someone if we need to?"

"We can," I promise. "We can do it right now."

But she's already shaking her head. "I don't want to ring the emergency services for something like this," she says. "They'll be busy enough as it is."

She stares out at the trees, tapping her finger against her arm as she thinks. If she wants me to get her home, I will. I'll get myself suited and booted and hike down the mountain until I can find someone to come out to us.

I just really wish she doesn't.

"We're going to miss Christmas," she says eventually.

"According to who?" I ask. "We've got movies. We've got food. People spend a lot of money to have Christmas here, and we get to do it for free."

"Only because Andrew's paid for all this stuff."

"And he's not going to be using it." Plus, I'll just pay him back, anyway. Now that the idea is in my head, it feels too good to let go. "Come on. You're telling me you don't want to try the hot tub?"

She crosses her arms even as she starts to smile. "I feel like you're one step away from giving me puppy-dog eyes."

"I'm not above them," I say. "But it's up to you, Meg."

Her expression softens at the nickname, and I know I've got her. "How are you okay with this?" she asks. "You wanted Christmas dinner with your family. I was going to big you up, remember?"

"Nah," I say. "What I wanted was to have a good Christmas."

And I have a feeling that's exactly what I've gotten.

TWENTY-SIX

MEGAN

"Let me get this straight," Frankie says. "You're trapped in a luxury romantic cabin for Christmas with your pretend boyfriend who has made it clear that he is one hundred percent attracted to you."

"Yes."

"And this is the same guy as before we're talking about."

"Yes."

"The super-hot one."

"*Yes*," I hiss, drawing the curtains closed.

"The super-hot guy you're trapped in a cabin with wants to bone you and you want to bone him, but instead of either of you doing that, you're hiding in your room and on the phone to me and are all like *oh no, my reasons*."

I pause. "Well, when you say it like that..."

Frankie groans. "Megan—"

"I know."

"Get your head out of your—"

"I *know*," I say, turning on the light. I woke to darkness five minutes ago after a much-needed nap and the first thing I did was call her. I'm beginning to regret it. She always did have a habit of getting straight to the point of things. "It's more complicated than it sounds."

"Only because you're complicating it."

"It was clearer before. We had rules." And now he said the rules have gone out the window, meaning I have no idea where we stand. "We still have to get through another week of this," I say. "I don't want to make it awkward."

"You're making it awkward right now," she tells me. "Just go for it. If it doesn't work, it doesn't work. Whatever. You move on. You cut your hair short and buy a bunch of books you're never going to read. *C'est la vie.*"

"I read at least two of those books last time."

"Megan, come on. Look at where you are right now. Where he is. You just brought him back from the brink of death! That's romantic."

"He had a migraine and I brought him water."

"And you still couldn't leave his side. It would be different if he'd kept his distance, but he hasn't. Do you want to explore this or not?"

I fall silent, sitting on the end of the mattress. "Maybe."

"Well, I guess that's a start," she says, sounding tired.

"I don't even know how I'd go about doing it."

"Easy. You take him to your bed and you—"

"Frankie."

"You flirt with the guy!" she exclaims. "You touch his arm. You look him in the eye. You smile and you laugh, and you tell him you're cold and give him no choice but to warm you. You're an excellent flirt, Megan. This should not be hard."

I make a face. "Maybe I should just go talk to him."

"No," she says firmly. "Talking's boring. Talking's for non-trapped people on bad first dates in mid-priced restaurants. Go get lost in the woods."

"No."

"Make him find you."

"I'm going to talk with him."

Like we should have done the other night. Before he got all... close.

We should have done it today too, but things got busy. First, we called our families to tell them what was going on and then spent thirty minutes trying to free the car just in case we could get down. We couldn't, of course, and Christian made me go inside and take a bath when I started shivering.

But the bath just made me sleepy and I decided to rest my eyes, and an hour later, I woke up. I'm not surprised, I barely slept at all yesterday. Christian didn't need much care other than forcing some painkillers down his throat and making sure he was hydrated, but I was still worried. I vaguely remember calling both our families and explaining what had happened, but the conversations are a blur. All my attention was on him. And seeing as how he slept for most of that time, it left me with nothing but my thoughts. And I had a lot of them.

Of him. Of me. Of everything.

What happened in the car after the fundraiser can be explained. A little pent-up frustration, some high emotions, both of us looking the best we ever looked. What were we going to do? *Not* make out? But to do that once can be laughed off. Twice...

I fall back on the bed, clutching the phone to my ear as Frankie gives me a detailed rundown of everything I should do, say, and before I can stop her, touch. Only then do I convince her to let me hang up, and when I do, I head over to the full-length mirror on the other side of the room to see what we have to work with.

I definitely don't look like I did the night of the party. I've traded a ball gown for the same sweatshirt and leggings I've been wearing for two days that the addition of a cabin robe does nothing to complement. I don't have my makeup. I don't even have a hairbrush.

But I also don't really care.

Christian's never shown any indication that he likes me to look or act a certain way. Be anyone other than who I am in any given moment and so, before I can chicken out, I open the bedroom door.

Night has fallen sharply in the last few hours, and the cabin is dark, bar a flickering light filtering up the stairs. The hallway smells rich and decadent, scented with garlic and onions and wine, and my mouth waters as I creep toward the banisters.

"Christian?"

There's no answer, but I hear the faint clang of pots that must be coming from the kitchen. I should probably go back until he's ready, but I'm too curious and too hungry to wait, so I tiptoe down the stairs, only to almost trip at the bottom when I see what awaits me.

The living room has been transformed. Gone is the swanky, magazine-spread feel, and in its place is a vision from a storybook.

Nat King Cole croons softly from the stereo, and the television plays an old black-and-white movie with the volume turned down low. The strings of fairy lights we'd found bundled in one of the cabinets have been detangled and strung both around the room and the furniture. Besides the roaring fire, they're the only source of light, and it casts the place in a warm, safe glow that makes me feel instantly at ease.

I walk over to the couch, running my fingers over the mound of blankets he'd draped over it, but I've barely taken a breath when Christian enters the room, stopping abruptly when he sees me.

"You're up."

He says it accusingly like I've foiled his plan.

"You did all this?"

"Me? Nah. It's a Christmas miracle."

"And what's that—" I blush as my stomach grumbles, cutting me off.

"Smell?" Christian asks with a knowing look. "That's the elves."

"You're cooking dinner?"

"I'm an incredible cook."

"And so humble," I croon, following him into the kitchen. "So humble and..."

Okay.

I didn't even know there was this much food in the house, which makes me think there must be some kind of secret underground cellar that he raided because holy shit.

The table is filled with dishes, all of it far too much for two people, and from the look of it, all vegetarian. Bread and cheese and bowls of different vegetables and salads. Dips and sauces are dotted in between the different foods, and I count at least three, no *four* different kinds of potatoes. The man has cooked us a feast.

"What was that?" Christian asks, putting his hand to his ear when I just gape at all. "Did you say something?"

"How did you—"

"It's all in the plating," he says, and steers me into a chair before snapping a napkin onto my lap. "And the fact that most of it came preprepared. But let's pretend I know how to rock a pestle and mortar, shall we?"

I don't even know where to start, but I decide to just go for the dish nearest me, pilling my plate with sweet parsnips and glazed carrots. The green beans are garlicky perfection, the broccoli a perfect texture. He's not happy with the potatoes, but to me, they're perfect, especially when I slather half of them in butter and drown the rest in gravy. He doesn't touch anything until I've finished piling high, even though he must be hungry. But he seems content to just watch me eat, and I'm too busy salivating to care.

"You want to watch a movie after this?" he asks. I give up trying to be ladylike as I eat a cob of corn and instead just start gnawing on the thing.

"There's a television here?"

"There's a hidden one in the bookcase."

"Shut up. No, there's not."

He only grins at my amazement. "I'm sorry. I know you were looking forward to it."

"Movie night?" I'm surprised he remembers. "That's okay. We'll make do."

"Even with no projector?"

"Even then," I say gravely. "Can we build a blanket fort?"

"I'd be disappointed if we didn't."

"Can we drink the champagne?"

"You mean the bottles I've had chilling in the fridge for three hours?"

I pop a carrot slice into my mouth, eyeing at the dark patio outside. "Can we use the hot tub?"

Christian pauses in digging into the baked camembert, his gaze shooting to mine.

I smile.

———

I do not fit into the bikini.

It's been a few years since I've worn it, but it was the only swimsuit of mine Mam still had in the house, and yikes. I spend a whole minute in front of the mirror rearranging it over my breasts, so I'm not spilling out of the damn thing, but there is still a definite risk of a nip-slip tonight.

I even think about wearing a T-shirt over it, but I don't want to wear a T-shirt over it. I want to wear the hot pink bikini in the big sexy hot tub, and I want Christian Fitzpatrick to look at me while I do it.

I force myself to stop fiddling with the straps and pull on the robe again. It doesn't help. I grow self-conscious as soon as I leave the room, and by the time I make it down the stairs, I'm seconds away from running back up them and changing. But Christian hears me and calls out, asking me to get the champagne from the fridge, and that's, like, the number one most important task of the night, so I do. I stride into the kitchen like nothing's wrong. I get the champagne, I turn around, and that's when I see Christian Fitzpatrick without his shirt on.

I don't know what I was expecting.

I mean, he told me he was a gym guy. He told me that it cleared his mind and that he was a little vain and liked keeping fit, but I never really thought about what that meant. I knew he looked good in clothes, but I thought that was a posture thing. A nice-clothes, good-posture thing, but it turns out it's also a nice-clothes, good-posture, *washboard*-abs thing.

I've never been with a guy who had washboard abs. Washboard abs belong in action movies or Instagram ads for protein shakes. Not on real people. And not on people who have made it exceedingly clear that they find me attractive and wouldn't mind taking things up a notch.

My mouth runs dry as I watch him walk around the hot tub, spreading blankets over chairs and texting someone on his phone. The skin on his chest is bare, with no tattoos or piercings or anything other than a happy little V-trail that disappears into his trunks, all the way down to... well, I can guess where it goes. I can picture it too. In fact, I picture it quite clearly as I linger in the shadows like a little creeping creeper and decide there and then that he should never wear a shirt ever again.

"Megan?"

"Coming," I yell, skirting around the island to the fridge. By the time I turn back around, champagne in hand, he's gotten into the tub, half-hidden in the bubbles but looking no less tempting.

Screw it.

I step forward, leaving my comforting robe behind... and freeze at the same time Christian does.

His eyes pin me in place before I've even left the kitchen, staring at me like I'd just been staring at him. Only he's not even trying to hide his interest, taking his time as his eyes rake over my body in a way that makes me want to press my thighs together, and I... love it.

I love it.

And so, what if I sway my hips a little as I step out onto the patio? So, what if I'm a flirt? Frankie's right.

I'm an excellent flirt.

TWENTY-SEVEN

CHRISTIAN

Maybe this isn't such a good idea.

I had nothing but the best intentions. All I was trying to do was thank her for taking care of me. To apologize for ruining her Christmas by dragging her up here. I wanted to make it up to her. To be her friend.

And then she walks onto the porch in that bikini, and the last thing I'm thinking about is being in any way platonic. I should have known. I could barely handle seeing her in a swimsuit, for God's sake, and that covered a lot more skin than she's showing now.

I don't know what it is about her that makes me feel like a teenager again trying to catch the eye of a girl for the first time, but I'm enormously glad I'm already in the water when she approaches, and I shift as subtly as I can, rearranging myself as she sets her drink on the side and climbs cautiously in.

The noise she makes when she relaxes back is just cruel.

"Okay," she says, closing her eyes. "All of that was worth it for this."

I couldn't agree more.

She sinks farther into the water, her cheeks flushing from

the heat, and I'm trying desperately to think of spreadsheets and emails and deposits and budgets and anything else, any*one* else, but her. But then her eyes snap open, finding me immediately, and she smiles a shy little smile that makes my heart pang.

The smile widens. "Almost forgot my champagne," she says, reaching for the glass. "I feel like a celebrity."

"You look like one. Do you want a picture of you and the—"

"Yes," she says, and I laugh as I reach for my phone. It takes her a few seconds to figure out her pose, settling on simply holding the flute up like she's toasting to someone.

I take two before she's happy, and then she insists on taking one of me. After that, neither of us sees any reason to stop, coming up with increasingly ridiculous poses as we make it through one glass of champagne and on to another.

"I feel bad about Andrew's proposal," she says, as I pour them out.

I don't. Call me a bad brother and a terrible person, but I am perfectly okay that Megan and I are here and they are not. Someone's got to be the selfish sibling.

"He'll find another moment," I say, ever the diplomat. "Molly didn't want to come up here, anyway."

"I guess." Our fingers brush as I hand her the glass, and she takes a quick sip. "How are you feeling?"

"Better," I say truthfully. "You know, for someone who never gets sick, you're really good at looking after people."

She shrugs, her shoulders dipping in and out of the water. "I watch a lot of medical dramas. And I once dated a guy who ran first aid courses."

"Is this where you tell me you used to practice CPR on each other?"

"I'm really good at wrapping gauze. I have a little kit."

"You have a gauze kit?"

"Of course, I have a gauze kit. I also dated a sommelier."

"Is this how you remember the men in your life?" I ask. "Occupation?"

"They all kind of blur into one otherwise. I had a type."

"Dare I ask?"

"Blonds," she says. "Bearded."

I raise a brow. "I am neither blond nor bearded."

"I'm aware. You're my type breaker."

"I'm honored."

"That was when I first moved to Dublin, though. I was very different."

"Hornier."

She smiles. "Maybe. But I was also just..." She trails off, growing thoughtful. "Remember when I said I wasn't ready for a relationship?"

"Extremely."

"Well, that was all I wanted back then."

"Of course it was," I say. "It was all you knew."

She nods, growing more confident. "I guess it never occurred to me to try being alone," she admits. "Even though I had no idea what I was looking for or what I even wanted. I never met anyone who lasted more than a few weeks, *maybe* a few months, and it got to the point where I thought something was wrong with me. Like I'd messed myself up somehow."

"But you worked through it?"

"I went to therapy," she says. "For as long as I could afford it. And it helped. At least with that part of everything. I stopped defining myself by my connection to other people, and... sorry, it sounds so cheesy when I say it out loud."

"It's not," I tell her, and she purses her lips.

"I learned that I needed to find myself before I could find someone else."

"And did you?"

Her smile slips back. "Yeah. Turns out I'm great."

"I could have told you that," I say. "What else?"

"That I like my job. Do you know how many people don't like their job? I love my job."

"I know you do."

"I like to make things. I like giving gifts and swimming in the sea. I like living in the city and meeting new people. I like that I don't know where I'm going to be in the next five years. I like that I try things even if I'm scared to." She pauses. "*Especially* when I'm scared to."

"And..."

She tilts her head. "And?"

"You also like me," I prompt, and she laughs this delighted laugh that makes me ache.

"And you," she says generously. "Sometimes."

"Sometimes, huh?" I watch a strand of her hair curl in the steam, twisting until it rests on her cheek.

"Sometimes I like you a whole lot," she says. "Sometimes you're all I think about."

You could set off a firework behind her, and I still wouldn't be able to look away, but she gets shy again, averting her gaze like she can no longer look at me. She reaches for her empty glass and then for the empty bottle. "Do you want me to get another one?" she asks, and I shake my head. "Do you want—"

"Megan," I interrupt softly. "Come here."

It's enough to make her stop breathing. At least I think she stops. She definitely stops moving, watching me with glittering eyes before slowly, carefully, she sets her glass on the side of the tub and crosses the small distance between us. I assumed she was just going to sit beside me, but instead, she places herself astride my lap, and the first thing I notice is how different it feels to when she did it at the pub, where she perched on me like she'd rather be doing anything else.

Now she drapes her thighs on either side of my legs, settling down like she's done this a hundred times before. Like my body is a familiar thing.

She straightens her spine, and she's close enough to kiss. But not yet. Not quite.

And now I'm the one who can't draw a breath.

We stay like that, unmoving for a long second before she trails one finger down my nose and traces my lips. I let her, giving her as much time and space as she wants. Whatever she wants, I'll give her. I realize that now. How I'll never be able to say no to this person.

How I'm completely at her mercy.

"This doesn't feel like pretend," she says quietly.

"Do you want it to be?"

She shakes her head, and I see the movement of her throat as she swallows. "But I don't know what this is yet."

"Me neither," I tell her. "But it doesn't have to be anything. We can just…"

Her lips pull up when I trail off. "You were going to say vibe, weren't you?"

"No," I lie.

"Yes." She laughs, looping her arms around my neck. "All the vibes," she whispers.

Her eyes flick over my face, gauging my reaction, but there's nothing unsure about her movements as her hand dips below the water and finds mine, bringing it to her hip. The strap of her bikini presses against my palm, and it takes supreme effort not to simply untie it right there and then.

I know she can feel my erection. *I* can certainly feel it, pushing up between her thighs, but when she doesn't hesitate or move away, I pull her tighter to me, tight enough that she groans, tight enough that I do too.

"This okay?" I ask, and she nods, pushing her hips into mine. My other hand finds her waist, but she catches it and brings it to her breast.

I swear I get even harder. I don't know why I thought she'd be shy about this. There was a moment after her mother's party that I felt like she was going to rip my clothes off, but this? The confidence in showing exactly what she wants and exactly how she wants it is making me lose control.

I cup her breast as directed, rolling her nipple under my thumb until her eyes flutter closed. I don't even dare to blink, scrutinizing her expression for the slightest change until the moment I take a gamble and pinch her.

Her entire body jolts as her heated gaze snaps to mine, and before I can do anything else, she's kissing me.

It's a hungry kiss, all tongues and teeth, and gasping breaths, and I don't think I've ever been so turned on in my life. I love kissing Megan. She does it with an enthusiasm I'm not used to. Like she's not scared to show how much she wants me. It's what I've always liked about her. She plays no games, no tricks.

Her hips start to move, instinctive, undulating motions until she's arching into me. My hand at her waist slips under the strap and starts to travel. I go slowly, pressing firmly so she's aware of my intentions and can give me plenty of opportunity to stop. And I think she's going to when her lips leave mine, but she only drops her mouth to my shoulder, kissing the skin she finds there.

I drag a finger through the heat of her, purposefully avoiding all the places I know she most wants me to go.

"You're wet," I tell her, rubbing her again.

"We're in the water," she mutters, and I grin as I slide one finger inside her.

"My mistake," I say, circling her clit with my thumb. Her breath comes out in a harsh gasp when I do, hot against my neck. "I'll work harder."

"Christian—"

I add a second finger, and she stops talking, her hold on me turning to a clutch. She whimpers into my ear, and I turn my focus back to her breast, multitasking like a champ as her movements grow more frantic. When I finally give her what she wants, curling my fingers in as far as they'll go, the noise she lets out makes my hips jerk, and she pushes harder against me until there's no space between us, just body against body, skin against skin.

I grab hold of her bun with nothing more than the intention of guiding her lips back to mine, but that little tug turns out to be just what she needs, and with a soft moan, I'm pretty sure I'll remember for the rest of my life, she stretches over me, going taut as a bowstring before her legs start to tremble. I stay right where I am, seeing her through it and only stopping when she begs me to, too sensitive to keep going. Even then, the urge to keep touching her is overwhelming, and I stroke her hair as she relaxes around me, feeling like I could stay like that forever. But then she sucks in a breath, nipping my ear as she rouses herself enough to reach a hand between us and, more boldly than I could ever dream of, grasps me through my trunks.

Yeah, forever can wait.

My head tips back as she sits up, and I watch through heavy-lidded eyes as she smiles a sexy little smile that tells me she knows exactly the power she has over me. I want to remind her that I'm the one who just rocked her world, but I'm also not an idiot and am rewarded for my silence with a kiss as she spears her fingers through my hair with one hand and slips under my waistband with the other.

"Tell me what you like," she murmurs, as she starts to explore, and I open my mouth to do just that when something inhuman shrieks in the darkness.

She freezes immediately, her eyes comically wide as they flick over my shoulder.

"What was that?" she asks, and then before I can answer: "Oh my God, it's a murderer, isn't it? Girls who have sex always die in horror-movie cabins."

The crankier part of me wants to point out to her that we

haven't exactly gotten to that part yet, but I rub her shoulder instead. "It's probably just an animal."

"Are you sure?"

"Positive."

But she doesn't move, still plastered against me as if she's waiting for something. Waiting for...

Okay.

"I'll go check."

I ease her off me and am halfway out of the tub, my erection quickly disappearing in the cold, when her hand grabs mine.

"What if it's a bear?"

"There are no bears in Ireland."

"There are in the *zoo*," she hisses, and I try not to laugh. She seems genuinely worried, and I have a feeling some teasing, no matter how well-meaning, will not go down well.

"I think we would have heard if there was a mass zoo break-out," I point out. "And I was thinking more along the lines of a fox."

"Christian—"

"Do you ever think about your tendency to jump to the darkest possible conclusions?"

"You mean my survival instinct?" she shoots back, looking around the porch as though searching for a weapon.

"I'm pretty sure it's a fox." I've heard enough of their shrieks in London to tell. "But I'll go check."

"Be careful," she pleads, as I take a few steps toward the trees. I don't need to go much further.

It *is* a fox.

I spy it instantly, sitting a few meters away from the cabin, just on the edge of the light.

"You have really bad timing," I tell it. "You know that?"

"Who are you talking to?" Megan whispers behind me.

"Peeping Tom over here."

"*What?*"

I press my lips together, trying not to smile as water sloshes in the tub. A second later, Megan appears at my side, drawing a towel around her as she pushes wet strands of hair from her face.

"Fox," I say, pointing to the animal that's still sitting there, staring up at us.

"Oh." She relaxes against me before tensing again. "Do you think it was watching us?" she asks, and she sounds so appalled that this time I can't help it.

I laugh so loud the animal runs away.

TWENTY-EIGHT

MEGAN

I mean, excuse me for not wanting woodland creatures watch me get my rocks off.

Once the fox disappears into the trees, we head back inside the house. I'm not too annoyed about it. The heat of the water has made the air even colder, and my fingers have pruned to a wrinkly, distinctly unsexy look. I feel bad about Christian, but he doesn't seem too mad, offering to start on the kitchen cleanup while I get changed. That I definitely *don't* feel bad about since he obviously likes cleaning and is already moving about the space with brisque precision as I pad back up the stairs.

I have a quick shower, my skin still buzzing, but when I put on my leggings and sweater again, I hesitate. Christian's gone to so much effort to make today special, meanwhile, I've shown up looking like someone who hasn't left her house in a week. It's Christmas Eve. It's Christmas Eve, and in a few hours, it will be Christmas Day, and if I don't get to wear the gold dress I'd bought especially for the occasion, then I'm going to wear the next best thing.

I don't have dressy clothes or even my makeup with me, but I do have my knitting gear which is full of many wonders. In my bag, I find a red ribbon to tie my hair back and even some glittery dust, which I pat lightly into my cheeks. I would kill for some mascara, but the effect is better than I expected and, impatient to continue the night, I grab the bag and rush downstairs.

Christian's waiting for me in the living room when I return and has changed back into his clothes from earlier. He's built up the fire again too, and it crackles happily in the hearth, bathing the room in a deep golden glow.

"You're just in time," he says when he sees me. "I know you said you didn't mind about the movie night, but I thought we could..." He trails off as I reach into the bag. "What's that?"

"I know we said no gifts, but technically I didn't *get* you anything," I say, taking out the hat. "Sorry, it's not wrapped."

He stares at the plain black beanie for a heartbeat before taking it from my outstretched hand.

"Is this what you were working on in the car?" he asks, fitting it over his hair.

"Yeah, but seeing you with it now makes me think about how I've never actually seen you wear one."

Doubt starts to creep in as he turns away from me, going to the mirror on the other side of the room. Yep. Not once. Not a hat guy. Why didn't I make him a scarf? Everyone loves scarves. Everyone loves—

"I need to make some adjustments."

"Whoa." He ducks out of my grasp when I try to take it off him. "You can't take a gift back once gifted. I love it, Megan. Thank you."

I shrug, pleased. Very pleased. Unusually pleased. I make things for people all the time. And I started this one as an afterthought, just to have something to give him in front of his family, but his genuine delight makes me feel all fluttery inside.

"I got you something as well," he says with a grimace. "But it's at home."

"Sure it is," I tease, and he laughs.

He goes back to the fire while I slip into the kitchen, pouring us some more of the red wine we had at dinner.

Christian's still wearing the hat when I return, something that, again, should not make me as happy as it does, and I try to play it cool as I smile at him.

"We have wineglasses, you know," he says when I hand him his drink.

"Wine is more fun in a mug. It's like eating food with a little spoon."

"How is that more fun?"

"It just is," I say, turning to the television setup. "I don't make the rules. Oh, hey." I pull open a drawer, finding a stack of DVDs. "Like the eighteen hundreds."

"Internet gets patchy up here," he says, plucking one from the pile. *It's a Wonderful Life*. "This one?"

"Then the Muppets."

"Then the Muppets," he promises and loads up the DVD player. I'm already too warm sitting so close to the fire, so I retreat to the couch, the one that looks like it could hold twenty people. It is incredibly comfy, and I tuck my legs up as Christian sits beside me.

"You're really good at Christmas," I tell him, and he shrugs.

"Runs in the family."

We start the film.

I do not pay attention.

It takes every bit of control I have not to fidget, supremely aware of the man beside me, of every breath he takes. But every time I go to make a move, I chicken out, and it's not until we're about halfway into the film, when I'm *finally* starting to watch it, that he speaks.

"We should count down," he says, his gaze on the grandfather clock by the mantelpiece. It's almost midnight.

"It's Christmas," I remind him. "Not New Year's."

He ignores me. "Eight."

"Christian."

"Seven."

"Oh my God."

"Six."

I can't fight my smile as he mutes the television, twisting his body to face me.

"Five."

He kisses me on the nose.

"Four."

Another on the lips.

"Three."

I close my eyes.

"Two."

One.

"Merry Christmas, Megan."

He brushes his mouth against me once more before pulling back. My eyes flutter open, my breath catching in my throat as I see him looking at me like... well, like I've never been looked at before.

"I want to make some more amendments to the contract," I whisper, and I swear the warmth in his eyes turns molten.

"I have a better idea," he says. "What about we forget the contract?"

"Our legally binding one?"

"We'll come up with a new one." He kisses my jaw before his mouth skims down my throat. "Or maybe we won't. Maybe we'll just start again."

"Again?"

He nods, and every thought in my head zeroes in on that sensitive spot where my neck meets my shoulder, where his tongue now swirls and his lips caress.

"Again," he confirms. "We'll get dinner."

"Are you asking me out on a date?"

"Are you going to say yes?"

"Maybe."

He pauses. "Maybe?"

"I'm pretty busy right—"

I yelp, giggling as he pulls me under him until I'm lying flat on my back.

"Go out with me," he demands.

"Or what?"

"Or you'll break my heart, Megan O'Sullivan." And just like that, my teasing mood vanishes.

"No more pretending," he whispers.

I nod, and he dips down to kiss me before climbing off the couch. I can only lie there, watching him as he stands to his full height. Watching as hands go to his belt, dropping it to the floor with a purposeful thud before starting on his jeans. I don't look away from his fingers as he pulls the zipper down, and I swear he's doing it slowly just to taunt me.

Not wanting to be left behind, I pull my socks off before tugging down my leggings as he grabs his wallet from his coat and comes back with a condom. He doesn't even make it back to the couch before divesting himself of more clothes, pulling his T-shirt off in one swift move before shoving his jeans to the ground.

The boxers go with them.

I freeze on the couch, swallowing as he reveals his erection.

"You alright there?" he asks, sounding amused, and I can't even summon a retort.

"Well done," I say seriously, and he rolls his eyes as he opens the condom packet, but *no, no, no.* No.

Driven purely by an instinct I didn't know I possessed, I lean forward, wrapping my hand around him before he can. He grunts when I do, a surprised, strangled sound that makes me smile.

He's shockingly warm in my palm, shockingly big too, and I

give an experimental tug, watching his abdomen move in and out as he takes a ragged breath.

"Megan," he warns. Or is it a plea?

I lean forward to lick a line across his stomach, obsessed with the way his muscles contract under my touch. Obsessed with him. Obsessed enough that I dip lower, moving my hand down as I close my mouth around his head.

Christian groans and his hand goes to my shoulder, clenching like he doesn't know whether to push me away or pull me closer.

My eyes flick up to find him staring down at me, his gaze heady and intense as I take him deeper, letting myself relax, savoring him as I start to move. But he barely lets me find a rhythm before he cups my cheek, pulling me gently off.

I start to protest when he swoops down, kissing the words from my lips. "You want this to be an early night or a late night?"

"Late night."

"Then stop touching me like that and get naked."

He straightens, and I scramble along the couch, making room for him as he rolls the condom on and joins me.

I'm panting before he even touches me.

"You want to go upstairs?" he asks, and I shake my head. "You want to stay here?"

"It's nice down here," I say, though nice is an understatement. I feel like I'm in a dream.

"Well, we gotta get rid of this first," he says, tugging on my sweater. His hands are warm when they slip under it, leaving a trail of heat as they glide up.

I inhale, trying to gather as much breath as I can into my lungs, and as I do, he encourages me to raise my arms, lifting the sweater over my head. He lays it gently to the side, even while his eyes flare at my lack of bra.

I bite back a smile. "Eyes up here, buddy."

"Nah, I'm good," he says, and laughs when I push him. The tension eases, simmering into something warm and familiar, and I run my hands up his chest and around his neck as he raises us up into a sitting position.

"You alright?" he murmurs, and I kiss him in response as I lift my hips, slipping my underwear off. It's a little awkward, but he helps, brushing the hair from my face as I settle back over his legs, and help nudge him in. We'd been completely compatible up to this point, so it never occurred to me that we wouldn't be, but the stretch I expected is more of a pinch, and when the pinch becomes a burn, I tense against him, sucking in a breath.

He stops immediately. "What?" he asks. "What's wrong?"

"Nothing," I say quickly, tightening my hold when he tries to move me off him. His grip on my ass is the only thing stopping gravity from doing its thing. But as I pant against his shoulder, I don't think even that would help right now.

He's bigger than I'm used to. I knew he was when I grinded up against him for several minutes in that freaking hot tub. I knew he was when I held him not moments before and even though I tell myself to relax, I, of course, don't.

"I'm fine," I add when he leans back to look at me. "Just give me a second."

Do they have lube in luxury cabins? I feel like that is a thing they should have. Or maybe—

I suck in a breath as Christian moves, tipping me back so I'm lying along the couch.

"What are you *doing*?" I hiss, as he loops my legs over his shoulders.

"What does it look like?" He tucks a pillow under my hips, moving me about just how he wants me, which I never thought I would find hot, but right now, I really, *really* do. "*Fine* is not a word a guy wants to hear."

"Christian—" I break off with a jolt as he presses a kiss right below my belly button.

"We've got all night," he says. "And if it takes all night, then you might as well be comfy."

"But—"

"Shhh," he whispers. "I'm seducing you."

I relax a bit more into the cushions. I've been with plenty of guys who get frustrated when things don't move along fast enough, and I'm well aware that we were interrupted earlier. But Christian seems to be telling the truth and doesn't look in any rush as he rubs slow circles into my skin, his touch soft and soothing and perfect.

"You say the word, and we stop, okay? Anytime."

"Okay," I say, and he rewards me with another one of those devastating smiles. "I want this," I add, as he settles between my legs. "I want you. I think ever since I kissed you in the parking lot."

"The parking lot, huh?" His voice is teasing as he trails a hand down my thighs. "Only then? I've wanted you a lot longer than that."

"Everything's a game to you, isn't it?" I ask, and he chuckles, a low and delicious sound that makes me writhe. Christian immediately tightens his grip, keeping my body where he wants it.

"The cocktail bar?" I guess, swallowing as he presses a kiss to the inside of my knee. I remember the intense way he looked at me in the candlelight, and just the thought of it sends a fizz of excitement through me.

But Christian shakes his head.

"Are you kidding me?" He inches up, nuzzling. "I wanted you the moment I saw you in that wedding dress."

Embarrassment seeps around the edges of that memory, just like it always does. Only now, it's quickly chased away by something hotter, something needy.

"Should have run away with you," he continues, and my heart starts to slam in my chest as his fingers find me once again, sinking deep. I groan at the sensation, hands fisting as he sucks on the skin of my thigh. "... let me?"

"Huh?" My mind scrambles for purchase. He asked me a question. He asked—

"Would you have let me?" he repeats, rotating his wrist until... oh *God*. "Let me take you away from there? Away from everything?"

"You barely knew me then."

"That's not what I asked."

I tilt my chin to my chest, watching him watch me with dark, heat-filled eyes and get the same mix of feelings I always get when he's around. Attraction. Curiosity. Trust. Trust, most of all. I trusted him when he asked to walk me home, when I agreed to our plan, when I grabbed him by the hair and kissed the living daylights out of him. I would trust Christian Fitzpatrick with my life, and lying here before him, I realize with complete certainty that I trust him with my heart too. Wherever that may lead me.

So yes. "I would have."

"Right answer," he says and skims his thumb over that sweet spot, wrenching a gasp from me.

"I'm ready," I pant, but he just tsks.

"I'll tell you when you're ready," he says in that infuriatingly confident way he says everything. Only this time, it doesn't sound infuriating at all. It sounds sexy and promising, and then his tongue meets his fingers, and I'm gone. Vanished. Dead. Goodbye.

The man knows what he's doing.

He kisses all around before focusing on my clit, blowing on it lightly before his lips close around the small nub, and if there's one thing I now know for sure, it's that nothing has ever, *ever* felt this good in my entire life. It's the kind of good that I never want to end, which of course means it does all too quickly.

It takes only a few minutes for me to unravel, but even then, he only stops when I tell him to, beg him to, too sensitive for so much as a kiss as he works his way back up to my lips.

He lifts up my leg, his fingers dimpling my thigh as he drapes it over his hip and lines our bodies together, eye to eye and chest to chest, and it's only when our gazes meet, when I tilt my chin to kiss him *yes*, that he moves.

He presses into me, going so slowly I can hardly bear it. I can certainly feel it, though, every inch of him a delicious stretch that I never want to end.

When he can finally go no more, he pauses, letting me get used to him. There are beads of sweat on his forehead, and his cheeks are flushed, but whether that's from the heat of the fire or not, I don't know. He dips his head to check on me, and his mouth curves as he does, amusement glinting in his eyes.

"What?" I whisper, and his smile widens.

"You've got glitter in your hair." And then he drops his control.

My breath catches as he speeds up, and all I can do is lift my hips, pushing against him fast as a wave of pleasure shoots through me.

The smile vanishes from his face as intensity takes over, and he starts to push deeper, harder until we're both panting from the effort.

Still, he doesn't take his eyes off me.

And the fire crackles and the fairy lights dance, and I feel so warm and so cherished and so *loved* that I know what this is, whatever we have, it's different.

It's different. It's different. It's different.

And the realization only makes me move more frantically, clenching around him until he curses and drops his forehead to my sweat-sheened shoulder and thrusts even deeper into me, setting all my nerves alight.

I tangle my fingers in his hair, holding him to me as my heart squeezes in my chest.

Don't cry during sex, Megan. Do *not* cry during sex. But even with that stern command, tears prick the corner of my eyes, the sensations too overwhelming to handle. It's like everything inside me just wants to let go, and my body is winding tighter and tauter and always *almost* there until finally, Christian pushes up just enough to capture my mouth with his, and as he sinks into me one final time, I squeeze my eyes shut, and give in.

TWENTY-NINE

CHRISTIAN

"This is the spoon. And this is the Nutella jar."

I can only stare as Megan places both items on the counter, her expression deadly serious.

"So when you said you couldn't cook," I begin, but she decides to demonstrate.

"The spoon goes *into* the Nutella jar—"

"Can you at least put it on some toast?"

"It's Christmas Day. If I can't eat chocolate spread for breakfast on Christmas Day, then when can I?" She taps the jar. "I feel like you're not in the festive spirit."

"I feel like you need to eat a bag of spinach."

She put the spoon in her mouth instead, pouting when I add my chopped banana to my oats.

"Do we have to clean the hot tub, or can we use it again?"

"It should be okay," I say, glancing outside. It's sunny now, and there was only a light flurry of snow this morning, meaning we should probably try and leave if we can, but neither of us has brought up that possibility. It's like if we don't mention it out loud, we can both pretend nothing exists outside our little winter hideaway. Nothing but these four walls and us.

I finish making my breakfast while Megan grabs our teas, the spoon still dangling from her mouth as she follows me back to the nest we've made in front of the fireplace.

She settles cross-legged on the cushions, completely at ease as she eats her terrible breakfast and gazes at an old sitcom on the television. She's semi-dressed but is wearing my sweater instead of hers, something that is several sizes too big for her and keeps slipping off her shoulder, revealing the freckles there.

I got to know her freckles intimately last night. Her freckles and her curves, and the scar just above her left knee. The tattoo on her hip. I especially liked that. A small smattering of stars that I discovered on one of my many inventories of her body. I couldn't stop touching her. Luckily for me, she didn't want me to.

"Stop staring at me," she says, as we dig into our breakfasts.

"Never."

"I'm eating."

"I know. The way you have Nutella all over your chin?"

"Yeah?"

"Hottest thing I've ever seen," I say, and she dips her spoon into the jar again. "You're really going to finish the whole thing, aren't you?"

"Most important meal of the day. And—" She gasps as I lean forward, closing my lips over the spoon. "A thief. That's what you are."

"You have to eat a banana now."

"So we're just making up rules now? We're just—" She smiles against my lips as I kiss her. Kiss her again and again and again. "You've got really long eyelashes," she says when I pull back.

"So, I've been told."

"And you've got a shadow," she adds, dragging her fingers across the stubble on my jaw before putting our food to the side. "And chocolate on your mouth," she whispers, licking it off as she climbs onto my lap. "Would it be weird if we stayed here forever?"

"No," I say instantly, and she laughs.

"Yes, it would."

"People have definitely done weirder stuff."

"I don't think we can afford it."

"I'm the boss." I shrug. "I'll say it's being fumigated."

She pushes me back until we're lying against the cushions, draping herself across my chest, and yeah, I could definitely stay here forever.

Megan falls silent, but I can tell something's on her mind, and sure enough after a few seconds, she shifts against me, her voice curious. "Can I ask you something personal?"

"Is this about that rash because I swear it's just—"

She bats my arm, smiling. But when she speaks next, her words are soft. "Why don't you get on with your dad?"

It takes every ounce of control within me not to tense, knowing she'd feel it if I did. "What do you mean?" I ask lightly.

"You never talk about him. Not like you do the others. And you... I don't know, you said you wanted someone to help you with your family, but from what I can see, they all love you. A lot. They just want you to be happy."

Happy. My father's words come back to me in a flash, and my chest grows tight. *I think you're unhappy*, he said to me, and I'd immediately rejected it. Lashed out, and...

"Christian?" Her head lifts up, and I stroke her hair back on instinct, addicted to the feel of her. "You get along with everyone," she says when I don't respond. "I've seen you. You're good at it. So why not with him?"

Maybe because he knows me better than I think he does. Or maybe because he doesn't put up with my pretense.

"Remember what you said about your mam?" I ask. "About how she tries to understand you?"

"Yeah."

"Well, so does my dad. He's always tried to. The problem is, I've never made it easy on him." I wind a strand of her hair around my finger, watching it glint in the sunlight.

"I wasn't that smart at school," I say. "People think I was, but all I did was remember stuff, and that's all they cared about it. I memorized what they told me, and I fed it back to them. I barely had to think about it, and it made everything so boring, and I guess that's why I..."

"Was such a dick?"

I grin. "I wasn't a dick."

"You were a troublemaker."

"But the small-town kind. I was endearing."

"Whatever you need to tell yourself," she mutters. "Didn't you put our teacher's house up for sale online?"

"No."

"You did!"

"Must have been someone else."

"And like thirty people showed up to the open viewing. Mam was furious because he didn't ask her to dress it for the photos."

"I have no recollection of that," I lie, smiling at the memory. That was the fun stuff. Harmless. Everything else... disappearing all night, drinking God knows what until dawn. I did my parents' heads in.

"I stopped all that when I moved to college," I say.

"Because you weren't bored anymore?"

"More like I was out of my depth. I spent my early twenties like a fish out of water. Only for the first time in my life, I wanted to fit in." I remember sitting in lecture halls, watching the other students, what they wore, how they spoke. "You'd be surprised how many places you can get to just by acting like you belong there," I add. "But you should have seen the first

Christmas I came home with a bit of money. I went overboard with the presents and the clothes and..." I pause. "I guess in hindsight it must have felt like I was rubbing it in."

"They'd never think that," Megan argues.

Maybe not. But looking back on it, it certainly feels like I did. "I thought they'd be impressed," I say quietly. "My dad especially. But he just treated me the same as he always did. Like I'd mess it all up somehow. And that's how it's always been since. No matter what I do. No matter my job or my salary or any of it. And it's fine most of the time, but at Christmas, I can't escape it and... Jesus, maybe I do have daddy issues."

Megan smiles, looking sad. But there's no pity in her expression. Just understanding. And it's because of that I carry on.

"I think he saw through me. I think he knew I was unhappy but pretending I wasn't, and that's what disappointed him. That's why the harder I tried, the worse it got between us."

"You're unhappy?" Megan asks, and I start to shake my head before hesitating.

"Maybe," I say. "Right now? No. I am the furthest from unhappy you could get. But yeah. I spent the last ten years working toward something that changed a lot on the outside and nothing on the inside. And I'm beginning to realize that maybe that meant I was chasing the wrong things the whole time."

"It doesn't mean it can't change," she points out. "Do you like anything about your life right now?"

"I like the money," I admit. "I like not having to worry about where I'm going to get next month's rent or what I'll do if there's an emergency. I like having a nice car and buying Liam's kids expensive stuff that makes his eye twitch. I don't think it's wrong to be in a job for the salary."

"But you hate it?" she guesses, and I pause. Do I?

"I don't know. I don't think so. I guess I never really thought too much about it because it's been just a step to me, but I like my team. I think I even like the work. Plus, there's room for growth, so I can—"

"Room for growth?"

"What?"

"You're not doing a job interview," she says, amused. "You don't have to grow. Not if you don't want to. This job doesn't have to be another rung on the ladder. It can just be a job. A job you go to and enjoy. It's more than a lot of people have." At my silence, her voice goes flat. "Please tell me you know this."

I shrug, uncomfortable. "Settling wasn't really a done thing with the people I hung around with."

"It's not settling, Christian. It's realizing what you actually want instead of what you think everyone else wants. Slow down, take stock, and focus on what fills that gap right there." She taps my chest, looking serious. "I give you permission."

"Permission, huh?"

"People who look like you shouldn't have to try so hard, anyway," she says, and I burst out laughing before rolling us, so I'm hovering over her.

"Thank you," I murmur.

"For what?"

"Listening." I sit back, reaching for the hem of the sweater. "Caring." I pull it off her, laying it to the side as she stretches out beneath me, shivering slightly when her bare skin meets the air. "You cold?"

"A little," she says, and I glance at the fire, wondering if I should build it up before we—

"Hello, hello!" A voice calls from outside. "Rescue team is here."

Our heads whip toward the door, but before either of us can do anything, it swings open, and Andrew steps inside. "Are you alive or are you— Oh."

Megan shrieks, gathering up the blankets to cover herself as Molly enters and slaps a hand over my brother's face.

"Sorry," he calls, as Megan scrambles up the stairs, her bare calves flashing with each step. "I thought it was locked."

"But you tried it anyway?" I ask, exasperated.

"We did call," Molly says. "And text. But looks like you two were too busy to check your— Christian!" She covers her own eyes as I get up, accidentally flashing her before I can remember my own lack of clothing.

"Put some clothes on," Molly complains. "I don't want to see you naked."

"Words I've never heard before."

"Christian," Andrew warns, and I shrug my jeans on.

"I'm decent."

"Glad to see you're feeling better," Andrew says, as I grab a T-shirt. "You giant liar."

"Ask Megan if you don't believe me. I was bedridden for a day."

"*Bedridden*, you say."

Molly sighs. "Okay."

"More like sheet-fort ridden."

"I'm going to help Megan," Molly says pointedly. "Your mother is worried enough as it is that we won't make it back for dinner, and we already got lost twice coming up here." She heads up the stairs, calling Megan's name, and I plug my phone in to charge to see I do indeed have several messages from them.

"You guys didn't have to come up," I say.

"And spend Christmas without you?" Andrew claps me on the back. "I want a refund, by the way."

"I think I can pull some strings." I glance toward the stairs, lowering my voice. "The proposal?"

"Tomorrow. Going to take her on a walk." His grin is mischievous. "She loves walks."

"You're really bad at this."

"The grumpier she is, the more she'll be surprised."

"You're also an idiot. But I'll make this up to you."

"Cottage with the pool?"

"Cottage with the pool."

Molly and a fully dressed Megan start bringing our bags down while Andrew helps me clean up the living room.

"We should be fine on the roads," he says when we're ready to go. "They were cleared this morning, but it seems everyone's using the snow as an excuse to stay inside. Mam is still insisting you come for dinner," he adds to Megan. "But I'm going to guess you want to head home."

"If you wouldn't mind," she says. "I'm sorry we took your surprise."

"Don't worry about it. If it had to be anyone else, I'm glad it was you two." He rubs his hands together, glancing around at the now spotless cabin. "We good to go?"

"As we'll ever be," I say, shouldering my bag. "I'll get Molly. I think she's still choosing what food she wants to keep."

Turns out that's exactly what she's doing. I poke my head in the kitchen to find her standing with her back to me next to several tubs of leftover food stacked on the counter. She doesn't hear me come in, lost in her own little world until I rap my knuckles on the door frame.

"Let's go, slowpoke," I say, as she spins around, startled. "If you wanted to stay here, you shouldn't have gone shopping." But she doesn't budge, distracted as she glances over her shoulder. "You okay?"

"I'm fine," she says in a not-fine voice. And then: "Did you bring all this stuff up yourself?"

"All the food? Nah, we just brought a change of clothes. This was Andrew overpreparing." I prop a shoulder against the wall, frowning when she just stands there. "I'll make it up to you guys, I promise."

"No, I just..." A strange look crosses her face. "Never mind. Let's go." She grabs the tubs, brushing past me without another word, and, confused, I round the island to see what she'd been looking at.

I don't see anything at first. Nothing but some empty cartons to be returned to the caterers, the recycling bags laid out for the cleaning crew... and the two boxes of untouched rose petals next to them, a sticker saying *Honeymoon Special* plastered to the side.

THIRTY

MEGAN

We all take Andrew's car since his rental is fitted out for the snow, and no one wants to risk getting stuck again. But we're only about ten minutes into the journey when I begin to regret the decision.

And it's because of Molly.

She's quiet the whole way down the mountain. Completely and utterly silent. She sits up front with Andrew while Christian and I take the back, and the air is so strained, I can practically feel it.

"What happened?" I whisper when we go forty minutes without anyone speaking. Christian just shakes his head, but in a *don't ask* rather than a *I don't know* way, so I nudge him with my foot and give him a pointed look until he caves.

"She saw the rose petals."

"What?"

"The rose petals," Christian murmurs, his voice barely audible over the music. "Andrew ordered them to propose."

"So?"

"So," he says, "how many situations can you think of where

your boyfriend whisks you away to a cabin getaway and orders two buckets of rose petals?"

"He could just be being romantic," I say, but Christian grimaces.

"She knows. Or guessed at least."

"But then why..." I trail off, looking at the rigid hold of her shoulders, at her head turned firmly to the side window. If she's guessed what Andrew was planning, she doesn't look very happy about it.

Andrew seems to think so too. He can't stop glancing at her. Nor can he stop tapping his fingers against the steering wheel, a nervous gesture that I doubt he's even aware of. But even if he wanted to, he can't do anything with Christian and me in the car.

He can only wait and wonder and probably think the worst.

"You couldn't have locked the front door?" I mutter, and Christian's lips twitch as his hand finds mine, holding it for the rest of the ride.

By the time we get to my house, things have gotten so awkward that I wouldn't be surprised if Christian asks to get out as well, but Andrew straightens halfway up the drive, his voice just a little *too* cheerful as he attempts to break the tension.

"Looks like you have guests!"

I lean forward as he slows to a halt, trying to see who it is and if I can avoid them. "Mam probably invited some... oh my God."

There are two unknown cars parked in front of my house. Two cars and three people. One is Sophie, who stands on the porch with her hand over her mouth, and the other two are Aidan and Isaac.

Who are currently in the middle of a fight.

They wrestle together on what should be the grass but is now just a thick lump of snow, something which severely hampers both their efforts, making the whole thing more ridiculous than it is violent, seeing as how they keep falling over their own feet.

Sophie's eyes widen when she sees us, and she hurries over as Andrew stops the car, and I scramble out.

"This is my fault," she says. "I'm so sorry, Megan."

"What are you talking about? *Hey!*" I shout, as the other two rush at each other. Aidan disappears briefly into the snow before getting back up again. "Break it up!"

Neither of them hear me.

"Aidan and I were talking," Sophie explains. "And then Isaac showed up and he wouldn't leave until he spoke with you, and I got angry at him and then he got angry at me and then Aidan got *really* angry and now they're fighting. They've been at it for ages. I don't know what to do."

"Would you call that fighting?" Andrew says mildly as they both fall again.

"*Aidan!*" I yell, finally getting his attention. "What the hell are you doing? Mam's going to kill you!"

I don't expect an answer, but what I really don't expect is for him to get distracted and look over just in time to catch a punch to the face.

Okay, it's not really a punch. More like a flailing hand that manages to make contact, but still. He rears back, clutching his jaw, and I give up.

"Don't just stand there," I say, gesturing at them as Christian does just that. "Do something."

"Like what?"

"Like *help*."

He looks surprised. "Aidan's holding his own."

Oh, for the love of— "I don't mean help *him*, I mean help *me*. We need to break them apart."

"They'll tire themselves out eventually," he says, only to sigh when I glare at him. "You could have at least waited until Aidan got a few hits in."

Neither man notices Christian's approach, and he examines them only briefly before diving in, grabbing Isaac by the back of his coat and hauling him back. Isaac immediately loses his footing and lands with a hard thump in the snow, but Christian pays him no heed as he reaches out a hand and helps Aidan up.

Aidan who has a split lip.

Sophie gasps beside me at the sight of blood, but it doesn't seem to bother my brother, who immediately tries to go after Isaac again. This time Christian's there, standing between them, and with a firm shove, keeps him away.

"We should probably go," Andrew says behind me. "Unless you need us to—"

"No," I say, embarrassed. "Go. This is all... It's just a misunderstanding."

"Uh-huh," he says, but he looks back at the car, to where Molly still sits, staring at us from the front seat. "Well. Merry Christmas, for what it's worth."

"Thanks, Andrew." I wait until he drives off before returning to the mess before me.

"Okay," I say calmly as Sophie shuffles her feet. "What the hell?"

"He's basically stalking you now," Aidan grumbles.

"Don't accuse people of things like that," I warn. "And where's Mam?"

"At his parents," he says tersely, glaring at Isaac. "He thought he'd take his chance. Said he wouldn't leave until he saw you. Even when I said you weren't here. Sophie can back me up."

"And why are you here?" I ask Sophie, who freezes before sharing a glance with Aidan.

"I—"

"Never mind," I say, holding my hands up. I don't have time for this. "Isaac," I call, and my ex-fiancé looks up from where he's brushing off snow from his knee. "Go home."

"I want to talk to you first."

Wrong thing to say. "Aidan," I caution, as my brother steps forward.

"I just need a minute," Isaac continues, and he has the brains to sound more contrite than before. "Please, Meg."

"Don't call her that," Aidan says and maybe I was wrong the other day. Maybe migraines are contagious. It certainly feels like I'm getting one now.

Christian catches my gaze, raising a questioning brow. *Whatever you want to do,* he seems to say. And I know he means it. If I want to go and talk with Isaac, then he'll deal with my brother, so I can. If I want to fight my own battles, he'll stand back and support. He's got me. Just like he said.

And maybe at some other time, in some other place, I'd get some closure. I'd have it out. I'd point my finger and accuse.

But the thing is, I don't want to do any of that.

I don't want to talk to Isaac. I don't want to look at him. I don't want to worry about him or *think* about him ever again. Five years since I left him, and he still occupies way too much of my mind. And it's time to put an end to it.

"If we can just—"

"No," I say, and he actually looks surprised. "Whatever you want to say to me, you can say it in front of everyone here."

"Megan—"

"Or leave," I add. "Which you'll be doing anyway in about sixty seconds because that's all I'm giving you."

He pauses, his eyes flitting between me and the others. Not one friendly face looks back at him.

His mouth twists unhappily. "I wanted to say that I'm sorry you felt that I..." He stops at Sophie's murderous look. "I'm sorry," he corrects. And that's it.

"Okay," I say after a beat. "Thanks. I don't accept."

His eyes dart back to me. "But—"

"No."

"Then tell me what you want me to say," he snaps, starting to get irritated, and I know it's less about truly apologizing to me and more about his own reputation. That's what he's always been the most concerned about. The perfect girlfriend. The perfect life.

"I don't want you to say anything," I tell him. "At least not to me. I want you to go home and I want you to tell your parents why I left. And I want you to know that I'm going to tell my mother. And anyone else who asks. I'm going to tell everyone who wants to know what really happened between us and I'm going to tell them the truth. And after that, I don't know what will happen, but I know I don't want you to come to this house again. I don't want to see you again. I want you gone."

He looks stricken. Like he genuinely thought I would welcome him back with open arms. Like this is all some big misunderstanding.

"Look," he starts, dropping his voice so only I can hear him. He doesn't dare step any closer to me, though. Not with Christian and Aidan watching his every move. "I'm sorry about the job. About everything. But that was a long time ago. I'm not that person anymore."

"Then you won't have any issue telling people what you did. Goodbye, Isaac. I'd like you to go now."

He stares at me for a long, weighted moment before he huffs out a breath and stalks past me to his car. No one says a word. It only takes a few seconds for him to leave, driving around the bend and out of my sight, but it feels like a lifetime.

Telling the truth won't magically solve everything. I know that. And I know it means I'll be forced to have the same conversations over and over again, to confront everything I've tried to pretend no longer eats at me. And I know it's going to be shit.

But maybe this time, when I'm ready, I'll come out the other side.

"Megan?"

Sophie lingers next to the house, and I glance at Christian, who nods in understanding.

"Let's go get you cleaned up," he says, clapping my brother on the shoulder, and to my surprise, Aidan doesn't shrug him off. He even goes with him, pressing his hand to his lip to stem the bleeding.

Sophie waits for them to head inside before turning to me. "I—"

"Are you dating my brother?"

"What?" she asks, startled. "No!"

"Are you sure?"

"He's one of Cormac's best friends," she says as if that explains everything. "I didn't come here to see him. I wanted to see if you were okay. Cormac did too, but we didn't want to..."

"Overwhelm me?" I guess, and she shrugs, looking uncomfortable.

"I wanted to apologize," she says. "For what I said in the pub. And for everything that came before it. I wanted to—"

"You don't need to apologize for Isaac."

"No, I know. I'm not. I'm just... I'm sorry you couldn't tell me what was going on," she says. "I couldn't sleep the other night thinking about it. That you felt you had to do it all by yourself. But you have to understand that when you left, it felt like our group was suddenly torn apart, and no one knew why. And it was so *unlike* you." She gives a shaky laugh. "Or maybe it was. Maybe it was the real you. But you weren't there and Isaac was, and he was so shattered and confused and it never occurred to me that you might be too. And that's on me. I'm so sorry, Megan."

Her words ring with sincerity, enough of it that some of my defenses start to crack. "I shouldn't have run off like I did," I tell her. "I shouldn't have assumed you'd just dismiss me."

"You felt that you didn't have a choice. I get that now. Especially if he..." Her expression darkens. "God, you should have seen it. When we overheard you the other day? I've never seen Cormac so angry. He just lost it. And Aidan..." She rolls her eyes slightly. "I'm surprised they didn't get into a fight sooner."

"I thought he might have convinced you I was lying," I admit, and she shakes her head, miserable.

"You must have felt so alone. And then to come back here and for me to freak out at you." She grimaces. "I was such a bitch at the pub. I just didn't expect to see you, and I was going through my own shit, and I took it out on you. That's not okay. That is the opposite of being a girl's girl. That's—"

"I'm sorry too," I interrupt before she can get herself worked up. "The truth should have come out years ago."

"Well, it's coming out now," she says, crossing her arms. "I can't believe you're dating Christian Fitzpatrick." Her eyes widen. "Shit. Sorry. I didn't mean to say that out loud. Sometimes things just pop out."

"I remember," I say with a small smile. "Don't worry. I can't believe I'm dating him either."

"I used to have such a crush on him," she continues before her face falls again. "Shit."

This time I just laugh. She grins when I do, her face lighting up just like it used to. Back when we were younger. Back when we were friends.

"It's completely fine to tell me no," she says. "But do you want to get a drink sometime? On me, obviously. We could... I don't know, catch up."

"I'd love to. Mam says you moved into the cottage by the church."

She nods. "It has asbestos and I'm pretty sure it's haunted."

"Wonderful."

Her smile is tentative, but it's there. "Okay then," she says. "I'll see you soon. Happy Christmas, Megan."

I murmur it back, and she leaves, picking her way carefully

across the snow. When she turns her car around, she beeps, and I wave, and it feels like the beginning of something. But the peace doesn't last long.

She's just turned the corner when Christian bursts back outside, looking tense.

Ah, crap.

"What did he say now?" I ask flatly as I look behind him for my brother, but Christian shakes his head.

"Andrew just messaged," he says, holding up his phone. "Molly definitely knows about the proposal. She started freaking out when it was just the two of them, and when they got back, she..." He trails off, wincing as he rereads the text.

"She what?" I ask, as Aidan steps out of the house with a bag of frozen peas against his lips.

Christian shoots me an apologetic look and shows me the screen so I can see for myself. "She ran."

THIRTY-ONE

CHRISTIAN

"What do you mean she *ran?*" I ask Andrew as he paces along our family's porch.

"I mean when we got here, she said something about needing to call Zoe and then she took off." He gestures down the lane. "Said she was going for a walk, and she hasn't been back. That was forty minutes ago."

"Should we go look for her?" Megan asks, peering up at the sky. It's stopped snowing, but the sun is setting soon and it's already pretty dark.

"Just give her a few more minutes," I say, checking the time. "She won't have gone far."

"She figured it out," Andrew says, dragging a hand down his face. "She's figured it out and she doesn't want me to propose."

"So don't," I say. "Just leave it." Megan shoots me a look. "What? Not everyone has to get married."

"I agree, but we don't even know that's what's going on here. Can you check in with Zoe?" she asks Andrew. "I'm sure if you just explain to her what you were planning, she'll tell you what happened."

"I should have just done it in public," he says. "I should have put her on the spot and forced her hand."

"He's joking," I tell Megan as I notice movement up ahead.

"Am I, Christian? Am I?"

"Andrew—"

"I could have got someone to film it, made us go viral. And then what can she do? *Not* cash in on our newfound fame?"

"*Andrew*," I hiss, and he finally pauses, following my gaze to see a very tired-looking Molly shuffle through the gate.

"What are you guys doing here?" she asks, looking to Megan as she makes her way toward us. "Is everything okay?"

"It's grand now," Megan says with a quick smile. "Just family stuff. Sorry."

"You're fine," she says, glancing at Andrew. Hope flickers across his face before she promptly looks away. "Cool. Well, I'm glad you're alright. If you guys don't mind; I think I'm going to have a shower. Try out this new hot water Colleen's been talking so much about."

She doesn't wait for a response, marching past us into the house. Andrew stares after her, stricken.

"Just let her go," I say quietly. "It might not be what you think. She might just— *Andrew*." I mutter a curse as he takes off after her, almost tripping up the steps.

"Uh-oh," Megan whispers, and she keeps pace with me as we follow them inside.

"Wait," Andrew clips out, and Molly stops in the middle of the hallway, whirling to face him.

"I need a shower."

"And you can have one as soon as you tell me what's wrong."

"What's going on?" Mam asks, appearing in the kitchen doorway. Dad joins her a moment later while Hannah peeks her head out of the living room.

"We don't have to talk about it," Andrew says, ignoring

everyone but Molly. "Whatever you think I was going to— If you're not ready, just forget about it, okay?"

She looks like she doesn't know whether she wants to laugh or cry. "It's not that."

"Then what? You can tell me. You can tell me anything. But at least tell me something because you're starting to worry me, and—"

"Andrew, *please.*"

"We talk, don't we? That's what we do. We talk to each other, and we tell each other when something's wrong."

"Nothing's wrong. Not like that."

"Then why are you—"

"Because I was going to propose!"

She exclaims the words so loud she almost yells them, and it's so quiet after it's like all the air has been sucked from the house.

No one moves. No one speaks.

And when five seconds pass, Megan tugs on my hand with a *do something* look, and I clear my throat. "Maybe we should give them some privacy," I say to my family.

I might as well have been speaking to the void.

"What do you mean?" Andrew asks eventually. Molly looks straight-up miserable.

"I wanted to surprise you."

"You were going to propose?"

"I picked out a ring," she explains, her skin flushing. "A stupid perfect ring, but I didn't know your size, and I... Do you remember last year when my parents brought over those Christmas crackers, and you got some plastic rings in yours, and they were a perfect fit? Well, I thought that could be a starting point, but it's hard to find Christmas crackers in the States, so I had to wait until we came back here, and then I had to find the same brand and—"

"Moll—"

"And then when we found them, I had to make an order with the jeweler to make it, and that's why Zoe came down. She came to collect me to get the ring, and we had to get it that day because they were closing for Christmas, and I was planning to propose on Christmas morning, but you were so disappointed about the cabin—"

"*Molly.*"

"So I panicked because when am I going to do it? I had this big plan, and then I was like, maybe I'll wait until the night before we leave, but you were acting so weird, and I thought you were mad that I didn't want to go, and then we drove up to the cabin, and I saw the rose petals, and it all clicked and I—" She takes a shaky breath. "And I realized what you were planning," she says, her voice breaking. "And that I'd messed it all up by planning the exact same thing. And I felt awful because I ruined your proposal."

"And I ruined yours." He doesn't sound very guilty about it. "You got my ring size from a Christmas cracker?"

"You said it fit you like a glove."

His mouth moves like he's trying not to smile. "I remember."

She rolls her eyes, hiccupping slightly. "You're laughing at me."

"Yeah," he says. "I am." He raises his arms in a stretch. "So, are we doing this or what?"

"What do you—"

Megan gasps beside me as Andrew lowers to one knee.

"No time like the present," he says, grinning up at Molly like he planned this all along. "Your turn."

It takes her a second to realize what's happening, and when she does, she blinks rapidly before moving jerkily to the floor, mirroring his stance.

Hannah makes a small noise across the hall. "I'm going to cry," she mumbles, waving her hands in front of her face.

I frown at her. "How does that help?"

"I don't know! It just does."

"*Shhh!*" Mam hushes, giving us a stern look that immediately softens when she turns back to the couple.

Neither Molly nor Andrew gives any indication that they hear us at all.

"Do you want to go first?" he prompts, but Molly shakes her head.

"You're better at this stuff."

"That's true," he says, straight-faced, and pulls out a small black box from his pocket.

"Oh my God," Megan breathes, clutching my hand so tight she's starting to cut off circulation.

"Molly Kinsella—"

Hannah squeaks.

But Andrew doesn't continue, his mouth slightly open as though he has so many things he wants to say to her, he doesn't even know where to start. But maybe that doesn't matter.

"I love you," he says simply. "And I want to spend the rest of my life with you. Will you marry me?"

Molly smiles through her tears, smiles at him, and then reaches into her coat for her own box.

"Yes," she says. "Will you marry me?"

His answer, which I can only presume was an affirmative, is lost as they kiss like they're the only two people in the world, and then they're exchanging rings, and Hannah is full-on sobbing, and Megan has tucked herself into my side and I'm smiling so hard my face hurts.

"Nothing's ever easy with you guys," I call, as they stand. "Is it?"

Andrew turns to me as Molly is quickly enveloped by my mother.

"She said yes."

"I heard," I say. "Congratulations, idiot."

"I want to be a bridesmaid," Hannah announces, as Megan kisses him on the cheek.

"Welcome to the family," I tell Molly as she embraces me next. "You guys still have dowries, right?"

"I'm such an idiot," she mutters into my shoulder.

"Yeah, but you're our idiot now."

And then she's pulled from my arms and back into Andrew's, and he spins her around with such joy you have to wonder if the whole world can feel it.

———

"You'll have to come over tomorrow," Mam says, pushing a foil-covered plate into Megan's hands. "We'll have plenty of leftovers."

"I will."

"And you're sure you can't stay? Or your mother is more than welcome to come over and—"

"Megan's got her own food at home," I interrupt as Mam adds a box of chocolates on top of the pile.

"I'll bring everyone over tomorrow," Megan promises, and that seems to appease her. With a final hug, and what looks to be a jar of chutney, she rushes back to the kitchen to rescue the dinner.

"So much for not stealing your thunder," Megan says, once she's gone. I shrug. It's not like I can be mad at Andrew and Molly for being the center of attention today.

"You sure you don't want me to go with you?"

She shakes her head, readjusting the food in her hands. "You should stay and celebrate," she says. "I promise you the O'Sullivan Christmas dinner won't be anywhere near as fun. Plus, I need to add something engagement themed to the sweaters."

"Oh God, I forgot."

"Late presents are the best presents," she says, and looks over her shoulder as headlights sweep down the drive. A second later, her mother pulls up with a wave.

"I better go," Megan says, but she doesn't. She lingers, and for the first time, a hint of awkwardness fills the silence.

"I'll see you tomorrow?" she asks eventually.

"Yeah." I force a smile. "Merry Christmas."

She gives me one last look, waiting, and then jogs to the car.

I know instantly that she's disappointed. That I messed up.

If this had been a few days ago, I wouldn't have any hesitation in going to her. And maybe it's seeing Andrew and Molly get engaged, but it feels different now between us. Newer. Like we've gone straight back to the beginning. With no idea what to do, or what the other wants.

And though I don't want to admit it, it scares me just a little.

After all, you don't have as many failed relationships as I do without getting a little cautious.

But maybe I should have kissed her goodbye.

I definitely should have kissed her goodbye.

I stand on the porch, annoyed with myself as I watch her drive off. But even when she's gone, I don't move. Even though it's freezing out.

And I know I should head inside and offer to help my parents with dinner. I should go change. I should. But I don't. Because I don't want to do any of that. For the first time in my life, the first time in all my Christmases, I wish I wasn't at home. I wish I was back in the cabin with Megan. We just spent several days cooped up together, but all I want to do is see her and touch her and breathe her in. I want it so much I can barely think.

I reach for my phone, intending to text her, but my fingers close around something else instead. A worn, crumpled packet that used to be the center of my universe.

I examine the cigarettes briefly before tapping one out,

more out of curiosity than necessity. And I'm pleased when I feel none of the usual pull toward it, none of the itch that's plagued me for the last few months. I go so far as to brush it across my lips, tempting all sorts of devils, but there's no impulse. No need. Not even a—

"Christian."

I spin, automatic guilt making my heart leap into my throat as I turn to see my father standing in the doorway.

"I wasn't going to—"

"I know," he says simply, and to my surprise, he lets the door fall behind him as he steps out in a simple fleece. If he feels the cold, he doesn't show it. "How long has it been?" he asks, nodding at the packet before I shove it back into my coat.

"A lifetime," I mutter before I pause. "Four months, two weeks, three days... four hours," I say, checking my watch. "But who's counting."

He doesn't smile at the joke. Nor does he order me inside, which I thought he was about to do. Instead, he takes a step forward, joining me.

"Thank you for the boiler," he says. "It was very generous of you."

Ah. "Yeah." I clear my throat. "Well."

"You're right. We needed to get it replaced years ago."

"It's not a big deal."

"It is," he says. "That's why you didn't tell us you were doing it."

Fair enough.

"Look, Dad—"

"It stuck with me. What you said the other day. About you being a disappointment."

I freeze, faint alarm bells ringing because I have no idea what to do with that. We usually don't argue on Christmas Day. That's the unspoken rule between us.

"Is that really what you think?" he asks and looks at me as if he really wants an answer. Like he genuinely doesn't know. But I don't rise to the bait, if that's what it is, and after a long moment of silence, he sighs, his breath misting in the night air.

"I didn't know what to do with you when you were young," he admits. "From the moment you learned to stand on your own two feet, you were walking rings around the lot of us. Liam was good as gold. Andrew was a nightmare. You couldn't leave him alone in the room without him sticking forks into sockets and climbing bookshelves. But you... sometimes you were so smart it scared me. I was relieved when you acted out because at least then I knew how to yell at you. At least then, I could feel like a parent. It was the only way I knew how to talk to you. And I guess that never stopped."

I stare at him, not daring to say a word. I think it's the most I've ever heard him speak in my entire life, and I'm afraid he's going to stop.

"Sometimes I feel like I pushed you away," he continues slowly. "And that's why you left. I won't lie and say that I didn't want you on the farm. I thought you'd be good at it. You're more ambitious than Liam, more disciplined than Andrew. It's hard work, but you're a hard worker. Even when you pretended you weren't. And I was so proud of you when you got that scholarship. I thought you'd finally find what you were looking for. That some of that restless energy would ease. But it never did. If anything, it got worse. And I didn't know how to help you." He turns to me then, his gaze as steady and calm as it always is. "You're not a disappointment, Christian. You never have been. But there's no point to any of this if you're not happy. And you can tell me if I'm wrong, but I don't think you are. And I don't think anything you've done these last few years has done anything to change that. And that's what eats at me. That's what worries me."

I swallow, my chest tight with some emotion I can't even begin to pick apart.

"You guys make me happy," I say gruffly. "Being back in Ireland makes me happy. My job some days. Running. Reading." I pause, and the tightness turns into an ache. "Megan."

"She's a nice girl, that one," Dad says. "I'm sorry I implied you didn't care for her."

"You weren't completely off base. Not like I ever had a real relationship before."

"Just because they weren't meant to last forever doesn't mean they weren't real."

"Doesn't mean they were good for me either," I say, remembering how I'd acted around previous girlfriends. Playing the role I thought they wanted me to. "Megan's not like that for me."

"You like her."

The words are such an understatement, I almost laugh. "Yeah. You could say that. I like her so much that I think I'm falling in love with her."

"You think?"

"I don't know. I've never been in love before. And if this is it, it's kind of shit, if I'm honest. Makes me feel like I'm losing my mind."

Dad doesn't say anything for a long moment, and I know, as always, he's weighing his words carefully.

"Did I ever tell you the story about how your mother and I met?"

"Yeah," I say, surprised. It's Mam's favorite story when she's had one sherry too many. "You were at a dance."

"Did I tell you she was there with someone else?"

"She was not," I say, impressed, and Dad nods.

"Graham Feeney."

"My real father?"

"That's the one," he says, faint humor in his eyes. "It was only their second date, but he was pretty taken by her." He speaks matter-of-factly, like he's discussing the weather, but I've never heard him talk about her like this before. "She was the most beautiful person I'd ever seen," he continues. "And she was a wonderful dancer. But I had two left feet and had always been shy, so I didn't dare approach her. Not at first."

"This isn't the part you tell me you threw her over your shoulder and carried her off into the night, is it? Because that stuff doesn't fly anymore."

"This is the part where I tell you I took lessons."

I stare at him. "You took dance lessons?"

"Every Saturday morning for two months."

"So you could dance with Mam?"

"So I'd have the courage to ask her. And it worked. I was only nineteen years old. I had my whole life ahead of me, but she was all I could think about. And the thought of letting her start a life with someone without even trying..." He shakes his head. "I'd never be able to live with myself. I did everything I could to get her to notice me, and when I did, it was like a whole new world opened up. If Megan's that person for you, then you need to let her know."

"She does."

"Does she?" His brows rise. "Have you told her?"

"Well, not in so many words, but she knows."

Dad just stares at me. Stares and stares and...

"Right," I sigh. "Okay."

"Go see her tonight."

"Tonight? It's Christmas."

"And she's clearly all you can think about," he says before stepping quietly back into the house. "They like gestures," he adds sagely.

Gestures. "I already learned to dance," I tell him.

"So think of something else. I'd think quick, though. The day after Christmas doesn't have the same ring to it."

THIRTY-TWO

MEGAN

"They're bath salts."

"Of course, they are!" Mam croons, examining the tub of pink crystals. "And they're French! How lovely."

Aidan gives me a look from across the room.

"Thank you both very much," she continues, and I roll my eyes.

"Okay. You're overdoing it."

"No, really," she says, reading the label. "I always say I need to take more baths."

Christ. I should have just made her another scarf.

The front room is strewn with discarded wrapping paper and Christmas cards as we each sit in our designated seats in the living room, a pile of presents beside us.

Mam gave me some beautiful earrings and Aidan an old watch that used to belong to our grandfather. In our annual tradition of bad gifts, my brother got me a book of slow-cooker recipes for one, which made me glad I'd gotten him a jazz compilation CD.

"I don't like jazz," he said. "Or have a CD player."

Mam told him off for being ungrateful.

I'd come home from Christian's to find Aidan had stuck a Band-Aid on his lip. Neither of us said anything about what happened, and Mam seemed blissfully ignorant as she finished cooking dinner and we all sat down to it. It was a surprisingly peaceful evening once that started. A surprisingly normal one too.

After the presents, Aidan disappears while I take a quick nap as the last few days catch up with me. I wake around forty minutes later, groggy and disorientated and not wanting to be alone, so I text Christian to see how his dinner went and then pull on a sweater and head downstairs. It's a little after eight p.m. now, and I find my mother in the kitchen, halfway through the washing up.

"We've got a dishwasher, you know."

"It relaxes me," she says, dipping her hands into the soapy water.

"Do you need some help?"

"You can pass me the plates on the table."

I do just that, lingering by her side. "I could dry," I offer, and she smiles.

"Well, you must be *very* bored."

I ignore her, grabbing a dishcloth and starting on the stack of plates. "If the snow's not too bad tomorrow, we should go for a walk. Maybe into the village?"

"Maybe," she agrees. "If Aidan feels up to it."

"What do you mean?"

"He fell, apparently," she says, her tone not changing as she rinses a wine glass and sets it to the side. "Tripped on the stairs." She squeezes the sponge. "Isaac fell in the snow too. I saw him when I was at his parents. He bruised his jaw. Says he hit a rock."

I fall silent, concentrating on polishing the smudges I pretend I see.

"That was your opening," she says after a minute, and my

throat tightens.

"Mam..." But I can't. I don't even know where to begin.

"I didn't invite him to the fundraiser," she continues when I don't. "I want you to know that."

"I know you didn't."

"I've had my suspicions these last few years looking back on everything, but I just—"

"I'm okay," I say softly, and she takes a breath, her hands stilling in the water. "I promise. But maybe we don't talk about this right now? Please? It's all a little..." I wave my fingers around my head, accidentally flicking suds everywhere.

"I guess you've had a long day," she says, finally lifting her gaze to mine. "But we'll talk soon."

"We will."

We watch each other for a moment, and then she hands me another glass. "Maybe you should go change."

"Change? Why?"

"Before we start with the movies."

"But we're just going to—" I jump, almost dropping the glass as something hits against the wall outside. "What was that?"

"Aidan's shoveling the snow," Mam says, unconcerned.

"By throwing it against the side of the house?"

Another thump, and I swear I hear muffled voices.

"Do we have guests?" I ask.

"I don't think so. Use a fresh towel for that one, would you?"

"Mam is someone—"

"*Megan.*" Aidan shouts my name through the house, and I scowl in his direction as Mam strips off her washing gloves.

"Go on," she says. "You're off the hook."

"But—"

"You know how he gets."

"He's not seven," I mutter, but I kiss her on the cheek, throwing in a hug for good measure.

"Happy Christmas, Mam."

"Happy Christmas," she tells me, and I head down the hall.

"Yell much?" I ask when I see my brother standing in the entranceway, blocking the open front door. "What the hell are you doing?"

"Supervising your boyfriend."

"What?" I edge around him, jostling him when he doesn't budge to see the Fitzpatrick family Jeep outside. A second later, Christian himself appears, taking a pile of blankets from the back.

"What's he doing?"

"Guy stuff."

"*Aidan.*" I grab my coat from the hook by the door, but he plants a foot against the frame before I can leave. "Move."

"No."

"Don't make me push you."

"I'd like to see you try."

I do. He doesn't even pretend to wobble.

"Would you just—"

"You should have told me about Isaac," he says, and I pause, watching him warily. "I wish you would have told me," he adds. "I would have believed you."

"I know."

"I would have helped you."

"I know you would have," I say. "I wish I had too."

He nods, satisfied. "You're good?"

"Yeah. Or I'm getting there."

"Is *he* good?" he asks, jerking his head outside.

"He's the best," I say. "And he has a really nice car."

Aidan snorts but relaxes a little as he grabs my hand, looping his pinkie finger briefly with mine.

I'm confused. "What was that?"

"I don't know," he says honestly. "But we don't have a secret handshake, so I thought we should do something."

"We could hug?"

"Eh." He glances back to the yard and drops his foot. "You can go now."

"That's it?"

"Christian told me to stall." He moves to the side before I can ask him what he's talking about and motions me out with a grand sweep of his arm.

I pull my hood up against the cold and hurry down the steps, rounding the house just as Christian does. I almost walk straight into him.

"What are you—"

"Not yet."

"What?"

"Not yet," he repeats. He takes me by the arms, walking me backward as he looks to Aidan, who's still waiting by the door. "I asked you to—"

"You try telling her what to do," he calls. "See how far you get."

He tsks. "Two seconds," he says to me and returns to the car, emerging with a black thermal flask.

"Hot chocolate," he explains, handing it over. "Molly says it's her special recipe."

"Special usually means it's spiked."

"I think she just adds cinnamon. I also got you this." He holds up a simple silver chain. "Happy Christmas."

I smile at him, taking it carefully between my fingers. "You drove over just to give me my present?"

"No. You cold?"

"Could be warmer."

He nods like that's the right answer. "Then right this way."

"What's going on?" I ask, hurrying to keep up as he brings me around the side again.

"It's a surprise. A big one."

"The last time you had a big surprise, you took me to see

taxidermy, and I don't— what the..." I trail off, gaping as he brings us to a stop.

The side of my house is no longer just the side of my house. It's a wonderland.

The projector sits behind us, playing *Home Alone* against the wall. Strings of fairy lights bracket the screen, but the real star of the show is the small bonfire set up in front, the flames flickering brightly inside a large ring of stones. Chairs of various shapes and sizes all face it, each one draped with blankets and cushions and hot water bottles to keep out the chill.

It's like something out of a movie.

"You said this is what you looked forward to most," he says when I stare at it. "So I wanted to make it extra special this year."

"I love it," I say. "It's gorgeous, Christian, but you didn't have to go to all this trouble."

"It's a gesture," he says as if that explains everything.

"And why are there so many chairs?"

"I invited both our families to join. Just later."

"Later?"

"I wanted to talk to you first."

"Okay..." He tugs at my hand, and I drag my attention from the movie on the wall as he leads me closer to the fire. "Oh, you know what we should do? We should get —"

"I have so many marshmallows, you will never want to eat one again," he tells me, and I beam.

"Great minds."

But he doesn't smile back. Just scratches the back of his neck, looking suddenly nervous. "Do you know what I was thinking earlier?" he asks. "When you left? I was thinking that I wish you hadn't. I was thinking that I wished you'd stayed. And I was thinking, what am I going to do if she wants to stick to the plan? If, in a couple of days, she shakes my hand, and we go our separate ways. What the hell am I going to do? Because the thing is, the biggest thing I've realized is that this is real to me. All of it. The cabin. The party. You. Me. Everything. And I've been trying to figure out when it stopped being pretend, but I can't put my finger on it. I think because a part of me has wanted this from the moment I bumped into you. It was like I couldn't leave you alone even then. I didn't want to." He clasps his hands gently on either side of my face, dipping his head slightly so he can look me straight in the eye. "I've been searching for something my whole life, and nothing's ever clicked. And I think it's because I was looking for you." His voice turns thick. "I'm falling in love with you," he says and my heart squeezes like a fist. "I'm falling hard and fast and I don't want to stop. But I don't expect you to feel the same way. I swear, I don't. We can take this slow, and if that means breaks or time apart, then we can do that. But I want you to know where I stand. I want to spend next Christmas with you, Megan. And every day in between. I want to wake up knowing I'm going to see you. I want to know everything there is to know about you and I want to start right now."

There are tears in the back of my eyes. I can feel them gathering, burning my lids, his words coupled with the exhaustion of the last few days, but when I go to speak, I find the burning has moved to my throat, and I can't talk. I can't even swallow. Can't do anything but look at him.

"I know it's fast," he adds haltingly, thrown by my lack of reaction. "But you've always felt right to me, and technically, we've known each other our whole lives, so—"

"Christian—"

"Plus, the sex is great, so we already—"

I laugh. Or at least I think I do. It comes out more like a strangled sob before I slam my hand over my mouth.

"It is great," I agree when I've regained control. "More than great. And I think I'm falling in love with you too."

His brows lower, his gaze searching my face like he's looking for the truth to my words, and then he holds me even tighter. Like he's scared I'll disappear.

"You let me say all that when you felt the same way?"

"You're clearly feeling so much," I tease. "It's good to get it off your chest." I pull back to look at him, though he doesn't let me go far. "There isn't anyone else in this world who could convince me into a fake relationship," I tell him. "And no one else who could turn it into a real one."

"My grand plan all along."

"I figured," I say with a smile, and he wipes my tears as they fall. "You want to try this? For real?"

"I do."

"No backing out?"

"No backing out," he says, and I tilt my chin as he kisses me, his lips moving against mine as though trying to prove everything he just said. When we finally break apart, I swear my mouth tingles with it.

"Take me on a date," I whisper. "A real one. Our first one."

"I can do that," he murmurs. "And then?"

And then?

"Everything," I tell him. "And then everything." I twine my arms around his neck, pressing as close to him as our coats allow. On the other side of the house, I hear a car drive up and then Hannah's voice calling hello before several other voices join in.

"On second thought, maybe this should have just been an us thing," Christian says, and I laugh.

"What's Christmas without your family annoying you?"

"A really good one?"

"Don't worry," I say, as the first person rounds the corner. "I'll be your backup."

And as the exclamations of wonder start behind us, as the bonfire crackles and the stars glint overhead, I lift my lips to his once more and seal it all with a kiss.

EPILOGUE

MEGAN

One Year later

"Everything okay?" Hannah asks.

Molly nods, even as she fiddles with fabric at her waist, smoothing out a nonexistent wrinkle. "Yes."

"No second thoughts?" Hannah continues and gives me a wicked grin over her shoulder. Molly doesn't notice, too busy staring at her reflection like she doesn't recognize the girl gazing back at her.

"You look stunning," I tell for her the millionth time, and I mean it. The dress is simple and perfect for her. A long white gown. No veil, no frills. Just a sweep of fabric down to the floor and a short train to make it look like she's gliding when she walks. Her blonde hair is pinned up and back and dotted with flowers, like she's stepped out of a fairy tale.

She's a beautiful bride.

And also, apparently, a hungry one.

With a sharp exhale, Molly turns abruptly from the mirror, almost making me drop the necklace I'm clasping at her neck as she crosses the hotel room to one of the many boxes of treats arranged on the table.

She barely glances at them before she pops a truffle in her mouth. And then another.

"Chocolate dehydrates your mouth," Hannah tells her. "You don't want a dry mouth."

"I don't want a wedding," Molly retorts. "Why did I agree to a big wedding?"

"Because you want to make my brother happy. And he is going to be very, very happy when he sees you walk down the aisle in this dress with no chocolate stains on your face." She takes out a tissue as she speaks, dabbing it at the corner of her lips.

They had a small civil ceremony in Chicago for their friends over there. But this is a proper Irish wedding. It's big. It's a party. And at Christmastime, no less. There's a lot of guests down there.

"I'm not good at talking in front of people," Molly continues.

"You talk in front of people all the time," Zoe says as she exits the bathroom. "It's literally your job. You stand in front of people, and you talk."

"I stand in front of *strangers,* and I talk about *food.*"

"We should start thinking about going downstairs," Hannah says, the official schedule keeper of the room. "They said eleven."

"I'm not ready."

"Yes, you are," I remind her. "There's no one but family and friends down there. And the man you love more than anyone else in the world."

"I just don't like attention."

"Would you like me to make a scene? Distract them a little?"

That gets a smile out of her. A small grateful one as she

squeezes my hand. "Can I have a minute instead?"

"You can have five," I say, as Hannah checks the time with a pointed look. "If you can't run the show on your wedding day, then when can you? I'll let everyone know."

"And I'll hide the chocolate," Zoe says, taking the box from Molly's hands.

I slip out of the room, grabbing the navy shrug that each of the bridesmaids has. Hannah made all our dresses, deep forest-green ones that she designed as a present to her brother, and as I head toward the hotel elevators, I delight as I always do in wearing something new, something beautiful. I've already decided to wear it again at our New Year's party. With the right shoes I can dress it down and maybe add some—

"Hi."

My eyes widen as the elevator doors slide open to reveal Christian standing inside.

"Where are you going in such a rush?" he asks, as he steps smoothly out into the hallway.

"Molly needs five more minutes."

"What a coincidence. So do I."

I'm confused for an instant before I catch the look on his face. "*No, we—*"

"Maybe ten." He grabs my hand, whisking me a few steps down the corridor and around a corner, where he brings me to a stop, my back against the wall. "I missed you last night."

"No, you didn't. You were playing minigolf with Andrew."

"But thinking of you the entire time."

"How romantic," I deadpan, but I can't help my smile. "How is he?"

"Andrew?" He shrugs. "Excited. Happy. Relishing the attention. But let's focus on you," he says, stealing a kiss before I can protest.

"My lipstick—"

"Tastes delicious," he says, kissing me again.

"You're a real charmer today."

"What can I say?" he murmurs. "Turns out I'm not great with the whole sleeping apart thing."

I smooth my hands down the front of his suit, flushing slightly. Zoe had arranged a girls' sleepover for Molly last night, meaning yesterday was one of the few days we hadn't shared a bed since we moved in together.

That happened pretty quickly when we came back after Christmas last year. I'd been hesitant at first, wondering if it was just the magic of the season that made everything feel that much *more*. But not even a dark, rainy January could dull whatever had flared between the two of us, and, as if sensing I might be doubting everything, Christian had been all over me. The two of us were inseparable, and by March, I was spending so much time at his that I had basically moved in. And when he officially asked me to one morning in bed, I said yes.

It wasn't all smooth sailing, though.

His apartment was just as fancy as I imagined it to be, and for the first few days, I was awkward as hell. He told me I could make myself at home, and I believed him, but it still felt like *his*. His furniture. His things. Even when he did his best to make me welcome, clearing out half his wardrobe and buying a whole new dresser, I still felt like I couldn't completely relax and only ended up bringing half my stuff with me so I wouldn't clutter the space.

I was walking around on tiptoes until one day, I came home from work to find he'd painted the bedroom a soft pink and added an incredibly comfy yet slightly ugly armchair to the living room. He put it next to the midcentury lounge chair by the bookcase, so I could knit while he read.

"We can change it," he'd said to me when I'd stood there wide-eyed. "Any of it. All of it. Don't be scared to talk to me."

Don't be scared.

I wasn't after that, meeting him halfway as, bit by bit, we

transformed the apartment from his into ours. Until it felt like my home too. I don't know if I want to stay there forever. I'd like a garden. I'd like a little room to work on my crafts. But it's enough for now. And it's exciting having something in the future to think about. A future with him.

But no sooner did both of us settle into our new lives together than something else happened to shake it up.

Three months ago, Aidan officially left Australia. It wasn't as easy as packing his bags. There was his notice period and his apartment, a life he had to unpack bit by bit. He was staying in Madrid now, crashing with a friend, but was due to come back to Ireland before the new year for some job that he tried to explain to me and I couldn't understand. With rent in Dublin being what it was, Christian immediately offered up our spare room until he got on his feet, but neither Aidan nor I was keen to enter that sitcom-esque territory just yet. We're probably going to kill each other. But still, it will be nice to have him closer. Nice to have him home.

"I get first dance, by the way," Christian says, snapping my attention back to the present. "And the last."

I hesitate. "I promised your dad I'd dance with him first, so—"

"Megan."

"I'm sorry! You've got to get in there quick. I'm in high demand."

"Apparently," Christian says, but he doesn't look too mad.

That's probably the unlikeliest of relationships to come out of all this. Or maybe it isn't. His dad has a soft spot for me. Christian said he'd never seen him take so much time away from the farm, and yet whenever we came to visit, he popped around. Taking me to see the animals, asking me about my knitting, my job, my life.

I enjoyed spending time with him. I looked forward to it, even. But a deeper part of me was grateful that it seemed to bring Christian closer to him too. I think he's spent more time with his dad in the last year than he ever did in his life, and the effect is noticeable. No more awkward conversations where they're both scared they're going to say something to set the other off, no more arguments, no more tension. They still might not know how to communicate fully with each other, but they're getting there. They understand each other better now and at the heart of it, his dad just wants to see Christian happy.

We have that in common.

"You nervous?" he asks now.

"Kind of," I say. "Not as much as Molly, but still. It's exciting, isn't it?"

"Extremely," he says, distracted as he runs his fingers up and down my arms. "You ever want to do this again one day?" he asks, and I don't need to ask what he's referring to.

"One day," I say softly. "Maybe."

He hesitates. "With me, right?"

"*Yes.*"

"Just checking."

He kisses me once more before reluctantly breaking away. "I'd better get back down there."

"I think the five minutes are up, anyway," I admit, checking his watch for the time. As soon as I do, I hear footsteps, and I peek around the corner to see Molly striding down the hallway with a determined look on her face.

"Okay," she announces. "I'm ready. Let's get this over with."

"Ah, true love," Christian sighs and we join the party for the elevators. It takes two trips to get everyone down and another five minutes to assemble before the ballroom doors. Christian leaves us with a wink at Molly, who barely notices him. She just keeps muttering her vows, her eyes trained on the ornate doors leading to the rest of her life. She still looks nervous. And while I don't know exactly what she's experiencing right now, seeing as I never made it this far, I can take a guess, so as Zoe brusquely schools the flower girls into order, I sidle up to her, clearing my throat.

"If you want to make a run for it, I know a shortcut."

Her eyes flash to mine, startled for one brief second before she laughs. "I'm good," she assures me. "But I appreciate it."

"Just keep your eyes on him. Only him and no one else. Because right now, the rest of us are just decoration."

Her dad approaches her then, offering her his arm, and she gives me a warm smile as I join Hannah at the front.

"How's my blush?" she asks.

"Impeccable."

"So is yours," she says and stares straight ahead, full of poise and purpose as the doors creak open. Hannah takes an audible breath, and I clutch my small bouquet to my chest as a lone cello starts to play something beautiful and lifting and perfect.

The flower girls go first, some of them visibly shaking with excitement as they start the long walk up the aisle. Hannah and I go next, and I concentrate on keeping my posture straight and my pace steady.

Dozens of faces smile back at me, before looking over my shoulder to see if they can glimpse the bride. All except one person, who can't seem to take his eyes off me.

Christian stands next to his brother with the biggest smile on his face, all his attention on me.

Hi, he mouths as I reach the front, and I find myself grinning back at him.

An excited murmur ripples through the guests, and the music changes, but I can't look away from the man opposite me. I don't want to.

I am, as I seem to be more and more lately, right where I want to be. Right where I need to.

And someday, I might be here again, and it will be me walking up that aisle. Me in that dress. And on that day, I'll have no doubts, no worries. I'll have nothing but hope and excitement for the future.

A future with the man who I love more than I thought was possible. Who'll stand beside me come what may.

Always and forever.

A LETTER FROM CATHERINE

Dear Reader,

Thank you so much for reading *Snowed In*! I hope you enjoyed Megan and Christian's story.

If you want to keep up to date with my latest releases, you can sign up for my mailing list at the following link. Your email address will never be shared and you can unsubscribe at any time

www.bookouture.com/catherine-walsh

If you liked *Snowed In*, and I really hope you did, I would be so grateful if you could spare the time to write a review. It makes such a difference in helping new readers to discover one of my books for the first time. I also love hearing from my readers—you can get in touch through social media or my website.

All my best,

Catherine

catherinewalshbooks.com

twitter.com/CatWalshWriter

instagram.com/catwalshwriter

ACKNOWLEDGMENTS

A massive thank you to me for once again doing the most work. Well done, me.

This book is dedicated to Lucy Baxter, who has asked at least twice when it's her turn for this and guess what! It's now! Lucy, thank you for your endless patience, your enthusiasm and devotion to boosting my social media engagement levels by replying to every single story I post. I love you a whole lot.

Thank you also to Hannah Cole for all the writing sessions (that are really just gossip sessions, but the laptops are there so it counts) and to all my friends and family who have learned to no longer ask me "how's the book going?" and instead just cheerfully buy it when it's out.

To my agent, Hannah Schofield, for replying with a resounding *yes* within an hour of me sending her the idea for this book. To the team at Bookouture for equaling her enthusiasm, and to my editor Susannah, for helping me find the heart of this story.

My biggest thank you as always is to all the bloggers and readers who continue to shout about my books. I am continually grateful for all your kind words, creativity, and thoughtfulness. It's been a real highlight getting to meet so many of you this year, and every time I sit down to write, it is you I think of first. I hope you enjoy this one.